Fiction Catalog

LOOK TO WINDWARD

LOOK TO WINDWARD

IAIN M. BANKS

POCKET BOOKS

NEW YORK   LONDON   TORONTO   SYDNEY   SINGAPORE

POCKET BOOKS, a division of Simon & Schuster, Inc.
1230 Avenue of the Americas, New York, NY 10020

Copyright © 2000 by Iain M. Banks

Quotation from "The Waste Land" taken from *Collected Poems 1909–1962* by T. S.
Eliot. Reprinted by permission of Faber and Faber Ltd.

Originally published in 2000 in Great Britain by Orbit

Library of Congress Cataloging-in-Publication Data

Banks, Iain.
    Look to windward / Iain M. Banks.
      p.   cm.
    ISBN 0-7434-2191-4
    I. Title.

  PR6052.A485 L66 2001
  823'.914—dc21   2001021833

First Pocket Books hardcover printing August 2001

10 9 8 7 6 5 4 3 2 1

For the Gulf War Veterans

Gentile or Jew
O you who turn the wheel and look to windward,
Consider Phlebas, who was once handsome and tall as you.
                    T. S. ELIOT,
                    "THE WASTE LAND," IV

CONTENTS

Prologue 1

1 The Light of Ancient Mistakes 7

2 Winter Storm 29

3 Infra Dawn 46

4 Scorched Ground 63

    Airsphere 79

5 A Very Attractive System 94

6 Resistance Is Character-Forming 113

7 Peer Group 126

8 The Retreat at Cadracet 140

    Dirigible 158

    The Memory of Running 173

9 Pylon Country 177

10 The Seastacks of Youmier 193

11 Absence of Gravitas 210

12 A Defeat of Echoes 232

    Flight 256

13 Some Ways of Dying 269

14 Returning to Leave, Recalling Forgetting 293

15   A Certain Loss of Control. 319

16   Expiring Light 336

      Space, Time 356

      Closure 363

Epilogue. 367

LOOK TO WINDWARD

Prologue

Near the time we both knew I would have to leave him, it was hard to tell which flashes were lightning and which came from the energy weapons of the Invisibles.

A vast burst of blue-white light leaped across the sky, making an inverted landscape of the ragged clouds' undersurface and revealing through the rain the destruction all around us: the shell of a distant building, its interior scooped out by some earlier cataclysm, the tangled remains of rail pylons near the crater's lip, the fractured service pipes and tunnels the crater had exposed, and the massive, ruined body of the wrecked land destroyer lying half submerged in the pool of filthy water in the bottom of the hole. When the flare died it left only a memory in the eye and the dull flickering of the fire inside the destroyer's body.

Quilan gripped my hand still tighter. "You should go. Now, Worosei." Another, smaller flash lit his face and the oil-scummed mud around his waist where it disappeared under the war machine.

I made a show of consulting my helm's readout. The ship's flyer was on its way back, alone. The display told me that no larger craft was accompanying it, while the lack of any communication on the open channel meant there was no good news to report. There would be no heavy lift, there would be no rescue. I flipped to the close-quarter tactical view. Nothing better to report there. The confused, pulsing schematics indicated there was great uncertainty in the representation (a bad enough sign in itself) but it looked like we were right in the line of the Invisibles' advance and we would soon be overrun. In ten minutes, maybe. Or fifteen. Or five. That uncertain. Still I smiled as best I could and tried to sound calm.

"I can't get to anywhere safer until the flyer gets here," I said quietly. "Neither of us can." I shifted on the muddy slope, trying to find a better footing. A series of booms shook the air. I crouched over Quilan, protecting his exposed head. I heard debris thudding onto the slope across from us, and something splashed into the water. I glanced at the level of the pool in the bottom of the crater as the waves slapped against the chisel shape of the land destroyer's fore armor and fell back again. At least the water didn't seem to be rising anymore.

"Worosei," he said. "I don't think I'm going anywhere. Not with this thing on top of me. Please. I'm not trying to be heroic and neither should you. Just get out now. Go."

"There's still time," I told him. "We'll get you out of there. You were always so impatient." Light pulsed above us again, picking out each lancing drop of rain in the darkness.

"And you were—"

Whatever he was going to say was drowned out by another fusillade of sharp concussions; the noise rolled over us as though the very air was being torn apart.

"Loud night," I said as I crouched over him again. My ears were ringing. More light flickered to one side and, close up, I could see the pain in his eyes. "Even the weather's against us, Quilan. Dreadful thunder."

"That was not thunder."

"Oh, it was! There! And that is lightning," I said as I crouched further over him.

"Go. Now, Worosei," he whispered. "You're being stupid."

"I—" I began. Then my rifle slipped from my shoulder and the stock hit him on the forehead. "Ouch," he said.

"Sorry." I shouldered the weapon again.

"My fault for losing my helmet."

"Still," I slapped one of the sections of track above us, "you gained a land destroyer."

He started to laugh, then winced. He forced a smile and rested one hand against the surface of one of the vehicle's guide wheels. "It's funny," he said. "I'm not even sure if it's one of ours or one of theirs."

"You know," I said, "neither am I." I looked up at its ruptured carcass. The fire inside seemed to be spreading; thin blue and yellow flames were starting to show in the hole where the main turret had been.

The crippled land destroyer had kept its tracks on this side as it had half trundled, half slid into the crater. On the far side, the stripped track lay flat on the crater's slope, a stride-wide strip of flat metal sections leading up like a ramshackle escalator almost to the hole's jagged lip. In front of us, huge guide wheels protruded from the war machine's hull; some supported the giant hinges of the tracks' upper course, others ran on the tracks beneath. Quilan was trapped beneath their lower level, squashed into the mud with only his upper torso free.

Our comrades were dead. There were only Quilan and me, and the pilot of the light flyer, returning to pick us up. The ship, just a couple of hundred kilometers above our heads, could not help.

I had tried pulling Quilan, ignoring his bitten-off moans, but he was held fast. I had burned out my suit's AG unit trying to shift the track sections trapping him, and cursed our supposedly wonderful nth generation projectile weapons; so good for killing our own species and penetrating armor, so useless for cutting through thick metal.

Noise crackled nearby; sparks flicked out of the fire in the turret aperture, rising and fading in the rain. I could feel the detonations through the ground, transmitted by the body of the wrecked machine.

"Ammunition, going off," Quilan said, his voice strained. "Time you went."

"No. I think whatever blew the turret off accounted for all the ammunition."

"And I don't. It could still blow up. Get out."

"No. I'm comfortable here."

"You're what?"

"I'm comfortable here."

"Now you're being idiotic."

"I am not being idiotic. Stop trying to get rid of me."

"Why should I? You're being idiotic."

"Stop calling me idiotic, will you? You're bickering."

"I am not bickering. I'm trying to get you to behave rationally."

"I am behaving rationally."

"This doesn't impress me, you know. It's your duty to save yourself."

"And yours not to despair."

"Not despair? My comrade and mate is acting like an imbecile and I've got a—" Quilan's eyes widened. "Up there!" he hissed, pointing behind me.

"What?" I twisted, bringing my rifle around and then going still.

The Invisible trooper was at the crater lip, peering down at the wreckage of the land destroyer. He had some sort of helmet on but it didn't cover his eyes and probably wasn't very sophisticated. I gazed up through the rain. He was lit by firelight from the burning land destroyer; we ought to be mostly in shadow. The trooper's rifle was held in one hand, not both. I stayed very still.

Then he brought something up to his eyes, scanning. He stopped, looking straight at us. I had raised the rifle and fired by the time he'd let the night sight drop and begun to bring his weapon to bear. He exploded in light just as another flash erupted in the skies above. Most of his body tumbled and slipped down the slope toward us, shorn of one arm and his head.

"Suddenly you're a half-decent shot," Quilan said.

"I always was, dear," I told him, patting his shoulder. "I just kept it quiet because I didn't want to embarrass you."

"Worosei," he said, taking my hand again. "That one will not have been alone. Now really is the time to go."

"I—" I began, then the hulk of the land destroyer and the crater around us shook as something exploded inside the wreck and glowing shrapnel whizzed out of the space where the turret had been. Quilan gasped with pain. Mud slides coasted down around us and the remains of the dead Invisible slid another few strides closer. His gun was still clutched in one armored glove. I glanced at my helm's screen again. The flyer was almost here. My love was right, and it really was time to go.

I turned back to say something to him.

"Just fetch me that bastard's rifle," he said, nodding at the dead trooper. "See if I can't take another one or two of them with me."

"All right," I said, and found myself scrambling up the mud and debris and grabbing the dead soldier's rifle.

"And see if he has anything else!" Quilan shouted. "Grenades; anything!"

I slid back down, overshooting and getting both boots in the water. "All he had," I said, handing him the rifle.

He checked it as best he could. "That'll do." He fitted the stock against his shoulder and twisted around as far as his trapped lower body would allow, settling into something approaching a firing position. "Now, go! Before I shoot you myself!" He had to raise his voice over the sound of more explosions tearing at the wreck of the land destroyer.

I fell forward and kissed him. "I'll see you in heaven," I said.

His face took on a look of tenderness just for a moment and he said something, but explosions shook the ground and I had to ask him to repeat what he'd said as the echoes died away and more lights strobed in the skies above us. A signal blinked urgently in my visor to tell me the flyer was immediately overhead.

"I said, there's no rush," he told me quietly, and smiled. "Just live; Worosei. Live for me. For both of us. Promise."

"I promise."

He nodded up the slope of the crater. "Good luck, Worosei."

I meant to say good luck in return, or just goodbye, but I found I could not say a thing. I just gazed hopelessly at him, looking upon my husband for that one last time, and then I turned and hauled myself upward, slithering on the mud but pulling myself away from him, past the body of the Invisible I had killed, along the side of the burning machine's hull and traversing its rear beneath the barrels of its aft turret while more explosions sent flaming wreckage soaring into the rain-filled sky and splashing into the rising waters.

The sides of the crater were slick with mud and oils; I seemed to slip down more than I was able to climb up and for a few moments I believed I would never make my way out of that awful pit, until I slid and hauled myself over to the broad metal ribbon that was the stripped track of the land destroyer. What would kill my love saved me; I used the linked sections of the embedded track as a staircase, at the end almost running to the top.

Beyond the lip, in the flame-lit distances between the ruined buildings and the squalls of rain, I could see the lumbering shapes of other great war machines, and the tiny, scurrying figures behind them, all moving this way.

The flyer swooped from the clouds; I threw myself aboard and we lifted immediately. I tried to turn and look back, but the doors slammed closed and I was thrown about the cramped interior while the tiny craft dodged rays and missiles aimed at it as it rose to the waiting ship *Winter Storm*.

I

The Light of Ancient Mistakes

The barges lay on the darkness of the still canal, their lines softened by the snow heaped in pillows and hummocks on their decks. The horizontal surfaces of the canal's paths, piers, bollards and lifting bridges bore the same full billowed weight of snow, and the tall buildings set back from the quaysides loomed over all, their windows, balconies and gutters each a line edged with white.

It was a quiet area of the city at almost any time, Kabe knew, but tonight it both seemed and was quieter still. He could hear his own footsteps as they sank into the untouched whiteness. Each step made a creaking noise. He stopped and lifted his head, sniffing at the air. Very still. He had never known the city so silent. The snow made it seem hushed, he supposed, muffling what little sound there was. Also tonight there was no appreciable wind at ground level, which meant that—in the absence of any traffic—the canal, though still free of ice, was perfectly still and soundless, with no slap of wave or gurgling surge.

There were no lights nearby positioned to reflect from the canal's black surface, so that it seemed like nothing, like an absolute absence on which the barges appeared to be floating unsupported. That was

7

unusual too. The lights were out across the whole city, across almost all this side of the world.

He looked up. The snow was easing now. Spinwards, over the city center and the still more distant mountains, the clouds were parting, revealing a few of the brighter stars as the weather system cleared. A thin, dimly glowing line directly above—coming and going as the clouds moved slowly overhead—was far-side light. No aircraft or ships that he could see. Even the birds of the air seemed to have stayed in their roosts.

And no music. Usually in Aquime City you could hear music coming from somewhere or other, if you listened hard enough (and he was good at listening hard). But this evening he couldn't hear any.

Subdued. That was the word. The place was subdued. This was a special, rather somber night ("Tonight you dance by the light of ancient mistakes!" Ziller had said in an interview that morning—with only a little too much relish) and the mood seemed to have infected all of the city, the whole of Xaravve Plate, indeed the entire Orbital of Masaq'.

And yet, even so, there seemed to be an extra stillness caused by the snow. Kabe stood for a moment longer, wondering exactly what might cause that additional hush. It was something that he had noticed before but never quite been bothered enough about to try and pin down. Something to do with the snow itself . . .

He looked back at his tracks in the snow covering the canal path. Three lines of footprints. He wondered what a human—what any bipedal—would make of such a trail. Probably, he suspected, they would not notice. Even if they did, they would just ask and instantly be told. Hub would tell them: those will be the tracks of our honored Homomdan guest Ambassador Kabe Ischloear.

Ah, so little mystery, these days. Kabe looked around, then quickly did a little hopping, shuffling dance, executing the steps with a delicacy belying his bulk and weight. He glanced about again, and was glad to have, apparently, escaped observation. He studied the pattern his dance had left in the snow. That was better . . . But what had he been thinking of? The snow, and its silence.

Yes, that was it; it produced what seemed like a subtraction of noise, because one was used to sound accompanying weather; wind sighed or roared, rain drummed or hissed or—if it was mist and too light to produce noise directly—at least created drips and glugs. But snow falling with no wind to accompany it seemed to defy nature; it was like watching a screen with the sound off, it was like being deaf. That was it.

Satisfied, Kabe tramped on down the path, just as a whole sloped roofload of snow fell with a muffled but distinct crump from a tall building onto ground nearby. He stopped, looked at the long ridge of whiteness the miniature avalanche had produced as a last few flakes fell swirling around it, and laughed.

Quietly, so as not to disturb the silence.

At last some lights, from a big barge four vessels away around the canal's gradual curve. And the hint of some music, too, from the same source. Gentle, undemanding music, but music nevertheless. Fill-in music; biding music, as they sometimes called it. Not the recital itself.

A recital. Kabe wondered why he had been invited. The Contact drone E. H. Tersono had requested Kabe's presence there in a message delivered that afternoon. It had been written in ink, on card and delivered by a small drone. Well, a flying salver, really. The thing was, Kabe usually went to Tersono's Eighth-Day recital anyway. Making a point of inviting him to it had to mean something. Was he being told that he was being in some way presumptuous, having come along on earlier occasions when he hadn't been specifically invited?

That would seem strange; in theory the event was open to all— what was not, in theory?—but the ways of Culture people, especially drones, and most especially old drones, like E. H. Tersono, could still surprise Kabe. No laws or written regulations at all, but so many little . . . observances, sets of manners, ways of behaving politely. And fashions. They had fashions in so many things, from the most trivial to the most momentous.

Trivial: that paper message delivered on a salver; did that mean that everybody was going to start physically moving invitations and even day-to-day information from place to place, rather than have such things transmitted normally, communicated to one's house, familiar, drone, terminal or implant? What a preposterous and deeply tedious idea! And yet just the sort of retrospective affectation they might fall in love with, for a season or so (ha! at most).

Momentous: they lived or died by whim! A few of their more famous people announced they would live once and die forever, and billions did likewise; then a new trend would start among opinion-formers for people to back up and have their bodies wholly renewed or new ones regrown, or to have their personalities transferred into android replicas or some other more bizarre design, or . . . well, anything; there was really no limit, but the point was that people would start doing that sort of thing by the billion, too, just because it had become fashionable.

Was that the sort of behavior one ought to expect from a mature society? Mortality as a life-style choice? Kabe knew the answer his own people would give. It was madness, childishness, disrespectful of oneself and life itself; a kind of heresy. He, however, was not quite so sure, which either meant that he had been here too long, or that he was merely displaying the shockingly promiscuous empathy toward the Culture that had helped bring him here in the first place.

So, musing about silence, ceremony, fashion and his own place in society, Kabe arrived at the ornately carved gangway that led from the quayside into the gently lit extravagance in gilded wood that was the ancient ceremonial barge *Soliton*. The snow here had been tramped down by many feet, the trail leading to a nearby sub-trans access building. Obviously he was odd, enjoying walking in the snow. But then he didn't live in this mountain city; his own home here hardly ever experienced snow or ice, so it was a novelty for him.

Just before he went aboard, the Homomdan looked up into the night sky to watch a V-shaped flock of big, pure white birds fly silently overhead, just above the barge's signal rigging, heading inland from the High Salt Sea. He watched them disappear behind the buildings, then brushed the snow off his coat, shook his hat and went aboard.

• • •

"It's like holidays."

"Holidays?"

"Yes. Holidays. They used to mean the opposite of what they mean now. Almost the exact opposite."

"What do you mean?"

"Hey, is this edible?"

"What?"

"This."

"I don't know. Bite it and see."

"But it just moved."

"It just *moved?* What, under its own power?"

"I think so."

"Well now, *there's* a thing. Evolve from a real predator like our friend Ziller and the instinctive answer's probably yes, but—"

"What's this about holidays?"

"Ziller was—"

"—What he was saying. Opposite meaning. Once, holidays meant the time when you went *away.*"

"Really?"

"Yes, I remember hearing that. Primitive stuff. Age of Scarcity."

"People had to do all the work and create wealth for themselves and society and so they couldn't afford to take very much time off. So they worked for, say, half the day, most days of the year and then had an allocation of days they could take off, having saved up enough exchange collateral—"

"Money. Technical term."

"—in the meantime. So they took the time off and they went away."

"Excuse me, are you edible?"

"Are you really talking to your food?"

"I don't know. I don't know if it is food."

"In very primitive societies there wasn't even that; they got only a few days off each year!"

"But I thought primitive societies could be quite—"

"Primitive industrial, he meant. Take no notice. Will you stop poking that? You'll bruise it."

"But can you eat it?"

"You can eat *anything* you can get into your mouth and swallow."

"You know what I mean."

"Ask, you idiot!"

"I just did."

"Not *it!* Grief, what are you *glanding?* Should you be out? Where's your minder, terminal, whatever?"

"Well, I didn't want to just—"

"Oh, I see. Did they all go away at once?"

"How could they? Things would stop working if they all did nothing at the same time."

"Oh, of course."

"But sometimes they had days when a sort of skeleton crew operated infrastructure. Otherwise, they staggered their time off. Varies from place to place and time to time, as you might expect."

"Ah ha."

"Whereas nowadays what we call holidays, or core time, is when you all stay home, because otherwise there'd be no period when you could all meet up. You wouldn't know who your neighbors were."

"Actually, I'm not sure that I do."

"Because we're just so flighty."

"One big holiday."

"In the old sense."

"And hedonistic."

"Itchy feet."

"Itchy feet, itchy paws, itchy flippers, itchy barbels—"

"Hub, can I eat this?"

"—itchy gas sacs, itchy ribs, itchy wings, itchy pads—"

"Okay, I think we get the idea."

"Hub? Hello?"

"—itchy grippers, itchy slime cusps, itchy motile envelopes—"

"Will you shut up?"

"Hub? Come in? Hub? Shit, my terminal's not working. Or Hub's not answering."

"Maybe it's on holiday."

"—itchy swim bladders, itchy muscle frills, itchy—mmph! What? Was there something stuck in my teeth?"

"Yes, your foot."

"I think that's where we kicked off."

"Appropriate."

"Hub? Hub? Wow, this has never happened to me before . . ."

"Ar Ischloear?"

"Hmm?" His name had been spoken. Kabe discovered that he must have gone into one of those strange, trance-like states he sometimes experienced at gatherings like this, when the conversation—or rather when several conversations at once—went zinging to and fro in a dizzying, alienly human sort of way and seemed to wash over him so that he found it difficult to follow who was saying what to whom and why.

He'd found that later he could often remember exactly the words that had been said, but he still had to work to determine the sense behind them. At the time he would just feel oddly detached. Until the spell was broken, as now, and he was awakened by his name.

He was in the upper ballroom of the ceremonial barge *Soliton* with a few hundred other people, most of them human though not all in human form. The recital by the composer Ziller—on an antique Chelgrian mosaikey—had finished half an hour earlier. It had been a restrained, solemn piece, in keeping with the mood of the evening, though its performance had still been greeted with rapturous applause. Now people were eating and drinking. And talking.

He was standing with a group of men and women centered on one of the buffet tables. The air was warm, pleasantly perfumed and filled with soft music. A wood and glass canopy arced overhead, hung with some ancient form of lighting that was a long way from anybody's full-spectrum but which made everything and everybody look agreeably warm.

His nose ring had spoken to him. When he had first arrived in the Culture he hadn't liked the idea of having com equipment inserted into his skull (or anywhere else for that matter). His family nose ring was about the only thing he always carried with him, so they had made him a perfect replica that happened to be a communications terminal as well.

"Sorry to disturb you, Ambassador. Hub here. You're closest; would you let Mr. Olsule know he is speaking to an ordinary brooch, not his terminal?"

"Yes." Kabe turned to a young man in a white suit who was holding a piece of jewelry in his hand and looking puzzled. "Ah, Mr. Olsule?"

"Yeah, I heard," the man said, stepping back to look up at the Homomdan. He appeared surprised, and Kabe formed the impression that he had been mistaken for a sculpture or an article of monumental furniture. This happened fairly often. A function of scale and stillness, basically. It was one hazard of being a glisteningly black three-and-a-bit-meter-tall pyramidal triped in a society of slim, matte-skinned two-meter-tall bipeds. The young man squinted at the brooch again. "I could have sworn this . . ."

"Sorry about that, Ambassador," said the nose ring. "Thank you for your help."

"Oh, you're welcome."

A gleaming, empty serving tray floated up to the young man, dipped its front in a sort of bow and said, "Hi. Hub again. What you have there, Mr. Olsule, is a piece of jet in the shape of a ceerevell, explosively inlaid with platinum and summitium. From the studio of Ms. Xossin Nabbard, of Sintrier, after the Quarafyd school. A finely wrought work of substantial artistry. But unfortunately not a terminal."

"Damn. Where is my terminal then?"

"You left all your terminal devices at home."

"Why didn't you tell me?"

"You asked me not to."

"When?"

"One hundred and—"

"Oh, never mind. Well, replace that, umm . . . change that instruction. Next time I leave home without a terminal . . . get them to make a fuss or something."

"Very well. It will be done."

Mr. Olsule scratched his head. "Maybe I should get a lace. One of those implant things."

"Undeniably, forgetting your head would pose considerable difficulties. In the meantime, I'll second one of the barge's remotes to accompany you for the rest of the evening, if you'd like."

"Yeah, okay." The young man put the brooch back on and turned to the laden buffet table. "So, anyway; can I eat this . . . ? Oh. It's gone."

"Itchy motile envelope," said the tray quietly, floating off.

"Eh?"

"Ah, Kabe, my dear friend. Here you are. Thank you so much for coming."

Kabe swiveled to find the drone E. H. Tersono floating at his side at a level a little above head height for a human and a little below that of a Homomdan. The machine was a little less than a meter in height, and half that in width and depth. Its rounded-off rectangular casing was made of delicate pink porcelain held in a lattice of gently glowing blue lumenstone. Beyond the porcelain's translucent surface, the drone's internal components could just be made out; shadows beneath its thin ceramic skin. Its aura field, confined to a small volume directly underneath its flat base, was a soft blush of magenta, which, if Kabe recalled correctly, meant it was busy. Busy talking to him?

"Tersono," he said. "Yes. Well, you did invite me."

"Indeed I did. Do you know, it occurred to me only later that you might misinterpret my invitation as some sort of summons, even as an imperious demand. Of course, once these things are sent . . ."

"Ho-ho. You mean it wasn't a demand?"

"More of a petition. You see, I have a favor to ask you."

"You do?" This was a first.

"Yes. I wonder if we might talk somewhere we'd have a little more privacy?"

Privacy, thought Kabe. That was a word you didn't hear very often in the Culture. Probably more used in a sexual context than any other. And not always even then.

"Of course," he said. "Lead on."

"Thank you," the drone said, floating toward the stern and rising to look over the heads of the people gathered in the function space. The machine turned this way and that, making it clear it was looking for something or someone. "Actually," it said quietly, "we are not yet quite quorate . . . Ah. Here we are. Please; this way, Ar Ischloear."

They approached a group of humans centered on the Mahrai Ziller. The Chelgrian was nearly as long as Kabe was tall, and covered in fur that varied from white around his face to dark brown on his back. He had a predator's build, with large forward-facing eyes set in a big, broad-jawed head. His rear legs were long and powerful; a striped tail, woven about with silver chain, curved between them. Where his distant ancestors would have had two middle-legs, Ziller had a single broad midlimb, partially covered by a dark waistcoat. His arms were much like a human's, though covered in golden fur and ending in broad, six-digit hands more like paws.

Almost as soon as he and Tersono joined the group around Ziller, Kabe found himself engulfed by another confusing babble of conversation.

"—of course you don't know what I mean. You have no context."

"Preposterous. Everybody has a context."

"No. You have a situation, an environment. That is not the same thing. You exist. I would hardly deny you that."

"Well, thanks."

"Yeah. Otherwise you'd be talking to yourself."

"You're saying we don't really live, is that it?"

"That depends what you mean by live. But let's say yes."

"How fascinating, my dear Ziller," E. H. Tersono said. "I wonder—"

"Because we don't suffer."

"Because you scarcely seem capable of suffering."

"Well said! Now, Ziller—"

"Oh, this is such an ancient argument . . ."

"But it's only the *ability* to suffer that—"

"Hey! I've suffered! Lemil Kimp broke my heart."

"Shut up, Tulyi."

"—you know, that makes you sentient, or whatever. It's not actually suffering."

"But she did!"

"An ancient argument, you said, Ms. Sippens?"

"Yes."

"Ancient meaning bad?"

"Ancient meaning discredited."

"Discredited? By whom?"

"Not whom. What."

"And that what would be . . . ?"

"Statistics."

"So there we are. Statistics. Now then, Ziller, my dear friend—"

"You are not serious."

"I think she thinks she is more serious than you, Zil."

"Suffering demeans more than it ennobles."

"And this is a statement derived wholly from these statistics?"

"No. I think you'll find a moral intelligence is required as well."

"A prerequisite in polite society, I'm sure we'd all agree. Now, Ziller—"

"A moral intelligence which instructs us that all suffering is bad."

"No. A moral intelligence which will incline to treat suffering as bad until proved good."

"Ah! So you admit that suffering can be good."

"Exceptionally."

"Ha."

"Oh, nice."

"What?"

"Did you know that works in several different languages?"

"What? What does?"

"Tersono," Ziller said, turning at last to the drone, which had lowered itself to his shoulder level and edged closer and closer as it had tried to attract the Chelgrian's attention over the past few moments, during which time its aura field had just started to shade into the blue-gray of politely held-in-check frustration.

Mahrai Ziller, composer, half outcast, half exile, rose from his crouch and balanced on his rear haunches. His midlimb made a shelf briefly and he put his drink down on the smoothly furred surface while he used his forelimbs to straighten his waistcoat and comb his brows. "Help me," he said to the drone. "I am trying to make a serious point and your compatriot indulges in word play."

"Then I suggest you fall back and regroup and hope to catch her again later when she is in a less trenchantly flippant mood. You've met Ar Kabe Ischloear?"

"I have. We are old acquaintances. Ambassador."

"You dignify me, sir," the Homomdan rumbled. "I am more of a journalist."

"Yes, they do tend to call us all ambassadors, don't they? I'm sure it's meant to be flattering."

"No doubt. They mean well."

"They mean ambiguously, sometimes," Ziller said, turning briefly to the woman he had been talking to. She raised her glass and bowed her head a fraction.

"When you two have entirely finished criticizing your determinedly generous hosts . . ." Tersono said.

"This would be the private word you mentioned, would it?" Ziller asked.

"Precisely. Indulge an eccentric drone."

"Very well."

"This way."

The drone continued past the line of food tables toward the stern of the barge. Ziller followed the machine, seeming to flow along the polished deck, lithely graceful on his single broad midlimb and two strong rear legs. The composer still had his crystal full of wine balanced effortlessly in one hand, Kabe noticed. Ziller used his other hand to wave at a couple of people who nodded to or greeted him as they passed.

Kabe felt very heavy and lumbering in comparison. He tried drawing himself up to his full height so as to appear less stockily massive, but nearly collided with a very old and complicated light fitting hanging from the ceiling.

• • •

The three sat in a cabin which extended from the stern of the great barge, looking out over the ink-dark waters of the canal. Ziller had folded himself onto a low table, Kabe squatted comfortably on some cushions on the deck and Tersono rested on a delicate-looking and apparently very old webwood chair. Kabe had known the drone Tersono for all the ten years he had spent on Masaq' Orbital, and had noticed early on that it liked to surround itself with old things; this antique barge, for example, and the ancient furniture and fittings it contained.

Even the machine's physical makeup spoke of a sort of antiquarianism. It was a generally reliable rule that the bigger a Culture drone appeared, the older it was. The first examples, dating from eight or nine thousand years ago, had been the size of a bulky human. Subsequent models had gradually shrunk until the most advanced drones had, for some time, been small enough to slip into a pocket. Tersono's meter-tall body might have suggested that it had been constructed millennia ago when in fact it was only a few centuries old, and the extra space it took up was accounted for by the separation of its internal components, the better to exhibit the fine translucency of its unorthodox ceramic shell.

Ziller finished his drink and took a pipe from his waistcoat. He sucked on it until a little smoke rose from the bowl while the drone exchanged pleasantries with the Homomdan. The composer was still trying to blow smoke rings when Tersono finally said, ". . . which brings me to my motive in asking you both here."

"And what would that be?" Ziller asked.

"We are expecting a guest, Composer Ziller."

Ziller gazed levelly at the drone. He looked around the broad cabin and stared at the door. "What, now? Who?"

"Not now. In about thirty or forty days. I'm afraid we don't know exactly who quite yet. But it will be one of your people, Ziller. Someone from Chel. A Chelgrian."

Ziller's face consisted of a furred dome with two large, black, almost semicircular eyes positioned above a gray-pink, furless nasal area and a large, partially prehensile mouth. There was an expression on it now that Kabe had never seen before, though admittedly he had known the Chelgrian only casually and for less than a year. "Coming here?" Ziller asked. His voice was . . . icy, was the word, decided Kabe.

"Indeed. To this Orbital, possibly to this Plate."

Ziller's mouth worked. "Caste?" he said. The word was more spat than pronounced.

"One of the . . . Tacted? Possibly a Given," Tersono said smoothly.

Of course. Their caste system. At least part of the reason that Ziller was here and not there. Ziller studied his pipe and blew more smoke. "Possibly a Given, eh?" he muttered. "My, you are honored. Hope you get your etiquette exquisitely correct. You'd better start practicing now."

"We believe this person may be coming here to see you," the drone said. It turned frictionlessly in the webwood seat and extended a maniple field to work the cords which lowered the gold cloth drapes over the windows, cutting off the view to the dark canal and the snow-enfolded quays.

Ziller tapped the bowl of his pipe, frowning at it. "Really?" he said. "Oh dear. What a shame. I was thinking of embarking on a cruise before then. Deep space. For at least half a year. Perhaps longer. In fact I had quite decided upon it. You will convey my apologies to whatever simpering diplomat or supercilious noble they're sending. I'm sure they'll understand."

The drone dropped its voice. "I'm sure they won't."

"Me too. I was being ironic. But I'm serious about the cruise."

"Ziller," the drone said quietly. "They want to meet with you. Even if you did leave on a cruise, they would doubtless attempt to follow you and meet up on the cruise ship."

"And of course you wouldn't try to stop them."

"How could we?"

Ziller sucked on his pipe for a moment. "I suppose they want me to go back. Do they?"

The drone's gunmetal aura indicated puzzlement. "We don't know."

"Really?"

"Cr. Ziller, I am being perfectly open with you."

"Really. Well, can you think of another reason for this expedition?"

"Many, my dear friend, but none of them are especially likely. As I said, we don't know. However, if I was forced to speculate, I'd tend to agree with you that requesting your return to Chel is probably the main reason for the impending visit."

Ziller chewed on his pipe stem. Kabe wondered if it would break. "You can't force me to go back."

"My dear Ziller, we wouldn't even think of suggesting to you that you do," the drone said. "This emissary may wish do so, but the decision is entirely yours. You are an honored and respected guest, Ziller. Culture citizenship, to the extent that such a thing really exists with any degree of formality, would be yours by assumption. Your many admirers, among whose number I count myself, would long ago have made it yours by acclamation, if only that would not have seemed presumptuous."

Ziller nodded thoughtfully. Kabe wondered if this was a natural expression for a Chelgrian, or a learned, translated one. "Very flattering," Ziller said. Kabe had the impression the creature was genuinely trying to sound gracious. "However, I am still Chelgrian. Not quite naturalized yet."

"Of course. Your presence is trophy enough. To declare this your home would be—"

"Excessive," Ziller said pointedly. The drone's aura field flushed a sort of muddy cream color to indicate embarrassment, though a few flecks of red indicated it was hardly acute.

Kabe cleared his throat. The drone turned to him.

"Tersono," the Homomdan said. "I'm not entirely sure why I'm here, but may I just ask whether, in all this, you are talking as a representative of Contact?"

"Of course you may. Yes, I am speaking on behalf of the Contact section. And with the full co-operation of Masaq' Hub."

"I am not without friends, admirers," Ziller said suddenly, staring at the drone.

"Without?" Tersono said, field glowing a ruddy orange. "Why, as I say, you have almost nothing but—"

"I mean among some of your Minds; your ships, Tersono the Contact drone," Ziller said coldly. The machine rocked back in its chair. A little melodramatic, thought Kabe. Ziller went on, "I might well be able to persuade one of them to accommodate me and provide me with my own private cruise. One which this emissary might find much more difficult to intrude upon."

The drone's aura lapsed back to purple. It wobbled minutely in the chair. "You are welcome to try, my dear Ziller. However, that might be taken as a terrible insult."

"Fuck them."

"Yes, well. But I meant by us. A terrible insult on our part. An insult so terrible that in the very sad and regrettable circumstances—"

"Oh, spare me." Ziller looked away.

Ah yes, the war, thought Kabe. And the responsibility for it. Contact would regard this as all very delicate.

The drone, misted in purple, went quiet for a moment. Kabe shifted on his cushions. "The point is," Tersono continued, "that even the most willful and, ah, characterful of ships might not accede to the sort of request you have indicated you might make. In fact I'd wager quite heavily on it that they wouldn't."

Ziller chewed some more on his pipe. It had gone out. "Which means that Contact has already fixed this, doesn't it?"

Tersono wobbled again. "Let's just say that the wind has been tested."

"Yes, let's. Of course, this is always assuming that none of your ship Minds were lying."

"Oh, they never lie. They dissemble, evade, prevaricate, confound, confuse, distract, obscure, subtly misrepresent and willfully misunderstand with what often appears to be a positively gleeful relish and are generally perfectly capable of contriving to give one an utterly unambiguous impression of their future course of action while in fact intending to do exactly the opposite, but they never lie. Perish the thought."

Ziller did a good stare, Kabe decided. He was quite glad that those big, dark eyes were not directed at him. Though, certainly, the drone seemed impervious.

"I see," the composer said. "Well then, I suppose I might as well just stay put. I imagine I could just refuse to leave my apartment."

"Why, of course. Not very dignified, perhaps, but that would be your prerogative."

"Quite. But if I'm given no choice don't expect me to be welcoming, or even polite." He inspected the bowl of his pipe.

"That is why I asked Kabe to be here." The drone turned to the Homomdan. "Kabe, we would be so grateful if you'd agree to help play host to our guest Chelgrian when he or she appears. You would be half of a double act with me, possibly with some assistance from Hub, if that's acceptable. We don't yet know how much time this will take up on a daily basis, or how long the visit will last, but obviously if it proved to be extended we would make additional arrangements." The machine's body tipped a few degrees to one side in the webwood chair. "Would you do this? I know it is a lot to ask and you needn't give a definitive answer quite yet; sleep on it if you please and ask for any further information you'd like. But you would be doing us a great favor, given Cr. Ziller's perfectly understandable reticence."

Kabe sat back on his cushions. He blinked a few times. "Oh, I can tell you now. I'd be happy to be of help." He looked at Ziller. "Of course, I wouldn't want to distress Mahrai Ziller . . ."

"I shall remain undistressed, depend on it," Ziller told him. "If you can distract this bile-purse they're sending you'll be doing me a favor, too."

The drone made a sighing noise, rising and falling fractionally above the seat. "Well, that is . . . satisfactory, then. Kabe, can we talk more tomorrow? We'd like to brief you over the next few days. Nothing too intense, but, considering the unfortunate circumstances of our relationship with the Chelgrians over recent years, obviously we don't want to upset our guest through any lack of knowledge of their affairs and manners."

Ziller made a noise like a snarled "Huh!"

"Of course," Kabe told Tersono. "I understand." Kabe spread all three of his arms. "My time is yours."

"And our gratitude yours. Now," the machine said, rising into the air. "I'm afraid I've kept us chattering in here for so long we've missed Hub's avatar's little speech and if we don't hurry we'll be late for the main, if rather sad, event of the evening."

"That time already?" Kabe said, rising too. Ziller snapped the cap shut on his pipe and replaced it in his waistcoat. He unfolded himself from the table and the three returned to the main ballroom as the lights were going out and the roof was rumbling and rolling back to reveal a sky of a few thin, ragged clouds, multitudinous stars and the bright thread of the Orbital's far side. On a small stage at the forward end of the ballroom, the Hub's avatar—in the shape of a thin, silver-skinned human—stood, head bowed. Cold air flowed in around the assembled humans and varied other guests. All, save for the avatar, gazed up at the sky. Kabe wondered in how many other places within the city, across the Plate and along this whole side of the great bracelet world similar scenes were taking place.

Kabe tilted his massive head and stared up too. He knew roughly where to look; Masaq' Hub had been quietly persistent in its pre-publicity over the last fifty days or so.

Silence.

Then a few people muttered something and a number of tiny chimes sounded from personal terminals distributed throughout the huge, open space.

And a new star blazed in the heavens. There was just the hint of a flicker at first, then the tiny point of light grew brighter and brighter, exactly as though it was a lamp on which somebody was turning up a dimmer switch. Stars nearby began to disappear, their feeble twin-klings drowned out by the torrent of radiation pouring from the newcomer. In a few moments the star had settled to a steady, barely wavering gray-blue glare, almost outshining the glowing string of Masaq's far-side plates.

Kabe heard one or two breaths nearby, and a few brief cries. "Oh, grief," a woman said quietly. Someone sobbed.

"Not even particularly pretty," Ziller muttered, so softly that Kabe suspected only he and the drone had heard.

They all watched for a few more moments. Then the silver-skinned, dark-suited avatar said, "Thank you," in that hollow, not loud but deep and carrying voice that avatars seemed to favor. It stepped down from the stage and walked away, leaving the opened room and heading for the quayside.

"Oh, we had a real one," Ziller said. "I thought we'd have an image." He looked at Tersono, which allowed itself a faint glow of aquamarine modesty.

The roof started to roll back, gently shaking the deck beneath Kabe's trio of feet as though the old barge's engines had woken again. The lights brightened fractionally; the light of the newly bright star continued to pour through the gap between the halves of the closing roof, then through the glass after the segments had met and locked again. The room was much darker than it had been before, but people could see well enough.

They look like ghosts, thought Kabe, gazing around the humans. Many were still staring up at the star. Some were heading outside, to the open deck. A few couples and larger groups were huddled together, individuals comforting one another. I didn't think it would affect so many so deeply, the Homomdan thought. I thought they might almost laugh it off. I still don't really know them. Even after all this time.

"This is morbid," Ziller said, drawing himself up. "I'm going home. I have work to do. Not that tonight's news has exactly been conducive to inspiration or motivation."

"Yes," Tersono said. "Forgive a rude and impatient drone, but might I ask what you've been working on lately, Cr. Ziller? You haven't published anything for a while but you do seem to have been very busy."

Ziller smiled broadly. "Actually, it's a commissioned piece."

"Really?" the drone's aura rainbowed with brief surprise. "For whom?"

Kabe saw the Chelgrian's gaze flick briefly toward the stage where the avatar had stood earlier. "All in due course, Tersono," Ziller said. "But it's a biggish piece and it'll be a while yet before its first performance."

"Ah. Most mysterious."

Ziller stretched, putting one long furred leg out behind him and tensing before relaxing. He looked at Kabe. "Yes, and if I don't get back to work on it, it'll be late." He turned back to Tersono. "You'll keep me informed about this wretched emissary?"

"You will have full access to all we know."

"Right. Good night, Tersono." The Chelgrian nodded to Kabe. "Ambassador."

Kabe bowed. The drone dipped. Ziller went softly bounding through the thinning crowd.

Kabe looked back up at the nova, thinking.

Eight-hundred-and-three-year-old light shone steadily down.

The light of ancient mistakes, he thought. That was what Ziller had called it, on the interview Kabe had heard just that morning. "Tonight you dance by the light of ancient mistakes!" Except that no one was dancing.

It had been one of the last great battles of the Idiran war, and one of the most ferocious, one of the least restrained, as the Idirans risked everything, including the opprobrium even of those they regarded as friends and allies, in a series of desperate, wildly destructive and brutal attempts to alter the increasingly obvious likely outcome of the war. Only (if that was a word one could ever use in such a context) six stars had been destroyed during the nearly fifty years the war had raged. This single battle for a tendril of galactic limb, lasting less than a hundred days, had accounted for two of them as the suns Portisia and Junce had been induced to explode.

It had become known as the Twin Novae Battle, but really what had been done to each of the suns had generated something more like a supernova on each. Neither star had shone upon a barren system. Worlds had died, entire biospheres had been snuffed out and billions of sentient creatures had suffered—albeit briefly—and perished in these twin catastrophes.

The Idirans had committed the acts, the gigadeathcrimes—their monstrous weaponry, not that of the Culture, had been directed first at one star, then the other—yet still, arguably, the Culture might have prevented what had happened. The Idirans had attempted to sue for peace several times before the battle started, but the Culture had continued to insist on unconditional surrender, and so the war had ground onward and the stars had died.

It was long over. The war had ended nearly eight hundred years ago and life had gone on. Still, the real space light had been crawling across the intervening distance for all these centuries, and by its relativistic standard it was only now that those stars blew up, and just at this moment that those billions died, as the outrushing shell of light swept over and through the Masaq' system.

The Mind that was Masaq' Orbital Hub had its own reasons for wanting to commemorate the Twin Novae Battle and had asked the indulgence of its inhabitants, announcing that for the interval between the first nova and the second it would be observing its own private term of mourning, although without affecting the execution of its duties. It had intimated there would be some sort of more upbeat event to mark the end of this period, though exactly what form this would take it hadn't yet revealed.

Kabe suspected he knew, now. He found himself glancing involuntarily in the direction Ziller had taken, just as the Chelgrian's gaze had strayed toward the stage earlier, when he'd been asked who had commissioned whatever he was working on.

All in due course, Kabe thought. As Ziller had said.

For tonight, all Hub had wanted was that people look up and see the sudden, silent light, and think; perhaps contemplate a little. Kabe had half expected the locals to take no notice whatsoever and just carry on with their busy little one-long-party lives as usual; however it appeared that, here at least, the Hub Mind's wish had been granted.

"All very regrettable," the drone E. H. Tersono said at Kabe's side, and made a sighing sound. Kabe thought it probably meant to sound sincere.

"Salutary, for all of us," Kabe agreed. His own ancestors had been the Idirans' mentors, and fought alongside the Idirans in the early stages of the ancient war. The Homomda felt the weight of their own responsibilities as keenly as the Culture did its.

"We try to learn," Tersono said quietly. "But still we make mistakes."

It was talking now about Chel, the Chelgrians and the Caste War, Kabe knew. He turned and looked at the machine as the people moved away in the steady, ghostly light.

"You could always do nothing, Tersono," he told it. "Though such a course usually brings its own regrets."

I am too glib, sometimes, Kabe thought, I tell them too exactly what they want to hear.

The drone tipped back to make clear that it was looking up at the Homomdan, but said nothing.

2

Winter Storm

The hull of the ruined ship bowed away on all sides, curving out and then back, arcing overhead. They had fitted lights in the center of what had become the ceiling, directly above the curious, glazed-looking floor; reflections glowed from the glassily swirled, distorted surface itself, and from the few stumps of unidentifiable equipment that protruded above it.

Quilan tried to find a place to stand where he thought he could distinguish what it was he was standing on, then switched off the suit's field pack and let his feet touch the surface. It was hard to tell through his boots, but the floor seemed to have the feel of what it looked like; glass. The spin they'd given the hull produced what felt like about a quarter gravity. He patted the fastenings securing his bulky backpack.

He looked up and around. The hull's interior surface looked hardly damaged. There were various indentations and a scattering of holes, some circular and some elliptical, but all quite symmetrical and smooth and part of the design; none went all the way through the hull material and none looked ragged. The only aperture which led to the outside was right in the nose of the craft, seventy meters away from where he stood, more or less in the center of the spoon-shaped

29

mass of floor. That two-meter-wide hole had been cut in the hull weeks ago to gain access after the hulk had been located and secured. That was how he had gained entry.

He could see various discolored patches on the hull's surface that didn't look right, and a few small dangling tubes and wires, up near the newly emplaced lights. Part of him wondered why they had bothered with the lights. The hull's interior was evacuated, open to space; nobody would be coming in here without a full suit, so they would have the concomitant sensory equipment that made lights unnecessary. He looked down at the floor. Maybe the technicians had been superstitious, or just emotional. The lights made the place seem a little less forbidding, less haunted.

He could understand that wandering around in here with only ambient radiations to impinge upon the augmented senses might well induce terror if you were of a sensitive nature. They'd found much of what they'd hoped to find; enough for his mission, sufficient to save a thousand or so other souls. Almost certainly not enough to fulfill his hopes. He looked about. It appeared they had removed all the sensory and monitoring equipment they'd been using to inspect the wreck of the privateer *Winter Storm*.

He felt a shudder through his boots. He glanced up to the side, as the sliced-off bow of the ship was put back in place. Enclosed, in this ship of the dead. At last.

~ *Isolation established, it says,* said a voice in his head. The machine in his backpack produced a faint vibration.

~ *It says the proximity of the suit's systems are interfering with its instruments. You'll have to switch your com off. Now it's saying, Please remove the pack from your back.*

~ Will we still be able to talk?

~ *You and I will be able to talk to each other, and it'll be able to talk to me.*

~ All right, he said, slipping the pack off. ~ The lights are all right? he asked.

~ *They're just lights, nothing else.*

~ Where shall I put—he started to say, but then the pack went light in his hands and began to tug away from him.

~ *It wants us to know it has its own motive power,* the voice in his head informed him.

~ Oh, yes, of course. Ask it to work fast, would you? Tell it we're pressed for time because there's a Culture warship braking toward our position as we speak, coming to—

~ *Think that'll make any difference, Major?*

~ I don't know. Tell it to be thorough, too.

~ *Quilan, I think it'll just do what it has to do, but if you really want me to—*

~ No. No, sorry. Sorry, don't.

~ *Look, I know this is hard on you, Quil. I'll leave you alone for a bit, okay?*

~ Yes, thanks.

Huyler's voice went off-line. It was as though a hiss right on the boundary of hearing had suddenly been removed.

He watched the Navy drone for a moment. The machine was silvery gray and nondescript, like the pack from an ancient space suit. It floated silently across the near-flat floor, keeping about a meter off its surface, heading for the near, bow end of the ship to start its search pattern.

It would be too much to ask, he thought to himself. The chances are too remote. It was a small miracle we discovered anything at all in here, that we are able to rescue those souls from such destruction a second time. To ask for more . . . was probably pointless, but no more than natural.

What intelligent creature possessed of wit and feeling could do otherwise? We always want more, he thought, we always take our past successes for granted and assume they but point the way to future triumphs. But the universe does not have our own best interests at heart, and to assume for a moment that it does, ever did or ever might is to make the most calamitous and hubristic of mistakes.

To hope as he was hoping, hoping against likelihood, against statistical probability, in that sense against the universe itself, was only to be expected, but it was also almost certainly forlorn. The animal in him craved something that his higher brain knew was not going to happen. That was the point he was impaled upon, the front on which he suffered; that struggle of the lower brain's almost chemical simplicities of yearning pitched against the withering realities revealed and comprehended by consciousness. Neither could give up, and neither could give way. The heat of their battle burned in his mind.

He wondered if, despite what he'd been told, Huyler could hear any hint of it.

~ All our tests confirm that the construct has been fully recovered. All error-checks have been completed. The construct is now available for interaction and downloading, the sister technician announced in his head. She seemed to be trying to sound more like a machine than machines ever did.

He opened his eyes and blinked into the light for a moment. The headset he wore was just visible from the corners of his eyes. The reclined couch he lay on felt firm but comfortable. He was in the medical facility of the Mendicant Sisters' temple ship *Piety*. Across the racks of gleaming, spotless medical gear, near the side of a stained, battered-looking thing about the size of a domestic chill cabinet, the sister technician talking to him was a youngster with a severe expression, dark brown fur and a head which had been partially shaved.

~ I'll download it now, she continued. ~ Do you wish to interact with it immediately?

~ Yes, I do.

~ A moment, please.

~ Wait, what will it—will he—experience?

~ Awareness. Sight, in the form of a human-compensated feed from this camera. She tapped a tiny wand protruding from the headset she wore. ~ Hearing, in the form of your voice. Continue?

~ Yes.

There was the very faintest impression of a hiss, and then a sleepy-sounding, deeply male voice saying,

~ . . . *seven, eight . . . nine . . . Hello? What? Where is this? What is this? Where—? What's happened?*

It was a voice that went from slurred sleepiness to suddenly fearful confusion and then onto a degree of control within just a few words. The voice sounded younger than he'd been expecting. He supposed there was no need for it to sound old.

~ Sholan Hadesh Huyler, he responded calmly. ~ Welcome back.

~ *Who is that? I can't move.* There was still a trace of uncertainty and anxiety in the voice. ~ *This isn't . . . the beyond. Is it?*

~ My name is Called-to-Arms-from-Given Major Quilan IV of Itirewein. I'm sorry you can't move but please don't worry; your personality construct is currently still inside the substrate you were originally stored within, in the Military Technology Institute, Cravinyr, on Aorme. At the moment the substrate you're inside is aboard the temple ship *Piety*. It's in orbit around a moon of the planet Reshref Four, in the constellation of the Bow, along with the hulk of the star cruiser *Winter Storm*.

~ *There you are. Ah. You say you're a major. I was an admiral-general. I outrank you.*

The voice was perfectly under control now; still deep, but clipped and crisp. The voice of somebody used to giving orders.

~ Your rank when you died was greater than mine now, certainly, sir.

The sister technician adjusted something on the console in front of her.

~ *Whose are those hands? They look female.*

~ Those belong to the sister technician who is looking after us, sir. Your point of view is from a headset she's wearing.

~ *Can she hear me?*

~ No, sir.

~ *Ask her to take the headset off and show me what she looks like.*

~ Sir, are you—?

~ *Major, if you would.*

Quilan felt himself sigh. ~ Sister technician, he thought. He asked her to do as Huyler had asked. She did, but looked annoyed about it.

~ *Sour-looking, frankly. Wish I hadn't bothered. So, what has been happening, Major? What am I doing here?*

~ A great deal has been happening, sir. You'll be given a full historical briefing in due course.

~ *Date?*

~ It is the ninth of spring, 3455.

~ *Just eighty-six years? I expected more, somehow. So, Major, why have I been resurrected?*

~ Frankly, sir, I do not entirely know myself.

~ *Then, frankly, Major, I think you'd better rapidly put me in touch with somebody who does know.*

~ There has been a war, sir.

~ *A war? Who with?*

~ With ourselves, sir; a civil war.

~ *This some sort of caste thing?*

~ Yes, sir.

~ *I suppose it was always coming. So, am I being conscripted? Are the dead being used as the reserves?*

~ No, sir. The war is over. We are at peace again, though there will be changes. There was an attempt to rescue you and the other stored personalities from the substrate in the Military Institute during the war—an attempt I was involved in—but it was only partially success-ful. Until a few days ago we thought it had been completely unsuc-cessful.

~ *So; am I being brought back to life to appreciate the manifest glories of the new order? To be re-educated? Tried for past incorrectness? What?*

~ Our superiors think that you may be able to help with a mission that lies before both of us.

~ *Before both of us? Uh-huh. And what exactly would that mission be, Major?*

~ I can't tell you that at the moment, sir.

~ *You seem worryingly ignorant to be the one who's pulling all the strings here, Major.*

~ I'm sorry, sir. I believe that my current lack of knowledge may be a safety procedure. But I would guess that your expertise regard-ing the Culture could be of some help.

~ *My thoughts on the Culture proved politically unpopular when I was alive, Major; that's one of the reasons I took the offer of being put into storage on Aorme, rather than either die and go to heaven or keep banging my head against a wall in Combined Forces Intelligence. Are you telling me the top brass have come around to my point of view?*

~ Perhaps, sir. Perhaps just your knowledge of the Culture would prove useful.

~ *Even if it's eight-and-a-half decades old?*

Quilan paused, then expressed something he'd been preparing for some days, since they'd rediscovered the substrate.

~ Sir, considerable thought and great effort went into both retrieving you and preparing me for my mission. I would hope that no part of that thought or effort was either wasted or without point.

Huyler was silent for a moment. ~ *There were about five hundred others besides me in that machine in the Institute. Did they all get out, too?*

~ The final figure for those stored was nearer a thousand, but yes, sir, they all appear to have come through, though only you've been revived so far.

~ *All right then, soldier, perhaps you should start by telling me what you do know about this mission.*

~ I know only what you might call our cover story, sir. I've been induced to forget the real mission goal for the time being.

~*What?*

~ It's a security measure, sir. You'll be briefed with the full mission details and you won't forget them. I ought to remember gradually what my mission is anyway, but in the event that something goes wrong, you'll be the back-up.

~ *They frightened somebody might read your mind, Major?*

~ I imagine so, sir.

~ *Though, of course, the Culture doesn't do that.*

~ So we're told.

~ *Extra precaution, eh? Must be an important mission. But if you can still remember that you have a secret mission in the first place . . .*

~ I am reliably informed that in a day or two I'll even forget that as well.

~ *Well, all very interesting. So, what would that cover story be?*

~ I will be on a cultural diplomatic mission to a world of the Culture.

~ *A Cultural cultural mission?*

~ In a sense, sir.

~ *Just an old soldier's lame joke, son. Relax that frozen sphincter a bit, won't you?*

~ I'm sorry, sir. I need to have your agreement both to undertake the mission and to be transferred into another substrate within myself. That process may take a little time.

~ *Did you say another machine inside you?*

~ Yes, sir. There is a device inside my skull, designed to look like an ordinary Soulkeeper, but able to accommodate your personality as well.

~ *You don't look that much of a fat-head, Major.*

~ The device is no larger than a small finger, sir.

~ *And what about your Soulkeeper?*

~ The same device functions as my Soulkeeper too, sir.

~ *They can make something that clever that small?*

~ Yes, sir, they can. There probably isn't time to go into all the technical details.

~ *Well I beg your pardon, Major, but take it from an old soldier that war in general, and limited personnel missions in particular, are often all about the technical details. Plus, you're rushing me, son. You have the advantage of being at the controls here. I've got eighty-six years of catching up to do. I don't even know that you're telling me the truth about any of this. It all sounds suspicious as hell so far. And about this being transferred inside you. You trying to tell me I don't even get my own god-damned body?*

~ I'm sorry there wasn't more time to brief you, sir. We thought we had lost you. Twice, in a sense. When we discovered that your substrate had survived, my mission had already been decided on. And yes, your consciousness would be transferred entirely into the substrate within my body; you would have access to all my senses and we would be able to communicate, though you would not be able to control my body unless I became deeply unconscious or suffered brain death. The only technical detail I know is that the device is a crystalline nanofoam matrix with links to my brain.

~ *So I'd just be along for the ride? What sort of itch-shit mission profile is that? Who's putting you up to this, Major?*

~ It would be a novel experience for both of us, sir, and one that I would consider a privilege. It is believed that your presence and advice would increase the likelihood of the mission's success. As to who put me up to it, I was trained and briefed by a team under the command of Estodien Visquile.

~ *Visquile? Is that old horror still alive? And made it to Estodien, too. I'll be damned.*

~ He sends his regards, sir. I carry a personal and private communication from him addressed to you.

~ *Let me hear it, Major.*

~ Sir, we thought you might like a little more time to—

~ *Major Quilan, I'm mightily suspicious that I'm being shovelled into something pretty damn dubious here. I'll be honest with you, youngster; it's not very likely that I'm going to agree to take part in your unknown mission even after I've heard Visquile's message, but I'm sure as shit not going willingly through your ears, up your ass, or anywhere else unless I do hear what that old whoreboy's got to say, and I might as well hear it now as later. Making myself clear here?*

~ Very, sir. Sister technician; please replay the message from Estodien Visquile to Hadesh Huyler.

~ Proceeding, said the female.

Quilan was left alone with his thoughts. He realized how tense he had become communicating with the ghost of Hadesh Huyler, and deliberately relaxed his body, easing his muscles and straightening his back. Again, his gaze swept over the gleaming surfaces of the medical facility, but what he was seeing was the interior of the hull of the ship they were floating alongside, the privateer cruiser *Winter Storm*.

He had been aboard the wreck once so far, while they were still trying to locate and extract Huyler's soul from the thousand or so others stored within the rescued substrate, which they'd located in the wreck with a specially adapted Navy drone. He had been promised that later, if there was time, he would be allowed to go back to the wreck with that drone and attempt to discover any other souls the original sweeps had missed.

Time was running out, though. It had taken time to get permis-

sion for what he wanted to do, and it was taking time for the Navy
technical people to adjust the machine. Meanwhile they'd been told
that the Culture warship was on its way, just a few days out. At the
moment the techs were pessimistic that they'd get the drone finished
in time.

The image of the wrecked ship's scooped-out hull seemed fixed in
his brain.

~ *Major Quilan?*

~ Sir?

~ *Reporting for duty, Major. Permission to come aboard.*

~ Just so, sir. Sister technician? Transfer Hadesh Huyler into the
substrate within my body.

~ Directly, the female said. ~ Proceeding.

He had wondered if he'd feel anything. He did: a tingling, then a
warmth in a small area on the nape of his neck. The sister technician
kept him informed; the transfer went well and took about two minutes. Checking it had gone perfectly took twice that time.

What bizarre fates our technologies dream up for us, he thought
as he lay there. Here I am, a male, becoming pregnant with the ghost
of an old dead soldier, to travel beyond the bounds of light older than
our civilization and carry out some task I have spent the best part of
a year training for but of which I presently have no real knowledge
whatsoever.

The spot on his neck was cooling. He thought his head felt very
slightly warmer than it had before. He might have been imagining it.

You lose your love, your heart, your very soul, he thought, and
gain—"a land destroyer!" he heard her say, so falsely, bravely cheerful
in his mind, while the rain-filled sky flashed above her and the vast
weight pinned him utterly. Some memory of that pain and despair
squeezed tears from his eyes.

~ Complete.

~ *Testing, testing,* said the dry, laconic voice of Hadesh Huyler.

~ Hello, sir.

~ *You okay, son?*

~ I'm fine, sir.

~ *Did that hurt you there, Major? You seem a little . . . distressed.*

~ No, sir. Just an old memory. How do you feel?

~ *Pretty damn strange. I dare say I'll get used to it. Looks like everything checks out. Shit, that female techie doesn't look any better through a male's eyes than she does through a camera.* Of course; what he could see, Huyler could see. Before he could reply, Huyler added, *You sure you're okay?*

~ Positive, sir. I'm fine.

He stood within the hulk of the *Winter Storm*. The Navy drone went back and forth across the strange, almost flat floor of the wreck, searching in a grid pattern. It passed the hole in the floor where the substrate from Aorme had been wrenched out.

In the two days since they'd found the substrate, Quilan had persuaded the techs that it was worth recalibrating the drone to look for substrates much smaller than the one Huyler had been in, substrates the size of a Soulkeeper, in fact. They had already performed a standard search, but he got them at least to try and look more closely. The Mendicant Sisters on the temple ship had helped with the persuading; any chance to rescue a soul had to be pursued to the utmost.

By the time the drone was ready, though, the Culture ship which would take him on the first leg of his journey was already starting to decelerate. The Navy drone would have time for one sweep and one sweep only.

He watched it make its passes, following its own unseen grid across the flat floor. He looked up and around the gaping shell of the ship's hull.

He tried to recreate in his mind the interior of the vessel as it had been when it had been intact, and wondered in what part of it she had stayed, where she had moved and where she had lain her head to sleep in the ship's false night.

The main drive units might be up there, filling half the ship, the flyer hangar was there, in the stern, the decks would spread here and here; individual cabins would have been over there, or over there.

Maybe, he thought, maybe there was still a chance, maybe the techs had been wrong and there was still something left to find. The hull only held because it was energised somehow. They still didn't understand everything about these great, gifted ships. Perhaps somewhere within the hull itself . . .

The machine floated up to him, clicking, ceiling lights glittering across its metallic carapace. He looked at it.

~ *Sorry to break in, Quil, but it wants you to get the hell out the way.*

~ Of course. Sorry. Quilan stepped to one side. Not too clumsily, he hoped. It had been a while since he'd worn a suit.

~ *I'll leave you alone again.*

~ No, it's all right. Talk if you want to talk.

~ *Hmm. Okay. I've been wondering.*

~ What?

~ *We've spent so much time doing technical, calibrating stuff, but we haven't touched on some of the basic assumptions being made here, like is it really true we can hear each other when we talk like this but not when we think? Seems a damn fine distinction to me.*

~ Well, that's what we've been told. Why, have you had any hint of—?

~ *No, it's just that when you look at something through another person's eyes and you think something, after a while you start to wonder if it's really what you think or some sort of bleed-over from what they're thinking.*

~ I think I see what you mean.

~ *So, think we should test it out?*

~ I suppose we could, sir.

~ *All right. See if you can catch what I'm thinking.*

~ Sir, I don't think . . . he thought, but there was silence, even as his own thoughts tailed off. He waited a few more moments. Then a few more. The drone continued on its search pattern, each time passing by further and further away.

~ *Well? Catch anything?*

~ No, sir. Sir, I—

~ *You don't know what you missed, Major. Okay, your turn. Go on. Think of something. Anything.*

He sighed. The enemy ship—no, he shouldn't think of them that way . . . The ship could be here by now. He felt that what he and

Huyler were doing right now was a waste of time, but on the other hand there was nothing they could do to make the drone carry out its task any faster, so they weren't really wasting any time at all. All the same, it felt like it.

What a strange interval, he thought, to be here in this hermetic mausoleum, standing in the midst of such forlorn desolation with another mind inside his own, trading absences in the face of a task he knew nothing about.

And so he thought of the long avenue at Old Briri in the fall, the way she scuffed through the amber drifts of fallen leaves, kicking golden explosions of leaves into the air. He thought of their marriage ceremony, in the gardens of her parents' estate, with the oval bridge reflected in the lake. As they'd made their vows a wind out of the hills had ruffled the reflection and taken it away, snapping at the awning above them, blowing off hats and making the priest clutch at her robes, but the same strong, spring-scented breeze had stroked the tops of the veil trees and sent a shimmering white cloud of blossom falling around them, like snow.

A few of the petals were still resting on her fur and eyelashes at the end of the service when he turned to her, removed his own ceremonial muzzle and hers, and kissed her. Their friends and family hurrahed; hats were thrown into the air and some were caught by another gust of wind, to land in the lake and sail off across the little waves like a dainty flotilla of brightly colored boats.

He thought again of her face, her voice, those last few moments. Live for me, he had said, and made her promise. How could they have known it would be a promise she could never keep, and he would still live to remember?

Huyler's voice broke in. ~ *Done your thinking, Major?*

~ Yes, sir. Did you catch anything?

~ *No. Just physiological stuff. Looks like we've still got some degree of privacy. Oh; the machine says it's finished.*

Quilan looked at the drone, which had arrived at the far end of the spoon of floor. ~ What does it . . . Look, Huyler, can I talk to that thing directly?

~ *I think I can set that up, now it's finished. I'll still be able to hear though.*

~ I don't mind, I just . . .

~ *There. Try that.*

~ Machine? Drone?

~ Yes, Major Quilan.

~ Are there any other personality constructs in here, anywhere within the hull?

~ No. Only the one I was tasked with discovering earlier which now shares coordinates with yourself, that of Admiral-General Huyler.

~ Are you sure? he asked, wondering if any hint of his hope and despair could color his communicated words.

~ Yes.

~ What about within the fabric of the hull material itself?

~ That is not relevant.

~ Have you scanned it?

~ I cannot. It is not open to my sensors.

The machine was merely clever, not sentient. It would probably not have been able to recognize the emotions behind his words anyway, even if they had been communicated.

~ Are you absolutely certain? Have you scanned everything?

~ I am certain. Yes. The only three personalities present within the ship's hull in any form appreciable to my senses are: you, the personality through which I am communicating to you, and my own.

He looked down at the sworl of floor between his feet. So there was no hope. ~ I see, he thought. ~ Thank you.

~ You are welcome.

Gone. Gone utterly and forever. Gone in a way that was new, bereft of the comforts of ignorance, and without appeal. Before, we believed that the soul might be saved. Now our technology, our better understanding of the universe and our vanguard in the beyond, has robbed us of our unreal hopes and replaced them with its own rules and regulations, its own algebra of salvation and continuance. It has given us a glimpse of heaven, and made more intense the reality of our despair when we know that truly it exists and that those we love will never be found there.

He switched on his communicator. There was a message waiting: THEY'RE HERE, said the letters on the suit's little screen. It was timed eleven minutes earlier. A lot more time had passed than he'd have estimated.

~ *Looks like our ride's arrived.*

~ Yes. I'll let them know we're ready.

~ *You do that, Major.*

"Major Quilan here," he transmitted. "I understand our guests have arrived."

"Major." It was the voice of mission CO, Colonel Ustremi. "Everything all right in there?"

"Everything is fine, sir." He looked across the glassy floor and around the huge empty space. "Just fine."

"Did you find what you were looking for, Quil?"

"No, sir. I did not find what I wanted."

"I'm sorry, Quil."

"Thank you, sir. You can open the hatchway again. The machine's finished its work. Let the techs see what else they can find by just digging."

"Opening now. One of our guests wants to come and say hello."

"In here?" he said, watching the tiny cone in the ship's bow hinge away.

"Yes. That okay with you?"

"I suppose." Quil looked back at the drone, which was hovering where it had completed its search. "Tell your machine to switch itself off first, will you?"

"Done."

The Navy drone settled to the floor.

"Okay, send them in when they're ready."

The figure appeared in the blackness of the removed hatchway. It looked human and yet could not be; one of them would have been no more able to survive in the vacuum without a suit than he was.

Quilan upped the magnification on the visor, zooming in as the creature began to walk down the slope of the hull's interior. The biped had what looked like jet black skin and its clothing was shiny gray. It looked very thin but then they all did. Its feet met the flat surface he was already standing on and brought it closer. It swung its arms as it walked.

~ *They'd look like prey if there was just more eating on them.*

He didn't reply. The zoomed window in the visor kept the creature at the same magnification until the distinction between the window and the rest of the view disappeared. The thing's face was narrow and pointed, its nose thin and sharp, and the eyes set in the night-black face were small and vividly blue surrounded by white.

~ *Shit. They don't look any more appetizing closer up.*

"Major Quilan?" the creature said. The skin above its eyes moved when it spoke to him, but not its mouth.

"Yes," he said.

"How do you do. I am the avatar of the Rapid Offensive Unit *Nuisance Value*. Pleased to meet you. I've come to take you on the first leg of your trip to Masaq' Orbital."

"I see."

~ *Quick suggestion; ask how to address it.*

"Do you have a name, or rank? What should I call you?"

"I am the ship," it said, raising and dropping its narrow shoulders. "Call me Nuisance, if you like." Its mouth twisted up at the edges. "Or Avatar, or just Ship."

~ *Or just abomination.*

"Very well, Ship."

"Okay." It held up its hands. "I just wanted to say hello personally. We'll be waiting for you. Let us know when you're ready to go." It let its gaze arc up and around. "They said it was all right to come in here. I hope I didn't interrupt anything."

"I had finished in here. I was looking for something but I didn't find it."

"I'm sorry."

~ *So you should be, you worm-fucker.*

"Yes. Shall we go?" He started toward the circle of night in the bow of the ship. The avatar fell into step alongside. Its gaze took in the floor briefly. "What happened to this ship?"

"We don't know exactly," he told it. "It lost a battle. Something hit it very hard. The hull survived but everything else inside it was destroyed."

The avatar nodded. "Compacted fused state," it stated. "And the crew?"

"We are walking on them."

"I'm sorry." The creature immediately floated off the floor by half a meter. It stopped making the walking motion and posed itself as though sitting. It crossed its legs and arms. "This happened in the war, I take it."

They came to the slope and started up it; he kept on walking. He turned briefly to the creature. "Yes, Ship, it happened during your war."

3

Infra Dawn

B ut you might die."
  "That's the whole point."
"Really. I see."
"No, I don't think you do, do you?"
"No."
The woman laughed and continued to adjust the flying harness.
All about them the landscape was the color of drying blood.

Kabe stood on a rugged but still elegant platform made from wood
and stone and perched on the edge of a long escarpment. He was
talking with Feli Vitrouv, a woman with wild black hair and deep
brown skin over hard-looking muscles. She wore a tight blue body
suit with a small belly pack and was in the process of strapping herself
into a wing harness, a complicated device full of compressed, slatted
fins that covered most of her rear surfaces, from ankles to neck and
down her arms. About sixty other people—half of them also wing-
fliers—were distributed about the platform, which was surrounded
by the blimp tree forest.

Dawn was just starting to break anti-spinwards, throwing long
slanting rays across the cloud-whisped indigo sky. The fainter stars
had long since been submerged in the slowly brightening vault;

barely a handful still twinkled. The only other heavenly objects visible were the lobed shape of Dorteseli, the larger of the two ringed gas giants in the system, and the wavering white point that was the nova Portisia.

Kabe looked around the platform. The sunlight was so red it almost looked brown. It shone from the vastly distant atmospheres above the Orbital's trailing plates, over the escarpment's edge, across the dark valley with its pale islands of mist and sank onward to the low rolling hills and the distant plains on the far side. The cries of the forest's nocturnal animals had slowly disappeared over the past twenty minutes or so, and the calls of birds were beginning to fill the night-chilled air above the low forest.

The blimpers were dark domes scattered amongst the taller ground-hugging trees. They looked threatening to Kabe, especially in this ruddy glow. The giant black gas sacs loomed, shriveled and deflated but still impressively rotund, over the bloated bulk of the banner reservoir, while their strangler roots snaked across the ground all around them like giant tentacles, establishing their territory and keeping ordinary trees at bay. A breeze stirred the branches of the ground trees and set their leaves rustling pleasantly. The blimpers at first appeared not to be affected by the wind, then moved slowly, creaking and crackling, adding to the effect of monstrousness.

The crimson sunlight was just starting to catch the tops of the more distant blimp trees, hundreds of meters away along the shallow side of the scarp; a handful of wing-fliers had already disappeared and headed down barely discernible paths into the forest. On the other side of the platform the view sank over cliffs, scree and forest into the shadows of the broad valley, where the meandering loops and oxbow lakes of Tulume River could be glimpsed through the slowly drifting patches of mist.

"Kabe."

"Ah, Ziller."

Ziller wore a close-fitting dark suit, with only his head, hands and feet showing. Where the suit's material covered the pad of his midlimb it had been reinforced with hide. It had been the Chelgrian who'd wanted to come out here originally to see the wing-fliers. Kabe had already watched this particular sport, albeit from a distance, a few years earlier, shortly after he'd first arrived on Masaq'. Then he'd been on a long articulated river barge heading down the Tulume for the Ribbon Lakes, the Great River and the city of Aquime, and had observed the distant dots of the wing-fliers from the vessel's deck.

This was the first time Kabe and Ziller had met since the gathering on the barge *Soliton* five days earlier. Kabe had completed or put on hold various articles and projects he had been working on and had just begun to study the material on Chel and the Chelgrians which the Contact drone E. H. Tersono had sent him. He had half expected Ziller not to contact him at all, and so had been surprised when the composer had left a message asking him to meet him at the wing-fliers' platform at dawn.

"Ah, Cr. Ziller," Feli Vitrouv said as the Chelgrian loped up and folded himself to a crouch between her and Kabe. The woman flicked an arm out above her. A wing membrane snapped out for a few meters, translucent with a hint of blue-green, then flipped back. She clicked her mouth, seemingly satisfied. "We still haven't succeeded in persuading you to have a go, no?"

"No. What about Kabe?"

"I'm too heavy."

"Fraid so," Feli said. "Too heavy to do it properly. You could fit him with a float harness, I suppose, but that would be cheating."

"I thought the whole point of this sort of exercise was to cheat."

The woman looked up from tightening a strap around her thigh. She grinned at the crouched Chelgrian. "Did you?"

"Cheating death."

"Oh, that. That's just a form of words, isn't it?"

"It is?"

"Yeah. It's cheat as in . . . deprive. Not cheating in the technical sense of agreeing to follow certain rules and then secretly not, while everybody else does."

The Chelgrian was silent for a moment, then said, "Uh-huh."

The woman stood up straight, smiling. "When are we going to get to a statement of mine you agree with, Cr. Ziller?"

"I'm not sure." He glanced about the platform, where the remaining fliers were completing their preparations and the others were packing up breakfast picnics and transferring to the various small aircraft hovering silently nearby. "Isn't all of this cheating?"

Feli exchanged shouts of good luck and last minute advice with a few of her fellow wing-fliers. Then she looked at Kabe and Ziller and nodded toward one of the aircraft. "Come on. We'll cheat and take the easy way."

The aircraft was a little arrowhead-shaped sliver of a thing with a large open cabin. Kabe thought it looked more like a small motorboat than a proper plane. He guessed it was big enough to take about eight humans. He weighed the same as three of the bipeds and Ziller was probably almost the mass of two so they should be under its maximum capacity, but it still didn't look up to the task. It wobbled very slightly as he stepped aboard. Seats morphed and rearranged themselves for the two non-human shapes. Feli Vitrouv swung into the lead seat with a sort of clacking noise from the stowed wing fins, which she flicked out of the way as she sat. She pulled a control grip from the cockpit's fascia and said, "Manual please, Hub."

"You have control," the machine said.

The woman clicked the grip into place and, after a look around, pulled, twisted and pushed it to send them gently backing out and away from the platform and then racing off just above the tops of the ground trees. Some sort of field prevented more than a gentle breeze from entering the passenger compartment. Kabe reached out and poked it with one finger, feeling an invisible plastic resistance.

"So, how is all of this cheating?" Feli called back.

Ziller looked over the side. "Could you crash this?" he asked casually.

She laughed. "Is that a request?"

"No, just a question."

"Want me to try?"

"Not particularly."

"Well then, no; I probably couldn't. I'm flying it, but if I did any-thing really stupid the automatics would take over and haul us out of trouble."

"Is that cheating?"

"Depends. Not what I call cheating." She angled the craft down toward a group of blimp trees in a large clearing. "I'd call it a reason-able combination of fun and safety." She turned back to glance at them. The craft wriggled fractionally in the air, aiming between two tall ground trees. "Though of course a purist might say I shouldn't be using an aircraft to get to my blimp in the first place."

The trees rushed past, one on either side, very close; Kabe felt himself flinch. There was a hint of a thud and when he looked back Kabe saw a few leaves and twigs whirling and falling in their slip-stream. The craft bellied down toward the largest blimp tree, aiming close in underneath the curve of the gas sac where the giant tentacle roots joined together and merged into the dark brown bulbous pod of the banner reservoir.

"A purist would walk?" suggested Ziller.

"Yup." The woman made a sort of tapping-down motion with the grip and the craft settled onto the roots. She stowed the grip control in the panel in front of her. "Here's our boy," she said, nodding up at the dark black-green balloon blotting out most of the morning sky.

The blimp tree towered fifteen meters over them, casting a deep shadow. The gas sac's surface was rough and veined and yet still looked thin as paper, giving the impression of having been sewn together, clumsily, from giant leaves. Kabe thought it looked like a thunder cloud.

"How would they get here in the first place, to this forest?" Ziller asked.

"I think I see what you're getting at," Feli said, jumping out of the craft and landing on a broad root. She checked her harness points again, squinting at them in the semi-darkness. "Most of them would come by underground," she said, glancing around at the blimp tree and then up at the ruby light sifting through the ground trees. "A few would power-glide," she added, frowning at the blimper, which seemed to be stretching, tautening. Kabe thought he detected sounds coming from the banner reservoir. "Some would take an aircraft," she went on, then flashed a smile at them and said, "Excuse me. I think it's time I got into place."

She took a pair of long gloves from the belly pack and pulled them on. Curved black nails half as long as her fingers extended from their tips when she flexed them, then she turned and clambered up the side of the reservoir pod until she was at its lip, where the springy material curled under the blimp. The tree was creaking loudly now, the gas sac expanding and becoming taut.

"Others might come by ground car or bike, or boat and then walk," Feli went on, settling down in a crouch on the lip of the reservoir. "Of course the real purists, the sky junkies, they live out here in huts and tents and survive off hunting and wild fruits and vegetables. They travel everywhere on foot or by wing and you never see them in town at all. They live for flying; it's a ritual, a . . . what do you call it? A sacrament, almost a religion with them. They hate people like me because we do it for fun. Lot of them won't talk to us. Actually, some of them won't talk to each other and I think some have lost the power of speech alto—Whoo!" Feli turned away as the blimp suddenly parted company with the banner reservoir and rose into the sky like a giant black bubble from a vast brown mouth.

Beneath the gas sac, attached to it by a thick mass of filaments, rose a broad green streamer of tissue-thin leaf, eight meters across and webbed with darker veins.

Feli Vitrouv stood, flicked out the claws in her gloves and flung herself at the mass of filaments just under the blimp, thumping into the great curtain of leaf and making it shudder and ripple. She kicked at it with her feet, and more blades punctured the membrane. The blimp hesitated in its ascent, then continued up into the sky.

Released from the shadow of the blimp, the air around the aircraft seemed to lighten as the huge shape swept into the still brightening sky with a noise like a sigh.

"Ha *ha!*" shouted Feli.

Ziller leaned over to Kabe. "Shall we follow her?"

"Why not?"

"Flying machine?" Ziller said.

"Hub here, Cr. Ziller," said a voice from their seats' headrests.

"Take us up. We'd like to follow Ms. Vitrouv."

"Certainly."

The aircraft rose almost straight up, smoothly and quickly, until they were level with the black-haired woman, who had twisted so that she faced out from the banner under the blimp. Kabe looked over the side of the craft. They were about sixty meters up by now, and gaining height at a respectable rate. Looking right down, he could see into the blimper's base pod, where the reams of banner leaf unfolded from their reservoir and were hauled rippling into the air.

Feli Vitrouv smiled broadly at them, her body being pulled this way and that as the banner leaf flapped and ruffled in the roaring wind of the plant's ascent. "Okay there?" she said, laughing. Her hair flew about her face and she kept shaking her head.

"Oh, I think we're fine," Ziller shouted. "And you?"

"Never better!" the woman yelled, looking up at the blimp and then down at the ground.

"To go back to this thing about cheating," Ziller said.

She laughed. "Yes? What?"

"This whole place is a cheat."

"How so?" She flicked one hand and hung dangerously by a single arm while her other hand, claws stowed, brushed her hair away from her mouth. The movement made Kabe nervous. If he'd been her he'd have worn a cap or something.

"It's made to look like a planet," Ziller shouted. "It's not."

Kabe was watching the still rising sun. It was bright red now. An Orbital sunrise, like an O sunset, took much longer than the same event on a planet. The sky above you brightened first, then the rising star seemed to coalesce out of the infrared, a shimmering vermilion specter emerging out of the haze line and then sliding along the horizon, shining dimly through the Plate walls and the distant abundances of air and only gradually gaining height, though, once it had properly begun, the daylight lasted longer than on a globe. All of which was arguably a gain, Kabe thought, as sunset and sunrises often produced the day's more spectacular and attractive vistas.

"So what?" Feli had both hands anchored again.

"So why bother with this?" Ziller shouted, indicating the blimp. "Fly up here. Use a floater harness—"

"Do it all in a dream, do it all in VR!" She laughed.

"Would it be any less false?"

"That's not the question. The question is, Would it be any less *fun?*"

"Well, would it?"

She nodded vigorously. "Abso-fucking-lutely!" Her hair, caught in a sudden updraught, swirled above her head like black flames.

"So you only think it's fun if there's a certain degree of reality involved?"

"It's more fun," she shouted. "Some people blimp jump as their main recreation, but they only ever do it in . . ." Her voice was lost as a gust of wind roared around them; the blimper shuddered and the aircraft trembled a fraction.

"In what?" Ziller bellowed.

"In dreams," she shouted. "There are VR wing-flier purists who make a point of never doing the real thing!"

"Do you despise them?" Ziller yelled.

The woman looked mystified. She leaned out from the rippling membrane, then detached one hand—this time she left the glove where it was, anchored in the thick filament membrane—dug in her belly pack and clipped something tiny to one nostril. Then she put her hand back into the glove and relaxed back. When she spoke again, it was in a normal speaking voice and—relayed through Kabe's own nose ring and whatever terminal set-up Ziller was using—it was as though she was sitting right beside each of them.

"*Despise* them, did you say?"

"Yes," said Ziller.

"Why in the world would I despise them?"

"They achieve with minimal effort and no risk what you have to gamble your life on."

"That's their choice. I could do that too if I wanted. And anyway," she said, glancing up at the blimp above her, then taking a longer look at the skies around, "it's not exactly the same thing you achieve, is it?"

"Isn't it?"

"No. You know you've been in VR, not reality."

"You could fake that too."

She appeared to sigh, then grimaced. "Look, sorry; it's time to fly, and I prefer to be alone. No offense." She took her hand out of the glove again, put the nose-stud terminal in her belly pack and, after a struggle, got her hand back in the glove. Kabe thought she looked cold. They were over half a kilometer above the escarpment now and the air spilling over the aircraft's fields felt chill on his carapace. Their rate of ascent had slowed appreciably, and Feli's hair was blowing out to one side rather than whipping all about her head.

"See you later!" she yelled through the air. Then she let go.

She leaned out, gloves coming free first, then boots; Kabe saw the shining claws flick back in, reflecting orange-yellow in the sunlight as she dropped away. Released, the blimp set off into the sky again.

Kabe and Ziller looked out over the same side of the aircraft; it pushed back, keeping level, then spun around so they could watch the woman as she swooped. She kicked her legs and threw out her arms; the wing slats deployed, turning her in a single flicker into a giant blue-green bird. Over the noise of the wind, Kabe heard her wild ya-hooing. She curved away, heading toward the sunrise, then kept on turning and disappeared momentarily behind the banner leaf. In the skies around them, Kabe could make out a handful of other fliers; tiny dots and shapes angling through the air beneath the tethered balloons of the risen blimp trees.

Feli was banking round, gaining height now, heading back on a rising curve that would take her underneath them. The aircraft swivelled slowly in the air, keeping her in view.

She passed twenty meters beneath them, performing a roll and yelling at them, a huge grin on her face. Then she swung back over to present her back to the sky and swooped again, pulling her wings in and tearing away and down. She seemed to be diving into the ground. "Oh!" Kabe heard himself say.

Suppose she died? He had already started to compose in his head the next voice-piece he would send to the Homomdan Far-Flung Correspondents News Service. Kabe had been sending these illustrated letters back home every six days for nearly nine years now and had built up a small but devoted band of listeners. He had never had to describe an accidental death in one of his recordings and he did not relish the idea of doing so now.

Then the blue-green wings flicked out again and the woman rose once more, a kilometer away, before finally disappearing behind a fence of banner leaves.

"Our angel is not immortal, is she?" Ziller asked.

"No," Kabe said. He was not sure what an angel was, but thought it would be rude to ask either Ziller or Hub for the information. "No, she's not backed-up."

Feli Vitrouv was one of about half of the wing-fliers for whom no recording of her mind-state existed to revive them if they dived into the ground and were killed. It gave Kabe an unpleasant feeling just thinking about it.

"They call themselves the Disposables," he said.

Ziller was silent for a moment. "Strange that people are happy to adopt epithets they would fight to the death to throw off had they been imposed." A yellow-orange highlight reflected off part of the aircraft's brightwork. "There is a Chelgrian caste called the Invisibles."

"I know."

Ziller looked up. "Yes, how are your studies going?"

"Oh, well enough. I've only had four days, and there were various pieces of my own I've had to finish. However, I've made a start."

"An unenviable task you've taken on, Kabe. I'd offer an apology on behalf of my species except I feel it would be superfluous as that is more or less what my entire body of work consists of."

"Oh, now," Kabe said, embarrassed. To feel such shame for one's own was, well, shameful.

"Whereas this lot," Ziller said, nodding over the side of the aircraft at the wheeling dots of the wing-fliers, "are just odd." He settled back in his seat and produced his pipe from a pocket. "Shall we stay here a while and admire the sunrise?"

"Yes," Kabe said. "Let's."

From up here they could see for hundreds of kilometers across Frettle Plate. The system's star, Lacelere, was still rising and slowly yellowing to full brightness, shining through the continents of air to anti-spinward, its radiance obliterating any detail on the lands still in shade. To spinward—beneath the fuzzily broad then sharp but slowly diminishing line of the Plates that had risen into full sunlight, hanging in the sky like a bright, beaded bracelet—the Tulier Mountains rose, capes of snow about their shoulders. Spin-right, the view just faded away across the savannas, disappearing into haze. Left, there was a hint of hills in the blue distance, one edge of a broad estuary where Masaq' Great River decanted into Frettle Sea, and the waters beyond.

"You don't think I bait the humans too much, do you?" Ziller asked. He sucked on his pipe, frowning at it.

"I think they enjoy it," Kabe said.

"Really? Oh." Ziller sounded disappointed.

"We help to define them. They like that."

"Define them? Is that all?"

"I don't think that's the only reason they like to have us here, certainly not in your case. But we give them an alien standard to calibrate themselves against."

"That sounds slightly better than being upper-caste pets."

"You are different, dear Ziller. They call you Composer Ziller, Cr. Ziller; an address mode I've never heard of before. They are intensely proud you chose to come here. The Culture as a whole and Hub and the people of Masaq' in particular, obviously."

"Obviously," Ziller murmured, pulling on his still stubbornly unlit pipe and staring across the plains.

"You are a star amongst them."

"A trophy."

"Of a sort, but very respected."

"They have their own composers." Ziller frowned into the bowl of the pipe, tapping it and tutting. "Dregs, one of their machines, their Minds, could out-compose all of them put together."

"But that," Kabe said, "would be cheating."

The Chelgrian's shoulder shook and he made a sort of *huh*ing noise that might have been a laugh.

"They wouldn't let me cheat to get away from this fucking emissary." He looked sharply at the Homomdan. "Any more news on that?"

Kabe already knew from Masaq' Hub that Ziller had been diligently ignoring anything to do with the envoy being sent from his home. "They have dispatched a ship to bring him or her here," Kabe said. "Well, to start the process. There appeared to be a sudden change of plan at the Chelgrian end."

"Why?"

"From what they tell me, they don't know. A rendezvous was agreed, then changed by Chel." Kabe paused. "There was something about a wrecked ship."

"What wrecked ship?"

"Ah . . . Hmm. We might have to ask Hub. Hello, Hub?" he said, tapping his nose ring unnecessarily and feeling foolish.

"Kabe, Hub here. What can I do for you?"

"This wrecked ship that the Chelgrian envoy was being picked up from."

"Yes?"

"Do you have any details?"

"It was an Itirewein clan articled privateer of the Loyalist faction, lost in the closing stages of the Caste War. The hulk was discovered near the star Reshref a few weeks ago. It was called the *Winter Storm.*"

Kabe looked at Ziller, who was obviously being included in the conversation. The Chelgrian shrugged. "Never heard of it."

"Is there any more information on the identity of the emissary they're sending?" Kabe asked.

"A little. We don't have his name yet, but apparently he is or was a moderately senior military officer who later took religious orders."

Ziller snorted. "Caste?" he asked heavily.

"We believe he is a Given of the house Itirewein. I have to point out that there is a degree of uncertainty in all this, however. Chel has not been very forthcoming with information."

"You don't say," Ziller said, looking across the rear of the aircraft to watch the yellow-white sun complete its rise.

"When do we expect the emissary to arrive now?" Kabe asked.

"In about thirty-seven days."

"I see. Well, thank you."

"You're welcome. I or Dn. Tersono will talk to you later, Kabe. I'll leave you guys in peace."

Ziller was adding something to the bowl of his pipe.

"Does it make a difference, the caste status of this envoy?" Kabe asked.

"Not really," Ziller said. "I don't care who or what they send. I don't want to talk to them. Certainly dispatching somebody from one of the more militant ruling cliques who happens also to be some sort of holy boot-boy shows they aren't trying particularly hard to ingratiate themselves with me. I don't know whether to feel insulted or honored."

"Perhaps he is a devotee of your music."

"Yes, maybe he doubles or triples as a musicology professor for one of the more exclusive universities," Ziller said, sucking on the pipe again. Some smoke drifted from the bowl.

"Ziller," Kabe said. "I'd like to ask you a question." The Chelgrian looked at him. He went on. "The extended piece you've been working on. Would it be to mark the end of the Twin Novae period, commissioned by Hub?" He found himself glancing without meaning to in the direction of Portisia's bright point.

Ziller smiled slowly. "Between ourselves?" he asked.

"Of course. You have my word."

"Then, yes," Ziller said. "A full-blown symphony to commemorate the end of Hub's period of mourning and encompass both a meditation on the horrors of the war and a celebration of the peace which has, with only the most trivial of blemishes, reigned since. To be performed live just after sunset on the day the second nova ignites. If my conducting is of its usual accurate standard and I time it right, the light should hit at the start of the final note." Ziller spoke with relish. "Hub thinks it's going to arrange some sort of light show for the piece. I'm not sure I'll allow that, but we'll see."

Kabe suspected the Chelgrian was relieved that somebody had guessed and he could talk about it. "Ziller, this is wonderful news," he said. It would be the first full-length piece Ziller had completed since his self-imposed exile. Some people, Kabe included, had worried that Ziller might never again produce anything on the truly monumental scale he had proved such a master of. "I look forward to it. Is it finished?"

"Nearly. I'm at the tinkering stage." The Chelgrian looked up at the light-point that was the nova Portisia. "It has gone very well," he said, sounding thoughtful. "Wonderful raw material. Something I could really get my teeth into." He smiled at Kabe without warmth. "Even the catastrophes of the other Involveds are somehow on another level of elegance and aesthetic refinement compared to those of Chel. My own species' abominations are efficient enough in terms of the death and suffering produced, but pedestrian and tawdry. You'd think they'd have the decency to provide me with better inspiration."

Kabe was silent for a few moments. "It is sad to hate your own people so much, Ziller."

"Yes, it is," Ziller agreed, looking out toward the distant Great River. "Though happily that hatred *does* produce vital inspiration for my work."

"I know there is no chance that you will go back with them, Ziller, but you should at least see this emissary."

Ziller looked at him. "Should I?"

"Not to do so will make it appear you are frightened of his arguments."

"Really? What arguments?"

"I imagine he will say that they need you," Kabe said patiently.

"To be their trophy instead of the Culture's."

"I think trophy is the wrong word. Symbol might be better. Symbols are important, symbols do work. And when the symbol is a person then the symbol becomes . . . dirigible. A symbolic person can to some extent steer their own course, determine not just their own fate but that of their society. At any rate, they will argue that your society, your whole civilization, needs to make peace with its most famous dissident so that it can make peace with itself, and so rebuild."

Ziller gazed levelly at him. "They chose you well, didn't they, Ambassador?"

"Not in the way I think you mean. I am neither sympathetic nor unsympathetic to such an argument. But it is likely to be one they would wish to put to you. Even if you really haven't thought about this, and haven't tried to anticipate their propositions, then nevertheless you must know that if you had you would have worked this out for yourself."

Ziller stared at the Homomdan. Kabe found that it was not quite as difficult as he'd imagined, meeting the gaze of those two large dark eyes. Nevertheless, it was not something he'd have chosen as a recreation.

"Am I really a dissident?" Ziller asked at last. "I've just got used to thinking of myself as a cultural refugee or a political asylum seeker. This is a potentially unsettling recategorization."

"Your earlier comments have stung them, Ziller. As have your actions, firstly coming here at all, and then staying on after the background to the war became clear."

"The background to the war, my studious Homomdan pal, is three thousand years of ruthless oppression, cultural imperialism, economic exploitation, systematic torture, sexual tyranny and the cult of greed ingrained almost to the point of genetic inheritability."

"That is bitterness, my dear Ziller. No outside observer would make such a hostile summation of your species' recent history."

"Three thousand years counts as recent history?"

"You are changing the subject."

"Yes, I find it comical that three millennia count as 'recent' to you. Certainly that's more interesting than arguing over the exact degree of culpability ascribable to my compatriots' behavior since we came up with our exciting idea for a caste system."

Kabe sighed. "We are a long-lived species, Ziller, and have been part of the galactic community for many millennia. Three thousand years are far from insignificant by our reckoning, but in the lifetime of an intelligent, space-faring species it does indeed count as recent history."

"You are disturbed by these things, aren't you, Kabe?"

"What things, Ziller?"

The Chelgrian pointed the stem of his pipe over the side of the aircraft. "You felt for that human female as she seemed to be about to plunge into the ground and splatter her un-backed-up brains across the landscape, didn't you? And you find it uncomfortable—at least—that I am, as you put it, bitter, and that I hate my own people."

"All that is true."

"Is your own existence so replete with equanimity you find no outlet for worry except on behalf of others?"

Kabe sat back, thinking. "I suppose it appears so."

"Hence, perhaps, your identification with the Culture."

"Perhaps."

"So, you would feel for it, in its current, oh, shall we say *embarrassment* regarding the Caste War?"

"Encompassing all thirty-one trillion of the Culture's citizens might stretch even my empathy a little."

Ziller smiled thinly and looked up at the line of the Orbital hanging in the sky. The bright ribbon began at the haze line to spinward, thinning and sweeping into the sky; a single strip of land punctuated by vast oceans and the ragged, ice-shored lines of the trans-atmospheric Bulkhead Ranges, its surface speckled green and brown and blue and white; waisted here, broadening there, usually hemmed by the Edge Seas and their scattered islands, though in places—and invariably where the Bulkhead Ranges reared—stretching right to the retaining walls. The line that was Masaq' Great River was visible in a few of the nearer regions. Overhead, the Orbital's far side was just a bright line, the details of its geography lost in that burnished filament.

Sometimes, if you had very good eyesight indeed and looked up to the far side directly above, you could just make out the tiny black dot that was Masaq' Hub, hanging free in space, one and a half million kilometers away in the otherwise empty center of the world's vast bracelet of land and sea.

"Yes," said Ziller. "They are so many, aren't they?"

"They could easily have been more. They have chosen stability."

Ziller was still gazing into the sky. "Do you know there are people who've been sailing the Great River since the Orbital was completed?"

"Yes. A few are on their second circuit now. They call themselves the Time Travellers because, heading against the spin, they are moving less quickly than everybody else on the Orbital, and so incur a reduced relativistic time dilation penalty, negligible though the effect is."

Ziller nodded. The great dark eyes drank in the view. "I wonder if anyone goes against the flow?"

"A few do. There are always some." Kabe paused. "None of them have yet completed a circuit of the entire Orbital; they would need to live a very long time to do so. Theirs is a harder course."

Ziller stretched his midlimb and arms and put his pipe away. "Just so." He made a shape with his mouth Kabe knew was a genuine smile. "Shall we return to Aquime? I have work to do."

4

Scorched Ground

~ *Are our own ships not good enough?*

~ Theirs are faster.

~ *Still?*

~ I'm afraid so.

~ *And I hate this chopping and changing. First one ship then another, then another, then a fourth. I feel like a delivery package.*

~ This wouldn't be some obscure form of insult, or way of trying to delay us, would it?

~ *You mean not giving us our own ship?*

~ Yes.

~ *I don't think so. In an obscure sort of way they may even be trying to impress us. They're saying that they're taking so much care to correct the mistakes they made that they won't spare any ships from normal duty for anybody.*

~ Sparing four ships at different times makes more sense?

~ *It does the way they'll have their forces set up. The first ship was very much a war craft. They're keeping those close to Chel in case the war should begin again. They may loop a certain distance out, for example to ferry us, but no further. The one we are on now is a Superlifter, a sort of fast tug. The one we're approaching is a General Systems Vehicle; a kind of giant depot or mother ship. It carries other warships they could deploy in the event of fur-*

ther hostilities, if they went beyond the scale their immediately available *matériel* could deal with. *The GSV can loop further out than the war vessel but still can't stray too far from Chelgrian space. The last ship is an old demilitarized war craft of a type commonly used throughout the galaxy for this sort of picket duty.*

~ Throughout the galaxy. Somehow that still always comes as a shock.

~ *Yes. Decent of them to take such an interest in our relatively puny well-being.*

~ If you believe them, that is all they were ever trying to do.

~ *Do you believe them, Major?*

~ I think I do. I am just not convinced that that is sufficient excuse for what happened.

~ *Damn right it isn't.*

The first three days of their journey had been spent aboard the Torturer class Rapid Offensive Unit *Nuisance Value*. It was a massive, cobbled-together object; a bundle of gigantic engine units behind a single weapon pod and a tiny accommodation section that looked like an afterthought.

~ *God that thing is ugly,* Huyler said when they first saw it, riding across from the wreck of the *Winter Storm* in the tiny shuttle with the ship's black-skinned, gray-suited avatar. ~ *And these people are supposed to be decadent aesthetes?*

~ There is a theory that they are ashamed of their weaponry. As long as it looks inelegant, rough and disproportionate they can pretend that it is not really theirs, or not really a part of their civilization, or only temporarily so, because everything else they make is so subtly refined.

~ *Or it could just be form following function. However I confess that's a new one on me. Which university whizz-kid came up with that theory?*

~ You will be glad to know, Hadesh Huyler, that we now have a Civilizational Metalogical Profiling Section in Naval Intelligence.

~ *I can see I have a lot of catching up to do with the latest terminology. What does metalogical mean?*

~ It is short for psycho-physio-philosophilogical.

~ *Well, naturally. Of course it is. Glad I asked.*

~ It is a Culture term.

~ *A fucking Culture term?*

~ Yes, sir.

~ *I see. And what the hell does this metalogical section of ours actually do?*

~ It tries to tell us how other Involveds think.

~ *Involveds?*

~ Also one of their terms. It means space-faring species beyond a certain technological level which are willing and able to interact with each other.

~ *I see. Always a bad sign when you start using the enemy's terminology.*

Quilan glanced at the avatar sitting in the seat next to him. It smiled uncertainly at him.

~ I would agree with that, sir.

He returned his gaze to the view of the Culture warship. It was, indeed, rather ugly. Before Huyler had expressed his own thoughts, Quilan had been thinking how brutally powerful the craft looked. How odd to have somebody else in your head who looked through the same eyes and saw exactly the same things you did and yet came to such different conclusions, experienced such dissimilar emotions.

The craft filled the screen, as it had since they had set off. They were approaching it quickly, but it had been a long way off; some few hundred kilometers. A read-out at the side of the screen was count-ing the magnification level back toward zero. Powerful, Quilan thought—entirely to himself—and ugly. Perhaps, in some sense, that was always the case. Huyler broke into his thoughts:

~ *I take it your servants are already aboard?*

~ I am not taking any servants, sir.

~ *What?*

~ I am going alone, sir. Apart from yourself, of course.

~ *You're going without servants? Are you some sort of fucking outcast or something, Major? You're not one of these embryonicist Caste Deniers, are you?*

~ No, sir. Partly, my not bringing servants reflects some of the changes that have occurred in our society since your body-death. These will no doubt be explained in your briefing files.

~ *Yes, well, I'll be taking a further look at those when I have the time. You wouldn't believe the amount of tests and stuff they've been putting me through, even while you were asleep. I had to remind them that constructs need naps, too, or they'd have burned me out in here. But look, Major; this thing about servants. I read up on the Caste War, but I thought it ended up a draw. Dear scum in heaven, does this mean we lost it?*

~ No, sir. The war ended in a compromise following the Culture's intervention.

~ *I know that, but a compromise which involves having no servants?*

~ No, sir. People still have servants. Officers still employ squires and equerries. However I am of an order which eschews such personal help.

~ *Visquile mentioned you were some sort of monk. I didn't realize you'd be quite so self-denying.*

~ There is another reason for traveling alone, sir. If I might remind you, the Chelgrian we are being sent to meet is a Denier.

~ *Oh, yeah, this Ziller guy. Some spoiled, fur-rending liberal brat who thinks it's his God-given duty to do the whining for those who can't be bothered whining for themselves. Best thing you can do with these people is kick them out. These shits don't understand the first thing about responsibility or duty. You can't renounce your caste anymore than you can renounce your species. And we're indulging this arse-leaf?*

~ He is a great composer, sir. And we didn't chuck him out; Ziller left Chel to go into self-exile in the Culture. He renounced his Given status and took—

~ *Oh, let me guess. He declared himself an Invisible.*

~ Yes, sir.

~ *Pity he didn't go the whole way and make himself a Spayed.*

~ At any rate, he is not well disposed to Chelgrian society. The idea was that by going without an entourage I might make myself less intimidating and more acceptable to him.

~ *We should not be the ones having to make ourselves acceptable to him, Major.*

~ We are in a position where we have no choice, sir. It has been decided at cabinet level that we must try to persuade him to return. I have accepted that mission, as indeed you have yourself. We cannot force him to return, so we must appeal to him.

~ *Is he likely to listen?*

~ I really have no idea, sir. I knew him when we were both children, I have followed his career and I have enjoyed his music. I have even studied it. However that is all I have to offer. I imagine people closer to him by family or conviction might have been asked to do what I am doing, but it would seem that none of them were prepared to take on the task. I have to accept that while I may not be the ideal candidate, I must be the best of those available for the job, and just get on with it.

~ *This all sounds a little forlorn, Major. I worry about your morale.*

~ My spirits are at something of a low ebb, sir, for personal reasons; however my morale and sense of purpose are more robust and, when all's said and done, orders are orders.

~ *Yes, aren't they just, Major?*

The *Nuisance Value* carried a human crew of twenty and a handful of small drones. Two of the humans greeted Quilan in the cramped shuttle hangar and showed him to his quarters, which comprised a single cabin with a low ceiling. His meager baggage and belongings were already there, transferred from the Navy frigate that had taken him to the hulk of the *Winter Storm*.

Something like a Navy officer's cabin had been created for him. One of the drones had been assigned to him; it explained that the cabin's interior could deform to create something closer to his desires. He told the drone he was content with the present arrangements and was happy to unpack and remove the rest of his vacuum suit by himself.

~ *Was that drone trying to be our servant?*

~ I doubt it, sir. It may do as we ask if we do so nicely.

~ *Huh!*

~ So far they all seem quite diffident and determined to be helpful, sir.

~ *Right. Suspicious as hell.*

• • •

Quilan was attended to by the drone, which to his surprise did indeed act as an almost silent and very efficient servant, cleaning his clothes, sorting his kit and advising him on the minimal—almost nonexistent—etiquette that applied on board the Culture vessel.

There was what passed for a formal dinner on the first evening.

~ *They still* don't *have uniforms? This is a whole society run by fucking dissidents. No wonder I hate it.*

The crew treated Quilan with fastidious civility. He learned almost nothing from them or about them. They seemed to spend a great deal of time in simulations and had little time for him. He wondered if they just wanted to avoid him, but didn't care if they did. He was happy to have the time to himself. He studied their archives through the ship's own library.

Hadesh Huyler did his own studying, finally absorbing the historical and briefing files that had been loaded along with his own personality into the Soulkeeper device within Quilan's skull.

They agreed a schedule that would allow Quilan some privacy; if nothing important was taking place then for the hour before sleep and the hour after waking, Huyler would detach from Quilan's senses.

Huyler's reactions to the detailed history of the Caste War, which against Quilan's advice he turned to first, went through amazement, incredulity, outrage, anger and finally—when the Culture's part became clear—sudden fury followed by icy calm. Quilan experienced these varying emotions from the other being inside his head over the course of an afternoon. It was surprisingly wearing.

Only afterwards did the old soldier go back to the beginning and study in chronological sequence all the things that had happened since his body-death and personality storage.

Like all revived constructs, Huyler's personality still needed to sleep and dream to remain stable, though this coma-like state could be achieved in a sort of fast-forward time which meant that instead of sleeping all night Huyler could get by on less than an hour's rest. The first night he slept in the same real-time as Quilan; the second night he studied rather than slept and partook of just that brief period of unconsciousness. The following morning, when Quilan re-established contact after his hour's grace, the voice in his head said, ~ *Major.*

~ Sir.

~ *You lost your wife. I'm sorry. I didn't know.*

~ It's not something I talk about much, sir.

~ *Was that the other soul you were looking for on the ship where you found me?*

~ Yes, sir.

~ *She was Army too.*

~ Yes, sir. Also a major. We joined up together, before the war.

~ *She must have loved you a lot to follow you into the Army.*

~ Actually it was more me following her, sir; enlisting was her idea. Trying to rescue the souls stored in the Military Institute on Aorme before the rebels got there was her idea too.

~ *She sounds like quite a female.*

~ She was, sir.

~ *I'm really sorry, Major Quilan. I was never married myself, but I know what it is to love and to lose. I just want you to know I feel for you, that's all.*

~ Thank you. I appreciate that.

~ *I think maybe you and I need to study a bit less and talk a bit more. For two people in such intimate contact we haven't really told each other that much about ourselves. What do you say, Major?*

~ I think that might be a good idea, sir.

~ *Let's start by dropping the "sir," shall we? Doing my homework, I did notice the bit of legalese attached to the standard wake-up briefing which basically says that my admiral-generalship lapsed with my body-death. My status is Reserve Honorary Officer and you're the ranking grade on this mission. If anyone's going to get called sir around here it should be you. Anyway, just call me Huyler, if you're happy with that; that's how people usually knew me.*

~ As you say, ah, Huyler, given our intimacy, perhaps rank isn't entirely relevant. Please call me Quil.

~ *Done deal, Quil.*

• • •

The few days passed without incident; they traveled at absurd speed, leaving Chelgrian space far, far behind. The ROU *Nuisance Value* passed them via its little shuttle craft to a thing called a Superlifter, another big, chunky ship, though with a less extemporized look to it than the war craft. The vessel, called the *Vulgarian,* greeted them by voice only. It had no human crew; Quilan sat in what looked like a little used open area where pleasantly bland music played.

~ Never married, Huyler?

~ *An accursed weakness for smart, proud and insufficiently patriotic females, Quil. They could always tell my first love was the Army, not them, and not one of those heartless bitches was prepared to put her male and her people before her own selfish interests. If I'd only had the basic common sense to have been taken with airheads I'd have been happily married with—and probably even more happily survived by—a doting wife and several grown-up children by now.*

~ Sounds like a narrow escape.

~ *I notice you're not specifying who for.*

The General Systems Vehicle *Sanctioned Parts List* appeared on the screen in the Superlifter's lounge as another point of light in the starfield. It became a silver dot and grew quickly to fill the screen, though there was no sign of detail on the shining surface.

~ *That'll be it.*

~ I suppose so.

~ *We've probably passed near several escort craft, though they wouldn't be making their presence so obvious. What the Navy calls a High Value Unit; you never send them out alone.*

~ I thought it might look a little more grand.

~ *They always look pretty unimposing from the outside.*

The Superlifter plunged into the center of the silver surface. Within it was like looking from an aircraft inside a cloud, then there was the impression of plunging through another surface, then another, then dozens more in quick succession, flicking past like thumbed paper pages in an antique book.

They burst from the last membrane into a great hazy space lit by a yellow-white line burning high above, beyond layers of wispy cloud. They were above and aft of the craft's stern. The ship was twenty-five kilometers long and ten wide. The top surface was parkland; wooded hills and ridges separated by and studded with rivers and lakes.

Bracketed by colossal ribbed and buttressed outriggers chevroned in red and blue, the GSV's sheer sides were a golden, tawny color, scattered with a motley confusion of foliage-covered platforms and balconies and punctured by a bewildering variety of brightly lit openings, like a glowing vertical city set into sandstone cliffs three kilometers high. The air swarmed with thousands of craft of every type Quilan had ever seen or heard of, and more besides. Some were tiny, some were the size of the Superlifter. Still smaller dots were individual people, floating in the air.

Two other giant vessels, each barely an eighth of the size of the *Sanctioned Parts List*, shared the envelope of the GSV's surrounding field enclosure. Riding a few kilometers off each side, plainer and more dense-looking, they were surrounded with their own concentrations of smaller flying craft.

~ It is a little more impressive on the inside, isn't it?

Hadesh Huyler remained silent.

He was made welcome by an avatar of the ship and a handful of humans. His quarters were generous to the point of extravagance; he had a swimming pool to himself and the side of one cabin looked out into the chasm of air whose far wall, a kilometer distant, was the GSV's starboard outrigger. Another self-effacing drone played the part of servant.

He was invited to so many meals, parties, ceremonies, festivals, openings, celebrations and other events and gatherings that the suite's engagement-managing ware filled two screens just listing the variety of different ways of sorting all his invitations. He accepted a few, mostly those featuring live music. People were polite. He was polite back. Some expressed regret about the war. He was dignified, placatory. Huyler fumed in his mind, spitting invective.

He walked and traveled through the vast ship, attracting glances everywhere—in a ship of thirty million people, not all of them human or drone, he was the only Chelgrian—but was only rarely forced into conversation.

The avatar had warned him that some of the people who would want to talk to him would be, in effect, journalists, and might broadcast his comments on the ship's news services. Huyler's indignation and sarcasm were an advantage in such circumstances. Quilan would have carefully measured his words before speaking them anyway, but he would also listen to Huyler's comments at such moments, seemingly lost in thought, and was quietly amused to see that he gained a reputation for inscrutability as a result.

One morning, before Huyler had made contact again after the hour of grace, he rose from his bed and went to the window which gave out onto the external view, and—when he ordered the surface transparent—was not surprised to see the Phelen Plains outside, scorched and cratered and stretching into the smoke-filled distance beneath an ashen sky. They were traversed by the punctured ribbon of the ruined road on which the blackened, crippled truck moved like a winter-slowed insect, and he realized that he had not awakened or risen at all, and was dreaming.

The land destroyer jerked and shook beneath him, sending waves of pain through his body. He heard himself groan. The ground must be shaking. He was supposed to be beneath the thing, trapped by it, not inside it. How had this happened? Such pain. Was he dying? He must be dying. He could not see, and breathing was difficult.

Every few moments he imagined that Worosei had just wiped his face, or had just sat him up to make him comfortable, or had just spoken to him, quietly encouraging, gently funny, but each time it was as though he had somehow—unforgivably—fallen asleep when she had done these things, and only woken up after she had slipped away from him again. He tried to open his eyes but could not. He tried to talk to her, to shout out to her and bring her back, but he could not. Then a few more moments would elapse, and he would jerk awake again, and feel certain once more that he had just missed her touch, her scent, her voice.

"Still not dead, eh, Given?"

"Who's that? What?"

People were talking around him. His head hurt. So did his legs.

"Your fancy armor didn't save you, did it? They could feed most of you to the chasers. Wouldn't even have to mince you up first." Somebody laughed. Pain jolted from his legs. The ground shook beneath him. He must be inside the land destroyer with its crew. They were angry that it had been hit and they had been killed. Were they talking to him? He must have dreamt it turretless and burning, or perhaps it was very big inside and he was in an undamaged part. Not all dead.

"Worosei?" said a voice. He realized it must be his own.

"Oo, Worosei! Worosei!" another voice said, mimicking him.

"Please," he said. He tried to move his arms again, but only pain came.

"Oo, Worosei, oo, Worosei, please."

In the old faculty building, beneath the Rebound courts, in the Military Technical Institute, Cravinyr City, Aorme. That's where they had stored them. The souls of the old soldiers and military planners. Unwanted in peace, now they were seen as an important resource. Besides, a thousand souls were a thousand souls, and worth saving from destruction by the rebel Invisibles. Worosei's mission; her idea. Daring and dangerous. She'd pulled strings to make it happen, the way she had before when they'd joined up, to make sure that she and Quilan would be posted together. Time to go: Move! Now! Jump!

Had they been there?

He seemed to remember the look of the place, the warren of corridors, the heavy doors, all dark and cold, glowing falsely in the helmet visor. The others; two squires, Hulpe and Nolica, his best, trusted and true, and the Navy special forces triune. Worosei nearby, rifle balanced, her movements graceful even in the suit. His own wife. He should have tried harder to stop her but she'd insisted. Her idea.

The substrate device was there, bigger than they'd been expecting, the size of a domestic chiller cabinet. We'll never get this onto the flyer. Not with us at the same time.

"Hey, Given? Help me get this off. Come on. It might help."
Somebody laughing.

Get this off. Never get this back. The flyer. And she'd been right.
Two of the Navy people went with the thing. They'd never get off.
Never. Was that Worosei? She'd just wiped his face, he could have
sworn. He struggled to call her back, to say anything.

"What's he saying?"

"No idea. Who cares?"

One arm was very sore. Left arm or right arm? He was angry at
himself for not being able to tell which. How absurd. Ow ow ow.
Worosei, why . . . ?

"You trying to tear it off?"

"Just the glove. Must come off. He'll have rings or stuff. They
always do."

Worosei murmured something in his ear. He'd fallen asleep. She'd
just gone. Worosei! he tried to say.

The Invisibles came, with heavy weaponry. They must have a ship,
probably escorted. The *Winter Storm* would try to stay hidden, then.
They were on their own. Waiting for the flyer to return for them.
Then the discovery, attack, and losing them all. Madness, flashes and
explosions all over as the Loyalist side shelled and counter-attacked
from who-knew-where away. They ran out into the rain; the building behind them burned and slumped and fell, turned to glowing slag
by the energy weapons. It was night by then and they were alone.

"Leave him alone!"

"We just—"

"You just do as you're fucking told or I'll drop you on the fucking road, understand? If he lives we're going to ransom him. Even
dead he's worth more than you two brain-dead fuckwits, so make
sure he's alive when we get to Golse or you'll be following him to
heaven."

"Make sure he's alive? Look at him! He'll be lucky if he lasts the
night!"

"Well, if we pick up any medics less fucked up than he is, we'll
make sure they deal with him first. In the meantime; you do it. Here.

Medpac. I'll see you get extra rations if he lives. Oh, and there's nothing worth taking."

"Hey! Hey, we want a cut in the ransom! Hey!"

They'd dived into the crater, sliding and falling. A big explosion had punched them half into the mud. Killed them if they hadn't been suited up. Something whacked into his helmet, sending the speakers crazy and filling the visor with blinding light. He pulled the helmet off; it rolled into the pool of water in the foot of the crater. More explosions. Stuck, jammed into the mud.

"Given, you're just a heap of fucking trouble, you know that?"

"What's this do?"

"Fuck knows."

The land destroyer, turretless, trailing smoke and leaving one wide segmented track unravelled on the slope behind it, ground and skidded and rumbled its way into the crater. Worosei had recovered first, hauling herself out of the ooze. She tried to pull him free, then fell back as the machine rolled down on top of him. He screamed as the huge weight pressed him into the ground and his legs caught against something hard, breaking bones, pinning him.

He saw the flyer leave, taking her to the ship, to safety. The sky was full of flashes, his ears were pounded by the concussions. The land destroyer shook the ground as its munitions detonated, each pulse making him cry out. Rain lashed down, soaking his face and fur, hiding his tears. The water in the crater was rising, offering an alternative way to die, until another explosion in the burning machine hammered the ground, and air blew out of the center of the filthy pool and it all frothed and drained away into a deep tunnel. That side of the crater collapsed into it as well, and the land destroyer's nose tipped down, its rear went up and it pivoted off him, thundering down into the steam of the hole and shaking with another series of explosions.

He tried to drag himself out with his hands, but could not. He started trying to dig his legs free.

The next morning, an Invisible search and recovery team found him in the mud, semi-conscious, surrounded by a shallow trench he'd dug around himself but still unable to free himself. One of them kicked his head a few times and put a gun against his forehead, but he had just enough wits left to tell them his rank and title, so they pulled him from the mud's embrace, ignoring his screams, dragged him up the slope and threw him into the back of a half-wrecked armored truck with the rest of the dead and dying.

They were the slowest of the slow, the expected-to-die consigned to a wagon which itself was not expected to complete the journey. The truck had lost its tail doors in whatever engagement had resulted in its being unable to travel at much more than walking speed. Once they'd moved him and cleaned the blood from his eyes he could look out to watch the Phelen Plains unroll behind. They were black and scorched as far as the eye could see. Sometimes smudges of smoke adorned the horizon. The clouds were black or gray and sometimes ash fell like soft rain.

Real rain pelted down only once when the truck was on a part of the road sunk below the level of the plains, turning the roadway into a greasy stream of rushing gray and washing over the tailgate and into the rear compartment. He had been lifted, mewing with pain, to a sitting position on one of the rear benches. He could move his head and one arm very weakly, and so watched helplessly as three of the wounded died struggling on their stretchers, drowned under the swirling gray tide. He and one of the others shouted, but it seemed that nobody heard.

The truck went light and slewed from side to side as it was nearly washed away in the flood. He stared wide-eyed at the battered ceiling as the filthy water swirled over the submerged bodies and around his knees. He wondered if he cared anymore whether he died or not, and decided that he did because there was just a chance he might see Worosei again. Then the truck settled and found traction and climbed slowly out of the waters and grumbled onward.

The slurry of ash and water drained out through the rear, exposing the dead, coated in gray as though by shrouds.

The truck took frequent detours around shell holes and larger craters. It crossed two makeshift bridges, swaying. A few vehicles whizzed past them going in the other direction, and once a pair of aircraft slammed overhead, supersonic, so low their passing raised dust and ash. Nothing overtook the wagon.

He was attended to, minimally, by the two Invisible orderlies who'd been told to look after him by their CO. They were really Unheards; a caste above Invisibles by the Loyalist way of thinking. The two seemed to veer unpredictably between relief that he was going to live and perhaps furnish them with part of his ransom, and spite that he had survived at all. He had named them Shit and Fart in his head, and took some pride in not being able to recall their real names at all.

He daydreamed. Mostly he daydreamed about catching up with Worosei without her having heard that he had survived, so that when she saw him it would come as a complete surprise. He tried to imagine the look on her face, the succession of expressions he might see.

Of course it would never happen that way. She would be like him, if their circumstances were reversed; she would try to find out for sure what had happened to him, hoping, no matter how hopelessly, that by some miracle he had survived. So she would find out, or she would be told, once news of his escape became known, and he would not see that look on her face. Still, he could imagine it, and spent hours doing just that, as the truck squealed and thumped and rumbled its way across the sintered plains.

He had told them his name, once he'd been able to speak, but they hadn't seemed to pay any attention; all that appeared to matter was that he was a noble, with a noblemale's markings and armor. He wasn't sure whether to remind them of his name or not. If he did, and it was communicated to their superiors, then Worosei might find out all the quicker that he was alive, but there was a superstitious, cautious part of him that was afraid of doing that, because he could imagine her being told—that hope against hope fulfilled—and imagine the look on her face at that point, but he could also imagine himself dying even yet, because they hadn't been able to treat his injuries properly and he was feeling weaker and weaker all the time.

That would be too cruel, to be told that he had survived against all the odds, and then discover later he had died of his wounds. So he did not press the point.

Had there been any chance of paying for rescue or even faster passage he might have made more of a fuss, but he had no immediate means of payment, and the Loyalist forces—along with any privateers that might have been acceptable to both sides—had dropped even further back into home space around Chel, regrouping. It didn't matter. Worosei would be there, with them. Safe. He kept on imagining the look on her face.

He lapsed into a coma before they got to what was left of the city of Golse. The ransom and transfer took place without him being aware that anything was going on. It was quarter of a year later, the war was over and he was back on Chel before he discovered what had befallen the *Winter Storm,* and that Worosei had died in it.

He left during the GSV's night, when the sun-line had dimmed and disappeared and a deep red light bathed the three great ships and the few lazily flying machines weaving about them.

He was on yet another vessel, a thing called a *Very Fast Picket,* on the last leg of his journey to Masaq' Orbital. The craft disappeared through the interior stern fields of the *Sanctioned Parts List* and a little later exited and separated from the silvery ellipsoid's exterior, curving away to set course for the star and system of Lacelere and leaving the GSV to begin its long loop back to Chelgrian space, a vast bright cave of air flashing through the void between the stars.

Airsphere

Uagen Zlepe, scholar, hung from the left-side sub-ventral foliage of the dirigible behemothaur Yoleus by his prehensile tail and his left hand. He held a glyph-writing tablet with one foot and wrote inside it with his other hand. His remaining leg hung loose, temporarily surplus to requirements. He wore baggy cerise pantaloons (currently rolled up above the knee) secured with a stout pocket-belt, a short black jacket with a stowed cape, chunky mirror-finish ankle-bracelets, a single chain necklace with four small, dull stones and a tasselled box hat. His skin was light green, he was about two meters standing straight on his hind legs and a little longer measured from nose to tail.

Around him, beyond the hanging fronds of the behemothaur's slipstream-ruffled skin foliage, the view faded away to a hazy blue nothing in every direction except up, where the creature's body filled the sky.

Two of the seven suns were dimly visible, one large and red to right and just above Assumed Horizon, one small and yellow-orange to left about a quarter off directly below. No other mega fauna were visible, though Uagen knew that there was one nearby, just above Yoleus' top surface. The dirigible behemothaur Muetenive was in heat and had been for the last three standard years. Yoleus had been following the other creature for all that time, diligently cruising after it, always hanging just below and behind, paying court, arguing its case, patiently waiting to reach its own season and insulting, infecting or just ramming out of the way all other potential suitors.

By dirigible behemothaur standards a three-year courtship indicated little more than an infatuation, arguably no more than a passing fancy, but Yoleus seemed committed to the pursuit and it was this attraction that had brought them so low in the Oskendari airsphere over the last fifty standard days; usually such mega fauna preferred to stay higher up where the air was thinner. Down here, where the air was so dense and gelatinous that Uagen Zlepe had noticed his voice sounded different, it took a great deal of a dirigible behemothaur's energy to control its buoyancy. Muetenive was testing Yoleus' ardor, and its fitness.

Somewhere above and ahead of the two—perhaps another five or six days at this slow rate of drift—was the gigalithine lenticular entity Buthulne, where the pair might eventually mate, but more likely would not.

It was far from certain that they would even get to the great living continent in the first place. Messenger birds had brought news of a massive convection bubble that was looking likely to well up from the airsphere's lower reaches in the next few days and which would, if intercepted correctly, provide a rapid and easy ascent to the floating world that was Buthulne; however the timing was tight.

Gossip amongst Muetenive and Yoleus' assorted populations of slaved organisms, symbiotes, parasites and guests indicated there was a good chance that Muetenive would dawdle for the next two or three days and then make a sudden maximum-speed dash for the air space just above the convection bubble, to see if Yoleus was capable of keeping up. If it was and they both made it, then they would make a splendidly dramatic entrance into Buthulne's presence, where a huge parliament of thousands of their peers would be able to witness their glorious arrival.

The problem was that over the last few tens of thousands of years

Muetenive had proved itself to be something of an incautious gam-
bler when it came to such matters. Often it left such sportive or mating sprints until too late.

So they might not make it to the appropriate region until the bubble had gone, and the two mega fauna and all their crawlers-inside,
hangers-on and floaters-about would be left with nothing but turbu-
lence or even—worse still—descending air currents, while the bubble rose upwards in the airsphere.

Even more alarmingly for those committed to Yoleus, given the
fabulous, legendary reputation of the gigalithine lenticular entity
Buthulne, the messenger birds reckoned it was going to be a particularly big bubble and that Buthulne was in the mood for a change of
scenery, and therefore likely to position itself directly above the upwelling air, to ride it to the airsphere's upper reaches. If that happened
it might be years or even decades before they encountered another
gigalithine lenticular entity, and centuries—possibly millennia—
before Buthulne itself hove into view again.

Yoleus' Invited Guests' Quarters consisted of a gourd-shaped
growth situated just ahead of the creature's third dorsal fin complex,
not far from its summit. It was inside this structure, which reminded
Uagen of a hollowed-out fruit, albeit one fifty meters across, that he
had his rooms.

Uagen had stayed there, observing Yoleus, the other mega fauna
and the entire ecology of the airsphere, for thirteen years. He was
now thinking about drastically altering both his life expectancy and
his shape to suit better the scale of the airsphere and the length of its
larger inhabitants' lives.

Uagen had been fairly human-basic for most of the ninety years
he'd lived in the Culture. His present simian form—plus the use of
some Culture technology, though no field-based science, which the
mega fauna had a never entirely specified objection to—had seemed
a sensible adaption strategy for the airsphere.

Recently, however, he had started wondering about being altered
to resemble something more like a giant bird, and living for, potentially, a very long time indeed, and possibly indefinitely; long enough,

for example, to experience the slow evolution of a behemothaur.

If, say, Yoleus and Muetenive did mate, exchanging and merging personalities, what would the two resulting behemothaurs be called? Yoleunive and Mueteleus? How exactly did this offspringless coupling affect the two protagonists? How would they each change? Was it an equal trade or did one partner dominate the other? Were there ever any offspring? Did behemothaurs ever die of natural causes? Nobody knew. These and a thousand other questions remained unanswered. The mega fauna of the airspheres were scrupulous in keeping their own counsel on such matters, and in all recorded history—or at least all that he'd been able to access through the notoriously immodest data reservoirs of the Culture—the evolution of a behemothaur had never been recorded.

Uagen would give almost anything to be the person who witnessed such a process and came up with those answers, but just the chance of doing so would mean a huge long-term commitment.

He supposed if he was to do any of this he'd have to go back to his home Orbital and talk it over with his professors, mother, relations, friends and so on. They were expecting him back for good in another ten or fifteen years, but he was increasingly certain that he was one of those scholars who devoted their lives to their work, rather than one of those who use a period of intense study to make themselves more rounded beings. He felt no great sense of loss at such a prospect; by original humanoid standards of life-expectancy he had already lived a long, full life by the time he'd decided to become a student in the first place.

The long trip back home, however, did seem slightly daunting. The airsphere Oskendari was not in regular contact with the Culture (or anybody else for that matter) and—the last Uagen had heard—the next Culture ship with a course schedule that brought it anywhere near the system wasn't due for another two years. There might be other craft calling by before then, but it would take even longer to get home if he had to start out on an alien vessel, assuming they'd take him.

Even taking a Culture ship, there would be at least a year traveling

home, say a year once he got there, and then for the return journey . . . no vessels had even course-scheduled that far ahead when
he'd last checked.

He had been offered his own ship, fifteen years earlier, when news
had arrived that a dirigible behemothaur had consented to play host
to a Culture scholar, but tying up a star craft for a single person who
would use it twice in twenty or thirty years had seemed, well, overly
profligate, even by Culture standards. Nonetheless, if he was going to
stay and possibly never see his friends and family alive again, then he
really had no choice about returning. In any event, he needed to
think about it.

Yoleus' Invited Guests' Quarters had been sited where they were
to give the creature's visitors a pleasant and airy view. With the
courtship of Muetenive, and Yoleus' tactic of following the other
creature just below and behind, the quarters had become overshad-
owed and oppressive. A lot of people had left, and the remaining
guests seemed excessively gossipy and nervous to Uagen, who was, in
the end, there to study. So he spent less time socializing than he had
done, and more time either in his study or roaming the behemothaur's bulbous surfaces.

He hung from the foliage, working quietly.

Flocks of falficores roamed the spin winds about the two huge
creatures; columns and clouds of infinitesimal dark shapes. It was the
flight of a falficore flock Uagen was attempting to describe in the
glyph-writing tablet.

Writing, of course, was hardly the right word for what Uagen was
doing. You did not merely write within a glyph-writing tablet; you
reached inside its holo'd space with the digital stylo and carved and
shaped and colored and textured and mixed and balanced and anno-
tated all at once. Glyphs of this sort were solid poetry, fashioned from
nothing solid. They were real spells, perfect images, ultimate cross-
system intellectualizations.

They had been invented by Minds (or their equivalent) and there
was an infamous rumor that they had only been thought up to provide a means of communication that humans (or their equivalent)
would be unable ever to understand or produce. People like Uagen

had devoted their lives to proving that the Minds were either not as differentially smart as they thought, or that the paranoid cynics had been wrong.

"There, finished," Uagen said, holding the tablet away from his face and squinting at it. He turned it and inclined his head. He showed the tablet to his companion, the Interpreter 974 Praf, who was hanging from a nearby branch at Uagen's shoulder.

974 Praf was a fifth-order Decider in the dirigible behemothaur Yoleus' 11th Foliage Gleaner Troupe who had been given upgraded autonomous intelligence and the title Interpreter when she'd been assigned to Uagen. She inclined her head at the same angle and stared into the tablet.

"I see nothing." She spoke in Marain, the Culture's language.

"You are hanging upside down."

The creature shook its wings. Her eye pit band looked straight at Uagen. "Does that make a difference?"

"Yes. It's polarized. Observe." Uagen turned the tablet straight onto the Interpreter and inverted it.

974 Praf flinched, her wings jerking halfway out and her body hunching as though getting ready to fly. She collected herself and settled back, swaying to and fro. "Oh yes, there they are."

"I was attempting to use the phenomenon whereby one is looking at a flock of—for example—falficores from a great distance but is unable to see them because of one's inability to distinguish individual creatures at such a range, whereupon they suddenly coalesce and flock together, gathering into a tighter grouping and becoming suddenly visible as though out of nothing, as a metaphor for the often equally precipitous experience of conceptual comprehension."

974 Praf turned her head, opened her beak, flicked out her tongue to groom a twisted skin-leaf straight, then looked at him again. "That is done how?"

"Umm. With great skill," Uagen said, and then gave a delicate, slightly surprised laugh. He stowed the stylo and clicked the tablet to store the glyph.

The stylo must not have been properly stowed, because it clicked

out of its housing in the side of the tablet and fell away into the blueness below.

"Oh, damn," Uagen said, "I knew I should have replaced that lan-
yard."

The stylo swiftly became a dot. They both watched it.

974 Praf said, "That is your writing instrument."

Uagen took hold of his right foot. "Yes."

"Do you have another?"

Uagen chewed on one of his toenails. "Umm. Not really, no."

974 Praf tilted her head. "Hmm."

Uagen scratched his head. "I suppose I'd better go after it."

"It is your only one."

Uagen let go with his hand and tail, dropping into the air to follow the instrument. 974 Praf released her claw holds and followed
him.

The air was very warm and thick; it roared around Uagen's ears,
buffeting.

"I am reminded," 974 Praf said as they plummeted together.

"What?" Uagen said. He clipped the writing tablet to his belt,
popped a pair of wind-goggles over his already watering eyes and
twisted in the air to keep an eye on the stylo, which was almost out
of sight. Such styli were small but very dense and also effectively, if
unintentionally, quite streamlined. It was falling alarmingly quickly.
His clothes fluttered and snapped like a flag in a gale.

Uagen's tasselled hat flew off; he grabbed at it but it floated away
upwards. Above, the cloud-sized bulk of the dirigible behemothaur
Yoleus drew slowly away as they fell.

"Shall I get your hat?" 974 Praf shouted over the wind roar.

"No, thank you," Uagen yelled. "We can retrieve it on the way
back up."

Uagen twisted back around and peered into the blue depths. The
stylo was tearing through the air like a crossbow quarrel.

974 Praf drifted closer to Uagen until her beak was close to his
right ear and her body feathers were fluttering in the disturbed air
just past his shoulder. "As I was saying," she said.

"Yes?"

"The Yoleus would know more of your conclusions regarding your theory on the effects of gravitational susceptibility influencing the religiosity of a species with particular reference to their eschatological beliefs."

Uagen was losing sight of the stylo. He glanced around, frowning at 974 Praf. "What, now?"

"I just remembered."

"Umm, well. Just wait a moment, can't you . . . ? I mean, this thing's fairly hurtling away down here." Uagen fingered a button on his left wrist cuff; his clothes sucked in about him and stopped flapping. He assumed a diving position, placing his hands together and wrapping his tail around his legs. By his side, 974 Praf drew her wings in tighter and also took on a more aerodynamic aspect.

"I cannot see the thing you dropped."

"I can. Just. I think. Oh, bugger and blast."

It was getting away from him. The stylo's air resistance must be just that little less than his, even in a head-down dive. He looked at the Interpreter for a moment. "I think I'll have to power down to it," he shouted.

974 Praf seemed to draw herself in, bringing her wings even closer to her body and stretching her neck. She gained very slightly on Uagen, starting to move past him downwards, then relaxed, and drifted back up. "I cannot go any faster."

"Right, then. I'll see you in a bit."

Uagen clicked a couple of buttons on his wrist. Tiny motors in his ankle bracelets swung out and revved up. "Keep clear!" he shouted to the Interpreter. The motors' propeller blades were expandable, and while he would not need much extra power to increase his rate of fall sufficiently to catch up with the stylo, he had a horror of accidentally mincing one of Yoleus' most trusted servants.

974 Praf had already angled a few meters away. "I shall attempt to catch your hat and try not to become eaten by falficores."

"Oh. Right."

Uagen's speed through the air increased; the wind howled in his ears and tiny popping, crackling sounds from his ears and skull cavities told him the pressure was increasing. He had lost sight of the stylo just for a moment and now it seemed to be quite gone, swallowed up by the oceanic blue of the apparently infinite sky.

If only he'd kept his eyes on it he was sure he'd still be able to see it now. There was a similarity here, perhaps, with the glyph of the suddenly visible falficores. Something to do with perceptual concentration, with the way that one's vision pulled meaning from the semi-chaos of the visual field.

Perhaps the stylo had drifted away to one side. Perhaps a well-camouflaged raptor, mistaking it for a meal, had swept in and gobbled it up. Perhaps he would not regain sight of it until—having started out so low—they both hit the in-sloping side of the sphere. He supposed he might see it bounce. How steep was the slope? The airsphere was not really a sphere, indeed neither of its two lobes was a sphere; at a certain level the bottom of the airsphere's curving sides inverted, dipping under the mass of the detritus neck.

How far away were they from the pole line of the airsphere? He recalled they'd been quite near; by all accounts the gigalithine lenticular entity Buthulne hadn't strayed far from the pole line for several decades. Perhaps he would have to land on the detritus neck! He peered downwards. No sign of anything solid ahead at all. Besides, he'd been told you'd have to fall for days before you'd even see it. And anyway, if the stylo fell into the rubbish and muck of the neck, he'd never find it. Gracious, there were *things* down there. He might, as 974 Praf had put it, become eaten.

What if he landed on the detritus neck just as it was about to eject! Then he would surely die. In vacuum! As part of a glorified dung ball! How horrible!

Airspheres migrated around the galaxy, orbiting once every fifty to a hundred million years, depending on how close they were to the center. They swept up dust and gas on their forward-facing sides, and from their bases, every few hundred thousand years, they passed the waste that their scavenger flora and fauna had not been able to process any further. Droppings the size of small moons issued from globular impossibilities as big as brown dwarfs, leaving a trail of detritus globes scattered through the spiral arms that dated the bizarre worlds' first appearance in the galaxy to one and a half billion years earlier.

People assumed airspheres must be the work of intelligence, but really nobody—or at least nobody willing to share their thoughts on the matter—had any idea. The mega fauna might know, but—frustratingly for scholars like Uagen Zlepe—creatures like Yoleus were so far, far beyond the term Inscrutable that for all practical purposes the word might as well have been a synonym of Forthright, or A Simple-Hearted Chatterbox.

Uagen wondered how fast he was falling now. Perhaps if he fell too fast he would fly straight into the stylo and impale and kill himself. How delightfully ironic! But painful. He checked his velocity on a little read-out in the corner of one eye-goggle. He was falling at twenty-two meters per second, and this rate of descent was smoothly increasing. He adjusted his speed to a constant twenty.

He turned his attention back to the blue gulf ahead and below, and saw the stylo, wobbling fractionally as it fell as though somebody invisible was doodling a spiral with it. He judged that he was drifting toward the thing at a satisfactory rate. When he was a few meters away he cut his speed still further, until he was catching up with the instrument no quicker than a feather might fall through still air.

Uagen reached out and caught the stylo. He tried to halt his fall the impressive way, the way a person of action might (Uagen, for all his studiousness, was a sucker for action adventures, however implausible), by swinging himself around so that his feet were underneath him and the propeller blades on his ankle bracelets were biting down into the air rushing up toward and past him. In retrospect, he had probably stood a good chance of mutilating himself with his own propellers, but instead he just lost all control and tumbled chaotically through the air, shouting and cursing, trying to keep his tail curled up tight and away from the propellers and letting go of the stylo again.

He spread out his limbs and waited until there was some sort of regularity to his tumble, then twisted back into a dive to regain control, and once more looked about for the stylo. He could see the vaguest hint of Yoleus' shape, high, high above, and a tiny outline—just close enough to be a shape and not a dot—also above and to one side. This looked like 974 Praf. And there was the stylo; now above him, just stopping tumbling and beginning to settle into its crossbow quarrel attitude. He used his wrist controls to reduce power to the propellers.

The wind roar decreased; the stylo fell gently into his hand. He attached it to the side of the writing tablet, then used his wrist controls to feather and then repitch the motors' blades. Blood rushed to his head, adding another roaring to that of the wind and making the blue view pulse and darken. His necklace—a gift from his aunt Silder, presented just before he left—slid down under his chin.

He let the propellers free-wheel for a bit, then fed in the power again. He still felt very head-down heavy, but that was the worst he experienced. His headlong plummet became a slow fall, the thick air stopped shaking him and the slipstream became a gentle breeze. Finally he stopped. He thought the better of trying to balance on the ankle bracelet motors. He would activate the cape and let it float him back up.

He hung there, head down, effectively motionless as the ankle motors spun lazily in the thick air.

His eyes narrowed.

There was something down there, something far below, almost but not quite lost in the haze. A shape. A very big shape, filling about the same part of his visual field as his hand would have, held outstretched, and yet still so far away that it was barely visible in the haze. He squinted, looked away and looked back.

There was definitely something there. From the finned airship shape, it looked like another behemothaur, though Yoleus had let it be known that Muetenive had taken them unfashionably, hurtfully, almost unprecedentedly and arguably disgracefully low, and so Uagen thought it very strange to see another of the giant creatures so much deeper still beneath the courting couple. The shape, also, did not look quite right. There were too many fins, and in plan—making the very reasonable assumption that he was looking down on its back—the thing looked asymmetrical. Very unusual. Even alarming.

There was a fluttering noise nearby. "Here is your hat."

He turned to look at 974 Praf, flapping her wings slowly in the dense air and holding his tasselled box hat in her beak.

"Oh, thank you," he said, and rammed the hat on tight.

"You have the stylo?"

"Umm. Yes. Yes, I do. Look; down there. Can you see something?"

974 looked down. Eventually she said, "There is a shadow."

"Yes, there is, isn't there? Does it look like a behemothaur to you?"

The Interpreter cocked her head. "No."

"No?"

The Interpreter turned her head the other way. "Yes."

"Yes?"

"No and yes. Both at once."

"Ah-ha." He looked down again. "I wonder what it can be."

"I wonder too. Shall we return to the Yoleus?"

"Umm. I don't know. Do you think we ought?"

"Yes. We have fallen a long way. I cannot see the Yoleus."

"Oh. Oh dear." He looked up. Sure enough, the creature's giant shape had disappeared in the haze above. "I see. Or rather, we can't see. Ha ha."

"Indeed."

"Umm. Still, I do wonder what that is down there."

The shadowy outline beneath appeared to be stationary. Air currents in the haze made it almost disappear for a few moments, so that all that was left was the bias in the eye, making the assumption that it must still be there. And then it was back, distinguishable, but still no more than a shape, a one-shade-deeper blue shadow against the colossal gulf of air below.

"We should return to the Yoleus."

"Do you think Yoleus will have any idea what it is?"

"Yes."

"It does look like a behemothaur, doesn't it?"

"Yes and no. Maybe sick."

"Sick?"

"Injured."

"Injured? What can—how can behemothaurs become injured?"

"It is very unusual. We should return to the Yoleus."

"We could take a closer look," Uagen said. He wasn't really sure he wanted to, but he felt he ought to say it. It was interesting, after all. On the other hand, it was a little disturbing, too. As 974 Praf had said, they had lost visual contact with Yoleus. It ought to be easy enough to find it again—Yoleus had not been moving quickly and so simply going straight back up would probably still bring them up almost underneath the creature—but, well, even so.

What if Muetenive decided to make a bolt for the anticipated convection bubble now, rather than in a day or two? Good grief, he and 974 Praf could both be left stranded. Yoleus might not have noticed that they'd gone. If it had realized they were no longer aboard, and then took off after a suddenly frisky Muetenive, it would probably leave some raptor scouts behind to protect them and escort them back. But there was no guarantee that it did know he and 974 Praf were not safely within its foliage.

Uagen looked around for falficores. He didn't even have a weapon; when he'd refused any sort of bodyguard device the university had insisted he at least take a pistol with him, but he'd never even unpacked the damn thing.

"We should return to the Yoleus." The Interpreter spoke very quickly, which was as close as she ever got to sounding nervous or disturbed. 974 Praf had probably never been in a position where she couldn't see the great creature that was her home, host, leader, parent and beloved. She must be afraid, if such beings felt fear.

Uagen was afraid, he could admit that. Not very afraid, but afraid enough to hope that 974 Praf would refuse to accompany him down to the huge shape below. And they would have to go down quite a long way further. He didn't like to think how many more kilometers.

"We should return to the Yoleus," she said again.

"You really think so?"

"Yes, we should return to the Yoleus."

"Oh, I suppose so. All right." He sighed. "Discretion, and all that. Best let Yoleus decide what to do."

"We should return to the Yoleus."

"Yes, yes." He used the wrist controls to activate the stowed cape. It unfurled, collapsed slowly into a ball, then—even more slowly— began to expand.

"We should return to the Yoleus."

"We are, Praf. We are. We're going now." He could feel himself starting to drift upwards, and a faint pull on his shoulders began to lift him toward the horizontal.

"We should return to the Yoleus."

"Praf, please. That's what we're doing. don't keep—"

"We should return to the Yoleus."

"We are!" He let the power to the bracelet-ankle motors tail off; the ballooning cape, still a perfect black sphere blossoming behind his head, slowly took all his weight and hoisted him upright.

"We should—"

"Praf!"

The propellers cut out and stowed themselves back in his ankle bracelets. He was floating upwards at last. 974 Praf beat her wings a little harder to keep up with him. She looked up at the still enlarging black sphere of the cape.

"Another thing," she said.

Uagen was staring down, between his boots. Already the vast shape beneath was starting to disappear into the haze. He glanced at the Interpreter. "What?"

"The Yoleus would like to know more of the vacuum dirigibles in your Culture."

He looked up at the black balloon above his head. The cape produced lift by compressing itself into a ball and then expanding its surface area while leaving a vacuum inside. That vacuum was lifting him by the shoulders, up into the sky.

"What? Oh, well." He wished he hadn't mentioned the damn things now. He also wished he'd brought a more complete technical library from the Culture. "I'm hardly an expert. I have been a tourist on them a few times, on my home Orbital."

"You mentioned pumping vacuum. How is that done?" 974 Praf seemed to be laboring to keep up with him now, flapping her wings as hard as the thickened atmosphere would allow.

Uagen adjusted the dimensions of the cape. His rate of climb tailed off. "Ah, well, as far as I understand it, you keep the vacuum in spheres."

"Spheres."

"Very thin-shelled spheres. You keep the spaces between the spheres full of, ah . . . well; helium or hydrogen, I think, depending on your inclination. Though I don't think you get a vast amount of extra lift compared to using hydrogen or helium alone; just a few percent. One of those things that tend to be done because they can be rather than because they need to be."

"One sees."

"Then you can pump it. Them. The spheres and the gas."

"One sees. And what is the manner of this pumping?"

"Umm . . ." He looked down again, but the great shadowy shape had gone.

5

A Very Attractive System

(Recording.)

"This is a great simulation."

"It's not a simulation."

"Yeah. Of course. Still, it is though, isn't it?"

"Push! Push!"

"I'm pushing, I'm pushing!"

"Well, push harder!"

"You don't think this is a fucking simulation, do you?"

"Oh no, not a *fucking* simulation."

"Look, I don't know what you're on but whatever it is it's the wrong stuff."

"The flames are coming up the shaft!"

"So get some water down it!"

"I can't reach the—"

"I'm *really* impressed."

"You are on something, aren't you?"

"He must be glanding. Nobody can be this stupid straight."

"I'm so glad we waited till night, aren't you?"

"Absolutely. Look at the day side! I've never seen it shimmer like that, have you?"

"Not that I can recall."

"Ha! I love this. Brilliant simulation."

"It's *not* a simulation, you buffoon. Will you *listen?*"

"We should get this guy out of here."

"What is that, anyway?"

"Who, not what; Homomdan guy. Called Kabe."

"Oh."

They were lava-rafting. Kabe sat in the center of the flat-decked craft, staring at the mottled yellow-bright flowing river of molten rock ahead and the darkly desolate landscape through which it ran. He could hear the humans talking but he wasn't paying much attention to who said what.

"He's already out of it."

"Just *brilliant.* Look at that! And the heat!"

"I agree. Get him zapped."

"It's on fire!"

"Pole on the dark bits, you idiot, not the bright bits!"

"Bring it in and put it out!"

"What?"

"Fuck, it's hot."

"Yeah, it is, isn't it? I never felt a sim this hot!"

"This is not a simulation, and you're getting zapped."

"Can anybody—?"

"Help!"

"Oh, throw it away! Grab another oar."

They were on one of Masaq's last eight uninhabited Plates. Here—and for three Plates to spinward and four anti-spinward— Masaq' Great River flowed dead straight through a seventy-five-thousand-kilometer-long base-material tunnel across a landscape still in the process of being formed.

"Wow! Hot hot hot! Some sim!"

"Get this guy out of here. He shouldn't have been invited in the first place. There are one-timers here with no savers. If this clown thinks we're in a sim he could do anything."

"Jump overboard, hopefully."

"Need more bods on the starboard side!"

"The what?"

"Right. The right. This side. This side here. Fuck."

"Don't even fucking joke about that. He's so twisted I wouldn't trust him to punch out if he did fall in."

"Tunnel ahead! Going to get hotter!"

"Oh, shit."

"It can't get hotter! They don't let it."

"Will you fucking *listen?* This is not a simulation!"

As was by now long-standing established practice for the Culture, asteroids from Masaq's own system—most of them collected and parked in planetary holding orbits several thousand years earlier when the Orbital had first been constructed—were tugged in by Lifter craft and lowered to the Plate's surface where any one of several energy delivery systems (planetary crust-busting weapons, if you insisted on looking on them that way) heated the bodies to liquid heat so that even more mind-boggling matter- and energy-manipulating processes either let the resulting slag flow and cool in certain designated directions or sculpted it to cloak the already existing morphology of the strategic base matter.

"On."

"What?"

"On. You fall on, not in. Don't look at me like that; it's the density."

"I bet you know all about fucking density. Got a terminal?"

"No."

"Implanted?"

"No."

"Me neither. Try and find somebody who does or is and get that cretin off here."

"It won't come out!"

"The pin! You have to knock the pin out first!"

"Oh, yeah."

People—especially Culture people, whether human, once human, alien or machine—had been building Orbitals like this for thousands of years, and not very long after the process had become a mature technology, still thousands of years earlier, some fun- (or at any rate risk-) loving individual had thought of using a few of the lava streams naturally generated by such processes as the medium for a new sport.

"Excuse me, I have a terminal."

"Oh. Yeah, Kabe, of course."

"What?"

"I have a terminal. Here."

"Ship oars! Mind your heads!"

"It's fucking glowing in there, man!"

"Sep; hit the cover!"

"Covering now!"

"Oh, wow!"

"Ship them or lose them!"

"Hub! See this guy? Sim-shitter! Zap him out now!"

"Done . . ."

And so lava-rafting became a pastime. On Masaq' the tradition was that you did it without the aid of field technology or anything clever in the way of material science. The experience would be more exciting and you would come closer to its reality if you used materials that were only just up to the demands being made in it. It was what people called a minimal-safety-factor sport.

"Watch that oar!"

"It's caught!"

"Well, push it!"

"Oh, shit!"

"What the—?"

"Aaah!"

"It's okay, it's okay!"

"Fuck!"

". . . You are all quite mad, by the way. Happy rafting."

The raft itself—a flat-decked platform four meters by twelve with meter-high gunwales—was ceramic, the cover protecting the rafters from the heat of the lava tunnel they were now shooting down was

aluminized plastic, and the steering oars were wood, to introduce a
note of the corporeal.

"My hair!"

"Oh! I want to go home!"

"Water bucket!"

"Where'd that guy—?"

"Stop whining."

"Good *grief!*"

Lava-rafting had always been exciting and dangerous. Once the
eight Plates had been filled with air, it had become more of a hard-
ship; radiated heat was joined by convected, and while people felt it
was somehow more authentic to raft without breathing gear, having
your lungs scorched was generally no more fun than it sounded.

"Ah! My nose! My nose!"

"Thanks."

"Sprays!"

"You're welcome."

"I'm with the other guy. I don't believe this."

Kabe sat back. He had to crouch; the wind-rippled undersurface
of the raft's foil cover was just above his head. The canopy was reflecting the heat of the tunnel's ceiling, but the air temperature was still
extreme. Some of the humans were pouring water over themselves
or spraying it onto each other. Coils of steam filled the little mobile
cave that the raft had become. The light was very dark red, spilling
from either end of the pitching, bucking craft.

"This hurts!"

"Well, stop it hurting!"

"Zap me out too!"

"Nearly out! . . . Oh-oh. We got hang-spikes."

The downstream mouth of the lava tunnel had teeth; it was strung
with jagged protrusions like stalactites.

"Spikes! Get down!"

One of the hang-spikes ripped the raft's flimsy protective cover
away and flung it onto the yellow-glowing surface of the lava stream.
The cover shrank, burst into flames and then, caught in the thermals

coming off the braided flow, rose flapping like a burning bird. A blast of heat rolled over the raft. People screamed. Kabe had to fling himself back flat to avoid being hit by one of the pendulous spears of rock. He felt something give beneath him; there was a snap and another scream.

The raft flew out of the tunnel into a broad canyon of craggy cliffs whose basalt dark edges were lit by the broad stream of lava coursing between them. Kabe levered himself back up. Most of the humans were throwing or spraying water around, cooling themselves after the final blast of heat; many had lost hair, some were sitting or lying looking singed but uncaring, staring blankly ahead, blissed out on some secretion. One couple were just sitting hunched up on the flat deck of the raft, crying loudly.

"Was that your leg?" Kabe asked the man sitting on the deck behind him.

The man was holding his left leg and grimacing. "Yes," he said. "I think it's broken."

"Yes. I think it is, too. I'm very sorry. Is there anything I can do?"

"Try not falling back like that again, not while I'm here."

Kabe looked forward. The glowing river of orange lava meandered into the distance between the canyon walls. There were no more lava tunnels visible. "I think I can guarantee that," Kabe said. "I do apologize; I was told to sit in the center of the deck. Can you move?"

The man slid back on one hand and his buttocks, still holding his leg with the other hand. People were calming down. Some were still crying but one was shouting that it was okay, there were no more lava tunnels.

"You all right?" one of the females asked the man with the broken leg. The woman's jacket was still smouldering. She had no eyebrows and her blond hair looked uneven and had crisped-looking patches.

"Broken. I'll live."

"My fault," Kabe explained.

"I'll get a splint."

The woman went to a locker near the stern. Kabe looked around.

There was a smell of burned hair and old-fashioned clothing and lightly crisped human flesh. He could see a few people with discolored patches on their faces, and a few had their hands submerged in water buckets. The crouched couple were still wailing. Most of the rest who hadn't blissed out were comforting each other, tear-streaked faces lit by the livid light reflected from the glass-sharp black cliffs. High above, twinkling madly in the brown-dark sky, the nova that was Portisia gazed balefully down.

And this is meant to be fun, Kabe thought.

~ Does it become anymore ridiculous?

"What?" somebody yelled from the raft's bows. *"Rapids?"*

~ Not really.

Somebody started sobbing hysterically.

~ I've seen enough. Shall we?

~ By all means. Once was probably enough.

(Recording ends.)

Kabe and Ziller faced each other across a large, elegantly furnished room lit by golden sunlight that spilled through the opened balcony windows, already filtered through the gently waving branches of an everblue growing outside. A myriad of soft needle-shadows moved on the creamily tiled floor, lay across the ankle-deep, abstractly patterned carpets and fluttered silently on the sculpted surfaces of gleaming wooden sideboards, richly carved chests and plumply upholstered couches.

The Homomdan and the Chelgrian both wore devices which looked like they might have been either protective helmets of dubious effectiveness or rather garish head-jewelry.

Ziller snorted. "We look preposterous."

"Perhaps that is one reason people take to implants."

They each took the devices off. Kabe, sitting on a graceful, relatively flimsy-looking chaise longue with deep bays designed especially for tripeds, placed his head-set on the couch beside him.

Ziller, curled on a broad couch, set his on the floor. He blinked a couple of times then reached into his waistcoat pocket for his pipe. He wore pale-green leggings and an enamelled groin plate. The waistcoat was hide, jewelled.

"This was when?" he asked.

"About eighty days ago."

"The Hub Mind was right. They are all quite mad."

"And yet most of the people you saw there had lava-rafted before and had just as awful a time. I have checked up since and all but three of the twenty-three humans you saw there have taken part in the sport again." Kabe picked up a cushion and played with the fringe. "Though it has to be said that two of them have experienced temporary body-death when their lava canoe capsized and one of them— a one-timer, a Disposable—was crushed to death while glacier-caving."

"Completely dead?"

"Very completely, and forever. They recovered the body and held a funeral service."

"Age?"

"She was thirty-one standard years old. Barely an adult."

Ziller sucked on his pipe. He looked toward the balcony windows. They were in a large house in an estate in the Tirian Hills, on Osinorsi Lower, the Plate to spinwards of Xaravve. Kabe shared the house with an extended human family of about sixteen individuals, two of them children. A new top floor had been built for him. Kabe enjoyed the company of the humans and their young, though he had come to realize that he was probably a little less gregarious than he'd thought he was.

He had introduced the Chelgrian to the half dozen other people present in and around the house and shown him around. From down-slope-facing windows and balconies, and from the roof garden, you could see, looming bluely across the plains, the cliffs of the massif that carried Masaq' Great River across the vast sunken garden that was Osinorsi Lower Plate.

They were waiting for the drone E. H. Tersono, which was on its way to them with what it called important news.

"I seem to recall," Ziller said, "that I said I agreed with Hub that they were all quite mad and you began your reply with the words 'And yet.'" Ziller frowned. "And then everything you said subsequently seemed to agree with what I had said."

"What I meant is that however much they appeared to hate the experience, and despite being under no pressure to repeat it—"

"Other than pressure from their equally cretinous peers."

"—they nevertheless chose to, because however awful it might have seemed at the time, they feel that they gained something positive from it."

"Oh? And what would that be? That they lived through it despite their stupidity in undertaking this totally unnecessary traumatic experience in the first place? What one should gain from an unpleasant experience should be the determination not to repeat it. Or at least the inclination."

"They feel they have tested themselves—"

"And found themselves to be mad. Does that count as a positive result?"

"They feel they have tested themselves against nature—"

"What's natural around here?" Ziller protested. "The nearest 'natural' thing to here is ten light minutes away. It's the fucking sun." He snorted. "And I wouldn't put it past them to have meddled with that."

"I don't believe they have. In fact it was a potential instability in Lacelere that produced the high back-up rate on Masaq' Orbital in the first place, before it became famous for excessive fun." Kabe put the cushion down.

Ziller was staring at him. "Are you saying the sun could explode?"

"Well, sort of, in theory. It's a very—"

"You're not serious!"

"Of course I am. The chances are—"

"They never told me *that!*"

"Actually, it wouldn't really blow up as such, but it might flare—"

"It *does* flare! I've seen its flares!"

"Yes. Pretty, aren't they? But there is a chance—no more than one in several million during the time the star spends on the main-sequence—that it might produce a flare sequence that Hub and the Orbital's defenses would be unable to deflect or shelter everyone from."

"And they built this thing here?"

"I understand it was a very attractive system otherwise. And besides, I believe that over time they've added extra protection under-Plate which could stand up to anything short of a supernova, though of course any technology can go wrong and, sensibly, the culture of backing-up as a matter of course is still common."

Ziller was shaking his head. "They could have mentioned this to me."

"Perhaps the risk is deemed so tiny they have given up bothering."

Ziller smoothed his scalp fur. He'd let his pipe go out. "I don't believe these people."

"The chances of disaster are very remote indeed, especially for any given year, or even sentient lifetime." Kabe rose and lumbered over to a sideboard. He picked up a bowl of fruit. "Fruit?"

"No, thank you."

Kabe selected a ripe sunbread. He had had his intestinal flora altered to enable him to eat common Culture foods. More unusually, he had had his oral and nasal senses modified so that he could taste food as a standard Culture human would. He turned away from Ziller as he popped the sunbread into his mouth, chewed the fruit a couple of times and swallowed. The action of averting his face from others when eating had become habitual; members of Kabe's species had very big mouths and some humans found the sight of him eating alarming.

"But to return to my point," he said, dabbing at his mouth with a napkin. "Let's not use the word 'nature' then; let us say they feel they have gained something from having pitted themselves against forces much greater than themselves."

"And this is somehow not a sign of madness." Ziller shook his head. "Kabe, you may have been here too long."

The Homomdan crossed to the balcony, gazing out at the view. "I would say that these people are demonstrably not mad. They live lives that seem quite sane otherwise."

"What? Glacier-caving?"

"That is not all they do."

"Indeed. They do lots of other insane things; naked blade-fencing, mountain free-climbing, wing-flying—"

"Very few do nothing but take part in these extreme pastimes. Most have otherwise fairly normal lives."

Ziller relit his pipe. "By Culture standards."

"Well, yes, and why not? They socialize, they have work-hobbies, they play in more gentle forms, they read or watch screen, they go to entertainments. They sit around grinning in one of their glanded drug states, they study, they spend time traveling—"

"Ah-hah!"

"—apparently just for the sake of it or they simply . . . potter. And of course many of them indulge in arts and crafts." Kabe made a smile and spread his three hands. "A few even compose music."

"They spend time. That's just it. They spend time traveling. The time weighs heavily on them because they lack any context, any valid framework for their lives. They persist in hoping that something they think they'll find in the place they're heading for will somehow provide them with a fulfilment they feel certain they deserve and yet have never come close to experiencing."

Ziller frowned and tapped at his pipe bowl. "Some travel forever in hope and are serially disappointed. Others, slightly less self-deceiving, come to accept that the process of traveling itself offers, if not fulfilment, then relief from the feeling that they should be feeling fulfilled."

Kabe watched a springleg bounce from branch to branch through the trees outside, its ruddy fur and long tail dappled with leaf shadows. He could hear the shrill voices of human children, playing and splashing in the pool at the side of the house. "Oh, come, Ziller. Arguably any intelligent species feels that to some extent."

"Really? Does yours?"

Kabe fingered the soft folds of the drapes at the side of the balcony window. "We are much older than the humans, but I think we probably did, once." He looked back at the Chelgrian, crouched on the wide seat as though ready to pounce. "All naturally evolved sentient life is restless. At some scale or stage."

Ziller appeared to consider this, then shook his head. Kabe was

not yet sure if this gesture meant that he had said something too preposterous to be worth dignifying with an answer, perpetrated an
appalling cliché, or made a point that the Chelgrian could not find
an adequate reply to.

"The point is," Ziller said, "that having carefully constructed their
paradise from first principles to remove all credible motives for conflict amongst themselves and all natural threats—" He paused and
glanced sourly at the sunlight flaring off the gilt border of his seat.
"—Well, almost all natural threats, these people then find their lives
are so hollow they have to recreate false versions of just the sort of terrors untold generations of their ancestors spent their existences
attempting to conquer."

"I think that is a little like criticizing somebody for owning both
an umbrella and a shower," Kabe said. "It is the choice that is important." He rearranged the curtains more symmetrically. "These people
control their terrors. They can choose to sample them, repeat them
or avoid them. That is not the same as living beneath the volcano
when you've just invented the wheel, or wondering whether your
levee will break and drown your entire village. Again, this applies to
all societies which have matured beyond the age of barbarism. There
is no great mystery here."

"But the Culture is so insistent in its utopianism," Ziller said,
sounding, Kabe thought, almost bitter. "They are like an infant with
a toy, demanding it only to throw it away."

Kabe watched Ziller puff at his pipe for a while, then walked
through the cloud of smoke and sat trefoil on the finger-deep carpet
near the other male's couch.

"I think it is only natural, and a sign that one has succeeded as a
species, that what used to have to be suffered as a necessity becomes
enjoyed as sport. Even fear can be recreational."

Ziller looked into the Homomdan's eyes. "And despair?"

Kabe shrugged. "Despair? Well, only in the short term, as when
one despairs of completing a task, or winning at some game or sport,
and yet later does. The earlier despair makes the victory all the
sweeter."

"That is not despair," Ziller said quietly. "That is temporary annoyance, the passing irritation of foreseen disappointment. I meant nothing so trivial. I meant the sort of despair that eats your soul, that contaminates your senses so that every experience, however pleasant, becomes saturated with bile. The sort of despair that drives you to thoughts of suicide."

Kabe rocked back. "No," he said. "No. They might hope to have put that behind them."

"Yes. They leave it in their wake for others."

"Ah." Kabe nodded. "I think we touch upon what happened to your own people. Well, some of them feel remorse close to despair about that."

"It was mostly our own doing." Ziller crumbled some smoke block into his pipe, tamping it down with a small silver instrument and producing further clouds of smoke. "We would doubtless have contrived a war without the Culture's help."

"Not necessarily."

"I disagree. Regardless; at least after a war we might have been forced to confront our own stupidities. The Culture's involvement meant that we suffered the war's depredations while failing to benefit from its lessons. We just blamed the Culture instead. Short of our utter destruction the outcome could hardly have been worse, and sometimes I feel that even that is an unjustified exception."

Kabe sat still for a while. Blue smoke rose from Ziller's pipe.

Ziller had once been Gifted-from-Tacted Mahrai Ziller VIII of Wescrip. Born into a family of administrators and diplomats, he had been a musical prodigy almost from infancy, composing his first orchestral work at an age when most Chelgrian children were still learning not to eat their shoes.

He had taken the designation Gifted—two caste levels below that he had been born into—when he dropped out of college, scandalizing his parents.

Despite garnering outrageous fame and fortune in his career he scandalized them still further, to the point of illness and breakdown, when he became a radical Caste Denier, entered politics as an Equalitarian and used his prestige to argue for the end of the caste system. Gradually public and political opinion began to shift; it started to look as though the long talked-about Great Change might finally happen. After an unsuccessful attempt on his life Ziller renounced his caste altogether, and so was deemed the lowest of the non-criminal low; an Invisible.

A second assassination attempt very nearly succeeded; it left him near death and in hospital for quarter of a year. It was moot whether his months out of the political scrum had made any crucial difference, but unarguably by the time he was recovered the tide had turned again, the backlash had begun and any hope of significant change appeared to have vanished for at least a generation.

Ziller's musical output had suffered during the years of his political involvement, in quantity at least. He announced that he was quitting public life to concentrate on composition, so alienating his former liberal allies and delighting the conservatives who had been his enemies. Even so, despite great pressure he did not renounce his Invisible status—though increasingly he was treated as an honorary Given— and he never gave any sign of support for the status quo, save for that studied silence on all matters political.

His prestige and popularity increased still further; cascades of prizes, awards and honors were lavished upon him; polls proclaimed him the greatest living Chelgrian; there was talk of him becoming Ceremonial President one day.

With his celebrity and prominence at this unprecedented crescendo of acclaim, he used what was supposed to be his acceptance speech for the greatest civilian honor the Chelgrian State could bestow—at a grand and glittering ceremony in Chelise, the Chelgrian State's capital, which would be broadcast over the whole sphere of Chelgrian space—to announce that he had never changed his views, he was and always would be a liberal and an Equalitarian, he was more proud to have worked with the people who still espoused such views than he was of his music, he had grown to loathe the forces of conservatism even more than he had in his youth, he still despised the state, the society and the people that tolerated the caste system, he was not accepting this honor, he would be returning all the others he had acquired, and he had already booked passage to leave the Chelgrian State immediately and forever, because unlike the liberal comrades he loved, respected and admired so much, he just did not have the moral strength to continue living in this vicious, hateful, intolerable regime any longer.

His speech was greeted with stunned silence. He left the stage to hisses and boos and spent the night in a Culture embassy compound with a crowd at the gates baying for his blood.

A Culture ship lifted him away the following day; he traveled extensively within the Culture over the next few years and finally made his home on Masaq' Orbital.

Ziller had remained on Masaq' even after the election of an Equalitarian President on Chel, seven years after he'd left. Reforms were put in place and the Invisibles and the other castes were fully enfranchised at last, but still, despite numerous requests and invitations, Ziller had not returned to his home, and had offered little in the way of explanation.

People assumed it was because the caste system would still exist. Part of the compromise which had sold the reforms to the higher castes was that titles and caste names would be retained as part of one's legal nomenclature and a new property law would give ownership of clan lands to the immediate family of the house chief.

In return, people of all levels of society were now free to marry and procreate with whoever would have them, partnered couples would each take the caste of the highest-designated of the two, their young would inherit that caste, elected caste courts would oversee the redesignation of applying individuals, there would no longer be a law to punish people who claimed to be of a higher caste, and so, in theory, anybody could claim to be whatever they wanted to be, though a court of law would still insist on calling them as they had been born or redesignated.

It was an enormous legal and behavioral change from the old system, but it still included caste, and it did not seem to be enough for Ziller.

Then the ruling coalition on Chel had elected a Spayed as President as an effective but surprising symbol of how much had changed. The regime survived a coup attempt by some Guards officers and appeared strengthened by the experience, with power and authority seemingly being distributed even more fully and irrevocably down the ladder of original castes, yet still Ziller, arguably more popular than ever, had not returned. He claimed to be waiting to see what would happen.

Then something terrible happened, and he saw, and still did not go home, even after the Caste War, which broke out nine years after he left and was, by its own admission, largely the Culture's fault.

Eventually Kabe said, "My own people fought the Culture once."

"Unlike us. We fought ourselves." Ziller looked at the Homomdan. "Did you profit from the experience?" he asked tartly.

"Yes. We lost much; many brave people and many noble ships, and we did not succeed in our initial war aims, directly, but we maintained our civilizational course, and gained in as much that we discovered that the Culture could be lived with honorably, and that it was what we had been worried it was not: another temperate dweller in the galactic house. Our two societies have since become companionable and we are occasionally allies."

"They didn't crush you utterly, then?"

"They didn't try to. Nor we them. It was never that sort of war, and besides, that is neither their way nor ours. It is not really anybody's way, these days. In any event, our dispute with the Culture was always a sideshow to the principal action, which was the conflict between our hosts and the Idirans."

"Ah yes, the famous Twin Novae Battle," Ziller said, sounding disparaging.

Kabe was surprised at the tone. "Is your symphony past the tinkering stage yet?"

"Pretty much."

"You're still pleased with it?"

"Yes. Very. There is nothing wrong with the music. However I do begin to wonder whether my enthusiasm got the better of me. Perhaps I was wrong to become so involved with our Hub Mind's memento mori." Ziller fidgeted with his waistcoat, then waved one hand dismissively. "Oh, take no notice. I always become a little disheartened when I've just finished something this size, and I will confess to a degree of nervousness at the prospect of standing up and conducting in front of the sort of numbers Hub is talking about. Plus I'm still not sure about all the extraneous stuff Hub wants to add around the music." Ziller snorted. "I may be more of a purist than I thought."

"I am sure it will go wonderfully well. When does Hub intend to announce the concert?"

"Very soon now," Ziller said, sounding defensive. "It was one of the reasons I came over here. I thought I might be besieged if I stayed home."

Kabe nodded slowly. "I am glad to be of service. And I cannot wait to hear the piece."

"Thank you. I'm pleased with it, but I can't help feeling complicit with Hub's ghoulishness."

"I wouldn't call it ghoulish. Old soldiers are rarely so. Depressed, disturbed and morbid sometimes, but not ghoulish. That is a civilian preoccupation."

"Hub isn't a civilian?" Ziller asked. "Hub might be depressed and *disturbed?* Is this something else they didn't tell me about?"

"Masaq' Hub has never been either depressed or disturbed to my knowledge," Kabe said. "However, it was once the Mind of a war-adapted General Systems Vehicle and it was there at the Twin Novae Battle at the end of the war and suffered near total destruction at the hands of an Idiran battle fleet."

"Not quite total."

"Not quite."

"They don't believe in the captain going down with the ship, then."

"I understand that being last to abandon it is considered sufficient. But do you see? Masaq' mourns and honors those it lost, those who died, and seeks to atone for whatever part it played in the war."

Ziller shook his head. "The scummer might have told me some of this," he muttered. Kabe pondered the wisdom of remarking that Ziller might have discovered all of this easily enough himself had he been so inclined, but decided against it. Ziller tapped his pipe out. "Well, let us hope it does not suffer from despair."

"Drone E. H. Tersono is here," the house announced.

"Oh, good."

"About time."

"Invite it in."

The drone floated in through the balcony window, sunlight dappling its rosy porcelain skin and blue lumenstone frame. "I noticed the window was open; hope you don't mind."

"Not at all."

"Eavesdropping outside, were we?" Ziller asked.

The drone settled delicately on a chair. "My dear Ziller, certainly not. Why? Were you talking about me?"

"No."

"So, Tersono," Kabe said. "It is very kind of you to visit. I understand we owe the honor to further news of our envoy."

"Yes. I have learned the identity of the emissary being sent to us by Chel," the drone said. "His full name is, and I quote, Called-to-Arms-from-Given Major Tibilo Quilan IV Autumn 47th of Itirewein, griefling, Sheracht Order."

"Good heavens," Kabe said, looking at Ziller. "Your full names are even longer than the Culture's."

"Yes. An endearing trait, isn't it?" Ziller said. He looked into his pipe, brows puckered. "So, our emissary's a warlord-priest. A rich broker boy from one of the sovereign families who's found a taste for soldiering, or been shunted into it to keep him out of the way, and then found Faith, or found it politic to find it. Parents traditionalists. And he's a widower, probably."

"You know him?" Kabe asked.

"Actually, I do, from a long time ago. We were at infant school together. We were friends, I suppose, though not particularly close. We lost touch after that. Haven't heard of him since." Ziller inspected his pipe and seemed to be contemplating lighting it again. Instead he replaced it in his waistcoat pocket. "Even if we weren't once acquainted though, the rest of the name rigmarole tells you most of what you need to know." He snorted. "Culture full names act as addresses; ours act as potted histories. And, of course, they tell you whether you should bow, or be bowed to. Our Major Quilan will certainly expect to be bowed to."

"You may be doing him a disservice," Tersono said. "I have a full biography you might be interested in—"

"Well, I'm not," Ziller said emphatically, turning away to look at a painting hanging on one wall. It showed long-ago Homomdans riding enormous tusked creatures, waving flags and spears and looking heroic in a hectic sort of way.

"I'd like to look at it later," Kabe said.

"Certainly."

"So that's, what, twenty-three, twenty-four days till he gets here?"

"About that."

"Oh, I do so hope he's having a pleasant journey," Ziller said in a strange, almost childish voice. He spat into his hands and smoothed the tawny pelt over each forearm in turn, stretching each hand as he did so, so that the claws emerged; gleaming black curves the size of a human's small finger, glinting in the soft sunlight like polished obsidian blades.

The Culture drone and the Homomdan male exchanged looks. Kabe lowered his head.

6

Resistance Is Character-Forming

Quilan wondered about their ship names. Perhaps it was some elaborate joke to send him on the final leg of his journey aboard a one-time warship—a Gangster class Rapid Offensive Unit which had been demilitarized to become a Very Fast Picket—called *Resistance Is Character-Forming.* It was a jokey name, yet pointed. So many of their ship names were like that, even if more were just jokey.

Chelgrian craft had romantic, purposeful or poetic names, but the Culture—while it had a sprinkling of ships with names of similar natures—usually went for ironic, meticulously obscure, supposedly humorous or frankly absurd names. Perhaps this was partly because they had so many craft. Perhaps it reflected the fact that their ships were their own masters and chose their own names.

The first thing he did when he stepped aboard the ship, into a small foyer floored with gleaming wood and edged with blue-green foliage, was to take a deep breath. "It smells like—" he began.

~ *Home,* said the voice in his head.

"Yes," Quilan breathed, and experienced a strange, weakening, pleasantly sad sensation, and suddenly thought of childhood.

~ *Careful, son.*

"Major Quilan, welcome aboard," the ship said from nowhere in particular. "I have introduced a fragrance into the air which should be reminiscent of the atmosphere around Lake Itir, Chel, during springtime. Do you find this agreeable?"

Quilan nodded. "Yes. Yes, I do."

"Good. Your quarters are directly ahead. Please make yourself at home."

He'd been expecting a cabin as cramped as the one he'd been given on the *Nuisance Value,* but was pleasantly surprised; the *Resistance Is Character-Forming*'s interior had been refitted to provide comfortable accommodation for about half a dozen people rather than cramped quarters for four times that number.

The ship was uncrewed and chose not to use an avatar or drone to communicate. It just spoke to Quilan out of thin air, and carried out mundane house-keeping duties by creating internal maniple fields, so that clothes, for example, just floated around, seeming to clean and fold and sort and store themselves.

~ *It's like living in a fucking haunted house,* Huyler said.

~ Good job neither of us is superstitious.

~ *And it means it's listening to you all the time, spying.*

~ That could be interpreted as a form of honesty.

~ *Or arrogance. These things don't choose their names out of a hat.*

Resistance is character-forming. If nothing else, as a motto it was a little insensitive, given the circumstances of the war. Were they trying to tell him, and through him Chel itself, that they didn't really care about what had happened, despite all their protestations? Or even that they did care, and were sorry, yet it had all been for their own good?

More likely the ship's name was coincidence. There was a sort of carelessness about the Culture sometimes, a reverse side to the coin of the society's fabled thoroughness and tenacity of purpose, as though every now and again they caught themselves being overly obsessive and precise, and tried to compensate by suddenly doing something frivolous or irresponsible.

Or might they not get bored being good?

Supposedly they were infinitely patient, boundlessly resourceful, unceasingly understanding, but would not any rational mind, with or without the capital letter, grow tired of such unleavened niceness eventually? Wouldn't they want to cause just a little havoc, just once in a while, just to show what they could do?

Or did such thoughts merely betray his own inheritance of animal ferocity? Chelgrians were proud of having evolved from predators. It was a kind of double pride, too, even if a few people regarded it as contradictory in nature; they were proud that their distant ancestors had been predators, but they were also proud that their species had evolved and matured away from the kind of behavior that inheritance might imply.

Maybe only a creature with that ancient inheritance of savagery would think the way he, in his mind, had accused the Minds of thinking. Maybe the humans—who could not claim quite such a purity of predatoriness in their past as Chelgrians, but who had certainly behaved savagely enough toward those of their own species and others since they began to become civilized—would also think that way, but their machines didn't. Perhaps that was even why they had handed over so much of the running of their civilization to the machines in the first place; they didn't trust themselves with the colossal powers and energies their science and technology had provided them with.

Which might be comforting, but for one fact that many people found worrying and—he suspected—the Culture found embarrassing.

Most civilizations that had acquired the means to build genuine Artificial Intelligences duly built them, and most of those designed or shaped the consciousness of the AIs to a greater or lesser extent; obviously if you were constructing a sentience that was or could easily become much greater than your own, it would not be in your interest to create a being which loathed you and might be likely to set about dreaming up ways to exterminate you.

So AIs, especially at first, tended to reflect the civilizational demeanor of their source species. Even when they underwent their own form of evolution and began to design their successors—with or without the help, and sometimes the knowledge, of their creators— there was usually still a detectable flavor of the intellectual character and the basic morality of that precursor species present in the resulting consciousness. That flavor might gradually disappear over subsequent generations of AIs, but it would usually be replaced by another, adopted and adapted from elsewhere, or just mutate beyond recognition rather than disappear altogether.

What various Involveds including the Culture had also tried to do, often out of sheer curiosity once AI had become a settled and even routine technology, was to devise a consciousness with no flavor; one with no metalogical baggage whatsoever; what had become known as a perfect AI.

It turned out that creating such intelligences was not particularly challenging once you could build AIs in the first place. The difficulties only arose when such machines became sufficiently empowered to do whatever they wanted to do, They didn't go berserk and try to kill all about them, and they didn't relapse into some blissed-out state of machine solipsism.

What they did do at the first available opportunity was Sublime, leaving the material universe altogether and joining the many beings, communities and entire civilizations which had gone that way before. It was certainly a rule and appeared to be a law that *perfect AIs always Sublime.*

Most other civilizations thought this perplexing, or claimed to find it only natural, or dismissed it as mildly interesting and sufficient to prove that there was little point in wasting time and resources creating such flawless but useless sentience. The Culture, more or less alone, seemed to find the phenomenon almost a personal insult, if you could designate an entire civilization as a person.

So a trace of some sort of bias, some element of moral or other partiality must be present in the Culture's Minds. Why should that trace not be what would, in a human or a Chelgrian, be a perfectly natural predisposition toward boredom caused by the sheer grinding relentlessness of their celebrated altruism and a weakness for the occasional misdemeanor; a dark, wild weed of spite in the endless soughing golden fields of their charity?

The thought did not disturb him, which itself seemed odd. Some part of him, some part that was hidden, dormant, even found the idea, if not pleasant, at least satisfactory, even useful.

He increasingly had the feeling that there was more to discover about the mission he had undertaken, and that it was important, and that he would be all the more determined to do whatever it was that had to be done.

He knew that he would know more about it, later; remember more, later, because he was remembering more now, all the time.

"And how are we today, Quil?"

Colonel Jarra Dimirj lowered himself into the seat by Quilan's bed. The Colonel had lost his midlimb and one arm in a flyer crash on the very last day of the war; these were regrowing. Some of the casualties in the hospital seemed unconcerned about wandering around with developing limbs exposed, and some, often the more grizzled and proudly scarred ones, even made a joke of the fact that they had what looked exactly like a child's arm or midlimb or leg attached to themselves.

Colonel Dimirj preferred to keep his rematuring limbs covered up, which—to the extent that he really cared about anything—Quilan found more tasteful. The Colonel seemed to have made it his duty to talk to all the patients in the hospital on a rota. Obviously it was his turn. He looked different today, Quilan thought. He seemed energized. Perhaps he was due to go home soon, or had been promoted.

"I'm fine, Jarra."

"Uh-huh. How's your new self coming along, anyway?"

"They seem happy enough. Apparently I'm making satisfactory progress."

They were in the military hospital at Lapendal, on Chel. Quilan was still confined to bed, though the bed itself was wheeled, powered and self-contained and could, had he wanted, have taken him throughout most of the hospital and a fair part of the grounds. Quilan thought this sounded like a formula for chaos, but allegedly the medical staff actually encouraged their charges to wander. It didn't matter; nothing mattered; Quilan hadn't used the bed's mobility at all. He left it where it was, just to the side of the tall window which, he was told, looked out across the gardens and the lake to the forests on the far shore.

He hadn't looked out of the window. He hadn't read anything, except for the screen when they tested his eyesight. He hadn't watched anything, except for the comings and goings of the medical staff, patients and visitors in the corridor outside. Sometimes, when the door was left closed, he only heard the people in the corridor. Mostly he just stared ahead, at the wall on the far side of the room, which was white.

"That's good, yes," the Colonel said. "When do they think you'll be out of that bed?"

"They think perhaps another five days."

His injuries had been severe. One more day in the half-wrecked truck struggling across the Phelen Plains on Aorme and he would have died. As it was he had been delivered to Golse City, triaged and transferred to an Invisible depot ship with only hours to spare. The depot vessel's hopelessly over-stretched medics did their best to stabilize him. Still, he nearly died several more times.

The Loyalist military and his family negotiated his ransom. A neutral medical shuttle craft from one of the Caring Orders took him to a Navy hospital ship. He was barely alive when he arrived. They had to throw away his body from the midriff down; necrosis had eaten as far as his midlimb and was busily destroying his internal organs. In the end they disposed of those too and amputated his midlimb, putting him on a total life-support machine until the rest of his body regrew, part by part; skeleton, organs, muscles and ligaments, skin and fur.

The process was almost complete, though he had recovered more slowly than they'd expected. He could not believe that he had come so close to dying so many times, and had been so unlucky not to.

Perhaps the thought of seeing Worosei, of surprising her, of seeing the expression on her face that he had daydreamed about in the crippled truck lurching across the plains; perhaps that had kept him going. He didn't know, because all he could remember after the first few days in the truck was in the form of momentary and disconnected sensations: pain, a smell, a flash of light, a sudden feeling of nausea, an overheard word or phrase. So he did not know what his thoughts—assuming he'd had any thoughts—had been during that fevered, scrambled time, but it seemed to him perfectly possible and even likely that only those daydreams of Worosei had sustained him and made exactly the difference between his death and his survival.

How cruel that thought was. To have been so close to a death he would now happily welcome, but prevented from embracing it by the misguided belief that he could ever see her alive again. He had only been told that she was dead after he'd arrived here in Lapendal. He'd been asking about her since he woke up from the first major operation on the Navy hospital ship, when they had reduced him to his head and upper trunk.

He had brushed aside the doctor's solemn, careful explanation of how radical they had had to be and how much of his body they had had to sacrifice in order to save his life, and he had demanded, through his confusion and nausea and pain, to know where she was. The doctor hadn't known. He'd said he would find out, but then never reappeared in person, and nobody else on the staff seemed to be able to find out either.

A chaplain from a Caring Order had done his best to determine the whereabouts of the *Winter Storm* and Worosei, but the war was still being waged, and discovering the location of a fighting ship, or anybody who might be on it, was not the sort of information you really expected to be told.

He wondered who had known then that the ship was missing, presumed lost. Only the Navy, probably. It was likely that not even their own clan had been informed before it became obvious. Had there been a time when he could have been told of Worosei's fate and still have been close enough to death to have stepped easily over that threshold? Perhaps. Perhaps not.

He'd finally been told by his brother-in-law, Worosei's twin, the day after the clan had been told. The ship was lost, presumed destroyed. It and its single escort craft had been surprised by an Invisible fleet a few days out of Aorme. The enemy attacked with what sounded like a sort of gravity-wave impactor weapon. The larger ship was hit first; the escort vessel reported that the *Winter Storm* suffered total internal destruction, almost instantaneously. There had been no trace of any souls being saved from it.

The escort craft tried to escape, was pursued and run down. Its own destruction terminated its last message before it could even give its position. A few souls had been saved from it; much later they confirmed the details of the engagement.

Worosei had died instantly, which Quilan supposed he ought to treat as some sort of blessing, but the calamity that had overtaken the *Winter Storm* had happened so quickly that there had been no time for the people aboard to be saved by their Soulkeepers, and the weaponry used against them had been specifically configured to destroy the devices themselves.

It would be half a year before Quilan was able to appreciate the irony that in tuning the attack to wreck Soulkeeper-scale technology, the impactor had left the old-tech substrate rescued from Aorme almost unharmed.

Worosei's twin had broken down and cried when he'd told Quilan the news. Quilan felt a kind of distant concern for his brother-in-law and made some of the noises of comforting, but he did not cry, and—trying to look into his own thoughts and feelings—all he could make out was a terrible barrenness, an almost complete lack of emotion, save for a feeling of puzzlement that he should experience so limited a reaction in the first place.

He suspected his brother-in-law felt ashamed of crying in front of Quilan, or was offended that Quilan did not show any sign of sorrow. In any event, he only ever came for that one visit. Others of Quilan's own clan made the journey to see him; his father and various other relations. He found it difficult to know what to say to them. Their visits tailed off and he was quietly relieved.

A grief counsellor was assigned to him but he didn't know what to

say to her either and felt he was letting her down, not being able to
follow her leads into emotional areas she said she thought he needed
to explore. Chaplains were no more comfort.

When the war ended, suddenly, unexpectedly, just a few days earlier, he'd thought something like, Well, I'm glad that's over, but he
realized almost immediately that he hadn't really felt anything. The
rest of the patients and the staff of the hospital wept and laughed and
grinned and those who could got drunk and partied into the night,
but he felt oddly dissociated from it all, and experienced only
resigned annoyance at the noise, which kept him awake after he'd
normally have been safely asleep. Now his only regular visitor, save
for the medical staff, was the Colonel.

"Don't suppose you've heard, have you?" Colonel Dimirj said. His
eyes seemed to shine and he looked, Quilan thought, like somebody
who has just escaped death, or won an unlikely bet.

"Heard what, Jarra?"

"About the war, Major. About how it started, who caused it, why
it ended so suddenly."

"No, I haven't heard anything about that."

"Didn't you think it stopped hell of a quick?"

"I didn't really think about it. I suppose I rather lost touch with
things while I was unwell. I didn't appreciate how quickly the war
ended."

"Well, now we know the reason why," the Colonel said, and
slapped the side of Quilan's bed with his good arm. "It was those bastard Culture people!"

"They stopped the war?" Chel had had contact with the Culture
for the last few hundred years. They were known to be widespread
throughout the galaxy and technologically superior—though without the Chelgrians' apparently unique link with the Sublimed—and
prone to allegedly altruistic interference. One of the more forlorn
hopes people had cleaved to during the war was that the Culture
would suddenly step in and gently prise the combatants apart, making everything all right again.

It hadn't happened. Neither had the Chelgrian-Puen, Chel's own advanced force amongst the Sublimed, stepped in, which had been an even more pious hope. What had happened, more prosaically but scarcely less surprisingly, was that the two sides in the war, the Loyalists and the Invisibles, had suddenly started talking and with surprising speed come to an agreement. It was a compromise that didn't really suit anybody but certainly it was better than a war that was threatening to tear Chelgrian civilization apart. Was Colonel Dimirj saying that the Culture somehow had intervened?

"Oh, they stopped it, if you want to look at it that way." The Colonel leaned close over Quilan. "You want to know how?"

Quilan did not particularly care, but it would be rude to say so. "How?"

"They told us and the Invisibles the truth. They showed us who the real enemy was."

"Oh. So they did intervene after all." Quilan was still confused. "Who is the real enemy?"

"Them! The Culture, that's who," the Colonel said, slapping Quilan's bedside again. He sat back, nodding, his eyes bright. "They stopped the war by confessing that they started it in the first place, that's what they did. Uh-huh."

"I don't understand."

The war had begun when the newly enfranchised and empowered Invisibles had turned all their recently acquired weaponry on those who had been their betters in the old enforced caste system.

New militias and Equalitarian Guard Companies had been created as a result of the abortive Guards' Revolt, when part of the Army had tried to stage a coup after the first Equalitarian election. The militias and Companies, and the accelerated training-up of the one-time lower castes so that they could take command of a majority of the Navy's ships, were part of an attempt to democratize Chel's armed forces and ensure that through a system of power balances no single branch of the armed forces could take control of the state.

It was an imperfect and expensive solution, and it meant that more people than ever before had access to vastly powerful weaponry, but all that had to happen for it to work was that nobody behaved insanely. But then Muonze, the Spayed caste President, had seemed to do just that, and been joined by half of those who had gained most through the reforms. How could the Culture have had anything to do with that? Quilan suspected the Colonel was determined to tell him.

"It was the Culture that got that Equalitarian idiot Kapyre elected President before Muonze," Dimirj said, leaning over Quilan again. "Their fingers were on the scales all the time. They were promising the parliamentarians the whole fucking galaxy if they voted for Kapyre; ships, habitats, technologies; the gods only know what. So in comes Kapyre, out goes common sense, out goes three thousand years of tradition, out goes the system, in comes their precious fucking equality and that ball-less cretin Muonze. And do you know what?"

"No. What?"

"They got him elected, too. Same tactics. Basic bribery."

"Oh."

"And what are they saying now?"

Quilan shook his head.

"They're saying they didn't know he was going to go crazy, that it never occurred to them that a bit of equality—exactly what these people had been shouting for all this time—might not be enough for them, that some of them might just be stupid and vicious enough to want revenge. Never dawned on them that their shit-caste friends might want to do some score-settling, no. That wouldn't make sense, that wouldn't be logical." The colonel almost spat that last word. "So when it all blew up in our faces they were still moving their own ships and military people away from us. Didn't have the forces to intervene, couldn't find nine-tenths of the people they'd been paying off and whispering to because they were dead, like Muonze, or being held hostage or in hiding."

The Colonel sat back again. "So our civil war wasn't really one at all; it was all these do-gooders' work. Frankly I don't know that even this is the truth. How do we really know they're as powerful and advanced as they claim? Maybe their science is little better than ours and they were getting frightened of us. Maybe they meant all this to happen."

Quilan was still trying to take all this in. After a few moments, while the Colonel sat there, nodding, he said, "Well, if they had they wouldn't suddenly admit it, would they?"

"Ha! Maybe it was about to come out anyway, so they tried to look as good as they could by confessing."

"But if they told both us and the Invisibles in the first place, to stop the war—"

"Same thing; maybe we were about to find out on our own. They were just making the best of a bad job. I mean," Dimirj said, tapping one claw on the side of Quilan's bed, "can you believe they've actually had the gall to quote figures, statistics at us? Telling us that this hardly ever happens, that ninety-nine percent or whatever of these 'interferences' go according to plan, that we've just been really unlucky and they're really sorry and they'll help us rebuild?" The Colonel shook his head. "The nerve of them! If we hadn't lost most of our best in that insane fucking war that *they* caused I'd be tempted to go to war with *them!*"

Quilan stared at the other male. The Colonel's eyes were wide, his head fur was standing straight as he shook his head. He found that his own head was shaking too, in disbelief. "Is all this true?" he asked. "Really?"

The Colonel stood up, as though impelled by his anger. "You should watch the news, Quil." He looked around, as though for something to take his rage out on, then took a deep breath. "Won't be the end of this, I tell you, Major. Not the end, not by a long, long way." He nodded. "I'll see you later, Quil. Goodbye for now." He slammed the door on his way out.

And so Quilan did switch on a screen, for the first time in months, and discovered that it was indeed all very much as the Colonel had said, and that the pace of change in his own society had truly been forced by the Culture, and it by its own confession had offered what they called help and others might have called bribes to get elected the people it thought ought to be elected, and advised and cajoled and wheedled and arguably threatened its way to what it thought was best for the Chelgrians.

It had started to slacken off its involvement, and stand down the forces it had secretly brought up to near the Chelgrian sphere of influence and colonization in case things went wrong, when, without any warning, it had all gone quite spectacularly wrong.

Their excuses were as the Colonel had laid out, though there was also, Quilan thought, a hint that they weren't as used to predator-evolved species as they were to others, and that had been a factor in their failure to anticipate either the catastrophic behavior change which started with Muonze and cascaded down through the restructured society, or the suddenness and ferocity with which it occurred once it had begun.

He could hardly believe it, but he had to. He watched a lot of screen, he talked to the Colonel and to some other patients who'd started to come to visit him. It was all true. All of it.

One day, the day before he was to be allowed out of his bed for the first time, he heard a bird singing in the grounds outside his window. He clicked at the buttons on the bed's control panel, and made it turn and raise him up so that he could look out of the window. The bird must have flown off, but he saw the cloud-scattered sky, the trees on the far side of the glittering lake, the breaking waves on the rocky shore, and the wind-stroked grasses of the hospital grounds.

(Once, in a market in Robunde, he had bought her a caged bird because it sang so beautifully. He took it to the room they were hiring while she completed her thesis paper on temple acoustics.

She thanked him graciously, walked to the window, opened the cage's door and shooed the little bird out; it flew away over the square, singing. She watched the bird for a moment until it disappeared, then looked around to him with an expression that was at once apologetic, defiant and concerned. He was leaning against the door frame, smiling at her.)

His tears dissolved the view.

7

Peer Group

Important visitors to Masaq' were usually trans-shipped by a giant ceremonial barge of gilded wood, glorious flags and generally fabulous aspect encased within an ellipsoid envelope of perfumed air sewn with half a million perfumed candle balloons. For the Chelgrian emissary Quilan, Hub thought that such flagrant ostentation might strike a discordant, overly celebratory note, and so instead a plain but stylish personnel module was sent to rendezvous with the ex-warship *Resistance Is Character-Forming*.

The welcoming party consisted of one of the Hub's thin, silver-skinned avatars, the drone E. H. Tersono, the Homomdan Kabe Ischloear and a human female representative from the Orbital's General Board called Estray Lassils who both looked and was old. She had long white hair, currently gathered into a bun, and a very tanned, deeply lined face, and for all her age she was tall and slim and carried herself very upright. She wore a formal-looking plain black dress with a single brooch. Her eyes were bright and Kabe formed the impression that a lot of the grooves on her face were smile and laughter lines. He immediately liked her, and—given that the General Board had been elected by the human and drone population of the Orbital, and itself had duly chosen her to represent it—decided that so must everybody else.

"Hub," Estray Lassils said in an amused-sounding voice. "Your skin looks more matte than usual."

The Orbital's avatar wore white trousers and a tight jacket over its silvery skin, which did indeed, Kabe thought, seem less reflective than it usually appeared.

The creature nodded. "There are Chelgrian source tribes which once had superstitious beliefs concerning mirrors," it said in its incongruously deep voice. Its wide black eyes blinked. Estray Lassils found herself looking at a pair of tiny images of herself depicted in the avatar's eyelids, which it had briefly turned fully reflective. "I thought, just to be on the safe side . . ."

"I see."

"And how is everybody on the Board, Ms. Lassils?" the drone Tersono asked. It appeared, if anything, more reflective than usual, its rosy porcelain skin and lacy lumenstone frame looking highly polished.

The woman shrugged. "As ever. I haven't seen them for a couple of months. The next meeting's . . ." She looked thoughtful.

"In ten days' time," supplied her brooch.

"Thank you, house," she said. She nodded at the drone. "There you are."

The General Board was supposed to represent the inhabitants of the Orbital to Hub at the highest level; it was pretty much an honorary office given that each individual could talk directly to Hub whenever they wanted, but as that carried even the most thinly theoretical possibility that a mischievous or deranged Hub could play every single person on an Orbital off against each to further some unspecified nefarious scheme, it was usually thought sensible to have a conventionally elected and delegated set-up as well. It also meant that visitors from more autocratic or layered societies were provided with somebody they could identify as an official representative of the whole population.

The main reason that Kabe decided he liked Estray Lassils was that despite being there in this arguably quite consequential ceremonial role—she did represent nearly fifty billion people, after all—she had, apparently on a whim, brought along one of her nieces, a six-year-old child called Chomba.

The girl was thin and blond and sat quietly on the padded edge of the central pool in the personnel module's circular main lounge area as it sped out to meet the still decelerating *Resistance Is Character-Forming.* She wore a pair of deep purple shorts and a loose jacket of vivid yellow. Her feet were dangling in the water, where long red fish swam amongst artfully arranged rocks and beds of gravel. They eyed the child's waggling toes with leery curiosity and were gradually approaching.

The others stood—or in Tersono's case floated—in a group in front of the lounge's forward screen section. The screen extended right around the circular wall of the lounge so that when it was all activated it looked as if you were riding through space standing on one large disc with another suspended over your head (the ceiling could act as a screen too, as could the floor, though some people found the full effect unsettling).

The tallest, deepest part of the screen faced directly forward and it was there that Kabe glanced now and again, but all it showed was the star field, with a slowly flashing red ring showing the direction the ship was approaching from. Two broad bands of Masaq' Orbital traversed the screen from floor to ceiling, and there was a big storm system of whorled clouds visible on one mostly oceanic Plate, but Kabe was more distracted by the sinuously swimming fish and the human child.

It was one of the effects of living in a society where people commonly lived for four centuries and on average bore just over one child each that there were very few of their young around, and—as these children tended to stick together in their own peer groups rather than be found distributed throughout the society—there seemed to be even fewer than there really were. It was more or less accepted in some quarters that the Culture's whole civilizational demeanor resulted from the fact that every single human in the society had been thoroughly, comprehensively and imaginatively spoiled as a child by virtually everyone around them.

"It's all right," the child said to Kabe when she noticed him looking at her. She nodded at the slowly swimming fish. "They don't bite."

"Are you sure?" Kabe asked, squatting trefoil to bring his head closer to the child's. She watched this maneuver with what looked like wide-eyed fascination, but seemed to think the better of commenting.

"Yes," she said. "They don't eat meat."

"But you have such very tasty-looking little toes," Kabe said, meaning to be funny but instantly worrying that he might frighten her.

She frowned briefly, then hugged herself and snorted with laughter. "You don't eat people, do you?"

"Not unless I'm terribly hungry," Kabe told her gravely, and then silently cursed himself again. He was starting to recall why he'd never been very good with children of his own species.

She looked uncertain about this, then—after one of those vacant expressions you got used to when people were consulting a neural lace or other implanted device—she smiled. "You're vegetarians, Homomdans. I just checked."

"Oh," he said, surprised. "Do you have a neural implant?" He'd understood that children didn't usually possess them; as a rule they had toys or avatar companions who fulfilled that sort of role. Being fitted with your first implant was about as close as some bits of the Culture got to a formal adult initiation rite. Another tradition was to move smoothly from a cuddly talking toy via other gradually less childish devices to a tasteful little pen terminal, brooch or jewel stud.

"Yes, I do have a lace," she said proudly. "I asked."

"She pestered," Estray Lassils said, coming to stand by the poolside.

The girl nodded. "Well beyond the established limit that any normal and reasonable child would have given up at or before," she said, in gruff tones that were probably meant to impersonate a man's voice.

"Chomba is seeking to redefine the term 'precocious,'" Estray Lassils told Kabe, ruffling the child's short blond curls. "With considerable success, so far." The girl ducked away under Estray's hand, tutting. Her feet splashed in the water, driving the circling fish further away.

"I hope you said hello properly to Ambassador Kabe Ischloear," Estray told the child. "You were uncharacteristically shy when I introduced you earlier."

The girl sighed theatrically and stood up in the water, putting out one tiny hand and taking the massive slab of hand that Kabe offered. She bowed. "Ar Kabe Ischloear, I'm Masaq'-Sintriersa Chomba Lassils dam Palacope, how do you do?"

"I do well," Kabe said, inclining his head. "How do you do, Chomba?"

"As she pleases, basically," the older female said. Chomba rolled her eyes.

"Unless I'm mistaken," Kabe said to the child, "your precocity hasn't extended to nominating a middle name yet."

The girl smiled with what was probably meant to be a sly expression. Kabe wondered if he'd used too many long words.

"She informs us she has," Estray explained, looking at the child through narrowed eyes. "She's just not telling us what it is yet."

Chomba turned her nose up and looked away, smirking. Then she grinned widely at Kabe. "Do you have any children, Ambassador?"

"Sadly, no."

"Are you just here by yourself, then?"

"Yes, I am."

"Don't you get lonely?"

"Chomba," Estray Lassils chided gently.

"It's all right. No, I don't get lonely, Chomba. I know too many people to become lonely. And I have so much to do."

"What do you do?"

"I study, I learn and I report."

"What, about us?"

"Yes. I set out many years ago to try to understand humans, and perhaps, therefore, people in general." He spread his hands slowly and tried to make a smile. "That quest continues. I write articles and essays and pieces of prose and poetry which I send back to my original home, seeking, where I can and my modest talents allow, to explain the Culture and its people more fully to my own. Of course both our societies know everything about the other in terms of raw data, but sometimes a degree of interpretation is required for sense to be extracted from such information. I seek to provide that personal touch."

"But isn't it funny, being surrounded by us?"

"Just say when this all starts to get too much, Ambassador," Estray Lassils said apologetically.

"That's quite all right. Sometimes it's funny, Chomba, sometimes baffling, sometimes very rewarding."

"But we're completely different, aren't we? We have two legs. You've got three. don't you miss other Homomdans?"

"Only one."

"Who's that?"

"Somebody I once loved. Unfortunately she did not love me."

"Is that why you came here?"

"Chomba . . ."

"Perhaps it is, Chomba. Distance and difference can heal. At least here, surrounded by humans, I need never see somebody I might mistake, even for an instant, for her."

"Wow. You must have loved her a lot."

"I suppose I must."

"Here we are," the Hub's avatar said. It turned to face the rear of the lounge. On the curve of screen-wall, the stubby cylinder of the *Resistance Is Character-Forming* was sliding across the darkness, from ahead to astern. There were hints of the craft's field complex becoming briefly visible, like layers of gauze the module seemed to be slipping through as it closed with the larger vessel.

The module went astern, floating toward the accommodation unit near the front of the ex-warship, where a rectangle of hull was picked out in small lights. There was an almost imperceptible thud as the two craft connected. Kabe watched the water in the pool; it didn't even ripple. The avatar walked up to the rear of the lounge, with the drone floating just behind its left shoulder. The view astern disappeared to show the module's wide rear doors.

"Dry your feet," Kabe heard Estray Lassils tell her niece.

"Why?"

The module's doors jawed open, revealing a plant-lined vestibule and a tall Chelgrian dressed in formal gray religious robes. Something that looked like a large tray floated at his side, carrying two modest bags.

"Major Quilan," the silver-skinned avatar said, walking forward and bowing. "I represent Masaq' Hub. You are very welcome."

"Thank you," the Chelgrian said. Kabe smelled something tangy as the atmospheres of the module and the ship mingled.

The introductions were made. The Chelgrian seemed polite but reserved, Kabe thought. He spoke Marain at least as well as Ziller— and with the same accent—and, like Ziller, really had learned the language rather than chosen to rely on an interpretation device.

Last to be presented was Chomba, who recited her almost full name to the Chelgrian, dug into a jacket pocket and presented the male with a small posy of flowers. "They're from our garden," she explained. "Sorry they're a bit crushed but they were in my pocket. Don't worry about that; it's just dirt. Do you want to see some fish?"

"Major, we are so very pleased you were able to come," the drone Tersono said, floating smoothly between the Chelgrian and the child. "I know I speak not just for all of us here but for every single person on the Orbital of Masaq' when I say we feel truly honored that you are visiting us."

Kabe thought this would be Major Quilan's opportunity to mention Ziller, if he was of a mind to puncture this rather unrealistic image of politeness, but the male just smiled.

Chomba was glaring at the drone. Quilan tilted his head to see past Tersono's body and look at her as Tersono, extending a blue-pink field in an arc toward the Chelgrian's shoulders, ushered him forward. The floating platform carrying Quilan's bags followed him into the module; the doors closed and became a screen again. "Now," said the drone, "we are all here to say welcome, obviously, but also to let you know that we are entirely at your disposal for the duration of your visit, however long that may be."

"I'm not. I've got stuff to do."

"Ha ha ha ha," said the drone. "Well, all of us who're grown up, at any rate. Tell me, how was your journey? Satisfactory, I hope."

"It was."

"Please; take a seat." They arranged themselves on some couches while the module moved off. Chomba went back to dip her feet in the pool. Behind, the *Resistance Is Character-Forming* did the ship equivalent of a back-flip, became a dot, and vanished.

Kabe was pondering the differences between Quilan and Ziller. They were the only two Chelgrians he had ever met face to face, though he had done a deal of studying of the species since Tersono had first asked him to help at the recital on the barge *Soliton*. He knew the major was younger than the composer, and thought he looked leaner and fitter, too. There was a sleek sheen to his light brown fur, and he had a more muscled frame. Even so, he appeared more care-worn around his large dark eyes and broad nose. Perhaps that was not so surprising. Kabe knew quite a lot about Major Quilan.

The Chelgrian turned to him. "Do you represent the Homomda officially here, Ar Ischloear?" he asked.

"No, Major," Kabe began.

"Ar Ischloear is here at Contact's request," Tersono said.

"They asked me to help play host to you," Kabe told the Chelgrian. "I am shamefully weak in the face of such flattery and so accepted immediately, even though I have no real diplomatic training. To tell the truth, I am more of a cross between a journalist, a tourist and a student than anything else. I hope you don't mind me mentioning this now. It's just in case I commit some terrible faux-pas of protocol. If I do I wouldn't want it to reflect on my hosts." Kabe nodded to Tersono, which gave a stiff little inclinatory bow.

"Are there many Homomdans on Masaq'?" Quilan asked.

"I'm the only one," Kabe said.

Major Quilan nodded slowly.

"The task of representing our average citizen falls to me, Major," Estray said. "Ar Ischloear is not representative. However he is very charming." She smiled at Kabe, who realized he had never come up with a translatable gesture to indicate humility. "I think," the woman continued, "that we probably asked Kabe to help play host to prove that we're not so awful on Masaq' that we frighten away all our non-human guests."

"Certainly Mahrai Ziller seems to have found your hospitality irresistible," Quilan said.

"Cr. Ziller continues to grace us with his presence," Tersono agreed. Its aura field looked very rosy against the cream of the couch it rested on. "Hub here is being very modest in not immediately extolling the numerous virtues of Masaq' Orbital, but let me assure you it is a place of almost innumerable delights. Masaq' Great—"

"I assume that Mahrai Ziller does know that I am here," Quilan said quietly, looking from the drone to the avatar.

The silver-skinned creature nodded. "He has been kept informed of your progress. Unfortunately he is not here to welcome you personally."

"I wasn't particularly expecting him to be," Quilan said.

"Ar Ischloear is one of Cr. Ziller's best friends," Tersono said. "I'm sure, when the time comes, you'll all find plenty to talk about."

"I think I can safely claim to be the best Homomdan friend he has on Masaq,' " agreed Kabe.

"I understand your own connection with Cr. Ziller goes further back, Major," Estray said. "To school, is that right?"

"Yes," Quilan said. "However we haven't met or talked since then. We are more one-time friends than old friends. How is our absent genius, Ambassador?" he asked Kabe.

"He is well," Kabe said. "Still busily writing away."

"Missing home?" the Chelgrian asked. There was just the suggestion of a smile on his broad face.

"He would claim not to be," Kabe said, "though I think in his music over the last few years I have detected a certain plaintive harking back to traditional Chelgrian folk themes, with hints of eventual resolution implicit in their serial development." From the corner of one eye, Kabe saw Tersono's aura field blush with pleasure as he said this. "Though that may mean nothing, of course," he added. The drone's field collapsed back to a frosty blue.

"You are a fan, I take it, Ambassador," the Chelgrian said.

"Oh, I think we all are," Tersono said quickly. "I—"

"I'm not."

"Chom," said Estray.

"The darling child may find the maestro's music still beyond her," the drone said. Kabe caught a hint of a blossoming purple field flattening and dissipating in the direction of the girl sitting on the edge of the pool. He saw Chomba's mouth work but suspected Tersono had thrown some sort of field wall between her and the rest of the party. He could just about hear that she had said something, but had no idea what it was. Chomba herself either hadn't noticed or didn't care. She was concentrating on the fish.

"I count myself one of Cr. Ziller's most fervent aficionados," the drone was saying loudly. "I have seen Ms. Estray Lassils applaud loudly at several of Cr. Ziller's concerts and recitals and I know that to this day Hub delights in occasionally reminding all of its near-neighbor Orbitals that your compatriot chose to make his second home here rather than on any of them. We are all positively quivering with anticipation at the prospect of listening to Cr. Ziller's latest symphony in a few weeks' time. I am quite certain it will be splendid."

Quilan nodded. He held his hands out. "Well, as I'm sure you've guessed, I've been asked to try to persuade Mahrai Ziller to return to Chel," he said, looking around the others but settling his gaze on Kabe. "I don't imagine that this will be an easy task. Ar Ischloear—"

"Please, call me Kabe."

"Well, Kabe, what do you think? Am I right in believing it's going to be an uphill struggle?"

Kabe thought.

"I can't imagine," began Tersono, "that Cr. Ziller would really dream of passing up the chance to meet with the first Chelgrian—"

"I think that you are absolutely right, Major Quilan," Kabe told him.

"—to set foot—"

"Please, call me Quil."

"—on Masaq' for—"

"Frankly, Quil, they've given you a stinker of a job."

"—all these many, many years."

"That's just what I thought."

~ *All right?*

~ Yes. Thank you for that.

~ *You are very welcome,* Huyler sent, impersonating the deep voice of the Hub avatar. *I was almost too busy taking stuff in to pass any comments anyway.*

~ Well, it wasn't really necessary as it turned out.

They had been worried that Quilan's welcome might be overwhelming either accidentally or deliberately. His momentary slip when they had first boarded the *Resistance Is Character-Forming* and had spoken aloud in reply to a transmitted thought of Huyler's had made them wary, and so they'd agreed that, for the first part of Quilan's reception at least, Huyler would stay in the background, keeping silent unless he spotted something alarming that he felt he had to draw Quilan's attention to.

~ So, Huyler; anything interesting?

~ *Bit of a menagerie, don't you think? Only one of them's human.*

~ What about the child?

~ *Well, and the child. If it really is a child.*

~ Let us not become paranoid, Huyler.

~ *Let us not become complacent either, Quil. Anyway, it looks like they're going for the cuteness angle rather than the top-brass approach.*

~ There is a sense in which Estray Lassils is President of the World. And the silver-skinned avatar is under the direct control of the god which holds the power of life or death over the Orbital and everybody on it.

~ *Yes, and there is a sense in which the woman is a powerless temporary figurehead and the avatar is just a puppet.*

~ And the drone, and the Homomdan?

~ *The machine claims to be from Contact so that may well mean it's from Special Circumstances. The big three-legged guy seems genuine so I'd give him the benefit of the doubt for now; they probably think he's a suitable host because he's got more than the number of legs they're used to. He's got three legs, we've got three counting the midlimb; it could be that simple.*

~ I suppose.

~ *Anyway, we're here.*

~ Indeed we are. And quite an impressive "here" it is, don't you think?

~ *It's all right, I suppose.*

Quilan smiled thinly. He leaned on the deck-side rail, and looked around. The river stretched into the distance, the view dropped away to either side.

Masq' Great River was a single loop of water stretching unbroken right around the Orbital and flowing slowly as a result of nothing more than the huge spinning world's coriolis effect.

Fed by tributary rivers and mountain streams throughout its length, it was depleted by evaporation where it ran through deserts, drained by overflow waterfalls and the run-offs into seas, swamps and irrigation networks, and absorbed into giant lakes, vast oceans and entire continent-wide river systems and networks of canals, only to reappear via great converse estuaries which eventually bundled it into a single gathered current once again.

It ran its unending course through labyrinths of caverns under raised continents, their depths lit sporadically by plunging holes and immense troughs deep as the roots of mountains. It traversed the slowly decreasing numbers of yet unformed Plate topographies within transparent tunnels which gave out onto landscapes still being molded and inscribed by the manufactured vulcanologies of Orbital terraforming techniques.

It disappeared under Bulkhead Ranges in colossal watery mazes slung beneath those hollow ramparts and slipped—flooding some-times for whole seasons—across entire horizon-wide plains before running through winding canyons kilometers deep and thousands long. It iced over from one end of a continent to another during the Orbital's aphelion or within the local winters produced by a Plate group's sun lenses set on disperse.

Its course took in dozens of neatly circumscribed or lushly sprawl-ing cities and—when it reached Plates like Osinorsi, whose median level was well below the stream's steady elevation—the river was car-ried above the plains, savannas, deserts or swamps on single or braided massifs towering hundreds or thousands of meters above the surrounding ground; hoisted ribbons of land crowned with cloud, edged with falls, strewn with hanging vegetation and vertical towns, punctured by caves and tunnels and—as here—with artfully carved and soaring arches that turned the monumental massifs into a more precise image of exactly what they were: vast aqueducts on a water course ten million kilometers long.

The parapet of the massif here, just a few kilometers from the cliffs and the plains that marked the beginning of Xaravve, was a flower-strewn grassy bank less than ten meters wide. From his vantage point here, standing on a raised forecastle of the ceremonial barge *Bariatricist,* Quilan could look down through wisps of cloud to rolling hills and meandering rivers unwinding through misty forests two kilometers below.

They had asked him whether he wanted to go straight to the house they had provided for him, or if he would like to take in part of Masaq' Great River, and one of its famous barges, where a small reception had been arranged. He'd said he would be happy to take them up on their kind offer. The Hub avatar had looked quietly pleased; the drone Tersono had positively glowed with rosy approval.

The personnel module had lowered itself gently toward the atmosphere of the Orbital. The craft's ceiling had also become a screen, showing off the soaring arc of the Orbital's evening and night far-side while the vessel submerged into the slowly warming morning air above Osinorsi Plate. The module had swung out over one end of the vastly elongated S shape of the central massif carrying the river above the Plate's lower level. They rendezvoused with the *Bariatricist* near the border of Xaravve.

At about four hundred meters, the barge was nearly twice as long as the river here was wide; it was a tall, beamy craft tiered with decks and studded with masts, some of which held highly decorated sails, most of which trailed banners and flags.

Quilan had seen lots of people, though the vessel was hardly crowded.

"This isn't all for me, is it?" he'd asked the drone Tersono as the module approached one of the barge's half-decks stern first.

"Well," it had said, sounding uncertain. "No. Why, would you prefer to have a private craft?"

"No, I was just wondering."

"There are various other receptions, parties and different events taking place on the barge just now," the avatar had told him. "Plus there are several hundred people for whom the vessel is their temporary or permanent home."

"How many people have come to see me?"

"About seventy," the avatar replied.

"Major Quilan," the drone had said. "If you've changed your mind—"

"No, I—"

"Major, might I make a suggestion?" Estray Lassils had said.

"Please do."

And so the module had positioned itself so that he could walk straight out onto the barge's high forecastle; Estray Lassils had disembarked at the same time and shown him the route to take; she'd hung back while he found his way across a sort of gantry, through a rather riotous party, and eventually fetched up on one of the set-back decks looking out over the vessel's bows.

There were a few humans there, mostly in couples. He had remembered a hot hazy day on a much smaller boat on a broad but almost infinitely tinier river, thousands of light years away now; her touch and smell, the weight of her hand on his shoulder . . .

The humans had looked at him with curiosity, but had left him alone. He'd gazed out, taking in the view. The day was bright but cool. The great river and the vast, stunning world flowed and revolved beneath him, taking him with them both.

8

The Retreat at Cadracet

After a while he turned away from the view.

Estray Lassils emerged from a dance at the noisy party—flushed and breathing heavily—and walked with him toward the section of the barge set aside for his reception.

"You're sure you're quite happy to meet all these people, Major?" she asked.

"Quite certain, thank you."

"Well, do say the instant you want to get away. We won't think you rude. I did some research into your order. You sound quite, ah, ascetic, and semi-trappist. I'm sure we'd all understand if you found our gibbering gaggle tiresome."

~ *Wonder just how much they were able to research.*

"I'm sure I'll survive."

"Good for you. I'm supposed to be an old hand at this sort of thing but even I find it pretty damn tedious sometimes. Still, receptions and parties are pan-cultural, so we're told. I've never been sure whether to be reassured or appalled by that."

"I suppose both are appropriate, depending on one's mood."

~ *Well said, son. Think I'll go back to hovering. You concentrate on her; this one's devious. I can feel it.*

"Major Quilan, I do hope you appreciate how sorry we are for

140

what happened to your people," the woman said, looking at her feet, then up at him. "You may all be heartily fed up hearing this by now, in which case I can only apologize for that as well, but sometimes you feel you just have to say something." She glanced away into the hazy depth of the view. "The war was our fault. We'll make what amends and reparations we can, but for what it's worth—and I realize it may not seem like very much—we do apologize." She made a small gesture with her old, lined hands. "I think all of us feel that we owe you and your people a particular debt." She looked down at her feet again for a moment, before catching his gaze once more. "Do not hesitate to call upon it."

"Thank you. I appreciate your sympathy, and your offer. I've made no secret of my mission."

Her eyes narrowed, then she gave a small, hesitant smile. "Yes. We'll see what we can do. You're not in too great a hurry, I hope, Major."

"Not too great," he told her.

She nodded and continued walking. In a lighter tone, she said, "I hope you like the house Hub's prepared for you, Major."

"As you say, my order is not renowned for its indulgence or its luxury I'm sure you will have provided me with more than I need."

"I imagine we probably have. Do let us know if there's anything else you require, including less of anything, if you know what I mean."

"I take it this house is not next door to Mahrai Ziller's."

She laughed. "Not even next Plate. You're two away. But I'm told it has a very nice view and its own sub-Plate access." She looked at him through narrowed eyes. "You know what all this stuff means? The terminology, I mean?"

He smiled politely. "I have done my own research, Ms Lassils."

"Yes, of course. Well, just let us know what sort of terminal or whatever you want to use. If you've brought a communicator of your own I'm sure Hub can patch you through, or it's certainly prepared to put an avatar or some other familiar at your disposal, or . . . well it's up to you. What would you prefer?"

"I think one of your standard pen terminals would suffice."

"Major, I strongly suspect by the time you get to your house there'll be one there waiting for you. Ah ha." They were approaching a broad upper deck scattered with wooden furniture, partially covered by awnings and dotted with people. "And it may well be a more welcome sight than this: a bunch of people all desperate to talk your ears off. Remember; bail out any time."

~ *Amen.*

Everybody turned to face him.

~ *We must join the fray, Major.*

There were indeed about seventy people there to meet him. They included three from the General Board—whom Estray Lassils recognized, hailed and went into a huddle with as soon as was decent—various scholars of matters Chelgrian or whose speciality description included the word *xeno*—mostly professors—and a handful of other non-humans, none of whose species Quilan had even heard of, who coiled, floated, balanced or splayed about the deck, tables and couches.

The situation was complicated by various other non-human creatures which, but for the avatar, Quilan might easily have mistaken for other sentient aliens but that turned out to be no more than animal pets. All this was in addition to a bewildering variety of other humans who had titles that were not titles and job descriptions that had nothing to do with jobs.

~ *Intra-cultural mimetic transcriptioneer? What the hell does that mean?*

~ No idea. Assume the worst. File under Reporter.

The Hub's avatar had introduced all of them; aliens, humans and drones, which really did seem to be treated as full citizens and people in their own right. Quilan nodded and smiled and nodded or shook hands and made whatever other gesture appeared appropriate.

~ *I supposed this silver-skinned freak is just about the perfect host for these people. It knows all of them. And knows all of them intimately, too; foibles, likes, dislikes, everything.*

~ Not what we were told.

~ *Oh, yes; all it knows is your name and that you're somewhere here within its jurisdiction. That's the tale. It only knows what you want it to know. Ha! don't you find that just a little hard to believe?*

Quilan didn't know how close a watch on all its citizens a Culture Orbital Hub kept. It didn't really matter. He did know a lot about such avatars, though, he realized, when he thought about it, and what Huyler had said about their social skills was perfectly true. Tireless, endlessly sympathetic, with a flawless memory and with what must seem like a telepathic ability to tell exactly who would get on with who, the presence of an avatar was understandably judged indispensable at every social occasion above a certain size.

~ *With one of these silvery things and an implant people here probably never have to actually remember the name of a single other person.*

~ *I wonder if they ever forget their own.*

Quilan talked, guardedly, to a lot of people, and nibbled from the tables loaded with food, all of it served on plates and trays which were image-coded to indicate what was suitable for which species.

He looked up at one point and realized that they had left the colossal aqueduct and were traveling across a great grassy plain punctuated by what looked like the frameworks of gigantically tall tents.

~ *Dome tree stands.*

~ Ah ha.

The river had slowed here and broadened to over a kilometer from bank to bank. Ahead, just starting to show above and through the haze, another sort of massif was beginning to make itself visible.

What he had earlier assumed were clouds in the far distance turned out to be the peaks of snow-covered mountains strung around the massif's top. Deeply corrugated cliffs rose almost straight up, bannered with thin white veils that might be waterfalls. Some of these slender columns stretched all the way down to the base of the cliffs, while other, still thinner white threads faded and disappeared part-way down or vanished into and merged with layered clouds drifting slowly across the great serrated wall of rock.

~ *Aquime Massif. Apparently this little creek of theirs goes around both sides and straight through. Aquime City, in the middle, on the shores of the High Salt Sea, is where our friend Ziller lives.*

He stared at the great folded sweep of snow-settled cliff and mountain as it materialized out of the haze, becoming more real with each beat of his heart.

In the Gray Mountains was the monastery of Cadracet, which belonged to the Sheracht Order. He went there on a retreat once he was released from the hospital, becoming a griefling. He was taking extended furlough from the Army, which allowed such compassion-ate leave at his rank. The offer of de-enlistment and an honorable dis-charge, plus a modest pension, had been left open for him.

He already had a batch of medals. He was given one for being in the Army at all, one for being a combatant who'd held a gun, another for being a Given who could easily have avoided fighting in the first place, another for being wounded (with a bar because he had been seriously wounded), yet another for having been on a special mission and a last medal which had been decreed when it had been realized that the war had been the Culture's responsibility, not that of the Chelgrian species. The soldiers were calling it the Not-Our-Fault prize. He kept the medals in a small box within the trunk in his cell, along with the posthumous ones awarded to Worosei.

The monastery sat on a rocky outcrop on the shoulder of a mod-est peak, within a small stand of sigh trees by a tumbling mountain stream. It looked across the forested gorge beneath to the crags, cliffs, snow and ice of the tallest peaks in the range. Behind it, crossing the stream by a modest but ancient stone bridge celebrated in songs and tales three thousand years old, passed the road from Oquoon to the central plateau, momentarily straightening from its series of precipi-tous hairpins.

During the war, a troupe of Invisible servants who had already put to death all their own masters at another monastery further up the road had taken over Cadracet and captured the half of the monks who had not fled—mostly the older ones. They had thrown them over the parapet of the bridge into the rock-strewn stream below. The fall was not quite sufficient to kill all the old males, and some suf-fered, moaning, throughout that day and into the night, only dying in the cold before dawn the following morning. Two days later, a unit of Loyalist troops had retaken the complex and tortured the Invisibles before burning their leaders alive.

It had been the same story of horror, malevolence and escalatory retribution everywhere. The war had lasted less than fifty days; many wars—most wars, even those restricted to one planet—barely properly began in that time because mobilizations had to be carried out, forces had to be put in place, a war footing had to be established within society and territory had to be attacked, captured and consolidated before further attacks could be prepared and the enemy could be closed with. Wars in space and between planets and habitats of any number could in theory effectively be over in a few minutes or even seconds but commonly took years and sometimes centuries or generations to come to a conclusion, depending almost entirely on the level of technology the civilizations involved possessed.

The Caste War had been different. It had been a civil war; a species and society at war with itself. These were notoriously amongst the most terrible conflicts, and the initial proximity of the combatants, distributed throughout the civilian and military population at virtually every level of institution and facility, meant that there was a kind of explosive savagery about the conflict almost the instant that it commenced, taking many of the first wave of victims utterly by surprise: noble families were knifed in their beds, unaware that any real problem existed, whole dormitories of servants were gassed behind locked doors, unable to believe those they'd devoted their lives to were murdering them, passengers or drivers in cars, captains of ships, pilots of aircraft or space vessels were suddenly assaulted by the person sitting next to them, or were themselves the ones who did the attacking.

Cadracet monastery itself had escaped relatively unscarred from the war, despite its brief occupation; some rooms had been ransacked, a few icons and holy books had been burned or desecrated, but there had been little structural damage.

Quilan's cell was at the back of the building's third courtyard, looking out onto the grooved cobbled roadway to the dank green mountainside and the sudden yellow of the gaunt sigh trees. His cell contained a curl-pad on the stone floor, a small trunk for his personal possessions, a stool, a plain wooden desk and a wash-stand.

There was no form of communication allowed in the cell apart from reading and writing. The former had to be conducted with script-string frames or books, and the latter—for those who like him had no facility with the knotting, beading and braiding of script-string—was restricted to that possible utilizing loose paper and an ink pen.

Talking to anyone else inside the cell was also forbidden and by the strictest interpretation of the laws even a monk who talked to himself or cried out in his sleep ought to confess as much to the monastery superior and accept some extra duty as punishment. Quilan had terrible dreams, as he had had since halfway through his stay in the hospital at Lapendal, and frequently woke up in a panic in the middle of the night, but he was never sure if he'd cried out or not. He asked monks in neighboring cells; they claimed never to have heard him. He believed them, on balance.

Talking was allowed before and after meals and during those communal tasks with which it was judged not to interfere. Quilan talked less than the others in the tiered fields where they grew their foods, and on the walks down the mountain paths to gather wood. The others didn't seem to mind. The exertions made him strong and fit again. They tired him out, too, but not sufficiently to stop him waking each night with the dreams of darkness and lightning, pain and death.

The library was where most studying was done. The reader screens there were intelligently censored so that monks could not fritter their time away on vapid entertainments or trivia; they allowed religious and reference works and scholarly troves to be accessed, but little else. That still left many lifetimes' worth of material. The machines could also act as links to the Chelgrian-Puen, the gone-before, the already Sublimed. It would, however, be a while before a newcomer like Quilan would be allowed to use them for that purpose.

His mentor and counsellor was Fronipel, the oldest monk left alive after the war. He had hidden from the Invisibles in an old grain-store drum deep in a cellar and had remained there for two days after the Loyalist troops detachment had retaken the monastery, not knowing that he was now safe. Too weak to climb back out of the drum, he had almost died of dehydration and was only discovered when the troops mounted a thorough search to flush out any remaining Invisibles.

Where it showed above his robes, the old male's pelt was scraggy and tufted with dark patches of thick, coarse fur. Other areas were almost bare, showing his creased, dry-looking gray skin beneath. He moved stiffly, especially when the weather was damp, which was often the case at Cadracet. His eyes, set behind antique glasses, looked filmed, as though there was some gray smoke within the orbs. The old monk wore his decrepitude with no hint of pride or disdain, and yet, in this age of regrown bodies and replacement organs, such decay had to be voluntary, even deliberate.

They talked, usually, in a small bare cell set aside for the purpose. All it contained was a single S-shaped curl-seat and a small window.

It was the old monk's prerogative to use the first name of those junior to him, and so he called Quilan "Tibilo," which made him feel like a child again. He supposed this was the desired effect. He in turn was expected to address Fronipel as Custodian.

"I feel . . . I feel jealous, sometimes, Custodian. Does that sound mad? Or bad?"

"Jealous of what, Tibilo?"

"Her death. That she died." Quilan stared out of the window, unable to look into the older male's eyes. The view from the little window was much the same as from that of his own cell. "If I could have anything at all I would have her back. I think I have accepted that is impossible, or very unlikely indeed, at the very least . . . but, you see? There are so few certainties anymore. This is something else; everything is contingent these days, everything is provisional, thanks to our technology, our understanding."

He looked into the old monk's clouded eyes. "In the old days people died and that was that; you might hope to see them in heaven, but once they were dead they were dead. It was simple, it was definite. Now . . ." He shook his head angrily. "Now people die but their Soulkeeper can revive them, or take them to a heaven we know exists, without any need for faith. We have clones, we have regrown bodies—most of me is regrown; I wake up sometimes and think, Am I still me? I know you're supposed to be your brain, your wits, your thoughts, but I don't believe it is that simple." He shook his head, then dried his face on the sleeve of his robe.

"You are envious of an earlier time, then."

He was silent for a few moments, then said, "That as well. But I am jealous of her. If I can't have her back then all I'm left with is a desire not to have lived. Not a desire to kill myself, but to have, through having no choice, died. If she can't share my life, I would share her death. And yet I can't, and so I feel envy. Jealousy."

"Those are not quite the same things, Tibilo."

"I know. Sometimes what I feel is . . . I'm not sure . . . a feeble yearning for something I don't have. Sometimes it is what I think people mean when they use the word envy, and sometimes it is real, raging jealousy. I almost hate her for having died without me." He shook his head, hardly believing what he was hearing himself saying. It was as though the words, at last expressed to another, gave final shape to thoughts he had not wanted to admit to harboring, even to himself. He stared through his tears at the old monk. "I did love her, though, Custodian. I did."

The older male nodded. "I'm sure you did, Tibilo. If you didn't you wouldn't still be suffering like this."

He looked away again. "I don't even know that anymore. I say I loved her, I think I did, I certainly thought I did, but did I? Maybe what I'm really feeling is guilt at not having loved her. I don't know. I don't know anything anymore."

The older male scratched at one of his bare patches. "You know that you are alive, Tibilo, and that she is dead, and that you might see her again."

He stared at the monk. "Without her Soulkeeper? I don't believe that, sir. I'm not sure I even believe I would see her again even if it had been recovered."

"As you pointed out yourself, we live in a time when the dead can return, Tibilo."

They knew now that there came a time in the development of every civilization—which lasted long enough—when its inhabitants could record their mind-state, effectively taking a reading of the person's personality which could be stored, duplicated, read, transmitted and, ultimately, installed into any suitably complex and enabled device or organism.

In a sense it was the most radically reductivist position made real; an acknowledgment that mind arose from matter, and could be fundamentally and absolutely defined in material terms, and as such it did not suit everyone. Some societies had reached the horizon of such knowledge and been on the brink of the control it implied, only to turn away, unwilling to lose the benefits of the beliefs such a development threatened.

Other peoples had accepted the exchange and suffered from it, losing themselves in ways that seemed sensible, even worthy at the time but which finally led to their effective extinction.

Most societies subscribed to the technologies involved and changed to deal with the consequences. In places like the Culture the consequences were that people could take back-ups of themselves if they were about to do something dangerous, they could create mind-state versions of themselves which could be used to deliver messages or undertake a multiplicity of experiences in a variety of places and in an assortment of physical or virtual forms, they could entirely transfer their original personality into a different body or device, and they could merge with other individuals—balancing retained individuality against consensual wholeness—in devices designed for such metaphysical intimacy.

Amongst the Chelgrian people the course of history had diverged from the norm. The device which was emplaced in them, the Soulkeeper, was rarely used to revive an individual. Instead it was used to ensure that the soul, the personality of the dying person, would be available to be accepted into heaven.

The majority of Chelgrians had long believed, like the majority of many intelligent species, in a place where the dead went after death.

There had been a variety of different religions, faiths and cults on the planet, but the belief system that came to dominate Chel and was exported out to the stars when the species achieved space travel—even if by then it was taken as having a symbolic rather than a literal truth—was one which still spoke of a mythical afterlife, where the good would be rewarded by an eternity of noble joy and the evil would be condemned—no matter what their caste had been in the mortal world—to servitude forever.

According to the carefully kept and minutely analyzed records of the galaxy's more nit-picking elder civilizations, the Chelgrians had persisted in their religiosity for a significant time after the advent of scientific methodology, and—in continuing to cleave to the caste system—were unusual in retaining such a manifestly discriminatory social order so long into post-contact history. None of this, though, prepared any of the observing societies for what happened not long after the Chelgrians became able to transcribe their personalities into media other than their own individual brains.

Subliming was an accepted if still somewhat mysterious part of galactic life; it meant leaving the normal matter-based life of the universe behind and ascending to a higher state of existence based on pure energy. In theory any individual—biological or machine—could Sublime, given the right technology, but the pattern was for whole swathes of a society and species to disappear at the same time, and often the entirety of a civilization went in one go (only the Culture was known to worry that such—to it—unlikely absoluteness implied a degree of coercion).

There were generally a host of warning signs that a society was about to Sublime—a degree of society-wide ennui, the revival of long-quiescent religions and other irrational beliefs, an interest in the mythology and methodology of Subliming itself—and it almost always happened to fairly well-established and long-lived civilizations.

To flourish, make contact, develop, expand, reach a steady state and then eventually Sublime was more or less the equivalent of the stellar Main Sequence for civilizations, though there was an equally honorable and venerable tradition for just quietly keeping on going, minding your own business (mostly) and generally sitting about feeling pleasantly invulnerable and just saturated with knowledge.

Again, the Culture was something of an exception, neither decently Subliming out of the way nor claiming its place with the other urbane sophisticates gathered reminiscing around the hearth of galactic wisdom, but instead behaving like an idealistic adolescent.

In any event, to Sublime was to retire from the normal life of the galaxy. The few real rather than imagined exceptions to this rule had consisted of little more than eccentricities: some of the Sublimed came back and removed their home planet, or wrote their names in nebulae or sculpted on some other vast scale, or set up curious monuments or left incomprehensible artifacts dotted about space or on planets, or returned in some bizarre form for a usually very brief and topologically limited appearance for what one could only imagine was some sort of ritual.

All this, of course, suited those who remained behind quite well, because the implication was that Subliming led to powers and abilities that gave those who had undergone the transformation an almost god-like status. If the process had been just another useful technological step along the way for any ambitious society, like nanotechnology, AI or wormhole creation, then everybody would presumably do it as soon as they could.

Instead Subliming seemed to be the opposite of useful as the word was normally understood. Rather than let you play the great galactic game of influence, expansion and achievement better than you could before, it appeared to take you out of it altogether.

Subliming was not utterly understood—the only way fully to understand it appeared to be to go ahead and do it—and despite various Involveds' best efforts studying the process it had proved astonishingly frustrating (it had been compared to trying to catch yourself falling asleep, whereas it was felt that it ought to be as easy as watching somebody else fall asleep), but there was a strong and reliable pattern to its likelihood, onset, development and consequences.

The Chelgrians had partially Sublimed; about six percent of their civilization had quit the material universe within the course of a day. They were of all castes, they were of all varieties of religious belief from atheists to the devout of diverse cults, and they included in their number several of the sentient machines Chel had developed but never fully exploited. No discernible pattern in the partial Subliming Event could be determined.

None of this was especially unusual in itself, though for any of them to have gone at all when the Chelgrians had only been in space for a few hundred years did seem—perversely—immature in the eyes of some. What had been remarkable, even alarming, was that the Sublimed had then maintained links with the majority part of their civilization which had not moved on.

The links took the form of dreams, manifestations at religious sites (and sporting events, though people tended not to dwell on this), the alteration of supposedly inviolate data deep inside government and clan archives, and the manipulation of certain absolute physical constants within laboratories. A number of long-lost artifacts were recovered, a host of careers were ruined when scandals were revealed and several unexpected and even unlikely scientific breakthroughs occurred.

This was all quite unheard of.

The best guess that anyone could make was that it was something to do with the caste system itself. Its practice down the millennia had ingrained in the Chelgrians the idea of being part and yet not part of a greater whole; the mind-set it implied and encouraged had hierarchic and continuant implications which had proved stronger than whatever processes drove the normal course of a Subliming Event and its aftermath.

For a few hundred days a lot of Involveds started watching the Chelgrians very carefully indeed. From being a not particularly interesting and arguably slightly barbaric species of middling abilities and average prospects, they suddenly acquired a glamor and mystique most civilizations struggled over millennia to develop. Across the galaxy, research programmes into Subliming were quietly instituted, dragged out of dormancy and re-energized, or accelerated as the horrible possibilities sank in.

The fears of the Involveds proved unfounded. What the Chelgrian-Puen, the gone-before, did with their still applicable super powers was to build heaven. They made matter of fact what had until then required an act of faith to believe in. When a Chelgrian died, their Soulkeeper device was the bridge that carried them across to the afterlife.

There was an inevitable vagueness associated with the whole procedure that Involveds throughout the galaxy had become used to when dealing with anything to do with Subliming, but it had been proved to the satisfaction of even the most skeptical of observers that the personalities of dead Chelgrians did survive after death, and could be contacted through suitably enabled devices or people.

Those souls described a heaven very similar to that of Chelgrian mythology, and even talked of entities which might have been the souls of Chelgrians dead long before the development of Soulkeeper technology, though none of these remote ancestor personalities could be contacted by the mortal world directly and the suspicion was that they were constructs of the Chelgrian-Puen, best guesses at what the ancestors might have been like if heaven had really existed from the start.

There could, however, be no real doubt that people were saved by their Soulkeeper and did indeed enter the heaven fashioned for them by the Chelgrian-Puen in the image of the paradise envisaged by their ancestors.

"But are the returned dead really the people we knew, Custodian?"

"They appear to be, Tibilo."

"Is that enough? Just appearing?"

"Tibilo, you might as well ask when we awake whether we are the same person who went to sleep."

He gave a thin, bitter smile. "I have asked that."

"And what was your answer?"

"That, sadly, yes we are."

"You say 'sadly' because you feel bitter."

"I say 'sadly' because if only we were different people with every wakening then the me that wakes up would not be the one who lost his wife."

"And yet we are different people, very slightly, with every new day."

"We are different people, very slightly, with every new eyeblink, Custodian."

"Only in the most trivial sense that time has passed during the moment of that blink. We age with every moment but the real increments of our experience are measured in days and nights. In sleep and dreams."

"Dreams," Quilan said, staring away again. "Yes. The dead escape death in heaven, and the living escape life in dreams."

"Is this something else you have asked yourself?"

It was not uncommon, nowadays, for people with terrible memories either to have them excised, or to retreat into dreams, and live from then on in a virtual world from which it was relatively easy to exclude the memories and their effects that had made normal life so unbearable.

"You mean have I considered it?"

"Yes."

"Not seriously. That would feel as though I was denying her." Quilan sighed. "I'm sorry, Custodian. You must get bored hearing me say the same things, day after day."

"You never say quite the same thing, Tibilo." The old monk gave a small smile. "Because there is change."

Quilan smiled too, though more as a polite response. "What does not change, Custodian, is that the only thing I really wish for with any sincerity or passion now is death."

"It is hard to believe, feeling as you do at the moment, that there will come a time when life seems good and worthwhile, but it will come."

"No, Custodian. I don't think it will. Because I wouldn't want to be the person who had felt as I do now and then walked—or drifted—away from that feeling until things felt better. That is precisely my problem. I prefer the idea of death to what I feel just now, but I would prefer to feel the way I do now forever than to feel better, because feeling better would mean that I am not the one who loved her anymore, and I could not bear that."

He looked at the old monk with tears in his eyes.

Fronipel sat back, blinking. "You must believe that even that can change and it will not mean you love her less."

Quilan felt almost as good at that point as he had since they had told him Worosei was dead. It was not pleasure, but it was a sort of lightness, a kind of clarity. He felt that he had at last come to some sort of decision, or was just about to. "I can't believe that, Custodian."

"Then what, Tibilo? Is your life to be submerged in grief until you die? Is that what you want? Tibilo, I see no sign of it in you, but there can be a form of vanity in grief that is indulged rather than suffered. I have seen people who find that grief gives them something they never had before, and no matter how terrible and real their loss they choose to hug that awfulness to them rather than push it away. I would hate to see you even seem to resemble such emotional masochists."

Quilan nodded. He tried to appear calm, but a frightful anger had coursed through him as the older male had spoken. He knew Fronipel meant well, and was sincere when he said that he did not think Quilan was such a person, but even to be compared to such selfishness, such indulgence, made him almost shake with fury.

"I would have hoped to have died with honor before such a charge might be levelled against me."

"Is that what you wish, Tibilo? To die?"

"It has come to seem the best course. The more I think about it, the better it becomes."

"And suicide, we are told, leads to utter oblivion."

The old religion had been ambivalent about taking one's own life. It had never been encouraged, but different views of its rights and wrongs had been taken over the generations. Since the advent of a real and provable heaven, it had been firmly discouraged—following a rash of mass suicides—by the Chelgrian-Puen, who made it clear that those who killed themselves just to get to heaven more quickly would not be allowed in there at all. They would be not even be held in limbo; they would not be saved at all. Not all suicides would necessarily be treated so severely, but the impression was very much that you'd better have an unimpeachable reason for showing up at the gates of paradise with your own blood on your hands.

"There would be little honor in that anyway, Custodian. I would rather die usefully."

"In battle?"

"Preferably."

"There is no great tradition of such martial severity in your family, Tibilo."

Quilan's family had been landowners, traders, bankers and insurers for a thousand years. He was the first son to carry anything more lethal than a ceremonial weapon for generations.

"Perhaps it's time such a tradition started."

"The war is over, Tibilo."

"There are always wars."

"They are not always honorable."

"One may die a dishonorable death in an honorable war. Why should the converse not apply?"

"And yet we are here in a monastery, not the briefing room of a barracks."

"I came here to think, Custodian. I never did renounce my commission."

"Are you determined to return to the Army, then?"

"I believe I am."

Fronipel looked into the younger male's eyes for some time. Finally, straightening himself in his side of the curl-chair, he said, "You are a major, Quilan. A major who would lead his troops when he wishes only to die might be a dangerous officer indeed."

"I would not want to force my decision on anyone else, Custodian."

"That is easily said, Tibilo."

"I know, and it is not so easily done. But I am not in any hurry to die. I am quite prepared to wait until I can be quite certain I am doing the right thing."

The old monk sat back, taking off his glasses and extracting a grubby-looking gray rag from a waistcoat. He breathed on the two large lenses in turn and then polished each. He inspected them. Quilan thought they looked no better than when he had started. He put them back with some care and then blinked at Quilan.

"This is, you realize, Major, something of a change."

Quilan nodded. "It feels more like a . . . like a clarification," he said. "Sir."

The old male nodded slowly.

Dirigible

Uagen Zlepe, scholar, was preparing an infusion of jhagel leaves when 974 Praf suddenly appeared on the window ledge of the small kitchen.

The simian-adapted human and the fifth-order Decider-turned-Interpreter had returned to the dirigible behemothaur Yoleus without mishap after retrieving the errant glyph stylo and spotting whatever it was they had spotted all that way below them in the airsphere's blue, blue depths. 974 Praf had immediately flown off to report to her superior. Uagen had decided to have a snooze after all the excitement. This proved difficult, so he forced himself to sleep with some glanded *shush*. On waking, after exactly one hour, he had smacked his lips and come to the conclusion that some jhagel tea might be in order.

The circular window of his little kitchen looked out across the sloping forest that was Yoleus' upper forward surface. The window had a series of gauzy curtains he could fasten over it, but he usually left those gathered to each side. The view had once been wonderful and airy but for the last three years it had been in shadow beneath the looming bulk of Muetenive, Yoleus' prospective mate. Yoleus' skin foliage was starting to look shrunken and anemic in the shade of the other creature. Uagen sighed and began the process of making the infusion.

The jhagel leaves were very precious to him. He had only brought a few kilos from home; he had about a third of that amount left now and he'd been rationing himself to one cup every twenty days to eke out his supply. He should have brought seeds as well, he supposed, but somehow he'd forgotten.

Making the infusion had become something of a ritual for Uagen. Jhagel tea was supposed to be calming, however it had occurred to him that the process of making it was itself quite relaxing. Perhaps when his supply was entirely gone he ought to go through the motions with some placebo mixture—stopping short of actually drinking it—to observe what degree of tranquillity might be induced just by the ceremony of preparation.

Frowning with concentration, he began to transfer some of the steaming pale green infusion into a warmed cup through a deep container which held twenty-three graduated layers of filters, variously chilled to between four and twenty-four degrees below.

Then Interpreter 974 Praf thudded onto his window ledge without warning. Uagen gave a start. Some of the hot liquid splashed over his hand.

"Ow! Umm. Hello, Praf. Umm, yes; ow."

He put the strainer and the pot down, then placed his hand under cold running water.

The creature hopped through the circular window, keeping its leathery wings tightly folded. In the small scullery, it suddenly seemed very big.

It looked at the puddle of splashed infusion. "A time for dropping," it observed.

"Eh? Oh, yes," Uagen said. He looked at his reddened hand. "What can I do for you, Praf?"

"The Yoleus would talk with you."

This was unusual. "What, now?"

"Immediately."

"What, face to—umm, well . . . ?"

"Yes."

Uagen felt just a little frightened. He could do with some calming down. He pointed at the pot simmering on his little cooker. "What about my jhagel tea?"

974 Praf looked at it, then him. "Its presence is not required."

"Are you sure, Yoleus? Umm. I mean, well . . ."

"Sufficiently sure. Do you desire a percentage to be expressed?"

"No. No, no need for that, it's just. This is awfully. I'm not sure that. It's very."

"Uagen Zlepe, scholar, you are not finishing your sentences."

"Amn't I? Well, I mean." Uagen felt himself go *gulp.* "Do you really think I need to go down there?"

"Yes."

"Oh."

"Umm. The. Umm. Whatever it is couldn't come up here, then?"

"No."

"And you're sure?"

"Sufficiently sure. That which it is thought that you would be best to experience is in a situation/setting similar to this."

"Ah. I see."

Uagen was standing, a little precariously, on what felt like a particularly wobbly bit of marsh. In fact he was deep inside the body of the dirigible behemothaur Yoleus, within a chamber he had only once ever seen before and had rather hoped he might not have to visit again during his stay.

The place was about the size of a ballroom. It was a hemisphere, with ribs and curves everywhere. Even the floor had curves, low swells and hollows. The walls looked like gigantic folded curtains, gathered into a sphincter shape at the summit. It was unlit and Uagen was having to use his in-built IR sense, which made everything look gray and grainy and even more frightening.

The smell was that of a sewer under an abattoir. Stuck to the wall were dead, living-dead and still living things. One of them—one of the latter category, thankfully—was 974 Praf. Underneath 974 Praf, dwarfing her, were the recently attached and now drained-looking carcasses of two falficores, their wings and talons hanging loosely. Alongside the Interpreter was the even bigger body of a raptor scout.

974 Praf didn't look too bad; she appeared perched, wings neatly folded, feet drawn up. The creature hanging by her side, whose body was nearly the size of Uagen's and whose wings were easily fifteen meters from tip to tip, looked limp and—if not dead—near death. Its eyes were half closed, its huge beaked head was slumped across its chest, its wings looked pinned to the in-curving wall of the chamber, and its legs hung slackly.

What looked like a root or cable led from the back of its skull and into the wall. Where the cable entered its head, something like blood had leaked out, soaking its dark, scaly skin. The creature trembled suddenly and let out a low moan.

"The raptor scout's report on the fellow-creature below is not sufficient," the dirigible behemothaur Yoleus said through 974 Praf. "The captured falficores knew less still; only that there was a recent rumor of food below. Your report might be sufficient."

Uagen swallowed. "Umm." He stared at the raptor scout. It had not been tortured or really mistreated, by the locally prevailing standards, but whatever had happened to it didn't look very pleasant. It had been dispatched to reconnoiter the shape that Uagen and 974 Praf had seen when they'd gone after the falling glyph stylo.

The raptor scout had dived into the depths, escorted by the rest of its wing. It had landed on what was apparently another dirigible behemothaur, but one which had been injured or damaged, which had possibly lost its way and probably lost its mind. It had investigated inside a little, then it had rushed as fast as it could back to Yoleus, who had listened to its report and then concluded that the creature was not articulate enough to explain properly what it had seen—the raptor scout had not even been able to determine the identity of the other behemothaur—and so had decided to look directly into its memories by burrowing in with a direct link between its mind and Yoleus' own—whatever and wherever that was.

There was nothing all that unusual about this, or even anything cruel; the raptor scout was, in a sense, a part of the dirigible behemothaur and would have had no sense of having had interests or even an existence separate from the vast creature; probably it would have been proud that the information it was carrying was of such importance that Yoleus wanted to look at it directly. Nevertheless, to Uagen it still looked like some poor wretch chained to a wall in a torture chamber after the torturer had extracted what he wanted. The creature moaned again.

"Umm. Yes," Uagen said. "Ah. I would be able to make this report, umm. Verbally, wouldn't I?"

"Yes," the dirigible behemothaur said through 974 Praf.

Uagen felt just a little relief.

Then the Interpreter sat back against the wall behind her. She blinked a few times and then said, "Hmm."

"What?" Uagen said, suddenly aware of a funny taste in his mouth. He was aware that he was fingering the necklace his aunt Silder had given him. He put his hands down by his sides. They were shaking.

"Yes."

"Yes what?"

"There would also be . . ."

"What? What?" He was aware that his voice was more of a yelp, now.

"Your glyph tablet."

"What?"

"The glyph tablet that belongs to you. If it might be used for the recording of the impressions you have, that would be of use to me."

"Ha! The tablet! Yes! Yes, of course! Yes!"

"Then you will go and are so agreed."

"Oh. Umm. Well, yes, I suppose. That is—"

"I release the fifth-order Decider of the 11th Foliage Gleaner Troupe which is now Interpreter 974 Praf." There was a sound like a noisy kiss, and 974 Praf hinged away from her perch on the wall, falling untidily for the first couple of meters before collecting herself in an undignified clatter of wings and looking wildly about as though she had just woken up. 974 Praf hovered in front of Uagen's face, wings beating the smell of something rotten against him. She cleared her throat. "Seven wings of raptor scouts will accompany you," she told him. "They will take a deep-light signalling pod with them. They await."

"What, now?"

"Soon equates to good, later to worse, Uagen Zlepe, scholar. Therefore, immediacy."

"Umm."

They fell en masse, hurtling mob-handed into the dark blue abyss of air. Uagen shivered and looked around. One of the suns had gone out. The other had moved. They were not real suns, of course. They were more like immense spotlights; eyeballs the size of small moons whose annihilatory furnaces switched on and off according to a pattern dictated by their slow dance around the vast world.

Sometimes they glowed just sufficiently to stop themselves from falling further into Oskendari's gravity faint well, sometimes they blazed, bathing the airsphere's nearest volumes in radiance while the pressure of that released light kicked them further up and out, so that they would have escaped the airsphere's pull altogether if they hadn't then swivelled and sent out a pulse of light that sent them falling back in again.

The sun-moons were worth lifetimes of study all on their own, Uagen knew, though probably they were more the province of somebody interested in physics, rather than someone like himself. He turned up the heating in his suit—Yoleus had been persuaded to allow him time to return to his quarters and put on something more in keeping with the role of explorer—but then he started to sweat. He wasn't really cold, he decided, just afraid. He turned the heating down again.

The three wings of raptor scouts fell all around him, their long dark bodies streamlined darts slowly twisting as they aimed their arm-long beaks plummeting down through the thick blue air. Uagen's ankle motors hummed gently, keeping his pace up to that of the sleekly profiled raptor scouts. 974 Praf clung to his back, her body laid along his from nape to rump, her wings wrapped around his chest. She would have held them up if she'd dived separately. Her embrace was tight, and Uagen had already felt himself becoming breathless and had to ask her to slacken her grip to let him breathe.

He had half hoped the other dirigible behemothaur might have disappeared, but it was suddenly there; an alarmingly extensive area of darker blue deep beneath them. Uagen felt his heart sink, and wondered if the creature clamped to his back could feel his fear.

He tried to decide if he was really ashamed of being afraid, and decided that he was not. Fear was there for a purpose. It was wired into any creature that had not completely turned its back on its evolutionary inheritance and so remade itself in whatever image it coveted. The more sophisticated you became, the less you relied on fear and pain to keep you alive; you could afford to ignore them because you had other means of coping with the consequences if things went badly.

He wondered how imagination fitted in. He had a feeling it ought to. Any organism could learn to avoid experiences of a sort that had earlier resulted in damage and therefore pain, but with real intelligence came a more sophisticated form of anticipation of damage to oneself which pre-empted the injury. There should be a set of glyphs in this, he decided. He would work on them later, assuming he survived.

He looked up. Yoleus was invisible, its vast bulk lost in the scattering haze of air above. All he could see up there was the blob that was the infrared signalling pod and its attendant raptor scouts, falling after the main force as fast as possible. Around him, tearing down toward the vast blue shadow beneath, two hundred sleek blue-black shapes rustled and whistled in the thick, warm air.

It seemed like only moments later that those shapes were all suddenly expanding, stretching out and grabbing at the atmosphere with their great, dark-ribbed wings. 974 Praf kicked away from his back and fell separately, wings half extended.

Uagen could see detail on the upper surface of the dirigible behemothaur beneath; scars and gouges on the forests of the creature's back and tattered fins a hundred meters tall trailing strips of gauzy material for kilometers behind in the creature's languid slipstream. Some fins were missing altogether, and toward the rear of the enormous shape a huge chunk appeared to have been scooped away, as though bitten out by something even larger.

"Looks pretty chewed up, doesn't it?" Uagen shouted to 974 Praf.

She turned her head slightly toward him, tacking slowly toward him as she said, "The Yoleus believes that such damage is unprecedented in living memory."

Uagen just nodded, then recalled that dirigible behemothaurs lived for tens of millions of years, at least. That was a fairly long time to be without precedent.

He looked down. The scarred, curved back of the unnamed behemothaur rose up to meet them. There was a lot of activity there now, Uagen saw. The dying creature had been discovered by more than just one diving human-simian and a few falficores.

It had been like a horrific cross between cancer and civil war. The entire ecosystem that was the dirigible behemothaur Sansemin was tearing itself apart. Now others were joining in.

They had discovered its name through description. 974 Praf had flown around it, recording any distinguishing marks not altered or obliterated by the destruction taking place, then landed on the little hummock of naked envelope skin high on its back where the raptor scout troupe had established its primary base. The Interpreter had communicated its findings via the giant seed-shaped signalling pod in the center of the hastily established compound. The pod's infrared light had found Yoleus, tens of kilometers above, and then received the reply a little later. According to the library memories Yoleus shared with its kind, the dying behemothaur was called Sansemin.

Sansemin had always been an outsider, a renegade, almost an outlaw. It had disappeared from polite society thousands of years ago and was presumed to be haunting the less hospitable and less fashionable volumes of the airsphere, perhaps alone, possibly in the company of

the small number of other misfit behemothaurs known to exist.
There had been a few hazy, unconfirmed sightings of the creature
over the first several centuries of its self-imposed exile, but nothing
for the last few.

Now it had been rediscovered, but it was at war with itself and
about to die.

Flocks of falficores surrounded the giant in squabbling clouds,
feeding off its foliage and outer skins. Smerines and phuelerids, the
largest winged creatures in the airsphere, divided their time between
the living flesh of the behemothaur and the swarming clusters of falficores driven to recklessness by the sheer glut of food on offer. The
sleekly bulbous bodies of two ogrine disseisors—a rare form of lithe
behemothaur only a hundred meters in length and the world's
largest predator—swam through the air in tremendous sinuous
flicks, dipping to tear pieces from the body of Sansemin and snapping up handfuls of careless falficores and even the occasional smerine and phuelerid.

Tendon-strutted fragments of behemothaur skin fell into the blueness below like dark sails torn from cyclone-struck clippers; puffs of
gas made brief, dispersing vapor clouds in the air as the colossal creature's outer ballonets and gas sacs were ruptured; the torn bodies of
falficores, smerines and phuelerids tumbled in bloody cart-wheeling
spirals into the abyss, their screams frighteningly close in the compacted depth of air yet nearly drowned out in the vast noise of fren-
zied feeding going on all about.

The raptor scouts, cloud attackers, envelopian defenders and
other creatures which were part of Sansemin's dispersed self and that
would normally easily have kept such aggressors at bay were
nowhere to be seen. The remains of a few had been discovered
where they had fallen and been picked clean by others. The most
telling pair of skeletons had been found with their jaws clamped
around the other's neck.

Uagen Zlepe stood on the seemingly solid surface of the dirigible
behemothaur's vast back, looking out over a landscape of tattered,
withered skin foliage being torn apart by falficore flocks. He stood

beside the seven-meter-wide bulk of the signaling pod. It was anchored to the envelope's surface by a dozen small hooks made from falficore talons and tended to by a handful of Deciders nearly identical to 974 Praf.

Spread in a circle about them were a hundred of Yoleus' raptor scouts, forming a living defensive barrier which was patrolled from above by another fifty or sixty of the creatures, flying slow circuits. So far they had repelled all attacks and had not lost any of their number; even one of the ogrine disseisors, obviously intrigued by the activity around the signalling pod, had turned tail when confronted by twenty of the raptor scouts in attack formation and returned instead to the easier pickings on offer all over the dying behemothaur's surface.

Two hundred meters away across Sansemin's back, near the knobbled ridge of a longeron spine, a smerine swooped down, scattering the smaller creatures in a blizzard of piercing cries; it thudded into a giant wound in the behemothaur's skin; Uagen saw the flesh around the tear ripple under impact. The predator flapped its twenty-meter wings and dipped its long head, flaying the exposed tissue.

A gas sac, severed from its supporting structure, wobbled out of the spreading wound and into the air. It began to climb. The smerine looked up but let it go; the falficore flock above attacked it, screeching, until it punctured and jetted slowly off, deflating in a long exhaling scream of gas and scattering enraged falficores behind it.

There was a thud at his feet. Uagen jumped. "Oh, Praf," he said as the Interpreter stowed its wings. It had gone with a dozen of the raptor scouts to investigate the interior of the behemothaur. "Find anything?" he asked.

974 Praf watched the distant gas sac as it finally fell deflated into the foliage forest near Sansemin's upper fore-fins. "We have found something. Come and look."

"Inside?" Uagen asked nervously.

"Yes."

"Is it safe? Umm, in there?"

974 Praf looked up at him.

"Umm. I mean, umm. The central gas bladders. The hydrogen core. I thought there was a possibility those might, that is, it might. Umm."

"An explosion is possible," 974 Praf said in a matter-of-fact manner. "This would be of a catastrophic nature."

Uagen felt himself gulp. "Catastrophic?"

"Yes. The dirigible behemothaur Sansemin would be destroyed."

"Yes. And. Umm. Us?"

"Too."

"Too?"

"We too would be destroyed."

"Yes. Well, then."

"This outcome will grow more likely with delay. Therefore delay is not wise. Expedition is advisable." 974 Praf shuffled its feet. "Extremely advisable."

"Praf," Uagen said, "do we have to do this?"

The creature rocked back on its heel talons and squinted up at him. "Of course. It is duty to the Yoleus."

"And if I say no?"

"What do you mean?"

"What if I refuse to go inside and look at whatever it is you've found?"

"Then our investigations will take longer."

Uagen stared at the Interpreter. "Longer."

"Of course."

"What *have* you found?"

"We do not know."

"Then—"

"It is a creature."

"A creature?"

"Many creatures. All dead but one. Of an unknown type."

"What sort of unknown type?"

"That is what is unknown."

"Well, what does it look like?"

"It looks a little like you."

•   •   •

The creature looked like an alien child's doll, thrown against a barbed wall and left hanging there. It was long, with a tail that was half its body length. The head was broad, furred and—he thought—striped, though in the darkness, using only his IR sense, he couldn't tell what colors its pelt might be. The creature's big, forward-facing eyes were closed. It had a thick neck, broad shoulders, two arms about the size of a large human's but with very wide, heavy hands which looked more like paws. Only a dirigible behemothaur or one of its acolytes would have imagined it looked much like Uagen Zlepe.

It was one of twenty similar forms strung out along one wall of the chamber. All the others were dead and rotting.

Below the creature's arms, supported by a second, still wider set of shoulders, rested what at first appeared to be a giant flap of furred skin. Looking closer, Uagen realized this was a limb. A dark pad of toughened skin extended across its end in an 8 shape, and stubby hints of toes or claws dotted the perimeter of the pad. Below the torso, two powerful-looking legs hung from a broad set of hips. A furred mound probably concealed genitals of some sort. The tail was striped. One of the root-cables Uagen had seen attached to the raptor scout in the similar chamber in Yoleus led from the back of the creature's head and into the ribbed wall behind.

The smell in here was even worse than it had been in Yoleus. The journey had been horrific. Dirigible behemothaurs were riddled with fissures, chambers, cavities and tunnels disposed so that their collection of tributary fauna could carry out their various tasks. Many of these were large enough to admit raptor scouts and it was down one of these that they had journeyed from an entrance behind the behemothaur's rear dorsal fin complex.

The effects of the creature's own attendant entities turning against it were everywhere. Great gouges and tears had been slashed through the tunnel's walls, making the curved floor slick with liquid in some places and cloyingly sticky in others; flaps of decaying tissue hung from the ceiling like obscene banners, and rents in the floor could swallow a leg, a wing, or even—certainly in Uagen's case—a whole body.

Here and there smaller creatures still feasted upon the body of the being they had served; other corpses littered the floor of the winding tunnel, and where the two raptor scouts accompanying 974 Praf and Uagen Zlepe down into the body of the behemothaur could do so without delaying their progress, they swiped out at the parasites and tore them to pieces, leaving them twitching on the floor behind.

Finally they had arrived at the chamber where the behemothaur sought knowledge from its self-kin and guests. A great tremor ran through the cavern just as they entered, making the walls shake and dislodging some of the half-rotted bodies.

Two of the specialist raptor scouts had clawed their way up the wall beside the creature which still appeared to be alive. They were intent on an examination of its head where the cable root disappeared into it. One of the raptor scouts held something small and glittering.

"Do you know the nature of this being?" 974 Praf asked.

Uagen stared up at the creature. "No," he said. "Well, not properly. It looks vaguely familiar. I might have seen it on screen or something. But I don't know what it is."

"It is not of your sort?"

"Well, of course not. Look at it. It's bigger, it's got enormous eyes and a totally different sort of head. I mean, umm, *I'm* not of my sort, not originally, if you know what I mean," he said, turning to Praf, who blinked up at him. "But the main thing, umm, difference, is that middle bit. That looks like a sort of extra leg and foot. Well, like two that have grown together. Do you see those, ah, ridges? I'll bet those are the bones of what used to be two separate legs in its forebears, before it evolved into a single limb."

"It is not known to you?"

"Hmm? Umm, sorry. No."

"Do you think if it can be made to speak it will be able to be understood in its talking by you?"

"What?"

"It is not dead. It is linked to the mind of the Sansemin but the mind of the Sansemin is dead. But the creature is not dead. If we are able to sever its link to the mind of the Sansemin, which is dead, then it might be able to speak. If this were to happen, would you be able to understand that which it says?"

"Oh. Umm. I doubt it."

"That is unfortunate." 974 Praf was silent for a moment. "And yet this means that we would be wise to sever its link soon rather than later, and that is good because then we would be less likely to die when the Sansemin suffers its catastrophic explosion."

"What?" Uagen yelped. The Interpreter started to repeat itself, talking slightly slower, but he waved both hands at it. "Never mind! Sever its links now; let's get out quick! I mean, quickly!"

"This will be done," 974 Praf said. It babbled and clicked at the two raptor scouts clinging to the wall by the side of the alien creature. They turned and jabbered back. There seemed to be a disagreement.

Another tremor shook the whole chamber. The floor under Uagen's feet quaked. He put his arms out to each side to balance himself and felt his mouth go dry. There was a draft, then a distinct breeze of warm air, scented with a smell he suspected was methane. It took most of the smell of rotting flesh away, but he felt sickened with terror. His skin had gone cold and clammy. *"Please* let's go," he whispered.

The raptor scouts on either side of the hanging creature did something behind its head. It slumped forward and down, then the thing trembled as though shivering and brought its head back up. It worked its jaw, then opened its eyes. They were very large and black.

It looked around, at the raptor scouts on either side, at the rest of the chamber, then at 974 Praf, then at Uagen Zlepe. It made a sound, or set of sounds, but it was no language that Uagen had ever heard before.

"This is not a speech-form which is known to you?" the Interpreter asked. On the barbed wall of living, dying tissue, the alien creature's eyes went suddenly wide.

"No," Uagen said. "Doesn't mean a thing to me, I'm afraid. Umm, look, can we please, please get the hell out of here?"

"You, you there," gasped the creature on the wall, in accented but recognisable Marain. It was staring at Uagen, who was staring right back. "Help me," it wheezed.

"Wh—wh—what?" Uagen heard himself say.

"Please," the creature said. "Culture. Agent." It swallowed with obvious pain and croaked, "Plot. Assassin. Need. Get word. Please. Help. Urgent. Very. Urgent."

Uagen tried to speak but could not. There was a smell of something burning in the wind blowing through the chamber.

974 Praf adjusted her footing as another huge tremor shook the chamber and made the floor swell. She looked from Uagen to the creature on the wall and back again. *"This* speech-form is known to you?" she asked.

Uagen nodded.

The Memory of Running

The figure seemed to coalesce out of nothing, out of the air. Anyone or anything watching would have needed more than natural senses to have noticed the slow fall of dust spread out over an hour of time and a radial kilometer of the grasslands; that anything out of the ordinary was happening would only have become obvious a little later when an odd sort of wind seemed to stir itself out of the gentle breeze, disturbing the grass on the broad plain and producing what appeared to be a slowly revolving dust devil, whirling quietly in the air and gradually shrinking and tightening and darkening and speeding up until, suddenly, it disappeared, and where it had been there stood what looked like a tall and graceful Chelgrian female, dressed in the country day clothes of the Given caste.

The first thing she did when she felt she was complete was to crouch down and dig into the earth beneath the grass with her fingers. Her claws slid out, spearing the ground. She ripped out a handful of the soil and grass. She held the handful of earth and vegetation up to her broad, dark nose, and sniffed slowly.

She was waiting. She had nothing better to do for the moment, and so she thought that she would take a good hard look and a good long sniff at the ground she stood on.

There were so many different tones and flavors to the smell. The grass held a spectrum of odors of its own, all of them fresher and brighter than the heavy notes of the soil, giving it a scent of the air and the winds rather than the ground.

She raised her head, letting the breeze ruffle her head fur. She took in the view. It was almost perfectly simple; ankle-high grass stretching in every direction. There was a hint of cloud to the far northeast, where the Xhesseli Mountains were. She had seen them on the way down. Above, and everywhere else in the sky, just aquamarine clarity. No sign of contrails. That was good. The sun was halfway up the southern sky. To the north, both moons shone full face, and a single day star twinkled near the eastern horizon.

She was aware of some part of her mind using the information in the sky to calculate her position, the time and the precise compass direction she was facing in. The resulting knowledge made its existence felt, but did not force itself upon her; it was like the presence of somebody in an anteroom, signaled by a polite knock on the door. She called up another layer of data and was presented with an overlay across the sky; suddenly she could see a grid superimposed across the heavens, and drawn on it were the paths of numerous satellites and a few sub-orbital transport craft, with identities attached and a further stratum of more finely detailed information on each implied. The satellites whose images were slowly flashing were the ones which had been interfered with.

Then she saw a couple of dots on the eastern horizon, and turned to them, her eyes adjusting. Inside her, something exactly like a heart thumped hard and fast for a single beat before she could control it again. Some of the earth fell from the handful she held.

The dots were birds, a few hundred meters away.

She relaxed.

The birds rose into the air, facing each other and flapping wildly. They were half displaying, half fighting. There would be a female sitting crouched in the grass nearby watching the two males. The scientific and common names of the species, their range, feeding and mating habits and a variety of other information about the creatures seemed to hover at the back of her mind. The two birds fell back into the grass again. Their calls came thinly through the air. She had never heard their voices before, but knew that they sounded as they ought to.

Of course, it was still possible that the birds were not as innocent and unthreatening as they appeared. They might be real but altered animals, or not biological at all; in either case they might be part of a surveillance system. Well, there was nothing to be done. She would go on waiting a little longer.

She returned her attention to the clump of turf she held, bringing it up to her eyes, soaking up the sight. There were many different types of grasses and tiny plants in the handful, most of them a pale yellow-green color. She saw seeds, roots, tendrils, petals, husks, blades and stems. The relevant information describing each different species duly made its existence known at the back of her mind.

She was, by now, also aware that the data presenting itself had already been evaluated by some other part of her mind. If anything had looked wrong or seemed out of place—if, for example, those birds had moved in a manner so as to imply that they were heavier than they were supposed to be—then her attention would have been drawn to the anomaly. So far, everything seemed to be reassuringly normal. The data was a distant, comforting awareness, patiently lingering on the outskirts of her perception.

A few tiny animals moved within the mass of soil and on the surfaces of the vegetation. She knew their names and details, too. She watched a pale, thread-thin worm waving about blindly in the humus.

She put the divot back, pressing the clump of soil into the hole it had left and patting it down. She dusted off her hands while she looked around once more. Still no sign of anything amiss. The birds in the distance rose into the air again, then descended. A warm wave of air unfolded itself across the surface of the grass and flowed around her, stroking her fur where it was not covered by her plain hide waistcoat and pants. She picked up her cloak and fastened it around her shoulders. It became part of her, just like the waistcoat and pants.

The wind came from the west. It was freshening, taking the cries of the displaying birds away, so that when they rose in the distance for a third time, they seemed to do so quite silently.

There was just a hint, a faint tang of salt in the wind. It was sufficient to decide her. Enough of waiting.

She looped the cloak's tail-loop over her long tawny tail, then turned her face to the wind.

She wished that she had chosen a name. If she had she would have spoken it now; voiced it to the clear air like some declaration of intent. But she did not have a name, because she was not what she appeared to be; not a Chelgrian female; not a Chelgrian, not even a biological creature at all. I am a Culture terror weapon, she thought; designed to horrify, warn and instruct at the highest level. A name would have been a lie.

She checked her orders, just to be sure. It was true. She had complete discretion in the manner. A lack of instruction could be interpreted as a quite specific instruction. She could do anything; she was off the leash.

Very well.

She leaned back on her rear legs and brought her arms up to slip them into the glove pouches at the top of her waistcoat, then—with an initial bound very like a pounce—she set off, settling quickly into an easy-looking lope that carried her away across the grass in a series of long, smoothly sinuous bounds that stretched and compressed her powerful back and brought her heavily muscled rear legs and broad midlimb almost together then pushed them flying apart with every surging leap.

She felt the joy of the run and understood the ancient rightness of the wind in her face and fur. To run, to chase, to hunt, to bring down and kill.

The cloak rippled across her back in the slipstream. Her tail flicked from side to side.

9

Pylon Country

I'd almost forgotten this place existed myself."

Kabe looked at the silver-skinned avatar. "Really?"

"Nothing much has happened here for two hundred years apart from gentle decay," the creature explained.

"Couldn't that be said of the whole Orbital?" Ziller asked, in what was probably meant to be a falsely innocent tone. The avatar pretended to look hurt.

The antique cable car creaked around them as it swung around a tall pylon. It rumbled and squeaked through a system of overhead points hanging from a ring around the mast's top and then tacked away on a new heading toward a distant pylon on a small hill across the fractured plain.

"*Do* you ever forget anything, Hub?" Kabe asked the avatar.

"Only if I choose to," it said in its hollow voice. It was half sitting, half lying on one of the plump red polished hide couches, its booted feet up on the brass rail which separated the rear passenger compartment from the pilot's control deck, where Ziller was standing, watching the various instruments, adjusting levers and fiddling with a variety of ropes that emerged from a slot in the car's floor and were tied off on cleats mounted on the forward bulkhead.

"And do you ever choose to?" Kabe asked. He was squatting tre-foil on the floor; there was just enough headroom for him in the ornate cabin like that. The car was designed to carry about a dozen passengers and two crew.

The avatar frowned. "Not that I can recall."

Kabe laughed. "So you might choose to forget something then choose to forget forgetting it?"

"Ah, but then I'd have to forget forgetting the original forgetting."

"I suppose you would."

"Is this conversation *going* anywhere?" Ziller shouted over his shoulder.

"No," said the avatar. "It's like this journey; drifting."

"We are not drifting," Ziller said. "We are exploring."

"You might be," the avatar said. "I'm not. I can see exactly where we are from Hub central. What do you want to see? I can provide detailed maps if you'd like."

"The spirit of adventure and exploration is obviously alien to your computer soul," Ziller told it.

The avatar reached out and flicked a speck of dust from the top of one boot. "Do I have a soul? Is that meant to be a compliment?"

"Of course you don't have a soul," Ziller said, pulling hard on one rope and tying it off. The cable car picked up speed, swaying gently as it crossed the scrub-strewn plain. Kabe watched the car's shadow as it undulated over the dustily fawn and red ground below. The dark outline slid away and lengthened as they crossed a dry, gravel-braided river bed. A gust of wind raised eddies of dust on the ground below, then hit the car and tipped it fractionally, making the glass windows rattle in their wooden frames.

"That's good," the avatar said. "Because I didn't think I had one and if I did I must have forgotten."

"Ah ha," said Kabe.

Ziller made an exasperated sound.

They were in a wind-powered cable car crossing the Epsizyr Breaks, a huge area of semi-wilderness on Canthropa Plate, nearly a quarter-way spinwards around the Orbital from Ziller and Kabe's homes on Xaravve and Osinorsi. The Breaks were a vast dried-up river system a thousand kilometers broad and three times that in length. From space they looked thrown across the dun plains of Canthropa like a million twisted lengths of gray and ocher string.

The Breaks rarely carried much water. There was the occasional rain shower over the plains, but the region remained semi-arid. Every hundred or so years a really big storm managed to cross the Canthrops, the mountain range between the plains and Sard Ocean which occupied the whole of the Plate to spinward, and only then did the river system live up to its name, transporting the fallen rain from the mountains to the Epsizyr Pans, which filled and shimmered for a few days and supported a brief riot of plant and animal life before drying to salty mud flats again.

The Breaks had been designed to be that way. Masaq' had been modeled and planned as carefully as any other Orbital, but it had always been envisaged as a big world, and a varied one. It contained just about every form of geography possible, given its apparent gravity and human-friendly atmosphere, and most of that geography was human-friendly too, but it was rare for any self-respecting Orbital Hub to be happy without at least some wilderness around. Humans tended to complain after a while, too.

Filling every available bit of each and every Plate with gently rolling hills and babbling brooks, or even spectacular mountains and broad oceans, was not seen as producing a properly balanced Orbital environment; there ought to be wastes, there should be badlands.

The Epsizyr Breaks were just one of hundreds of different types of wasteland scattered about Masaq'. They were dry and windy and barren but otherwise one of the more hospitable badlands. People had always come to the Breaks; they came to walk, to camp out under the stars and the far-side light and feel themselves apart from things for a while, and though a few people had tried living there, almost nobody had stayed for more than a few hundred days.

Kabe was looking out over Ziller's head through the front windscreen of the car. From the tall pylon they were heading for, cables stretched away in six different directions along lines of masts disappearing into the distance, some in straight lines, others in lazy curves. Looking out over the fractured landscape all around, Kabe could see the pylons—each between twenty and sixty meters high and shaped like an inverted L—everywhere. He could see why the Epsizyr Breaks were also known as Pylon Country.

"Why was the system built in the first place?" Kabe asked. He had been quizzing the avatar about the cable-car system when it had made its remark about almost forgetting the place existed.

"All down to a man called Bregan Latry," the avatar said, stretching out across the couch and clasping its hands behind its head. "Eleven hundred years ago he got it into his head that what this place really needed was a system of sailing cable cars."

"But why?" Kabe asked.

The avatar shrugged. "No idea. This was before my watch, don't forget; back in the time of my predecessor, the one who Sublimed."

"You mean you didn't inherit any records from it?" Ziller asked incredulously.

"Don't be ridiculous, of course I inherited a full suite of records and archives." The avatar stared up at the ceiling and shook his head. "Looking back, it's very much as though I was there." It shrugged. "There just wasn't any record of exactly why Bregan Latry decided to start covering the Breaks in pylons."

"He just thought there should be . . . this . . . here?"

"Apparently."

"Perfectly fine idea," Ziller said. He pulled on a line, tightening one of the sails underneath the car with a squeak of wheels and pulleys.

"And so your predecessor built it for him?" Kabe asked.

The avatar snorted derisively. "Certainly not. This place was designed as wilderness. It couldn't see any good reason to start running cables all over it. No, it told him to do it himself."

Kabe looked around the haze horizon. He could see hundreds of pylons from here. "He built all this *himself?*"

"In a manner of speaking," the avatar said, still staring up at the ceiling, which was painted with scenes of ancient rustic life. "He asked for manufacturing capacity and design time and he found a sentient airship which also thought it would be a hoot to dot pylons all over the Breaks. He designed the pylons and the cars, had them manufactured and then he and the airship and a few other people he'd talked into supporting the project started putting the pylons up and stringing the cables in between."

"Didn't anyone object?"

"He kept it quiet for a surprisingly long time, but yes, people did object."

"There are always critics," Ziller muttered. He was studying a huge paper chart through a magnifying glass.

"But they let him go ahead?"

"Grief, no," the avatar said. "They started taking the pylons down. Some people like their wilderness just as it is."

"But obviously Mr. Latry prevailed," Kabe said, looking around again. They were approaching the mast on the low hill. The ground was rising toward the car's lower sails and their shadow was growing closer all the time.

"He just kept building the pylons and the airship and his pals kept planting them. And the Preservationeers—" the avatar turned and glanced at Kabe, "they had a name by this time; always a bad sign— kept taking them down. More and more people joined in on both sides until the place was swarming with people putting up pylons and hanging cable off them, rapidly followed by people tearing every-thing down and carting it away again."

"Didn't they vote on it?" Kabe knew this was how disputes tended to be settled in the Culture.

The avatar rolled its eyes. "Oh, they voted."

"And Mr. Latry won."

"No, he lost."

"So, how come—?"

"Actually they had lots of votes. It was one of those rolling cam-paigns where they had to vote on who would be allowed to vote; just people who'd been to the Breaks, people who lived on Canthropa, everybody on Masaq', or what?"

"And Mr. Latry lost."

"He lost the first vote, with those eligible to vote restricted to those who'd been to the Breaks before—would you believe there was one proposal to weight everybody's votes according to how many times they'd been here, and another to give them a vote for each day they'd been here?" The avatar shook its head. "Believe me; democracy in action can be an unpretty sight. So he lost that one and in theory my predecessor was then mandated to stop the manufacturing, but then the people who hadn't been allowed to vote were complaining and so there was another ballot and this time it was the whole Plate population, plus people who'd been to the Breaks."

"And he won that one."

"No, he lost that one, too. The Preservationeers had some very good PR. Better than the Pylonists."

"They had a name too by this time?" Kabe asked.

"Of course."

"This isn't going to be one of those idiotic local disputes that end up being put to a vote of the whole Culture, is it?" Ziller said, still poring over his chart. He looked up briefly at the avatar. "I mean, that doesn't *really* happen, does it?" he asked.

"It really happens," the avatar said. Its voice sounded particularly hollow. "More often than you'd think. But no, in this case the quarrel never went out of Masaq's jurisdiction." The avatar frowned, as though finding something objectionable in the painted scene overhead. "Oh, Ziller, by the way; mind that pylon."

"What?" the Chelgrian said. He glanced up. The pylon on the hill was only five meters away. "Oh, shit." He dropped the chart and the magnifying glass and moved quickly to adjust the levers controlling the car's overhead steering wheels.

There was a clanking, grinding noise from overhead; the stubby pylon whooshed past to starboard, its foametal girders streaked with bird droppings and dotted with lichen. The cable car shook and rattled as it crunched over the first set of points while Ziller loosened his ropes, letting the sails flap free. The car was now on a sort of ring around the top of the pylon from which the other cable routes left; a set of vanes on the top of the pylon powered a chain drive set into the ring, pulling the car around.

Ziller watched a pair of hanging metal boards go past; they bore large numbers in fading, flaking paint. At the third board, he shoved one of the steering levers forward; the car's overhead wheels reconnected and, with a screech of metal and a sudden jolt, it slipped onto the appropriate cable, sliding down by gravity alone at first until Ziller hauled on his ropes and reconfigured the sails to haul the swaying, gently bouncing car along a long bowed length of cable that led to another distant hillock.

"There," Ziller said.

"But eventually Mr. Latry got his way," Kabe said. "Obviously."

"Obviously," the avatar agreed. "In the end he just got enough people sufficiently enthused about the whole ridiculous scheme. The final vote was over the whole Orbital. The Preservationeers saved face by getting him to agree he wouldn't clutter up any other wildernesses, even though there was no evidence to show he had any plans to do so in the first place.

"So he went ahead, planting pylons, spinning cables and producing cars to his heart's content. Lots of people helped; he had to form separate teams with a couple of airships each, and some went their own way, though they mostly worked under a general plan drawn up by Latry.

"The only interruptions came during the Idiran War and—once I'd taken over—in the Shaladian Crisis, when I had to commandeer all the spare production capacity to be ready to build ships and military stuff. Even then he kept building pylons and spinning cables using home-made machinery some of his followers had built. By the time he'd finished, six hundred years after he'd started, he'd covered almost the whole of the Breaks in pylons. And that's why it's called Pylon Country."

"That's three million square kilometers," Ziller said. He had retrieved the chart and the magnifying glass and gone back to studying one through the other.

"Near enough," the avatar said, uncrossing then recrossing its legs.

"I counted the number of pylons once and totted up the kilometrage of cable."

"And?" Kabe asked.

The avatar shook its head. "They were both very big numbers, but otherwise uninteresting. I could search them out for you if you wanted, but . . ."

"Please," Kabe said. "Not on my account."

"So, did Mr. Latry die with his life's work completed?" Ziller asked. He was staring out of a side window now, and scratching his head. He held the map up and turned it one way, then the other.

"No," the avatar said. "Mr. Latry was not one of life's diers. He spent a few years traveling the cables in a car, all by himself, but eventually he grew bored with it. He did some deep space cruising then settled on an Orbital called Quyeela, sixty thousand years away from here. Hasn't been here or even inquired about the cable-car system to my knowledge for over a century. Last I heard he was trying to persuade a pack of GSVs to take part in a scheme to induce patterns of sunspots on his local star so they'd spell out names and mottoes."

"Well," Ziller said, staring at the chart again. "They say a man should have a hobby."

"At the moment yours seems to be keeping about two million kilometers between you and our Major Quilan," the avatar observed.

Ziller looked up. "Heavens. Are we really that far from home?"

"Pretty much."

"And how is our emissary? Is he enjoying himself? Has he settled in to his billet? Has he sent any souvenir cards back home yet?"

It was six days after Quilan had arrived on the *Resistance Is Character-Forming*. The Major had liked his quarters in Yorle City, on the Plate of the same name, well enough. Yorle was two Plates, two continents away from Aquime City, where Ziller lived. The Major had visited Aquime a couple of times since, once accompanied by Kabe, once alone. On each occasion he had announced his intention and asked Hub to tell Ziller what he was doing. Ziller wasn't spending much time at home anyway; he was visiting parts of the Orbital he hadn't seen before, or, as today, places he'd been to before and been taken with.

"He has settled in very well," Hub said through the avatar. "Shall I tell him you were asking after him?"

"Better not. We don't want him getting too excited." Ziller gazed through the side windows as the swaying car tipped in a gust of wind and then, still creaking and rattling, picked up speed along the monofil cable. "Surprised you're not with him, Kabe," Ziller said, glancing at the Homomdan. "I thought the idea was you had to hold his hand while he's here."

"The Major hopes that I might be able to persuade you to grant him an audience," Kabe said. "Obviously I can't do much persuading if I never leave his side."

Ziller inspected Kabe over the top of the chart. "Tell me, Kabe, is that him trying to be disarmingly honest through you, or just your usual naïveté?"

Kabe laughed. "A little of each, I think."

Ziller shook his head. He tapped at the chart with the magnifying glass. "What do all these cable lines cross-hatched in pink and red mean?" he asked.

"The pink lines have been judged unsafe," the avatar said. "The red ones are the stretches that have fallen down."

Ziller held up the chart toward the avatar. He indicated one area the size of his hand. "You mean you can't use these bits at all?"

"Not in a cable car," the avatar agreed.

"You just let them fall down?" Ziller said, staring at the chart again and sounding, Kabe thought, distinctly peeved.

The avatar shrugged. "Like I said; they weren't my responsibility in the first place. Nothing to do with me whether they stand or fall, unless I choose to adopt them as part of my infrastructure. And given that hardly anybody uses them these days, I'm not about to. Anyway, I kind of enjoy their gradual entropic decay."

"I thought you people built to last," Kabe said.

"Oh," said the avatar brightly, "if I'd built the pylons I'd have anchored them into the base material. That's the main reason the lines have collapsed or are unsafe; the pylons have been washed away in floods. They weren't founded on the substrate, just the geo-layer, and not very far into that. A big flood comes along after a super-cyclone and—whumf—a bunch of them fall down. Plus the monofil's so strong it can drag whole lines down once the first one or two pylons get washed into the flood streams; they didn't put enough safety breaks into the cables. There have been four big storms since the system was finished. I'm surprised more of it hasn't been compromised."

"Still, it does seem a shame to let it all fall into such disrepair," Kabe said.

The avatar looked up at him. "You really think so? I thought there was something rather romantic about it crumbling slowly away. For a work of such self-referential artifice to be attritionally sculpted by what passes for the forces of nature around here seemed appropriate to me."

Kabe thought about this.

Ziller was studying the chart again. "What about these lines hatched in blue?" he asked.

"Oh," said the avatar, "those just might be unsafe."

Ziller's face took on an expression of consternation. He held up the chart. "But we're *on* a blue line!"

"Yes," the avatar said, looking up through the glass panels in the center of the rustic painting, where the car's guide and steering wheels could be seen sliding along the cable. "Hmm," it said.

Ziller put the chart down, crumpling it. "Hub," he said. "Are we in any danger?"

"No, not really. There are safety systems. Plus if there was a failure and we fell off the wire I could zap down an AG platform before we'd fallen more than a few meters. So as long as I'm all right, we all are."

Ziller looked suspiciously at the silver-skinned creature lying on the couch, then returned to his chart.

"Have we settled on a venue for the first performance of my symphony yet?" he asked, not looking up.

"I thought the Stullien Bowl, on Guerno," the avatar said.

Ziller looked up. Kabe thought he looked both surprised and pleased. "Really?"

"I think I have little choice," the avatar said. "Been a lot of interest. Need a maximum-capacity venue."

Ziller smiled broadly, and looked to be about to say something, then he smiled, almost bashfully, Kabe thought, and buried his head in the chart again.

"Oh, Ziller," the avatar said. "Major Quilan has asked me to ask you if you'd mind him moving to Aquime City."

Ziller put the chart down. "What?" he hissed.

"Yorle is very nice but it's quite different from Aquime," the avatar said. "It's warm, even at this time of year. He wants to experience the same conditions you do up there on the massif."

"Send him to the top of a Bulkhead Range," Ziller muttered, taking up the magnifying glass again.

"Would it concern you?" the avatar asked. "You're hardly there these days anyway."

"It's still where I prefer to lay my head most nights," Ziller said. "So, yes, it would concern me."

"Then I should tell him you'd prefer he didn't move there."

"Yes."

"Are you sure? He wasn't asking to move in next door. Just somewhere in the city center."

"Still too close for comfort."

"Hub," Kabe began.

"Hmm," the avatar said. "He said he'd be happy to let you know where he was so you wouldn't bump into—"

"Oh dear fucking god!" Ziller threw the chart down and shoved the magnifying glass into a waistcoat pocket. "Look! I don't want the guy here, I don't want him anywhere near me, I don't want to meet him and I don't like being told that even if I want to I can't get away from the son of a bitch."

"My dear Ziller," Kabe said, then stopped. I'm starting to sound like Tersono, he thought.

The avatar brought its boots down off the top of the couch and swung itself into a sitting position. "Nobody's forcing you to meet the fellow, Ziller."

"Yes, but nobody's letting me get as far away from him as I'd like, either."

"You're a long way from him now," Kabe pointed out.

"And how long did it take us to get from there to here?" Ziller asked. They had come by sub-Plate car that morning; the whole journey had taken just over an hour.

"Hmm, well . . ."

"I'm practically a prisoner!" Ziller said, spreading his arms.

The avatar's face contorted. "No, you're not," it said.

"I might as well be! I haven't been able to write a note since that bastard showed up!"

The avatar sat up, looking alarmed. "But you have finished the—?"

Ziller waved one hand exasperatedly. "It's complete. But I usually wind down with shorter pieces after something this big, and this time I haven't been able to. I feel constipated."

"Well," Kabe said, "if you might as well be forced into contact with Quilan, why not see him and get it over with?"

The avatar groaned and flopped back on the couch. It put its feet up again.

Ziller was staring at Kabe. "Is that it?" he asked. "Is that you using your powers of argument to convince me I should see this piece of shit?"

"From your tone," Kabe said, voice rumbling, "I take it you are not persuaded."

Ziller shook his head. "Persuasion. What's reasonable. Would I mind? Am I concerned? Would I be insulted? I may do as I please but then so may he." Ziller pointed angrily at the avatar. "You people are polite to the point of it becoming worse than any direct insult. All this pussy-footing, mealy-mouthed bullshit, dancing around each other after-you-no-after-you-no-after-*you!*" He waved his arms around as his voice rose to a shout. "I hate this hopeless congealment of fucking good *manners!* Can't anyone just *do* something?"

Kabe thought about saying something, then decided not to. The avatar looked mildly surprised. It blinked a few times. "Such as what?" it inquired. "Would you prefer that the major called you out and challenged you to a duel? Or moved in next door?"

"You could kick him out!"

"Why would I do that?"

"Because he's annoying me!"

The avatar smiled. "Ziller," it said.

"I feel hunted! We're a predator species; we're only used to hiding when we're stalking. We're not used to feeling like *prey.*"

"You could move home," Kabe suggested.

"He'd follow me!"

"You could keep moving."

"Why should I? I like my apartment. I like the silence and the views, I even like some of the people. There are three concert halls in Aquime with perfect acoustics. Why should I be driven from the place just because Chel sends this military bag-boy to do god-knows-what."

"What do you mean, god-knows-what?" asked the avatar.

"Maybe he isn't here just to talk me into going back with him; maybe he's here to kidnap me! Or kill me!"

"Oh, really," Kabe said.

"Kidnap's impossible," Hub said. "Unless he brought a fleet of warships I've missed." The avatar shook its head. "Murder is almost impossible." It frowned. "Attempted murder is always possible, I suppose, but, if you were worried, I could make sure that if and when you did meet there would be a few combat drones and knife missiles and that sort of thing around. And of course you could be backed-up."

"I am not," Ziller said, deliberately, "going to need combat drones and knife missiles or backing-up. Because I am not going to meet him."

"But he's obviously annoying you just by being here," Kabe said.

"Oh, does it show?" Ziller asked, snarling.

"So, assuming that he's not going to get bored and go away," Kabe went on, "you'd almost be better off agreeing to see him and getting it over with."

"Will you just stop this 'getting it over with' nonsense?" Ziller shouted.

"Talking of not being able to get away from people," the avatar said heavily, "E. H. Tersono has discovered our whereabouts and would like to drop by."

"Ha!" Ziller said, whirling around to look out of the windscreen again. "I can't get away from that damn machine either."

"It means well," Kabe said.

Ziller looked around, appearing genuinely mystified. *"So?"*

Kabe sighed. "Is Tersono nearby?" he asked the avatar.

It nodded. "It's already on its way here. About ten minutes away. Flying in from the nearest tunnel port."

More than just the terrain made the Breaks wasteland; there were only a few sub-Plate access points and they were all on the outskirts of the area, so to get deep into the barrens at more than walking-trail pace you either had to use the cable-car system, or fly.

"What does it want?" Ziller checked the wind gauge, then loosened two ropes and tightened another, to no appreciable effect.

"Social visit, it says," the avatar told him.

Ziller tapped a gimbaled horizontal dial. "You sure this compass works?"

"Are you accusing me of not having a viable magnetic field?" the Hub asked.

"I was asking you if this thing works." Ziller tapped the instrument again.

"Should do," the avatar said, putting its clasped hands behind its head again. "Very inefficient way of determining your heading, though."

"I want to head into the wind on the next turn," Ziller said, looking ahead to the hill they were approaching and the stubby pylon at its scrubby summit.

"You'll need to start the propeller."

"Oh," Kabe said. "They have propellers?"

"Big two-bladed thing stowed at the back," the avatar said, nodding to the rear, where two curved windows cupped a broad paneled section. "Battery-powered. Should be charged up if the generator vanes are working."

"How do I determine that?" Ziller asked. He pulled his pipe from a waistcoat pocket.

"See the big dial on the right just under the windscreen with a lightning flash symbol?"

"Ah, yes."

"Is the needle in the brown-black section or the bright blue section?"

Ziller peered. He stuck his pipe in his mouth. "There is no needle."

The avatar looked thoughtful. "That could be a bad sign." It sat up and looked about. The pylon was about fifty meters away; the ground was rising underneath them. "I'd ease off on that mizzen sheet."

"The what?"

"Slacken the third rope from the left."

"Ah." Ziller loosened the rope and tied it off again. He pulled on a couple of the levers, braking the car and readying the steering wheels above. He clicked a couple of large switches and looked hopefully toward the rear of the car.

He caught the avatar's gaze. "Oh, let the fucking emissary move to Aquime," he said in an exasperated voice. "See if I care. Just keep us apart."

"Certainly," the avatar said, grinning. Then its expression changed. "Oh-oh," it said. It was staring straight ahead.

Kabe felt a spark of worry leap in his breast.

"What?" Ziller said. "Is Tersono here already?" Then he was thrown off his feet as, with a crashing, tearing noise, the cable car decelerated rapidly and came to a shuddering, swaying stop. The avatar had slid along the couch. Kabe had been thrown forward, only stopping himself from falling on his face by putting out one arm and bracing himself on the brass rail separating the passenger compartment from the crew's area. The brass rail bent and came away from the bulkhead on one side with a creak and a bang. Ziller ended up sitting on the floor between two of the instrument binnacles. The car rocked to and fro.

Ziller spat out a piece of his pipe. "What the fuck was that?"

"I think we snagged a tree," the avatar said, sitting upright. "Everybody all right?"

"Fine," said Kabe. "Sorry about this rail."

"I've bitten my pipe in half!" Ziller said. He picked one half of his severed pipe up from the floor.

"It'll repair," the avatar said. It pulled back the carpet between the couches and lifted open a wooden door. Wind gusted in. The creature lay on the floor and stuck its head out. "Yes, it's a tree," it shouted. It levered itself back inside. "Must have grown a bit since the last time anybody used this line."

Ziller was picking himself up. "Of course it wouldn't have happened if you'd been responsible for the system, would it?"

"Of course not," the avatar said breezily. "Shall I send a repair drone or shall we try and fix it ourselves?"

"I have a better idea," Ziller said, smiling as he looked out of a side window. Kabe looked too, and saw a mainly rose-colored object flying through the air toward them. Ziller slid open a window on that side and turned to his two companions with a smile before hailing the approaching drone. "Tersono! Good to see you! Glad you're here! See that mess down below?"

10

The Seastacks of Youmier

And was Tersono equal to the task?"

"More than equal physically, Hub tells me, despite its protestations that it risked tearing itself apart. However I think protestations that whatever empowers its will is also charged with maintaining its dignity and so is normally pretty much fully occupied with that."

"But was it able to free your car from the tree?"

"Yes, finally, though it took its time and it made a terrible mess of things. It shredded the car's mainsail, broke the mast and cut away half the tree."

"And what of Ziller's pipe?"

"Bitten in half. Hub repaired it for him."

"Ah. I was wondering if I might have made him a present of a replacement."

"I'm not sure he'd take it in the spirit it was meant, Quil. Especially as it's something he would be putting in his mouth."

"You suspect he might think I was trying to poison him?"

"It might occur to him."

"I see. I still have a way to go, don't I?"

"Yes, you do."

"And how much further do we have to go here, on our walk?"

"Another three or four kilometers." Kabe looked up at the sun. "We should be there nicely in time for lunch."

Kabe and Quilan were walking along the cliff tops of the Vilster Peninsula on Fzan Plate. To their right, thirty meters below, Fzan Ocean beat against the rocks. The haze horizon swam with scattered islands. Closer in, a few sailboats and larger craft cut through the spreading patterns of the waves.

A cool wind came off the sea. It whipped Kabe's coat about his legs and Quilan's robes snapped and fluttered about him as he led the way along the narrow path through the tall grass. To their left the ground sloped away to deep grassland and then a forest of tall cloudtrees. Ahead, the land rose to a modest headland and a ridge heading inland notched with a cleft for one branch of the path they were on. They were taking the more strenuous and exposed route along the cliff top.

Quilan turned his head to look down toward the waves falling against tumbled rocks at the cliff's base. The smell of brine was the same here.

~ *Remembering again, Quil?*

~ Yes.

~ *You're close to the edge. Mind you don't fall.*

~ I will.

Snow was falling in the courtyard of the monastery of Cadracet, sinking gently from a silent gray sky. Quilan had brought up the rear of the firewood foraging detail, preferring to walk in solitude and silence as the others trudged up the trail ahead. The other monks had all gone inside to the warmth of the great hall's hearth by the time he closed the postern door behind him, scuffed through the light covering of snow on the courtyard's stones and dumped his basket of wood with the rest under the gallery.

He dallied a moment, soaking up the fresh, clean smell of the wood—he remembered a time when they'd taken a hunting cabin in the Loustrian Hills, just the two of them. The axe that came with the cabin was blunt; he'd sharpened it with a stone, hoping to impress her with his handiness, but then when he'd come to swing it at the first piece of wood the head had sailed off and disappeared into the trees. He could still exactly recall her laughter, and then, when he must have looked hurt, her kiss.

They had slept under furs on a platform of moss. He remembered one cold morning when the fire had gone out overnight and it was freezingly cold in the cabin and they had coupled, him straddling her, his teeth nipped gently in the fur at the nape of her neck, moving slowly over and in her, watching the smoke of her breath as it billowed in the sunlight and rolled out across the room to the window, where it froze in curving, recursive motifs; a coalescence of pattern out of chaos.

He shivered, blinking away cold tears.

When he turned away he saw the figure standing in the center of the courtyard, looking at him.

It was a female, dressed in a cloak falling half-open over an Army uniform. The snow fell between them in soundless spirals. He blinked. Just for an instant . . . He shook his head, brushed his hands together and walked out to her, putting up the hood of his griefling robe.

He realized as he made those few steps that he hadn't even seen a female in the flesh for half a year.

She did not look like Worosei at all; she was taller, her fur was darker and her eyes looked more narrowed and wizened. He guessed she was ten or so years older than him. The pips on her cap identified her as a colonel.

"Can I help you, ma'am?" he asked.

"Yes, Major Quilan," she said in a precise, controlled voice. "Perhaps you can."

Fronipel brought them both goblets of mulled wine. His office was about twice the size of Quilan's cell, and cluttered with papers, screens and the ancient fraying string frames which were the holy books of the order. There was just enough room for the three of them to sit.

Colonel Ghejaline warmed her hands around the goblet. Her cap lay on the desk at her side, her cloak across the seat back. They had exchanged a few pleasantries about her journey up the old road by mount and her role during the war in charge of a space artillery section.

Fronipel settled himself slowly into his second-best curl-chair—the best had been given to the Colonel—and said, "I asked Colonel Ghejaline to come here, Major. She is familiar with your background and history. I believe she has a proposal for you."

The Colonel looked as though she would have been happy to have spent rather more time approaching the reason for her visit, but gave a shrug of good grace and said, "Yes, Major. There is something you might be able to do for us."

Quilan looked at Fronipel, who was smiling at him. "Who would the 'us' here be, Colonel?" he asked her. "The Army?"

The Colonel frowned. "Not really. The Army is involved, but this would not strictly speaking be a military assignment. It would be more like the one you and your wife undertook on Aorme, though even further afield and on a quite different level of security and importance. The 'us' I refer to would be all Chelgrians, but especially those whose souls are currently held in limbo."

Quilan sat back in his seat. "And what would I be expected to do?"

"I can't tell you exactly yet. I am here to find out if you will even consider undertaking the mission."

"But if I don't know what it is . . ."

"Major Quilan," the Colonel said, taking a small sip of her steaming wine and then—after a minimal nod to Fronipel to acknowledge the drink—putting the goblet down on the desk, "I'll tell you all I can." She drew herself up a little straighter in the seat. "The task we would ask you to undertake is one that is very important indeed. That is almost all I know about that aspect of it. I do know a little more but I'm not allowed to talk about it. The mission would require that you undergo a considerable amount of training. Again, I can't say much more about that. The clearance for the mission comes from the top of our society." She took a breath. "And the reason that it doesn't matter too much at this stage exactly what it is you are being asked to do is that in one sense what's being asked of you is as bad as it gets." She looked into his eyes. "This is a suicide mission, Major Quilan."

He had forgotten the sheer pleasure of staring into a female's eyes, even if she was not Worosei, and even if that pleasure, like some emotional internalization of physical law, created an equal and opposite feeling of grief and loss and even guilt. He gave a small, sad smile. "Oh, in that case, Colonel," he said, "I'll definitely do it."

"Quil?"

"Hmm?" He turned to face the tall, triangular bulk of the Homomdan, who had bumped into him.

"Are you all right? You stopped very suddenly there. Did you see something?"

"Nothing. No, I'm fine. I just . . . I'm fine. Come on. I'm hungry."

They walked on.

~ I just recalled. The Lady Colonel told me this is a one-way mission.

~ *Ah, yes, there is that.*

~ It is all coming back, isn't it?

~ *Unlike us, yes. That's the way they've arranged it. That's what we both agreed to. It seems to have worked so far.*

~ You knew, too, then.

~ *Yes. That was part of Visquile's briefing.*

~ Which is why they kept you backed-up in that substrate.

~ *Which is why they kept me backed-up in that substrate.*

~ Well. I can't wait for the next installment.

He reached the summit of the cliff path and saw the town; a scimitar of white towers and spires lying cradled in a bowl of wooded valley bordered by rising chalk cliffs, its bay protected from the sea by a spit of sand. Waves beat whitely on the strand. The Homomdan joined him, standing massively at his side and all but blocking out the wind. There was a hint of rain in the air.

• • •

The following day she left her mount in the monastery stables with her uniform. She dressed in the waistcoat and leggings of a Handed; he was to impersonate a Crafted, so wore trousers and an apron. They both put on nondescript gray winter cloaks. He said goodbye to Fronipel but to nobody else.

They waited until all the work parties had left before leaving the monastery, then they walked down the lower path through the falling snow and the bare husks of spall trees, past the distant wood-gatherers—their songs heard through the quietly falling snow, as though they were the voices of ghosts—down through a level of wispy cloud where the Colonel's gray cloak seemed almost to disappear at times and then through the drumming rain beneath and the dripping forest of dark leaves that descended toward the valley floor, where they turned and followed the deeply shaded track above the river rushing whitely in the chasm below.

The rain slackened and ceased.

A group of Tallier caste hunters in an old All-Terrain on their way back from the forests after stalking jhehj offered them a lift, but they refused politely. The trailer behind the All-Terrain was piled with the carcasses of the animals. It bounced down the track into the gloom with its cargo of the dead, so that from then on they followed a line of fresh blood-spots.

Finally, in the foothills of the Grey Mountains, toward sunset, they came out onto the Girdling turnpike, where cars and trucks and buses hummed past, trailing spray. A large car was waiting for them by the roadside. A young male who looked uncomfortable in civilian clothes opened the door for them and completed three-quarters of a salute to the Colonel before remembering. The vehicle's interior was warm and dry; they took off their cloaks. The car swung out onto the road and set off down the route toward the plains.

The Colonel plugged into a military com set in a briefcase on the rear seat and left him to his own thoughts as she sat with eyes closed, communicating. He watched the traffic; the outskirts of the city of Ubrent sparkled out of the gloom. It looked in better repair than the last time he'd seen it.

Within an hour they had reached the airport, and a sleek black sub-orbiter sitting on the mist-curdled runway. He was about to reach out and touch the Colonel to let her know they'd arrived when she opened her eyes, slipped the induction coil from the back of her head and nodded at the aircraft as though to say, "We're here."

The acceleration pressed him firmly back into the frame-seat. He saw the lights of the coastal cities of Sherjame, the mid-ocean islands of Delleun and the small sparks of oceanic ships. Above, the stars became bright and steady and looked very close in the ghostly silence of near-vacuum flight.

The sub-orbiter plunged back into the atmosphere in a gathering roar. There were a few lights, then a smooth touchdown and deceleration. He dozed in the closed transport which took them away from the private field.

When they transferred to a helicopter he could smell sea. They flew briefly in darkness and rain and clattered down into a great circular courtyard. He was shown to a small, comfortable room and fell promptly asleep.

In the morning, waking to a thudding, not quite regular booming noise and the distant screeches of birds, he opened the shutters to look down over a sheer gulf of air at a blue-green sea streaked with foam and breaking waves boiling around a jagged coastline fifty meters away and a hundred down. A line of cliffs vanished into the distance on either side, and immediately opposite him there was a huge double bowl cut out of the cliffs, so that the drop from the bottom of the bowl to the sea was only thirty meters or so. Clouds of seabirds wheeled in the sunlight like scraps of foam blown up from the fretful sea.

He recognized this place. He had seen it in books and on screen.

The seastacks at Youmier were part of an extensive cliff system on Mainland, one of the Tail-Quiff Islands which lay in a long curved line to the east of Meiorin. The cliffs dropped between two and three hundred meters into the ocean and the seventeen seastacks—

the remains of great arches that the ocean's swells and waves had first created and then destroyed—rose like the fingers of two drowning people.

Local legend had once held that they were the fingers of a pair of drowning lovers who'd thrown themselves from the cliffs rather than be forced to marry others.

The stacks were named as though they were fingers, and the last and smallest of them, which was only forty meters above the waves, was called the Thumb. The others ranged between one and two hundred meters in height and were about the same circumference where the sea washed incessantly around their bases, tapering slightly to their basalt summits.

Building had begun upon them four thousand years earlier, when the area's ruling family had constructed a single small stone castle on the stack nearest the cliff top and linked the two by a wooden bridge. As the family's power had grown, so had the castle, until work was started on another stack, and then another and another.

The fortress complex spread across the various rocky pinnacles, linked by a succession of bridges—at first wood, later stone, then later still iron and steel—and became a center of government, a place of worship and pilgrimage and a seat of learning. Over the centuries and millennia every stack except the Thumb had been permanently settled in some form or another, and it had even been a fortress for a while, equipped with heavy naval guns for a century or so. Gradually the seastacks had grown to become a city with its greatest part ashore, spreading out over the heathland behind the cliffs.

It had duly suffered the same fate as a handful of cities around the globe during the Last Unification War fifteen hundred years earlier, falling to a scatter of nuclear warheads which demolished one stack completely, halved the height of another, and had left a crater shaped like a giant 8 scooped out of the cliffs where most of the mainland districts had been.

The city was never rebuilt. The seastacks, cut off from the mainland by the twin craters, were derelict for centuries, a place for ghoulish tourism and home only to a few hermits and a million sea birds. Two of the stacks became a monastery during one of Chel's more religious phases, then the Combined Services had commandeered all of them as a training base and rebuilt almost everything save for the bridges to the mainland before moving off-world before the whole complex was finished and leaving the Stacks mothballed with only a caretaker staff behind.

Now it was his home.

Quilan leaned on a parapet and looked down to the white ruff of surf washing the Male's Middle Finger's base, three hundred meters below. The water looked slow from up here, he thought. As though each wave was tired from its long journey across the ocean, from wherever waves were born.

He had been here for a two-moon month. They were training him and assessing him. He still knew no more about the task beyond the fact that it was supposed to be a suicide mission. It was still not certain that he would be going on it. He knew that he was one of several contenders for the dubious honor. He had already agreed that if he was not chosen he would submit to a memory wipe which would leave him, apparently, just another war-traumatized monk in Cadracet Retreat struggling to come to terms with his experiences.

Colonel Ghejaline was present about half the time, overseeing his training. His principal instructor in the arts and crafts of most things martial was a scarred, stocky and taciturn male called Wholom. He seemed obviously Army or ex-Army, but would admit to no rank. Quilan's other tutor was called Chuelfier; a frail, white-furred old male whose years and infirmity seemed to drop away from him when he was teaching.

There were a few Army specialists he saw every few days who obviously also lived in the complex, a handful of servants of various castes and a number of Blinded Invisibles who had remained faithful to the old ways through the Caste War.

Quilan watched the Blinded go about their duties, their upper faces covered by the green band of their rank, feeling their way with an easy familiarity or using the high-pitched clicks they made with their claws to navigate their way amongst the concrete and rock-carved spaces of the stack. To be Blinded here, with the drop to the rocks and the ocean, was, he thought, to put your faith forever in walls and thoughtful design.

He was not allowed off this stack. He strongly suspected that some of his unseen comrade-adversaries—the others who might be chosen to go on the mission rather than him—were on some of the other stacks, across the long, locked bridges the Combined Services had thrown between the rocky columns.

He held up one arm and studied his unsheathed claws. He turned his arm left and right. He had never been so muscled, so fit. He wondered if he really needed to be at such a physical peak for this mission, or whether the Army—or whoever was really behind this—just trained you up like this as a matter of course.

A large circular parade ground was located high up on the seaward side of the stack. It was open at the sides but roofed by white awnings like old-fashioned ship sails. There they had taught him fencing, trained him with a crossbow and with projectile weapons and early laser rifles. They inculcated in him the finer and less fine points of fighting with knives, and with teeth and claws. The point had been made that close-in fighting would differ when you tackled species other than your own, but it had been left at that.

A small team of medics flew in one day and took him to a big but obviously rarely used hospital hollowed out of the rock deep beneath the stack's buildings. They equipped him with an improved Soulkeeper, but that was the only implant they touched or introduced. He had heard of agents and people on special missions being fitted with brain-linked communications rigs, poison-detection nasal glands, poison-producing sacs, subcutaneous weapon systems . . . the list was long but he, apparently, was going to receive none of these. He wondered why.

At one point there was a hint that whoever undertook the mission might not be entirely alone. He wondered about that, too.

Not all his training and education was martial; at least half of each waking day was spent being a student again, sitting in a curl-chair learning through screens or listening to Chuelfier.

The old male instructed him in Chelgrian history, in religious phi-

losophy both before and after the partial Sublimation of the
Chelgrian-Puen, and in the discovered history of the rest of the
galaxy and its other sentient beings.

He learned more than he'd ever imagined wanting or needing to
know of what Soulkeepers did and how they did it, and what limbo
and heaven were like. He learned where the old religion had been
overly fanciful or just plain wrong in its assumptions and tenets,
where it had inspired the Chelgrian-Puen and so been made real,
and where it had been superseded. He had no direct contact with any
of the gone-before, but he came to understand the afterlife better
than he ever had before. Sometimes, knowing that it was almost
beyond doubt that Worosei would never experience anything of this
created glory, he felt that they had chosen him only to torture him,
that all of this was an elaborate and cruel charade to find the knife of
Worosei's loss that was forever buried in his flesh and twist it with all
their might.

He learned all there was to know about the Caste War and the
Culture's involvement in the changes that had led to it.

He learned about the personalities who had contributed to the
War's background, and listened to some of the music of Mahrai
Ziller, at turns so achingly full of loss he cried, at others so full of
anger he wanted to smash something.

A number of suspicions and possible scenarios began to form in his
mind, though he kept them to himself.

Sometimes now he dreamt of Worosei. In one dream they were
being married here on the seastack, and a great wind off the sea
whipped people's hats away; he went to grab hers as it flew toward
the parapet and then crashed into the whitewashed concrete, tipping over it with her hat still just out of reach. He started to fall
toward the sea, and felt himself gather in the breath for a scream,
then recalled that of course Worosei wasn't really here, and could
not be here; she was dead, and he might as well be. He smiled at the
waves as they rushed up to meet him, and woke before he hit with
a feeling of somehow having been cheated, the salty dampness on
his pillow like sea.

• • •

One morning he was walking across the parade ground beneath the snapping white tents of the awnings, heading toward Chuelfier's class room for the first lecture of the day, when he saw a small group of people directly ahead. Colonel Ghejaline, Wholom and Chuelfier were standing talking to the white-and black-clothed figure in the middle of the group.

There were five others, three on the right of the central group, two on the left. All were males dressed as clerks. The male in the middle was small and old-looking, with a sort of sideways hunch to his stance. It was something of a shock for Quilan to realize that the male was dressed in the black and white striped robe of an Estodien, one of those who went between this world and the next. He wore a lop-sided smile and held onto a long mirror staff. His fur looked slick, as though it had been oiled.

Quilan was about to greet the Colonel, but as he approached the three people he knew dropped back to let the Estodien take a couple of small steps forward.

"Estodien," Quilan said, bowing deeply.

"Major Quilan," the old male said in a soft, smooth voice. He reached his hand out to Quilan, who had become aware that the male standing on the extreme right of the group bulked out his clerical robes differently to the rest, and that this same male had started moving around to the side, as if starting to circle behind him. When the male disappeared from his view, the semi-shadow he cast by the attenuated light coming through the white awnings suddenly moved faster.

What finally made Quilan certain he might be about to be attacked was something about the way that the old Estodien stretched when he reached out his hand. He was frail, and could not help but keep his distance from something that might prove violent.

Quilan made as though to take the older male's hand, then ducked and spun, went back on his haunches and brought his midlimb and hands out in the classic pounce-defense stance.

The bulky-looking male dressed as a clerk had been about to strike; he had rocked back on his haunches and his sleeves were rolled back to reveal tightly muscled arms, though his claws were only half exposed. There was a radiant, almost feral look on his white-furred face that lasted for a moment and even brightened for an instant as Quilan turned to confront him but then he glanced at the Estodien and relaxed, sitting back and lowering his arms and his head in what might have been a bow.

Quilan stayed exactly as he was, his head turning slightly to and fro, his gaze flicking as far behind him as he could manage without losing sight of the white-furred male. There did not appear to be any other movement or threat.

There was a frozen moment when nothing happened, save for the distant calls of the sea birds, the far-away thudding of the waves. Then the Estodien clicked his staff on the parade ground's concrete once, and the white-furred male rose and turned in one fluid movement and went to stand where he had before.

"Major Quilan," the old male said again. "Please, stand." He held out his hand once more. "No more unpleasant surprises, at least not for today, I give you my word."

Quilan took the Estodien's hand and rose from his crouch.

Colonel Ghejaline came forward. She looked pleased, Quilan thought. "Major Quilan, this is Estodien Visquile."

"Sir," Quilan said as the older male released his hand.

"And this is Eweirl," Visquile said, indicating the white-furred male to his left. The bulky-looking male nodded and smiled. "I hope you have the wit to realize you passed two little tests there, Major, not one."

"Yes, sir. Or the same one, twice, sir."

Visquile's smile broadened, revealing small, sharp teeth. "You don't really have to call me 'sir,' Major, though I confess I rather like it." He turned to Wholom and Chuelfier, and then to Colonel Ghejaline. "Not bad." He looked back to Quilan, looking him down then up. "Come along, Major, we'll have a talk, I think."

"We are told it is very unusual for them to make such a mistake. We are told that we should feel flattered they took such an interest in us in the first place. We are told that they respect us. We are told that it is an accident of development and the evolution of galaxies, stars, planets and species that we meet them on less than equal technological terms. We are told that what happened is unfortunate but that we may eventually gain from it. We are told they are honorable people who only wished to help and now feel that they are in our debt because of their carelessness. We are told that we may profit more through their crushing guilt than we might have gained thanks to their easy patronage." The Estodien Visquile smiled his thin, sharp smile. "None of this matters."

The Estodien and Quilan sat alone in a small tower perched out over the side of one of the stack's lowest levels of superstructure. Air and sea showed on three sides and the warm wind blew in through one glassless window and out another, laden with the scent of brine. They sat curled on grass mats.

"What matters," the old male went on, "is what the Chelgrian-Puen have decided."

There was a pause. Quilan suspected he was supposed to fill it, and so said, "And what would that be, Estodien?"

The old male's fur had the odor of expensive perfume. He sat up and back on his mat, looking out of a window toward the long swells of the sea. "It has been a consistent article of our faith for twenty-seven hundred years," he said casually, "that the souls of the departed are held in limbo for a full year before being accepted into the glory of heaven. That has not changed since we—our gone-before—made heaven real. Nor have many of the other doctrines associated with such matters. They have become rules, in a sense." He turned and smiled again at Quilan before looking away through the window once more.

"What I'm about to tell you is known to very few people, Major Quilan. It must stay that way, do you understand?"

"Yes, Estodien."

"Colonel Ghejaline does not know, and nor do any of your tutors."

"I understand."

The old male turned to him suddenly. "Why do you want to die, Quilan?"

He rocked back, thrown. "I—in a way I don't, Estodien. I just don't particularly want to live. I want to be no more."

"You want to die because your mate is dead and you are pining for her, is that not the truth?"

"I would put it a little stronger than pining for her, Estodien. But it was her death that took the meaning out of my life."

"The lives of your family and your society in this time of need and restructuring; these mean nothing to you?"

"Not nothing, Estodien. But not enough, either. I wish that I could feel otherwise, but I cannot. It is as though all the people I care about but feel I ought to care about more are already in another world from the one I inhabit."

"She was just a female, Quilan, just a person, just one individual. What makes her so special that her memory—forever irretrievable, apparently—outranks the more pressing needs of those still alive for whom something can still be done?"

"Nothing, Estodien. It is—"

"Nothing indeed. It is not her memory; it is yours. It is not her specialness or uniqueness that you celebrate, Quilan, but your own. You are a romantic, Quilan. You find the idea of tragic death romantic, you find the idea of joining her—even if it is joining her in oblivion—romantic." The old male drew himself up as though getting ready to go. "I hate romantics, Quilan. They do not really know themselves, but what is worse they do not really want to know themselves—or, ultimately, anybody else—because they think that will take the mystery out of life. They are fools. You are a fool. Probably your wife was a fool, too." He paused. "Probably you were both romantic fools," he said. "Fools who were doomed to a life of disillusionment and bitterness when you discovered that your precious romanticism faded away after the first few years of marriage and you were left to confront not just your own inadequacies but those of your mate. You were lucky she died. She was unlucky it was her and not you."

Quilan looked at the Estodien for a few moments. The old male was breathing a little deeper and harder than should have been necessary, but otherwise he was controlling any fear he felt very well. He would be thoroughly backed-up, and as an Estodien he would be reborn or reincarnated as and when he wished. That, however, would not prevent the animal self from contemplating being bundled through a window and falling to the sea with anything other than terror. Of course this assumed the old male wasn't wearing some sort of AG harness, in which case he might simply be afraid of Quilan ripping his throat out before Eweirl or anybody else could do anything about it.

"Estodien," Quilan said evenly, "I have thought of all of that and been through all of that. I have accused myself of all of these things that you mention, and in rather less temperate language than you have used. You find me at the end of the process you might have wished to initiate with such assertions, not the start."

The Estodien looked at him. "Quite good," he said. "Speak more honestly, more fully."

"I am not to be riled into violence by someone who never knew her calling my wife a fool. I know she was not, which is enough. And I think you just wanted to find out how easy I might be to anger."

"Perhaps not easy enough, Quilan," the old male said. "Not all tests are passed or failed as one might expect."

"I am not trying to pass your tests, Estodien. I am trying to be honest. I assume your tests are good ones. If they are and I do my best and fail while somebody else succeeds then that is better than me succeeding by telling you what I think you want to hear rather than what I feel."

"That is calm to the point of smugness, Quilan. Perhaps this mission requires somebody with more aggression and cunning than that reply indicates you to be in possession of."

"Perhaps it does, Estodien."

The old male kept his gaze locked on Quilan for some time. Eventually he looked away out of the window again. "The war dead will not be allowed into heaven, Quilan."

He had to listen to the comment in his head, replaying it, to be sure he had heard correctly. He blinked. "Estodien?"

"It was a war, Major, not a civilian disturbance or a natural disaster."

"The Caste War?" he asked, and immediately felt stupid.

"Yes, of course the Caste War," Visquile snapped. He composed himself again. "The Chelgrian-Puen have told us that the old rules apply."

"The old rules?" He thought he already knew what was meant.

"They must be avenged."

"A soul for a soul?" This was the stuff of barbarism, of the old cruel gods. The death of each Chelgrian had to be balanced by the death of an enemy, and until that balance had been achieved the fallen warriors were held from heaven.

"Why ought one to leap to the idea of a one-to-one correspondence?" the Estodien asked, with a cold smile. "Perhaps one death would be all that might be required. One important death." He looked away again.

Quilan was silent for a while, and motionless. When Visquile did not look back to him from the window and the view, he said, "One death?"

The Estodien fixed him with his gaze again. "One important death. Much might result from that." He looked away, humming a tune. Quilan recognized the melody; it was by Mahrai Ziller.

11

Absence of Gravitas

The point is: what happens in heaven?"

"Unknowable wonderfulness?"

"Nonsense. The answer is nothing. Nothing can happen because if something happens, in fact if something *can* happen, then it doesn't represent eternity. Our lives are about development, mutation and the possibility of change; that is almost a definition of what life is: change."

"Have you always thought that?"

"If you disable change, if you effectively stop time, if you prevent the possibility of the alteration of an individual's circumstances—and that must include at least the possibility that they alter for the worse—then you don't have life after death; you just have death."

"There are those who believe that after death the soul is recreated into another being."

"That is conservative and a little stupid, certainly, but not actually idiotic."

"And there are those who believe that, upon death, the soul is allowed to create its own universe."

"Monomaniacal and laughable as well as probably wrong."

"Then there are those who believe that the soul—"

"Well, there are all sorts of different beliefs. However, the ones that interest me are those concerning the idea of heaven. That's the idiocy it annoys me that others cannot see."

"Of course, you could just be wrong."

"Don't be ridiculous."

"In any case, even if heaven did not exist originally, people have created it. It does exist. In fact, lots of different heavens exist."

"Pa! Technology. These so-called heavens will not last. There will be war in them, or between them."

"And the Sublimed?"

"At last; something beyond heaven. And unfortunately therefore useless. But a start. Or rather an end. Or a start, again, of another sort of life, so proving my point."

"You've lost me."

"We're all lost. We are found dead."

". . . Are you really a professor of divinity?"

"Of course I am! You mean it isn't obvious?"

"Mr. Ziller! You met the other Chelgrian yet?"

"I'm sorry, have we met?"

"Yeah, that's what I'm asking."

"No, I meant have you and I met?"

"Trelsen Scofford. We met at the Gidhoutan's."

"Did we?"

"You said what I said about your stuff was 'singular' and 'uniquely viewpointed.' "

"I think I hear myself in there somewhere."

"Great! So, you met this guy yet?"

"No."

"No? But he's been here twenty days! Someone said he only lives—"

"Are you really as ignorant as you appear, Trelsen, or is this some sort of bizarre act, perhaps even meant to be amusing?"

"Sorry?"

"You should be. If you paid more than the most passing—"

"I just heard there was another Chelgrian—"

"—attention to what's going on you'd know that the 'other Chelgrian' is a feudal tough, a professional bully come to attempt to persuade me to go back with him to a society I despise. I have no intention of meeting the wretch."

"Oh. I didn't realize."

"Then you're simply ignorant rather than malevolent. Congratulations."

"So you're not going to meet him at all?"

"That's right; not at all. My plan is that after keeping him waiting for a few years he'll either get fed up and slope home to be ritually chastised or he'll gradually become seduced by Masaq' and its many attractions in particular and by the Culture and all its wonderful manifestations in general, and become a citizen. Then I might meet him. Brilliant strategy, don't you think?"

"You serious?"

"I'm always serious, never more so than when I'm being flippant."

"Think it'll work?"

"I neither know nor care. It's just amusing to contemplate, that's all."

"So why do they want you to go back?"

"Apparently I'm the true Emperor. I was a foundling swapped at birth by a jealous godmother for my long-lost evil twin, Fimmit."

"What? Really?"

"No, of course not really. He's here to deliver a summons for a minor traffic violation."

"You're kidding!"

"Drat, you guessed. No, the thing is I have this secretion that comes from my anterior glands; every Chelgrian clan has one or two males in each generation who produce this substance. Without it the males of my clan can't pass solids. If they don't lick the appropriate spot at least once per tidal month they start to experience terrible wind. Unfortunately my cousin Kehenahanaha Junior the Third recently suffered a bizarre grooming accident which left him unable to produce the vital secretion, so they need me back there before all

the males in my family explode from compressed shit. There is a sur-
gical alternative, of course, but sadly the medical patent rights are
held by a clan we haven't acknowledged for three centuries. Dispute
over a mistimed bid caused by an involuntary eructation during a
bride-bidding auction, apparently. We don't like to discuss it."

"You . . . you're not serious?"

"I really can't get a thing past you, can I? No, it's really about an
unreturned library book."

"You really are just kidding me now, aren't you?"

"Yet again you've seen right through me. It's almost as though I
needn't be here."

"So you really don't know why they want you back?"

"Well, what reason could there possibly be?"

"Don't ask me!"

"That's just what I was thinking!"

"Hey; why not just ask?"

"Better still, as it's you who seems to care, why don't you ask the
one you charmingly call the Other Chelgrian to tell you why they
want me back?"

"No, I meant ask Hub."

"Well, it does know everything, after all. Look, there's its avatar
over there!"

"Hey, right! Let's . . . Oh. Ah, see you, then, ah . . . Oh, hi. You
must be the Homomdan."

"Well spotted."

"So, what does this woman actually do?"

"She listens to me."

"She listens? Is that it?"

"Yes. I talk and she listens to what I say."

"Well? So? I mean, I'm listening to you now. What does this
woman do that's so special?"

"Well, she listens without asking the sort of question you've just
asked, frankly."

"What do you mean? I was just asking—"

"Yes, but don't you see? You're already being aggressive, you've made up your mind that somebody just listening to somebody else is—"

"But is that all she does?"

"More or less, yes. But it's very helpful."

"Haven't you got friends?"

"Of course I have friends."

"Well, isn't that what they're for?"

"No, not always, not for everything I want to talk about."

"Your house?"

"I used to talk about things with my house, but then I realized I was just talking to a machine that not even the other machines pretend to think is sentient."

"What about your family?"

"I especially do not want to share everything with my family. They figure largely in what I need to talk about."

"Really? That's terrible. You poor thing. Hub, then. It's a good listener."

"Well, I understand, but there are those of us who think that it only seems to care."

"What? It's *designed* to care."

"No, it's designed to *seem* to care. With a person you feel that you're communicating on an animal level."

"An animal level?"

"Yes."

"And that's supposed to be a good thing?"

"Yes. It's sort of instinct to instinct."

"So you don't think Hub cares?"

"It's just a machine."

"So are you."

"Only in the widest sense. I feel better talking to another human. Some of us feel that Hub controls our lives too much."

"Does it? I thought if you wanted to have nothing to do with it, you could."

"Yes, but you still live on the O, don't you?"

"So?"

"Well, it runs the Orbital, that's what I mean."

"Yeah, well, somebody's got to run it."

"Yes, but planets don't need anybody to run them. They're just sort of . . . there."

"So you want to live on a planet?"

"No. I think I'd find them a bit small and weird."

"Aren't they dangerous? don't they get hit by stuff?"

"No, planets have defense systems."

"So those need running."

"Yes, but you're missing the point—"

"I mean, you wouldn't want a *person* in charge of stuff like that, would you? That'd be scary. That would be like the old days, like barbarism or something."

"No, but the point is, wherever you live you can accept that something has to be minding the infrastructure, but it shouldn't run your life as well. That's why we feel we need to talk amongst ourselves more, not to our houses or to Hub or drones or anything like that."

"That's deeply weird. Are there a lot of people like you?"

"Well, no, not many, but I know a few."

"Do you have a group? Do you hold meetings? Have you got a name yet?"

"Well, yes and no. There have been a lot of ideas for names. There was a suggestion we call ourselves the fastidians, or the cellists, or the carboniphiles, or the rejectionists or the spokists, or the rimmers or the planetists or the wellians or the circumferlocuans or circumlocuferans, but I don't think we should adopt any of those."

"Why not?"

"Hub suggested them."

". . . Sorry."

". . . Who was that?"

"The Homomdan ambassador."

"Bit monstrous, don't you think? . . . What? *What?*"

"They have very good hearing."

• • •

"Hey! Mr. Ziller! I forgot to ask. How's the piece?"

". . . Trelsen, isn't it?"

"Yeah, of course."

"What piece?"

"You know. The music."

"Music. Oh yes. Yes, I've written quite a lot of that."

"Oh, stop joshing. So, how's it coming along?"

"Do you mean generally, or did you have a particular work in mind?"

"The new one, of course!"

"Ah yes, of course."

"So?"

"You mean at what stage of preparation is the symphony?"

"Yes, how's it coming along?"

"Fine."

"Fine?"

"Yes. It's coming along fine."

"Oh. Great! Well done. Look forward to hearing it. Great. Right."

". . . Yes, fuck off through the crowd, you cretin. Hope I didn't use too many technical terms . . . Oh, hello, Kabe. You still here? How are you, anyway?"

"I am well. And yourself?"

"Beset by idiots. Good job I'm used to it."

"Present company excepted, I hope."

"Kabe, if I suffered only one fool gladly, I assure you it would be you."

"Hmm. Well, I shall take that as I hope you meant it rather than as I suspect; hope is a more pleasing emotion to the spirit than suspicion."

"Your reservoir of graciousness astonishes me, Kabe. How was the emissary?"

"Quilan?"

"I believe that's what he answers to."

"He is resigned to a long wait."

"I heard you took him walking."

"Along the coastal path at Vilster."

"Yes. All those kilometers of path and not a single slip. Almost beggars belief, doesn't it?"

"He was a pleasant walking companion and seems a decent sort of person. A little dour, perhaps."

"Dour?"

"Reserved and quiet, quite serious, with a sort of stillness in him."

"Stillness."

"The sort of stillness there is in the center of the third movement of 'Tempest Night,' when the steel-winds fall silent and the basses hold those long, descending notes."

"Oh, a symphonic stillness. And is this mooted affinity with one of my works supposed to endear him to me?"

"That was the entirety of my purpose."

"You are a quite shameless procurer, aren't you, Kabe?"

"Am I?"

"Don't you feel even the slightest shame at doing their bidding like this?"

"Whose bidding?"

"Hub's, the Contact Section, the Culture as a whole, not to mention my own enchanting society and splendid government."

"I don't think your government is bidding me do anything."

"Kabe, you don't know what sort of help they asked for or demanded from Contact."

"Well, I—"

"Oh, grief."

"Did I hear our name mentioned? Ah, Cr. Ziller. Ar Ischloear. Dear friends, so good to see you."

"Tersono. You look positively polished."

"Thank you!"

"And a very pleasant crowd you've gathered, as ever."

"Kabe, you are one of my most important weathervanes, if I may elevate and reduce you at the same time. I rely utterly on you to tell me whether something is genuinely going well or whether people are just being polite, so I'm so glad that you feel that way."

"And Kabe is glad that you are glad. I was asking him about our Chelgrian chum."

"Ah, yes, poor Quilan."

"Poor?"

"Yes, you know; his wife."

"No, I don't know. What? Is she particularly ugly?"

"No! She's dead."

"A condition that rarely attends an improvement in looks."

"Ziller! Really! The poor fellow lost his wife in the Caste War. Didn't you know?"

"No."

"I think Ziller has been as assiduous in avoiding all knowledge of Major Quilan as I have been in accumulating it."

"And you haven't shared that knowledge with Ziller, Kabe? For shame!"

"My shame seems an especially popular subject this evening. But no, I have not. I might have been about to just before you arrived."

"Yes, it was all terribly tragic. They hadn't been married long."

"At least they can look forward to a reunion in the absurd blasphemy of our manufactured heaven."

"Apparently not. Her implant was not able to save her personality. She is gone forever."

"How very careless. And what of the Major's implants?"

"What of them, dear Ziller?"

"What are they? Have you checked him for any unusual ones? The sort of things that special agents, spies, assassins tend to have. Well? Have you checked him over for that sort of thing?"

". . . It's gone quiet. Do you think it's broken?"

"I think it's communicating elsewhere."

"Is that what those colors mean?"

"I don't think so."

"That's just gray, isn't it?"

"I think technically it's gunmetal."

"And is that magenta?"

"More violet. Though of course your eyes are different from mine."

"Ahem."

"Oh, you're back."

"Indeed. The answer is that Emissary Quilan was scanned several times on the way here. Ships don't let people aboard without inspecting them for anything that might be dangerous."

"You're certain?"

"My dear Ziller, he's been transported by what are in effect three Culture warships. Do you have any idea how nanoscopically fanatical those things can be about potential-harm hygiene?"

"What about his Soulkeeper?"

"Not scanned directly; that would imply reading his mind, which is *terribly* impolite."

"Ah-ha!"

"Ah-ha what?"

"Ziller is worried that the Major might be here to kidnap or murder him."

"That would be preposterous."

"Nevertheless."

"Ziller, my dear friend, please, if that is what is preying on your mind, have no fears. Kidnap is . . . I can't tell you how unlikely. Murder . . . No. Major Quilan has brought nothing with him more harmful than a ceremonial dagger."

"Ah! So I might be put to death ceremonially. That's different. Let's meet up tomorrow. We could go camping. Share a tent. Is he gay? We could fuck. I'm not but it's been a while, aside from Hub's dream-houris."

"Kabe, stop laughing; you ought not to encourage him. Ziller, the dagger is a dagger, no more."

"Not a knife missile, then?"

"Not a knife missile, not even in disguise or memoryform. It is simple, solid steel and silver. It's little better than a letter-opener really. I'm sure if we asked him to leave it—"

"Forget the stupid dagger! Maybe it's a virus; a disease or something."

"Hmm."

"What do you mean, 'Hmm'?"

"Well, our medicine effectively became perfect about eight thousand years ago, and we've had all that time to get used to evaluating other species rapidly to develop a full understanding of their physiology, so any ordinary disease, even a new one, is unable to establish a foothold thanks to the body's own defenses and will certainly be utterly helpless against external medical resources. However, somebody did once develop a genetic signature-keyed brain-rotting virus which worked so quickly it proved effective on more than one occasion. Five minutes after the assassin had sneezed in the same room as the intended victim their brains—and only theirs—were turning to soup."

"And?"

"So we look for that sort of thing. And Quilan is clean."

"So, there's nothing here but the pure, cellular him?"

"Apart from his Soulkeeper."

"Well, what about this Soulkeeper?"

"It's a simple Soulkeeper, as far as we can tell. Certainly it's the same size and has a similar outward appearance."

"A similar outward appearance. As far as you can *tell?*"

"Yes, it's—"

"And these people, my Homomdan friend, have established a reputation for thoroughness throughout the galaxy. Incredible."

"Was it thoroughness? I thought it was eccentricity. Well, there you are."

"Ziller, let me tell you a story."

"Oh, must you?"

"It appears I must. Somebody once thought of a way they might outwit the security of Contact."

"Serial numbers instead of ridiculous ship names?"

"No, they thought they could smuggle a bomb aboard a GCU."

"I've met one or two Contact ships. I confess the idea has occurred to me, too."

"The way they did it was to create a humanoid who appeared to have a form of bodily defect called hydrocephaly. Have you heard of such a condition?"

"Water on the brain?"

"Fluid fills the fetus' head and the brain grows smeared in a thin layer around the inside of the adult's skull. Not something you see in a developed society, but they had a plausible excuse for this individual having it."

"A milliner's mascot?"

"A prophet-savant."

"I was close."

"The point was that this individual carried a small anti-matter bomb in the center of his skull."

"Oh. Wouldn't you hear it bumping around when he shook his head?"

"Its containment vessel was tethered by atomic monofil."

"And?"

"Don't you see? They thought that by hiding it inside his skull, surrounded by his brain, it would be safe from any Culture scan, because we famously do not look inside people's heads."

"So they were right, it worked, it blew the ship to smithereens and I'm supposed to feel reassured?"

"No."

"I didn't really think so."

"They were wrong, the device was spotted and the ship sailed serenely on."

"What happened? It came loose, he sneezed and out it embarrassingly popped?"

"A standard Mind scan looks at something from hyperspace, from the fourth dimension. An impenetrable sphere looks like a circle. Locked rooms are fully accessible. You or I would look flat to them."

"Flat? Hmm. I have experienced certain critics who must have had access to hyperspace. Obviously I owe numerous apologies. Damn."

"The ship did not read the unfortunate creature's brains—it had no need to scan at such detail—but it was as obvious that he was carrying a bomb as if he'd balanced it on the top of his head."

"I have the feeling this is all just a long-winded way of telling me not to worry."

"If I have been long-winded, I apologize. I was seeking only to reassure you."

"Consider me reassured. I no longer imagine that this piece of shit is here to assassinate me."

"So you'll see him?"

"Absolutely no fucking way whatsoever."

"All Through With This Niceness And Negotiation Stuff."

"Yeah. Like it. Offensive Unit?"

"But of course."

"Had to be."

"Yeah. Your turn."

"Someone Else's Problem."

"Hmm."

" 'Hmm'? Just 'Hmm'?"

"Yeah, well. Doesn't do it for me. How about *Lacking That Small Match Temperament.*"

"Bit obscure."

"Well, I've just always liked it."

"Poke It With A Stick."

"OU?"

"GCU."

"I Said, I've Got A Big Stick."

"Sorry?"

"It's called, I Said, I've Got A Big Stick. You have to say it quietly. When you write it, it's in small type. An OU, as you might imagine."

"Oh, right."

"Probably my favorite. I think that's just the best."

"No, not as good as *Hand Me The Gun And Ask Me Again.*"

"Well, that's okay, but not as subtle."

"Well, but less derivative."

"On the other hand, *But Who's Counting?*"

"Yeah. *Germane Riposte.*"

"We Haven't Met But You're A Great Fan Of Mine."

"Oh? Yeah? What?"

"No, I just meant, isn't this fun?"

"Yes. Well, I'm glad you finally agree."

"What do you mean, finally agree?"

"I mean finally agree that the names are worth mentioning in polite company."

"What are you talking about? I was quoting you ship names for years before you started noticing."

"Let me quote you one back: *All The Same, I Saw It First.*"

"What?"

"You heard."

"Ha! Well then; *Ravished By The Sheer Implausibility Of That Last Statement.*"

"Oh, come on. You have *Zero Credibility.*"

"And you're *Charming But Irrational.*"

"While you're *Demented But Determined.*"

"And *You May Not Be The Coolest Person Here.*"

"You're making these up."

"No I'm . . . hold on, sorry; was that a ship name?"

"No, but here's one: you're talking *Lucid Nonsense.*"

"*Awkward Customer.*"

"*Thorough But . . . Unreliable.*"

"*Advanced Case Of Chronic Patheticism.*"

"*Another Fine Product From The Nonsense Factory.*"

"*Conventional Wisdom.*"

"*In One Ear.*"

"*Fine Till You Came Along.*"

"*I Blame The Parents.*"

"*Inappropriate Response.*"

"*A Momentary Lapse Of Sanity.*"

"*Lapsed Pacifist.*"

"*Reformed Nice Guy.*"

"*Pride Comes Before A Fall.*"

"*Injury Time.*"

"*Now Look What You've Made Me Do.*"

"*Kiss This Then.*"

"Look, if you two are going to fight, do it outside."

". . . Is that one?"

"Don't think so. Should be."

"Yeah."

"Hub."

"Ziller. Good evening. Are you enjoying yourself?"

"No. How about you?"

"Of course."

"Of course? Can real happiness be so . . . foregone as that? How depressing."

"Ziller, I am a Hub Mind. I have an entire—and if I may say so—quite fabulous Orbital to look after, not to mention having fifty billion people to tend to."

"Certainly I wasn't going to mention them."

"Right now I'm observing a fading supernova in a galaxy two and a half billion years away. Closer to home, a thousand years off, I'm watching a dying planet orbiting inside the atmosphere of a red giant sun as it spirals slowly down toward the core. I can also watch the results of the planet's destruction on the sun, a thousand years later, via hyperspace.

"In-system, I'm tracking millions of comets and asteroids, and directing the orbits of tens of thousands of them, some to use as raw material for Plate landscaping, some just to keep them out of the way. Next year I'm going to let a big comet come right through the Orbital, between the Rim and the Hub. That should be pretty spectacular. Several hundred thousand smaller bodies are speeding toward us right now, earmarked to provide an over-the-top light show for the first night of your new orchestral work at the end of the Twin Novae period."

"It was that—"

"At the same time, of course, I'm in simultaneous communication with hundreds of other Minds; thousands, over the course of any given day; ship Minds of every type, some approaching, some just having left, some old friends, some sharing interests and fascinations similar to my own, plus other Orbitals and university Sages, amongst others. I have eleven Roving Personality

Constructs, each one flitting over time from place to place in the greater galaxy, rooming with other Minds in the processor substrates of GSVs and smaller vessels, other Orbitals, Eccentric and Ulterior craft and with Minds of various other types; what they will be like, and how these once identical siblings might change me when they return and we consider remerging, I can only imagine and look forward to."

"It all sounds—"

"While I am at the moment hosting no other Minds, I look forward to that, as well."

"—fascinating. Now—"

"Additionally, sub-systems like manufactury process-overseeing complexes keep up a constant and fascinating dialogue. Within the hour, for example, in a shipyard in a cavern under the Buzuhn Bulkhead Range, a new Mind will be born, to be emplaced within a GCV before the year is out."

"No no; keep going."

"Meanwhile, via one of my planetary remotes I'm watching a pair of cyclonic systems collide on Naratradjan Prime and composing a glyph sequence on the effects of ultra-violent atmospheric phenomena on otherwise habitable ecospheres. Here on Masaq' I'm watching a series of avalanches in the Pilthunguon Mountains on Hildri, a tornado whirling across the Shaban Savannah on Akroum, a sworl-island calving in the Picha Sea, a forest fire in Molben, a seiche bore funnelling up Gradeens River, a firework display above Junzra City, a wooden house frame being hoisted into place in a village in Furl, a quartet of lovers on a hilltop in—"

"You've made your—"

"—Ocutti. Then there are drones and other autonomous sentients, able to communicate directly and at speed, plus the implanted humans and other biologicals also able to converse immediately. Plus of course I have millions of avatars like this one, the majority of them talking with and listening to people right now."

". . . Have you finished?"

"Yes. But even if all the other stuff seems a bit esoteric, just think of all those other avatars at all those other gatherings, concerts, dances, ceremonies, parties and meals; think of all that talk, all those ideas, all that sparkle and wit!"

"Think of all that bullshit, the nonsense and non-sequiturs, the self-aggrandisement and self-deception, the boring stupid nonsense, the pathetic attempts to impress or ingratiate, the slow-wittedness, the incomprehension and the incomprehensible, the gland-addled meanderings and general suffocating dullness."

"That is the chaff, Ziller. I ignore that. I can respond politely and where necessary felicitously to the most intense bore forever without flagging and it costs me nothing. It's like ignoring all the boring bits in space between the neat stuff like planets and stars and ships. And even that's not completely boring anyway."

"I cannot tell you how glad I am that you live such a full life, Hub."

"Thank you."

"May we talk about me for just a little while?"

"As long as you like."

"A terrible, terrible thought has just occurred to me."

"What would that be?"

"The first night of *Expiring Light.*"

"Ah, you have a title for your new work."

"Yes."

"I'll let the relevant people know. As well as the meteorite showers I mentioned earlier we'll have a conventional laser and firework show, plus there will be troupe dancing and a holo-image interpretation."

"Yes, yes, I'm sure my music will provide suitable aural wallpaper for all this spectacle."

"Ziller, I hope you know it will all be done with exquisite taste. It will all fade for the end, when the second nova ignites."

"That's not what I'm worried about. I'm sure it will all go splendidly."

"Then, what?"

"You're going to invite that son-of-a-prey-bitch Quilan, aren't you?"

"Ah."

"Yes, 'ah.' You are, aren't you? I knew it. I can just feel the tumorous pus-brain circling in. I should never have said he could move to Aquime. Don't know what I was thinking of."

"I think it would be very bad form not to invite emissary Quilan. The concert will probably be the single most important cultural event on the whole Orbital this year."

"What do you mean, 'probably'?"

"All right, definitely. There has been a vast amount of interest. Even using the Stullien Bowl the number of people who are going to have to be disappointed in the matter of live tickets is going to be immense. I've had to run competitions to make sure your keenest fans are there and then randomize almost all the rest of the distribution. There's a good chance that nobody from the Board will be able to make it to the event live, unless some ingratiate gives up their seat. The transmit audience over the whole O could be ten billion or more. I personally have exactly three tickets at my disposal; the allocation is so tight I'll have to use one if I want one of my own avatars to attend."

"So, a perfect excuse for not inviting this Quilan character."

"You and he are the only two Chelgrians here, Ziller; you composed it and he's our honored guest. How can I not invite him?"

"Because I won't go if he does, that's why."

"You mean you won't attend your own first night?"

"Correct."

"You won't conduct?"

"That's right."

"But you always conduct the first night's performance!"

"Not this time. Not if he's going to be there."

"But you have to be there!"

"No I don't."

"But who'll conduct it?"

"Nobody. These things don't really need conducting. Composers conduct to feed their own ego and to feel part of the performance rather than just the preparation."

"That's not what you said before. You said there were nuances that could not be programmed, decisions that a conductor could make at the time on the night in response to the audience's on-going reactions which required a single individual to collate, analyze and react to, functioning as a focal point for the distributed—"

"I was bullshitting you."

"You seemed as sincere then as you do now."

"It's a gift. The point is, I won't conduct if this mercenary whore-boy is there. I won't be anywhere near the place. I'll be at home, or somewhere else."

"That would be very embarrassing for all concerned."

"So keep him away if you want me there."

"How could I possibly do that?"

"You are a Hub Mind, as you've recently explained in exhausting detail. Your resources are almost infinite."

"Why can't we just keep the two of you apart on the night?"

"Because it won't happen. An excuse will be found to bring us together. An encounter will be manufactured."

"What if I give you my word that I will make sure that Quilan and you are never brought face to face? He will be there, but I'll ensure that you are kept apart."

"With one avatar? . . . Have you put a sound field around us?"

"Just around our heads, yes. This avatar's lips will no longer move and its voice will alter slightly as a result; don't be alarmed."

"I'll try to hold my terror in check. Go on."

"If I really have to I can make sure there are several avatars there at the concert. They don't always have to have silver skin, you know. And I'll have drones present, too."

"Big bulky drones?"

"Better; small, mean ones."

"No good. No deal."

"And knife missiles."

"Still no."

"Why not? I do hope you are not going to say that you don't trust me. My word is my word. I never break it."

"I do trust you. The reason that it's no deal is because of the people who would want this meeting to happen."

"Go on."

"Tersono. Contact. Grief, Special fucking Circumstances, for all I know."

"Hmm."

"If they want the two of us to meet—I mean really, determinedly want—could you definitely, certainly stop it from happening, Hub?"

"Your question could apply to any moment since Quilan's arrival."

"Yes, but until now a seemingly chance meeting would have been too artificial, too obviously contrived. They'd have expected me to react badly, and they'd have been absolutely right. Our meeting must look like fate, like it was inevitable, as though my music, my talent, my personality and very being have made it pre-ordained."

"You could always go and if you're forced to meet still react badly."

"No. I don't see why I should. I don't want to meet him; simple as that."

"I give you my word I will do everything I can to make sure that you do not meet."

"Answer the question: if SC were determined to force a meeting, could you stop them?"

"No."

"As I thought."

"I'm not doing very well here, am I?"

"No. However there is one thing that might change my mind."

"Ah. What's that?"

"Look into the bastard's mind."

"I can't do that, Ziller."

"Why not?"

"It is one of the very few more-or-less unbreakable rules of the Culture. Nearly a law. If we had laws, it would be one of the first on the statute book."

"Only more-or-less unbreakable?"

"It is done very, very rarely, and the result tends to be ostracism. There was a ship called the *Grey Area*, once. It used to do that sort of thing. It became known as the *Meatfucker* as a result. When you look up the catalogs that's the name it's listed under, with its original, chosen name as a footnote. To be denied your self-designated name is a unique insult in the Culture, Ziller. The vessel disappeared some time ago. Probably it killed itself, arguably as a result of the shame attached to such behavior and resulting disrespect."

"All it is is looking inside an animal brain."

"That's just it. It is so easy, and it would mean so little, really. That is why the not-doing of it is probably the most profound manner in which we honor our biological progenitors. This prohibition is a mark of our respect. And so I cannot do it."

"You mean you won't do it."

"They are almost the same thing."

"You have the ability."

"Of course."

"Then do it."

"Why?"

"Because I won't attend the concert otherwise."

"I know that. I mean what would I be looking for?"

"The real reason he's here."

"You really imagine he might be here to harm you?"

"It's a possibility."

"What would stop me saying I would do this thing and then only pretend to do it? I could tell you I had looked and found nothing."

"I'd ask you to give your word you would really do it."

"Have you not heard of the idea that a promise made under duress does not count?"

"Yes. You know you could have said nothing there."

"I wouldn't want to deceive you, Ziller. That too would be dishonorable."

"Then it sounds like I'm not going to that concert."

"I will still hope that you might, and work toward it."

"Never mind. You could always hold another competition; the winner gets to conduct."

"Let me think about this. I'll release the sound field. Let's watch the dune riders."

· · ·

The avatar and the Chelgrian turned from facing each other to stand with the others by the parapet of the trundling feast hall's viewing platform. It was night, and cloudy. Knowing the weather would be so, people had come to the dune slides of Efilziveiz-Regneant to watch the biolume boarding.

The dunes were not normal dunes; they were titanic spills of sand forming a three-kilometer-high slope from one Plate to another, marking where the sands from one of the Great River's sandbank spurnings were blown across toward the Plate's spinward edge to slip down to the desert regions of the sunken continent below.

People ran, rolled, boarded, ski'd, skiffed or boated down the dunes all the time, but on a dark night there was something special to be seen. Tiny creatures lived in the sands, arid cousins of the plankton that created bioluminescence at sea, and when it was very dark you could see the tracks left by people as they tumbled, twisted or carved their way down the vast slope.

It had become a tradition that on such nights the freeform chaos of individuals pleasing only themselves and the occasional watching admirer was turned into something more organized, and so—once it was dark enough and sufficient numbers of spectators had turned up on the crawler-mounted viewing platforms, bars and restaurants—teams of boarders and skiers set off from the top of the dunes in choreographed waves, triggering sand-slip cascades in broad lines and vees of scintillating light descending like slow, ghostly surf and weaving gently sparkling trails of soft blue, green and crimson tracks across the sighing sands, myriad necklaces of enchanted dust glowing like linear galaxies in the night.

Ziller watched for a while. Then he sighed and said, "He's here, isn't he?"

"A kilometer away," the avatar replied. "Higher up on the other side of the run. I'm monitoring the situation. Another one of me is with him. You are quite safe."

"This is as close as I ever want to get to him, unless you can do something."

"I understand."

12

A Defeat of Echoes

~ *So unterritorial.*

~ I suppose when you have this much territory you can afford to be.

~ *Do you think I'm old-fashioned to be disturbed by it?*

~ No. I think it's quite natural.

~ *They have too much of everything.*

~ With the possible exception of suspicion.

~ *We can't be sure of that.*

~ I know. Still; so far, so good.

Quilan closed the lockless door to his apartment. He turned and looked out at the floor of the gallery, thirty meters below. Groups of humans strolled amongst the plants and pools, between the stalls and bars, the restaurants and—well; shops, exhibitions? It was hard to know what to call them.

The apartment they had given him was near the roof level of one of Aquime City's central galleries. One set of rooms looked out across the city to the inland sea. The other side of the suite, like this glazed lobby outside, looked down into the gallery itself.

Aquime's altitude and consequently cold winters meant that a lot of the life of the city took place indoors rather than out, and as a result what would have been ordinary streets in a more temperate city, open to the sky, here were galleries, roofed-over streets vaulted with anything from antique glass to force fields. It was possible to walk from one end of the city to the other under cover and wearing summer clothes, even when, as now, there was a blizzard blowing.

Free of the driving snow that was bringing visibility down to a few meters, the view from the apartment's exterior was delicately impressive. The city had been built in a deliberately archaic style, mostly from stone. The buildings were red and blond and gray and pink, and the slates covering the steeply pitched roofs were various shades of green and blue. Long tapering fingers of forest penetrated the city almost to its heart, bringing further greens and blues into play and—with the galleries—dicing the city into irregular blocks and shapes.

A few kilometers in the distance, the docks and canals would glitter under a morning sun. Spinward of those, on a gentle slope of ridge rising to the outskirts of the city, Quilan could, when it was clear, see the tall buttresses and towers of the ornately decorated apartment building which contained the home of Mahrai Ziller.

~ *So could we just go and walk into his apartment?*

~ No. He got somebody to make him locks when he heard I was coming. Apparently this was mildly scandalous.

~ *Well, we could have locks, too.*

~ I think it better not to.

~ *Thought you might.*

~ We wouldn't want it to look like I have something to hide.

~ *That would never do.*

Quilan swung open a window, letting the sounds of the gallery into the apartment. He heard tinkling water, people talking and laughing, birdsong and music.

He watched drones and people in float harnesses waft by beneath him but above the other humans, saw people in an apartment on the other side of the gallery wave—he waved back almost without thinking—and smelled perfumes and the scent of cooking.

He looked up at the roof, which was not glass but some other more perfectly transparent material—he supposed he could have asked his little pen-terminal to find out exactly what it was, but he had not bothered—and he listened in vain for any sound of the storm swirling and blowing outside.

~ *They do love their little insulated existence, don't they?*

~ Yes, they do.

He remembered a gallery not so dissimilar to this, in Shaunesta, on Chel. It was before they had married, about a year after they had met. They had been walking hand-in-hand, and had stopped to look in a jeweller's window. He had gazed in casually enough at all the finery, and wondered if he might buy something for her. Then he'd heard her making this little noise, a sort of appreciative but barely audible, "Mmm, mmm, mmm, mmm."

At first he'd assumed she was making the noise for his amusement. It had taken him a few moments to realize that not only was she not doing that, but she was not aware that she was making the noise at all.

He realized this and suddenly felt as though his heart would burst with joy and love; he turned, swept her into his arms and hugged her, laughing at the surprised, confused, blinkingly happy look on her face.

~ *Quil?*

~ Sorry. Yes.

Somebody laughed on the gallery floor below; a high, throaty, female laugh, unrestrained and pure. He heard it echo around the hard surfaces of the closed-in street, remembering a place where there were no echoes at all.

They'd got drunk the night before they left; Estodien Visquile with his extended entourage including the bulky, white-furred Eweirl, and he. He had to be helped from his bed the next morning by a laughing Eweirl. A drenching under a cold shower just about brought him round, then he was taken straight to the VTOL, then to the field with the sub-orbital, then to Equator Launch City, where a commercial flight hoisted them to a small Orbiter. A demilled ex-Navy privateer was waiting. They'd left the system headed for deep space before his hangover started to abate, and he realized that he had been selected as the one to do whatever it was he had to do, and remembered what had happened the night before.

They were in an old mess hall, decorated in an antique style with the heads of various prey animals adorning three of the walls; the fourth wall of glass doors opened onto a narrow terrace which looked out to sea. There was a warm wind blowing and the doors were all opened, bringing the smell of the ocean into the bar. Two Blinded Invisible servants dressed in white trousers and jackets attended them, bringing the various strengths of fermented and distilled liquors a traditional drinking binge required.

The food was sparse and salty, again as dictated by tradition. Toasts were proposed, drinking games indulged in, and Eweirl and another of the party, who seemed nearly as well built as the white-furred male, balanced their way along the wall of the terrace from one end to the other, with the two-hundred-meter drop to one side. The other male went first; Eweirl went one better by stopping halfway along and downing a cup of spirit.

Quilan drank the minimum required, wondering quite what it was all in aid of and suspecting that even this apparent celebration was part of a test. He tried not to be too much of a wet blanket, and joined in several of the drinking games with a forced heartiness he thought must easily be seen through.

The night wore on. Gradually people went off to their curl-pads. After a while, only Visquile, Eweirl and he were left, served by the larger of the two Invisibles, a male even bulkier than Eweirl who maneuverd his way amongst the tables with surprising adroitness, his green-banded head swinging this way and that and his white clothes making him look like a ghost in the dim light.

Eweirl tripped him up a couple of times, on the second occasion causing him to drop a tray of glasses. When this happened Eweirl put his head back and laughed loudly. Visquile looked on like the indulgent parent of a spoiled child. The big servant apologized and felt his way to the bar to bring back a dustpan and broom.

Eweirl sank another cup of spirit and watched the servant lift a table out of the way one-handed. He challenged him to an arm-wrestling contest. The Invisible declined, so Eweirl ordered him to take part, which eventually he did, and won.

Eweirl was left panting with exertion; the big Invisible put his jacket back on, inclined his green-banded head, and resumed his duties.

Quilan was slumped in his curl-seat watching events with one eye closed. Eweirl did not look happy that the servant had won the contest. He drank some more. Estodien Visquile, who did not seem very drunk at all, asked Quilan some questions about his wife, his military career, his family and his beliefs. Quilan remembered trying not to appear evasive. Eweirl watched the big Invisible go about his duties, his white-furred body looking tensed and coiled.

"They might find the ship yet, Quil," the Estodien told him. "There may still be wreckage. The Culture; their consciences. Helping us look for the lost ships. It might turn up yet. Not her, of course. She is quite lost. The gone-before say there is no sign, no hint of her Soulkeeper having worked. But we might yet find the ship, and know more of what happened."

"It doesn't matter," he said. "She is dead. That's all that matters. Nothing else. I don't care about anything else."

"Not even your own survival after death, Quilan?" the Estodien asked.

"That least of all. I don't want to survive. I want to die. I want to be as she is. No more. Nothing more. Ever again."

The Estodien nodded silently, his eyelids drooping, a small smile playing across his face. He glanced at Eweirl. Quilan looked too.

The white-furred male had quietly changed seats. He waited until the big Invisible was approaching, then stood up suddenly in his path. The servant collided with him, spilling three cups of spirit over Eweirl's waistcoat.

"You clumsy fuck! can't you see where you're going?"

"I'm sorry, sir. I didn't know you'd moved." The servant offered Eweirl a cloth from his waistband.

Eweirl knocked it away. "I don't want your rag!" he screamed. "I said, can't you see where you're going?" He picked at the lower edge

of the green band covering the other male's eyes. The big Invisible
flinched instinctively, pulling back. Eweirl had hooked a leg behind
him; he stumbled and fell and Eweirl went down with him in a flurry
of crashing glasses and tumbling chairs.

Eweirl staggered to his feet and jerked the big male after him.
"Attack me, would you? Attack me, would you?" he yelled. He had
pulled the servant's jacket down across his shoulders and over his arms
so that he was half helpless, though the servant anyway did not seem
to be putting up any fight. He stood impassively as Eweirl screamed
at him.

Quilan didn't like this. He looked at Visquile, but the Estodien
was looking on tolerantly. Quilan pushed himself up from the table
they were curled at. The Estodien put a hand on his arm, but he
pulled it away.

"Traitor!" Eweirl bellowed at the Invisible. "Spy!" He pulled the
servant around and pushed him this way and that; the big male
crashed into tables and chairs, staggering and nearly falling, unable to
save himself with his trapped arms, each time using what leverage he
had from his midlimb to fend off the unseen obstacles.

Quilan started to make his way around the table. He tripped over
a chair and had to fall across the table to avoid hitting the floor. Eweirl
was spinning and pushing the Invisible, trying to disorient him or
make him dizzy as well as get him to fall over. "Right!" he shouted
in the servant's ear. "I'm taking you to the cells!" Quilan pushed
himself away from the table.

Eweirl held the servant before him and started marching not to the
double doors which led from the bar but toward the terrace doors.
The servant went uncomplainingly at first, then must have regained
his sense of direction or maybe just smelled or heard the sea and felt
the open air on his fur, because he pushed back and started to say
something in protest.

Quilan was trying to get in front of Eweirl and the Invisible, to
intercept them. He was a few meters to the side now, feeling his way
around the tables and chairs.

Eweirl reached up with one hand, pulled the green eye-band

down—so that for an instant Quilan could see the Invisible's two empty sockets—and forced it over the servant's mouth. Then he whipped the other male's legs from under him and while he was still trying to stagger back to his feet ran him out across the terrace to the wall and up-ended the Invisible over the top and into the night.

He stood there, breathing heavily, as Quilan came stumbling up to his side. They both looked over. There was a dim white ruff of surf around the base of the seastack. After a moment Quilan could see the pale shape of the tiny falling figure, outlined against the dark sea. After a moment more, the faint sound of a scream floated up to them. The white figure joined the surf with no visible splash and the scream stopped a few moments later.

"Clumsy," Eweirl said. He wiped some spittle from around his mouth. He smiled at Quilan, then looked troubled and shook his head. "Tragic," he said. "High spirits." He put one hand on Quilan's shoulder. "High jinks, eh?" He reached out and brought Quilan into a hug, pressing him hard into his chest. Quilan tried to push away, but the other male was too strong. They swayed, close to the wall and the drop. The other male's lips were at his ear. "Do you think he wanted to die, Quil? Hmm, Quilan? Hmm? Do you think he wanted to die? Do you?"

"I don't know," Quilan mumbled, finally being allowed to use his midlimb to push himself away. He stood looking up at the white-furred male. He felt more sober now. He was half terrified, half care-less. "I know you killed him," he said, and immediately thought that he might die too, now. He thought about taking up the classical defensive position, but didn't.

Eweirl smiled and looked back at Visquile, who still sat where he had been throughout. "Tragic accident," Eweirl said. The Estodien spread his hands. Eweirl held onto the wall to stop himself swaying, and waved at Quilan. "Tragic accident."

Quilan felt suddenly dizzy, and sat down. The view started to dis-appear at the edges. "Leaving us too?" he heard Eweirl inquire. Then nothing till the morning.

● ● ●

"You chose me, then?"

"You chose yourself, Major."

He and Visquile sat in the privateer's lounge area. Along with Eweirl, they were the only people aboard. The ship had its own AI, albeit an uncommunicative one. Visquile claimed not to know the craft's orders, or its destination.

Quilan drank slowly; a restorative laced with anti-hangover chemicals. It was working, though it might have worked more quickly.

"And what Eweirl did to the Blinded Invisible?"

Visquile shrugged. "What happened was unfortunate. These accidents happen when people drink freely."

"It was murder, Estodien."

"That would be impossible to prove, Major. Personally I was, like the unfortunate concerned, unsighted at the time." He smiled. Then the smile faded. "Besides, Major, I think you'll find Called-To-Arms Eweirl has a certain latitude in such matters." He reached out and patted Quilan's hand. "You must not concern yourself with the unhappy incident any further."

Quilan spent a lot of time in the ship's gym. Eweirl did, too, though they exchanged few words. Quilan had little he wanted to say to the other male, and Eweirl didn't seem to care. They worked and hauled and pulled and ran and sweated and panted and dust-bathed and showered alongside each other, but barely acknowledged the other's presence. Eweirl wore earplugs and a visor, and sometimes laughed as he exercised, or made growling, appreciative noises.

Quilan ignored him.

He was brushing the dust-bath off one day when a bead of sweat dropped from his face and spotted in the dust like a globule of dirty mercury, rolling into the hollow by his feet. They had mated once in a dust-bath, on their honeymoon. A droplet of her sweet sweat had fallen into the gray fines just so, rolling with a fluid silky grace down the soft indentation they had created.

He was suddenly aware he had made a keening, moaning noise. He looked out at Eweirl in the main body of the gym, hoping he would not have heard, but the white-furred male had taken his plugs and visor off, and was looking at him, grinning.

The privateer rendezvoused with something after five days' travel. The ship went very quiet and moved oddly, as though it was on solid ground but being slid around from side to side. There were thudding noises, then hisses, then most of the remaining noise of the craft died. Quilan sat in his little cabin and tried accessing the exterior views on his screens; nothing. He tried the navigation information, but that had been closed off too. He had never before lamented the fact that ships had no windows or portholes.

He found Visquile on the ship's small and elegantly spare bridge, taking a data clip from the craft's manual controls and slipping it into his robes. The few data screens still live on the bridge winked out.

"Estodien?" Quilan asked.

"Major," Visquile said. He patted Quilan on the elbow. "We're hitching a ride." He held up a hand as Quilan opened his mouth to ask where to. "It's best if you don't ask with whom or to where, Major, because I'm not able to tell you." He smiled. "Just pretend we're still under way using our own power. That's easiest. You needn't worry; we're very secure in here. Very secure indeed." He touched midlimb to midlimb. "See you at dinner."

Another twenty days passed. He became even fitter. He studied ancient histories of the Involveds. Then one day he woke and the ship was suddenly loud about him. He turned on the cabin screen and saw space ahead. The navigation screens were still unavailable, but he looked all about the ship's exterior views through the different sensors and viewing angles and didn't recognize anything until he saw a fuzzy Y shape and knew they were somewhere on the outskirts of the galaxy, near the Clouds.

Whatever had brought them here in only twenty days must be much faster than their own ships. He wondered about that.

The privateer craft was held in a bubble of vacuum within a vast blue-green space. A wobbling limb of atmosphere three meters in diameter flowed slowly out to meet with their outer airlock. On the far side of the tube floated something like a small airship.

The air was briefly cold as they walked through, turning gradually warmer as they approached the airship. The atmosphere felt thick. Underneath their feet, the tunnel of air seemed as pliantly firm as wood. He carried his own modest luggage; Eweirl toted two immense kit bags as though they were purses, and Visquile was followed by a civilian drone carrying his bags.

The airship was about forty meters long; a single giant ellipsoid in dark purple, its smooth-looking envelope of skin lined with long yellow strakes of frill which rippled slowly in the warm air like the mantle of a fish. The tube led the three Chelgrians to a small gondola slung underneath the vessel.

The gondola looked like something grown rather than constructed, like the hollowed-out husk of an immense fruit; it appeared to have no windows until they climbed aboard, making the ship tip gently, but gauzy panels let in light and made the smooth interior glow with a pastel-green light. It held them comfortably. The tube of air dissipated behind them as the gondola's door irised shut.

Eweirl popped his earplugs in and put on his visor, sitting back, seemingly oblivious. Visquile sat with his silvery stave planted between his feet, the round top under his chin, gazing ahead through one of the gauzy windows.

Quilan had only the vaguest idea where he was. He had seen the gigantic, slowly revolving elongated 8-shaped object ahead of them for several hours before they'd rendezvoused. The privateer ship had closed very slowly, seemingly on emergency thrust alone, and the thing—the world, as he was now starting to think of it, having come to a rough estimate of its size—had just kept getting bigger and bigger and filling more and more of the view ahead, yet without betraying any detail.

Finally one of the body's lobes had blotted out the view of the other, and it was as though they were approaching an immense planet of glowing blue-green water.

What looked like five small suns were visible revolving with the vast shape, though they seemed too small to be stars. Their positioning implied there would be another two, hidden behind the world. As they got very close, matching rotational speed with the world and coming near enough to see the forming indentation they were heading for, with the tiny purple dot immediately behind it, Quilan saw what looked like layers of clouds, just hinted at, inside.

"What is this place?" Quilan said, not trying to keep the wonder and awe out of his voice.

"They call them airspheres," Visquile said. He looked warily pleased, and not especially impressed. "This is a rotating twin-lobe example. Its name is the Oskendari airsphere."

The airship dipped, diving still deeper into the thick air. They passed through one level of thin clouds like islands floating on an invisible sea. The airship wobbled as it went through the layer. Quilan craned his neck to see the clouds, lit from underneath by a sun far beneath them. He experienced a sudden sense of disorientation.

Below, something appearing out of the haze caught his eye; a vast shape just one shade darker than the blueness all around. As the airship approached he saw the immense shadow the shape cast, stretching upwards into the haze. Again, something like vertigo struck him.

He'd been given a visor too. He put it on and magnified the view. The blue shape disappeared in a shimmer of heat; he took the visor off and used his naked eyes.

"A dirigible behemothaur," Visquile said. Eweirl, suddenly back with them, took off his visor and shifted over to Quilan's side of the gondola to look, imbalancing the airship for a moment. The shape below looked a little like a flattened and more complicated version of the craft they were in. Smaller shapes, some like other airships, some winged, flew lazily about it.

Quilan watched the smaller features of the creature emerge as they dropped down toward it. The behemothaur's envelope skin was blue and purple, and it too possessed long lines of pale yellow-green frills which rippled along its length, seemingly propelling it. Giant fins protruded vertically and laterally, topped with long bulbous protrusions, like the wing-tip fuel tanks of ancient aircraft. Across its summit line and along its sides, great scalloped dark-red ridges ran, like

three enormous, encasing spines. Other protrusions, bulbs and hummocks covered its top and sides, producing a generally symmetrical
effect that only broke down at a more detailed level.

As they drew still closer, Quilan had to press himself against the
frame of the little airship's gondola window to see both ends of the
giant below them. The creature must be five kilometers long, perhaps more.

"This is one of their domains," the Estodien went on. "They have
seven or eight others distributed around the outskirts of the galaxy.
No one is entirely sure quite how many there are. The behemothaurs
are as big as mountains and as old as the hills. They are sentient,
allegedly, the remnant of a species or civilization which Sublimed
more than a billion years ago. Though again, only by repute. This
one is called the Sansemin. It is in the power of those who are our
allies in this matter."

Quilan looked inquiringly at the older male. Visquile, still
hunched over holding his glittering stave, made a shrugging motion.

"You'll meet them, or their representatives, Major, but you won't
know who they are."

Quilan nodded, and went back to looking out the window. He
considered asking why they had come to this place, but thought the
better of it.

"How long will we be here, Estodien?" he asked instead.

"For a while," Visquile said, smiling. He watched Quilan's face for
a moment, then said, "Perhaps two or three moons, Major. We
won't be alone. There are already Chelgrians here; a group of about
twenty monks of the Abremile Order. They inhabit the temple ship
Soulhaven, which is inside the creature. Well, most of it is. As I understand it only the fuselage and life support units of the temple ship are
actually present. The vessel had to leave its drive units behind, somewhere outside, in space." He waved one hand. "The behemothaurs
are sensitive to force-field technologies, we're told."

The superior of the temple ship was tall and elegant and dressed in
a graceful interpretation of the order's simple robes. He met them on
a broad landing platform at the rear of what looked like a giant,

gnarled, hollowed-out fruit stuck onto the behemothaur's skin. They stepped from the airship.

"Estodien Visquile."

"Estodien Quetter." Visquile made the introductions.

Quetter bowed fractionally to Eweirl and Quilan. "This way," he said, indicating a cleft in the behemothaur's skin.

Eighty meters along a gently sloping tunnel floored with something like soft wood they came to a giant ribbed chamber whose atmosphere was oppressively humid and suffused with a vaguely charnel smell. The temple ship *Soulhaven* was a dark cylinder ninety meters in length and thirty across, taking up about half of the damp, warm chamber. It appeared to be tethered by vines to the chamber's walls, and what looked like creepers had grown over much of its hull.

Quilan had, over the years of his soldiering, become used to encountering makeshift camps, temporary command posts, recently requisitioned command HQs and so on. Some part of him took in the feel of the place—the extemporised organization, the mix of clutter and orderliness—and decided that the *Soulhaven* had been here for about a month.

A pair of large drones, each the shape of two fat cones set base to base, floated up to them in the dimness, humming gently. Visquile and Quetter both bowed. The two floating machines tipped briefly toward them.

"You are Quilan," said one. He could not tell which.

"Yes," he said.

Both machines floated very close to him. He felt the fur around his face stand on end, and smelled something he could not identify. A breeze blew around his feet.

QUILAN MISSION GREAT SERVICE HERE TO PRE-PARE TEST LATER TO DIE AFRAID?

He was aware that he had flinched backwards and had almost taken a step away. There had been no sound, just the words ringing in his head. Was he being spoken to by the gone-before?

AFRAID? the voice said in his head once more.

"No," he said. "Not afraid, not of death."

CORRECT DEATH NOTHING.

The two machines withdrew to where they had hovered before.

WELCOME ALL. SOON PREPARE.

Quilan sensed both Visquile and Eweirl rock back as if caught in a sudden gust of wind, though the other Estodien, Quetter, did not budge. The two machines made the tipping motion again. Apparently they were dismissed; they returned down the tunnel to the outside.

Their own quarters were, mercifully, here on the exterior of the giant creature, in the giant hollowed-out bulb they had landed near. The air was still cloyingly humid and thick, but if it smelled of anything it smelled of vegetation and so seemed fresh in comparison to the chamber where the *Soulhaven* rested.

Their luggage had already been off-loaded. Once they had settled, they were taken on a tour of the behemothaur's exterior by the same small airship they'd arrived on. Anur, a gangly, awkward-looking young male who was the *Soulhaven's* most junior monk, escorted them, explaining something of airspheres' legendary history and hypothesized ecology.

"We think there are thousands of the behemothaurs," he said as they slid under the bulging belly of the creature, beneath hanging jungles of skin foliage. "And almost a hundred megalithine and gigalithine globular entities. They're even bigger; the biggest are the size of small continents. People are even less sure whether they're sentient or not. We shouldn't see any of those or the other behemothaurs because we're so low in the lobe. They pretty well never descend this far. Buoyancy problems."

"How does the Sansemin manage to stay down here?" Quilan asked.

The young monk looked at Visquile before answering. "It's been modified," he said. He pointed up at a dozen or so dangling pods large enough to contain two full-grown Chelgrians. "Here you can see some of the subsidiary fauna being grown. These will become raptor scouts when they bud and hatch."

• • •

Quilan and the two Estodiens sat with bowed heads in the innermost recessional space of the *Soulhaven,* a nearly spherical cavity only a few meters in diameter and surrounded by two-meter-thick walls made from substrates holding millions of departed Chelgrian souls. The three males were arranged in a triangle facing inward, fur-naked.

It was the evening of the day they had arrived, by the time the *Soulhaven* kept. To Quilan it felt like the middle of the night. Outside, it would be the same eternal but ever changing day as it had been for a billion and a half years or more.

The two Estodiens had communicated with the Chelgrian-Puen and their on-board shades for a few moments without Quilan being involved, though even so he had experienced a sort of incoherent back-wash from their conversations while they'd lasted. It had been like standing in a great cavern and hearing people talking somewhere in the distance.

Then it was his turn. The voice was loud, a shout in his head.

QUILAN. WE ARE CHELGRIAN-PUEN.

They had told him to try to think his answers, to sub-vocalize. He thought, ~ I am honored to speak to you.

YOU: REASON HERE?

~ I don't know. I am being trained. I think you might know more about my mission than I do.

CORRECT. GIVEN PRESENT KNOWLEDGE: WILLING?

~ I will do what is required.

MEANS YOUR DEATH.

~ I realize that.

MEANS HEAVEN FOR MANY.

~ That is a trade I am willing to make.

NOT WOROSEI QUILAN.

~ I know.

QUESTIONS?

~ May I ask whatever I like?

YES.

~ All right. Why am I here?

TO BE TRAINED.

~ But why particularly this place?

SECURITY. PROPHYLACTIC MEASURE. DENIABILITY. DANGER. INSISTENCE OF ALLIES IN THIS.

~ Who are our allies?

OTHER QUESTIONS?

~ What am I to do at the end of my training?

KILL.

~ Who?

MANY. OTHER QUESTIONS?

~ Where will I be sent?

DISTANT. NOT CHELGRIAN SPHERE.

~ Does my mission involve the composer Mahrai Ziller?

YES.

~ Am I to kill him?

IF SO, REFUSE?

~ I haven't said that.

QUALMS?

~ If it was to be so, I would like to know the reasoning.

IF NO REASONS GIVEN, REFUSE?

~ I don't know. There are some decisions you just can't anticipate until you must really make them. You're not going to tell me whether my mission involves killing him or not?

CORRECT. CLARIFICATION IN TIME. BEFORE MISSION BEGINS. PREPARATION AND TRAINING FIRST.

~ How long will I be here?

OTHER QUESTIONS?

~ What did you mean by danger, earlier?

~ PREPARATION AND TRAINING. OTHER QUESTIONS?

~ No, thank you.

WE WOULD READ YOU.

~ What do you mean?

LOOK IN YOUR MIND.

~ You want to look into my mind?

CORRECT.

~ Now?

YES.

~ Very well. Do I have to do any—

—thing?

He was briefly dizzy, and was aware of swaying in his seat.

DONE. UNHARMED?

~ I think so.

CLEAR.

~ You mean . . . I am clear?

CORRECT.   TOMORROW: PREPARATION   AND
TRAINING.

The two Estodiens sat smiling at him.

He could only sleep fitfully, and woke from another dream of drowning to blink into the strange thick darkness. He fumbled for his visor and with the gray-blue image of the small room's curved walls before him, rose from the curl-pad and went to stand by the single window, where a warm breeze trickled slowly in and then seemed to die, as though exhausted by the effort. The visor showed a ghostly image of the window's rough frame, and, outside, the vaguest hint of clouds.

He took off the visor. The darkness appeared utter, and he stood there letting it soak into him until he thought he saw a flash, somewhere high above and blue with distance. He wondered if it was lightning; Anur had said it happened between cloud and air masses when they passed each other, rising and falling along the thermal gradients of the sphere's chaotic atmospheric circulation.

He saw a few more flashes, one of them of an appreciable length, although still seeming far, far away. He slipped the visor back on and held his hand up with claws extended, bringing two tips almost together; just a couple of millimeters apart. There. The flash had been that long.

Another flash. Seen with the visors, it was so bright the visor's optics turned the center of the tiny flash black to protect his night vision. Instead of just the minuscule spark itself, he saw the whole of a cloud system light up as well, the rolls and towers of the piled and distant vapor picked out in a remote blue wash of luminescence that vanished almost as soon as he became aware of it.

He took the visor off again and listened for the noise produced by those flashes. All he heard was a faint, enveloping noise like a strong wind heard from far away, seeming to come from all around him and course up through his bones. It appeared to contain within it frequencies deep enough to be distant rumbles of thunder, but they were low and continuous and unwavering, and try as he might he could not detect any change or peak in that long slow flow of half-felt sound.

There are no echoes here, he thought. No solid ground or cliffs anywhere for sound to reflect off. The behemothaurs absorb sound like floating forests, and inside them their living tissues soak up all noise.

Acoustically dead. The phrase came back to him. Worosei had done some work with the university music department, and had shown him a strange room lined with foam pyramids. Acoustically dead, she'd told him. It felt and sounded true; their voices seemed to die as each word left their lips, every sound exposed and alone, without resonance.

"Your Soulkeeper is more than a normal Soulkeeper, Quilan," Visquile told him. They were alone in the innermost recessional space of the *Soulhaven,* the following day. This was his first briefing. "It performs the normal functions of such a device, keeping a record of your mind-state; however it also has the capacity to carry another mind-state within it. You will, in a sense, have another person aboard when you undertake your mission. There is still more to come, but do you have anything you would like to say or ask about that?"

"Who will this person be, Estodien?"

"We are not certain yet. Ideally—according to the mission-profiling people in Intelligence, or rather according to their machines—it would be a copy of Sholan Hadesh Huyler, the late Admiral-General who was amongst those souls you were charged with recovering from the Military Institute on Aorme. However as the *Winter Storm* is lost, presumed destroyed, and the original substrate was aboard the vessel, we will probably have to go with a second choice. That choice is still being discussed."

"Why is this considered necessary, Estodien?"

"Think of it as having a co-pilot aboard, Major. You will have somebody to talk to, somebody to advise you, to talk things over with, while you are on your mission. This may not seem necessary now, but there is a reason we believe it may be advisable."

"Do I take it that it will be a long mission?"

"Yes. It may take several months. The minimum duration would be about thirty days. We can't be any more precise because it depends partly on your mode of transport. You may be taken to your destination aboard one of our own craft, or on a faster vessel from one of the older Involved civilizations, possibly one belonging to the Culture."

"Does the mission involve the Culture, Estodien?"

"It does. You are being sent to the Culture world Masaq', an Orbital."

"That is where Mahrai Ziller lives."

"Correct."

"Am I to kill him?"

"That is not your mission. Your covering story is that you are going there to try to convince him to return to Chel."

"And my real mission?"

"We will come to that in due course. And therein lies a precedent."

"A precedent, Estodien?"

"Your true mission will not be clear to you when you start it. You will know the covering story and you will almost certainly have a feeling that there is more to your task than that, but you will not know what it is."

"So am I to be given something like sealed orders, Estodien?"

"Something like that. But those orders will be locked inside your own mind. Your memory of this time—probably from some time just after the war to the end of your training here—will only gradually come back to you as you near the completion of your mission. By the time you recall this conversation—at the end of which you will know what your mission really is, though not yet exactly how you will accomplish it—you should be quite close, though not in exactly the correct position."

"Can memory be drip-fed so accurately, Estodien?"

"It can, though the experience may be a little disorienting, and that is the most important reason for giving you your co-pilot. The reason we are doing this is specifically because the mission involves the Culture. We are told that they never read people's minds, that the inside of your head is the one place they regard as sacrosanct. You have heard this?"

"Yes."

"We believe that this is probably true, but your mission is of sufficient importance for us to take precautions in case it is not. We imagine that if they do read minds, the most likely time this will happen will be when the subject concerned boards one of their ships, especially one of their warships. If we are able to arrange that you are taken to Masaq' on such a vessel, and it does look inside your head, all it will find, even at quite a deep level, is your innocent covering story.

"We believe, and have verified through experiments, that such a scanning process could be carried out without your knowledge. To go any deeper, to discover the memories we will initially hide even from you, this scanning process will have to reveal itself; you will be aware that it is taking place, or at the very least you will know that it has taken place. If that should happen, Major, your mission will end early. You will die."

Quilan nodded, thinking. "Estodien, has any sort of experiment been carried out on me yet? I mean, have I already lost any memories, whether I agreed to such a thing or not?"

"No. The experiments I mentioned were carried out on others. We are very confident that we know what we are doing, Major."

"So the deeper I go into my mission the more I'll know about it?"

"Correct."

"And the personality, the co-pilot, will it know everything from the start?"

"It will."

"And it cannot be read by a Culture scan?"

"It can, but it would require a deeper and more detailed reading than that required for a biological brain. Your Soulkeeper will be like your citadel, Quilan; your own brain is the curtain wall. If the citadel has fallen, the walls are either long since stormed, or irrelevant.

"Now. As I said, there is more to tell about your Soulkeeper. It contains, or will contain, a small payload and what is commonly known as a matter transmitter. Apparently it does not really transmit matter, but it has the same effect. I freely confess the importance of the distinction escapes me."

"And this is in something the size of a Soulkeeper?"

"Yes."

"Is this our own technology, Estodien?"

"That is not something that you need to know, Major. All that matters is whether it works or not." Visquile hesitated, then said, "Our own scientists and technologists make and apply astonishing new discoveries all the time, as I'm sure you are aware."

"Of course, Estodien. What would the payload you mentioned be?"

"You may never know that, Major. At the moment, I myself do not know exactly what it is either, though I will be told in due course, before your mission properly begins. At the moment all I know is something of the effect it will have."

"And that would be what, Estodien?"

"As you might imagine, a degree of damage, of destruction."

Quilan was silent for a few moments. He was aware of the presence of the millions of gone-before personalities stored in the substrates around him. "Am I to understand that the payload will be transmitted into my Soulkeeper?"

"No, it was put in place along with the Soulkeeper device."

"So it will be transmitted from the device?"

"Yes. You will control the transmission of the payload."

"I will?"

"That is what you are here to be trained for, Major. You will be instructed in the use of the device so that when the time comes you are able to transmit the payload into the desired location."

Quilan blinked a few times. "I may have fallen a little behind with recent advances in technology, but—"

"I would forget about that, Major. Previously existing technologies are of little importance in this matter. This is new. There is no precedent that we know of for this sort of process; no book to refer to. You will be helping to write that book."

"I see."

"Let me tell you more about the Culture world Masaq'." The Estodien gathered his robes about him and settled himself further into the cramped curl-pad. "It is what they call an Orbital; a band of matter in the shape of a very thin bracelet, orbiting around a sun—in this case the star Lacelere—in the same zone one would expect to find an habitable planet.

"Orbitals are on a different scale from our own space habitats; Masaq', like most Culture Orbitals, has a diameter of approximately three million kilometers and therefore a circumference of nearly ten million kilometers. Its width at the foot of its containing walls is about six thousand kilometers. Those walls are about a thousand kilometers high, and open at the top; the atmosphere is held in by the apparent gravity created by the world's spin.

"The size of the structure is not arbitrary; Culture Orbitals are built so that the same speed of revolution which produces one standard gravity also creates a day-night cycle of one of their standard days. Local night is produced when any given part of the Orbital's interior is facing directly away from the sun. They are made from exotic materials and held together principally by force fields.

"Floating in space in the center of the Orbital, equidistant from all places on its rim, is the Hub. This is where the AI substrate that the Culture calls a Mind exists. The machine oversees all aspects of the Orbital's running. There are thousands of subsidiary systems tasked with overseeing all but the most critical procedures, but the Hub can assume direct control of any and all of them at the same time.

"The Hub has millions of human-form representative entities called avatars with which it deals on a one-to-one basis with its inhabitants. It is theoretically capable of running each of those and every other system on the Orbital directly while communicating individually with every human and drone present on the world, plus a number of other ships and Minds.

"Each Orbital is different and each Hub has its own personality. Some Orbitals have only a few components of land; these are usually square parcels of ground and sea called Plates. On an Orbital as broad as Masaq' these are normally synonymous with continents. Before an Orbital is finished, in the sense of forming a closed loop like Masaq', they can be as small as two Plates, still three million kilometers apart but joined only by force fields. Such an Orbital might have a total population of just ten million humans. Masaq' is toward the other end of the scale, with over fifty billion people.

"Masaq' is known for the high rate of back-up of its inhabitants. This is sometimes held to be because a lot of them take part in dangerous sports, but really the practice dates from the world's inception, when it was realized that Lacelere is not a perfectly stable star and that there is a chance that it could flare with sufficient violence to kill people exposed on the surface of the world.

"Mahrai Ziller has lived there for the last seven years. He appears to be content to remain on the world. As I say, you will, seemingly, be going there to attempt to persuade him to renounce his exile and return to Chel."

"I see."

"Whereas your real mission is to facilitate the destruction of Masaq' Hub and so cause the deaths of a significant proportion of its inhabitants."

The avatar was going to show him around one of the manufacturies, beneath a Bulkhead Range. They were in an underground car, a comfortably fitted-out capsule which sped beneath the underside of the Orbital's surface, in the vacuum of space. They had swung half a million kilometers around the world, with the stars shining through panels in the floor.

The underground car line spanned the gap beneath the gigantic A-shape of the Bulkhead Range on a monofil-supported slingbridge two thousand kilometers long. Now the car was hurtling to a stop near the center, to ascend vertically into the factory space, hundreds of kilometers above.

~ *You all right, Major?*

~ Fine. You?

~ *The same. Mission target just come through?*

~ Yes. How am I doing?

~ *You're fine. No obvious physical signs. You sure you're all right?*

~ Perfectly.

~ *And we're still Go status?*

~ Yes, we're still Go.

The silver-skinned avatar turned to look at him. "You're sure you won't be bored seeing a factory, Major?"

"Not one producing starships, not at all. Though you must be running out of places to distract me with," he said.

"Well, it's a big Orbital."

"There's one place I would like to see."

"Where's that?"

"Your place. The Hub."

The avatar smiled. "Why, certainly."

Flight

"Are we nearly there yet?"

"Uncertain. That which the creature said. It meant?"

"Never mind that! Are we *there* yet?"

"This is hard to know with certitude. To return to that which the creature said. Is its meaning yet known to you?"

"Yes! Well, sort of! Please, can we go any *faster?*"

"Not really. We proceed as fast as is possible given the circumstances and therefore I thought our time might be employed by the telling of that which you understand from the creature's sayings. What would you then say was the import of such?"

"It doesn't matter! Well, it does, but! Just. Oh. Hurry! Faster! Go faster!"

They were inside the dirigible behemothaur Sansemin, Uagen Zlepe, 974 Praf and three of the raptor scouts. They were squeezing their way down a sinuous, undulating tube whose warm, slime-slick walls pulsed alarmingly every few moments. The air moving past them from ahead stank of rotting meat. Uagen fought the urge to gag. They could not go back to the outside the way they had come; it had been blocked off by some sort of rupture which had trapped and suffocated two of the raptor scouts who'd gone ahead of them.

Instead they had—after the creature had said what it had to Uagen and after an agonizingly long and absurdly relaxed discussion amongst the raptor scouts and the 974 Praf—taken another route out of the interrogatory chamber. This route initially led deeper and further into the quivering body of the dying behemothaur.

Two of the three raptor scouts insisted on going ahead in case of trouble, but they were squeezing their way through the convolutions of the twisting passage with some difficulty and Uagen was convinced that he could have gone quicker by himself.

The passage was deeply ribbed underfoot, making it hard to walk without supporting oneself on the wet and quivering walls. Uagen wished he'd brought gloves. His partial IR sense could make out little detail here because everything seemed to be the same temperature, reducing all he could see to a nightmarish monochrome of shadows upon shadows; it was, Uagen thought, worse than being blind.

The raptor scout in the lead came to a fork in the passage and stopped, apparently thinking.

There was a sudden concussive thud from all around them, then a pulse of fetid air swirled over them from behind, momentarily overcoming the flow of air from ahead and producing a still greater stench that very nearly made Uagen throw up.

He heard himself yelp. "What was that?"

"This is unknown," the Interpreter 974 Praf told him. The head wind resumed. The leading raptor scout chose the lower left-hand passage and shouldered its wings down the narrow cleft. "That way," 974 Praf said helpfully.

I'm going to die, Uagen thought, quite clearly and almost calmly. I'm going to die stuck inside this rotting, bloating, incinerating ten-million-year-old alien airship, a thousand light years from another human being and with information that might save lives and make me a hero.

Life is so unfair!

The creature on the wall in the interrogatory chamber had lived just long enough to tell him something which also might kill him, of course, if it was true, and even if he did get out of here. From what it had said, the knowledge he now possessed made him a target for people who wouldn't think twice about killing him or anybody else.

"You're Culture?" he said to the long, five-limbed thing hanging on the wall in the chamber.

"Yes," it said, trying to keep its head up as it talked to him. "Agent. Special Circumstances."

Uagen felt himself go *gulp* again. He'd heard of SC. He'd dreamt about being a Special Circumstances agent when he'd been a child. Dammit, he'd dreamt about being one when he'd been a young adult. He'd never really imagined he'd meet a real one. "Oh," he said, feeling infinitely foolish even as he said, "How do you do."

"You?" the creature said.

"What? Oh! Umm. Scholar. Uagen Zlepe. Scholar. Pleased to. Well. Probably not. Umm. I just. Well." He was fingering the necklace again. It must sound like he was twittering. "Doesn't matter. Can we get you down from there? This whole place, well, thing, is—"

"Ha. No. don't think so," the creature said, and might even have been trying to smile. It made a gesture with its head like a backward nod, then grimaced with pain. "Hate to tell you. Only me holding this together, such as it is. Through this link." It shook its head. "Listen, Uagen. You have to get out."

"Yes?" At least that was good news. The chamber floor wobbled underfoot as another rumbling detonation shook the puppet-like shapes of the dead and dying attached to the wall. One of the raptor scouts jerked its wings out to steady itself and knocked 974 Praf over. She made a clicking noise with her beak and glared at the offending beast.

"You have communicator?" the creature asked him. "Signal outside the airsphere?"

"No. Nothing."

The creature grimaced again. "Fuck. Then have to . . . get away from Oskendari. To ship, habitat; anywhere. Somewhere you can contact Culture, understand?"

"Yes. Why? To say what?"

"Plot. Not a joke, Uagen, not a drill. Plot. Serious fucking plot. Think it's to destroy . . . Orbital."

"What?"

"Orbital. Full Orbital, called Masaq'. Heard of?"

"Yes! It's famous!"

"They want to destroy it. Chelgrian faction. Chelgrian being sent. Don't know name. Doesn't matter. On his way, or will be soon. Don't know when. Attack happens. You. Get out. Get away. Tell Culture." The creature suddenly stiffened and bowed out from the wall of the chamber, its eyes closing. A tremendous shudder whipped through the cavity, tearing a couple of the dead bodies from the chamber's walls to send them falling limply to the quaking floor. Uagen and two of the raptor scouts were thrown onto their backs. Uagen struggled back to his feet.

The creature on the wall was staring at him. "Uagen. Tell SC, or Contact. My name is Gidin Sumethyre. Sumethyre, got that?"

"Got it. Gidin Sumethyre. Umm. That all?"

"Enough. Now get away. Masaq' Orbital. Chelgrian. Gidin Sumethyre. That's all. Out now. I'll try and hold this . . ." The creature's head dropped slowly to rest on its chest. Another titanic convulsion shook the chamber.

"That which the creature has just said," 974 Praf began, sounding puzzled.

Uagen stooped and picked the Interpreter up by her dry, leathery wings. "Get out!" he screeched into her face. "Now!"

They had hit a slightly wider part of the now steeply descending passage when the wind soughing past them from ahead suddenly picked up and became a gale. The two raptor scouts in front of Uagen, their folded wings acting like sails in the howling torrent of air, tried to wedge themselves against the rippling, buckling walls. They began to slide back toward him while Uagen also tried to brace himself against the damp tissues of the tube.

"Oh," 974 Praf said matter-of-factly from behind and below Uagen. "This development is not an indication of good."

"Help!" Uagen screamed, watching the two raptor scouts, both still desperately clutching at the passage's walls, slide closer toward him. He tried to make an X of himself, but the walls were now too far apart.

"Down here," Interpreter 974 Praf said. Uagen looked down between his feet. 974 Praf was holding onto the ribbed floor, flattened against it as best she could.

He looked up as the nearest raptor scout skidded to within touching distance. "Good idea!" he gasped. He dived. His forehead bounced off the heel spur of the raptor scout. He grabbed at the ribs on the floor as both the raptor scouts slid over him. The wind howled and tugged at his suit, then faded away. He untangled himself from 974 Praf and looked back. A painful-looking tangle of beaks, wings and limbs, the two raptor scouts were wedged further up in the passage with the one which had been bringing up the rear, in the narrow part they had recently forced their way through. One of the winged creatures clacked something.

974 Praf clacked back, then jerked to her feet and scuttled down the passage. "It is the case that the raptor scouts of the Yoleus will try to remain wedged there and so block the conflagration-feeding wind while we complete the journey which we make to the outside of the Sansemin. This way, Uagen Zlepe, scholar."

He stared after her retreating back, then scrambled after her. He was getting an odd feeling in his stomach. He tried to place it, then realized. It was like being in an inertia-subject lift or craft. "Are we sinking?" he said, whimpering.

"The Sansemin would appear to be losing height rapidly," 974 Praf said, bouncing from rib to rib down the steeply pitched floor ahead of him.

"Oh, shit." Uagen looked back. They were around a bend and out of sight of the raptor scouts. The passage dipped still further; it was now like descending a steeply pitched flight of stairs.

"Ah ha," the Interpreter said, as the wind tugged at them again.

Uagen felt his eyes widen. He stared ahead. "Light!" he screamed. "Light! Praf! I can see . . ." His voice trailed away.

"Fire," the Interpreter said. "Down on the floor, Uagen Zlepe, scholar."

Uagen turned and flung himself to the steps a moment before the fireball hit. He had time to take one deep breath and try to bury his face in his arms. He felt 974 Praf on top of him, wings extended, covering him. The blast of heat and light lasted a couple of seconds. "Up again," the Interpreter said. "You first."

"You're on fire!" he yelled as she pushed him with her wings and he stumbled down the steps of ribs.

"This is the case," the Interpreter said. Smoke and flames curled behind her wings as she prodded and pushed Uagen downwards. The wind was growing stronger and stronger; he had to fight against it to make any headway, forcibly walking down the ribbed side of the now almost vertical shaft as though they were somehow back on the level.

Looking ahead, Uagen could see light again. He groaned, then saw that it was blue-white, not yellow this time.

"We approach the outside," 974 Praf gasped.

They dropped from the belly of the dying behemothaur, falling not much faster than what was left of the vast creature itself as it burned and disintegrated and collapsed and descended all at once. Uagen held 974 Praf to him, smothering the flames eating at her wings, then used his ankle motors and balloon cape to halt their fall, and after an eternity of falling amongst flaming, fluttering wreckage and injured animals, brought the two of them around from underneath the massive, V-shaped ruin that was the dying behemothaur, into clear air space where the remains of the Yoleus' expeditionary force of raptor scouts found them moments before an ogrine disseisor could swoop in to swallow them whole.

The dazed, silent Interpreter shivered in his arms, the smell of her burned flesh filling his nose as they rose slowly with the raptor scout troupe back to the dirigible behemothaur Yoleus.

"Go?"

"Yes; away. Go. Depart. Leave."

"You wish to go away, depart, leave, now?"

"As soon as possible. When's the next ship? Of anybody's? Well, not, umm. Chelgrian. Yes; not Chelgrian."

Uagen had never imagined that Yoleus' interrogatory chamber would seem remotely homely, but it did now. He felt bizarrely safe here. It was just a pity he had to leave.

Yoleus was talking to him via a connecting cable and an Interpreter called 46 Zhun. The bulkier body of the nominally male 46 Zhun was perched on a ledge beside 974 Praf, who was stuck to the chamber wall looking singed and limp and dead but apparently beginning her reconstitution and recovery. 46 Zhun closed his eyes. Uagen was left standing there on the soft warm floor of the chamber. He could still smell the odor of burning coming off his clothes. He shivered.

46 Zhun opened his eyes again. "The next departing object is due to leave from the Second Tropic of Inclination Secessionary Portal in the Yonder lobe in five days," the Interpreter said.

"I'll take it. Wait; is it Chelgrian?"

"No. It is a Jhuvuonian Trader."

"I'll take it."

"There is not from now sufficient time for you to journey to and arrive at the said Tropic of Inclination Secessionary Portal."

"What?"

"There is not from now sufficient time for you to—"

"Well, how long would it take?"

The Interpreter closed its eyes again for a few moments, then opened them and said, "Twenty-three days would be the minimum time of requirement for a being such as you to journey to and arrive at the Second Tropic of Inclination Secessionary Portal from this point."

Uagen could feel a terrible gnawing in his guts; it was a sensation he hadn't felt since he was a very young child. He tried to remain calm. "When is the next ship after that?"

"That is not known," the Interpreter replied immediately.

Uagen fought back the urge to cry. "Is it possible to signal from Oskendari?" he asked.

"Of course."

"At beyond-light speed?"

"No."

"Could you signal for a ship? Is there any way for me to get off in the near future?"

"The definition of near future. This would be what?"

Uagen suppressed a moan. "In the next hundred days?"

"There are no objects known to be arriving or departing within that time period."

Uagen put his hands into his head-hair and pulled at it. He roared out of frustration, then stopped, blinking. He'd never done that. Never done either. Pulled at his hair or roared with frustration. He stared up at the blackened, crippled-looking body of 974 Praf, then dropped his head and stared at the chamber floor beneath his feet. His little ankle motors gleamed mockingly back up at him.

He raised his head. What had he been thinking of?

He checked what he knew about Jhuvuonian Traders. Only semi-Contacted. Fairly peaceful, quite trustworthy. Still in the age of scarcity. Ships capable of a few hundred lights. Slow by Culture standards, but sufficient. "Yoleus," he said calmly. "Can you signal the Second Secessionary Tropic of Inclinatory Portal or whatever it's called?"

"Yes."

"How long would that take?"

The creature closed its eyes and opened them. "One day plus one quarter of a day would be required for the outward signal and a similar amount of time would be required for a replying signal."

"Good. Where is the nearest Portal to where we are now and how long would it take for me to get there?"

Another pause. "The nearest Portal to where we are now is the Ninth Tropic of Inclination Secessionary Portal, Present lobe. It is two days plus one three-fifths of a day's flying time from here by raptor scout."

Uagen took a deep breath. I'm Culture, he thought to himself. This is what you're meant to do in such a situation, this is what it's all supposed to be about.

"Please signal the Jhuvuonian Trader vessel," he said, "and tell them they will be paid an amount of money equivalent to the worth of their vessel if they will pick me up at the Ninth Tropic of Inclination Secessionary Portal, Present lobe, in four days' time and take me to a destination I will disclose to them when they meet me there. Also mention that their discretion would be appreciated."

He considered leaving it at that, but this ship sounded like his only chance and he couldn't afford to risk its masters dismissing him as a crank. And if they were committed to that departure date then there wasn't time to indulge in a conversation by signal to convince them, either. He took another deep breath and added, "You may inform them that I am a citizen of the Culture."

He never did get a chance to say goodbye properly to 974 Praf. The Decider foliage-gleaner turned Interpreter was still unconscious and attached to the wall of the Interrogatory Chamber when he left, a day later.

He packed his bags, made sure that a record of his research notes, glyphs and all that had happened in the last couple of days was left in safe keeping with Yoleus, and made a particular point of finally preparing and drinking a glass of jhagel tea. It didn't taste very good.

A flight of raptor scouts escorted him to the Ninth Tropic of Inclination Secessionary Portal. His last glimpse of the dirigible behemothaur Yoleus was looking back over his shoulder watching the giant creature fading away into the greeny-blue distance above the shadow of a cloud complex, still faithfully following below and beneath the bulk of its desired mate, Muetenive. He wondered if they would yet make their dash for the predicted upwelling still building somewhere through the haze horizon ahead, to claim their free ride upwards to the manifold splendours of the gigalithine globular entity Buthulne.

He felt a sort of sweet sadness that he would not be there to share either that ride or arrival with them, and experienced a pang of guilt at feeling even the hint of a wish that the Jhuvuonian Trader craft would reject his offer and not show up, so leaving him no real choice but to attempt to return to Yoleus.

The two behemothaurs disappeared in the airily cavernous shadows above the cloud system. He turned back to face forward again. His ankle motors whirred, the cloak adjusted itself minutely to accommodate his altered orientation, still tensed to make a wing. The wings of the raptor scouts beat the air around him in a syncopated rhythm of stuttering sound, creating a curiously restful effect. He looked over at 46 Zhun, clasped to the neck and back of the raptor scout troupe leader, but the creature appeared to be asleep.

The Ninth Tropic of Inclination Secessionary Portal proved a little short of facilities. It was just a patch about ten meters in diameter on the side of the airsphere's fabric where the layers of containment material met and fused to produce a clear window into space. Around this circular area was clustered a handful of what looked like the mega fruit husks which grew on the behemothaurs and in one of which, until a day earlier, he had made his home. They provided a place for the raptor scouts to perch and get their strength back and for him to sit and wait. There was some food, some water, but that was all.

He passed the time by looking out at the stars—the Portal patches were the only truly clear areas on the airsphere's surface; the rest was only translucent in comparison—and composing a poeglyph trying to describe the sensation of terror he'd felt just the day before, trapped inside the dying body of the behemothaur Sansemin.

It was a frustrating process. He kept on putting down the stylo—the same damn stylo that had led to him being here now waiting on an alien spaceship that might never come—and tried to work out what had happened to Sansemin, why the Culture agent—if that was truly what he or she had been—had been here in the first place, whether there really was a plot of the sort that had been described to him, and what he ought to do if it transpired that the whole thing was some sort of joke, hallucination or figment of a mad and tormented creature's mind.

He had napped twice, scrubbed six attempts at the poeglyph and (having come to the tentative conclusion that it was marginally more likely that he had gone mad than that the events of the last few days had been real) was debating with himself the relative merits of suicide, Storage, transcorporation into a group entity or a request to return to Yoleus and resume his studies—suitably physically altered and with the elongated lifespan he'd been considering earlier—when the Jhuvuonian Trader ship, an unlikely arrangement of tubes and spars, hove to on the far side of the Portal.

Jhuvuonian Traders were not at all what he imagined. For some reason he had expected squat, rough-looking hairy humanoids wearing skins and furs, when in fact they resembled collections of very large red feathers. One of them floated through the Portal, encased within a mostly transparent bubble itself held inside a finger-like intrusion of air forming a tunnel reaching back to the Portal and the tubular vessel outside. He met it on a terrace of the mega fruit husk. 46 Zhun grasped the parapet at his side, watching the encased alien approach with the air of a creature sizing up potential nest-building material.

"You are the Culture person?" the creature in the bubble said, once it was hovering level with him. The voice was faint, the Marain accent tolerable.

"Yes. How do you do?"

"You will pay the worth of our ship to be taken to your destination?"

"Yes."

"It is a very fine ship."

"So I see."

"We would have another identical."

"You shall."

The alien made a series of clacking noises, talking to the Interpreter at Uagen's side. 46 Zhun clacked back.

"What is your destination?" the alien said.

"I need to send a signal to the Culture. Just get me in range to do that, initially, then take me to wherever I might meet with a Culture ship."

It had crossed Uagen's mind that the ship might be able to do this from here, without having to take him anywhere, though he doubted he would be so lucky. Still, in the next few moments he experienced a frisson of hope and nervousness until the creature said, "We could travel next to the Beidite entity Critoletli, where such communication and congregation might both be accomplished."

"How long would that take?"

"Seventy-seven standard Culture days."

"There is nowhere closer?"

"There is not."

"Could we signal ahead to the entity on our approach?"

"We could."

"How soon would we be in range to do that?"

"In about fifty standard Culture days."

"Very well. I'd like to set off immediately."

"Satisfactory. Payment to us?"

"From the Culture upon my safe delivery. Oh. I should have mentioned."

"What?" the alien said, its assemblage of red filaments fluttering inside the bubble.

"There may be an additional reward involved, beyond the payment we have already agreed."

The creature's feathery body rearranged itself again. "Satisfactory," it repeated.

The bubble floated up to the parapet. There was a second bubble forming beside the one enclosing the alien. It was, Uagen reflected, just like watching a cell divide. "Atmosphere and temperature are adjusted for Culture standard," the alien told him. "Gravity within ship will be less. This is acceptable to you?"

"Yes."

"You can provide your own sustenance?"

"I'll manage," he said, then thought. "You do have water?"

"We do."

"Then I'll survive."

"You will come aboard, please."

The twinned bubble bumped against the parapet. Uagen stooped, picked up his bags and looked at 46 Zhun. "Well, goodbye. Thank you for your help. Wish Yoleus all the best."

"The Yoleus wishes me to wish you a safe journey and a subsequent life which is pleasing to you."

Uagen smiled. "Tell it thank you, from me. I hope to see it again."

"This will be done."

13

Some Ways of Dying

The ship lift sat underneath the falls; when it was needed, its counter-weighted cradle swung slowly up and out from the swirling pool at the foot of the torrent, trailing veils and mists of its own. Behind the plunging curtain of water, the giant counter-weight moved slowly down through its subterranean pool, balancing the dock-sized cradle as it rose until it slotted into a wide groove carved into the lip of the falls. Once home, its gates gradually forced themselves open against the current, so that the cradle presented a sort of balcony of water jutting out beyond the river's kilometer-wide drop-off point.

Two bullet-shaped vessels powered upstream from either side like giant fish; they trailed long booms which stretched out to form a wide V that funnelled the oncoming barge toward the cradle. Once the gates had closed again and the barge was safely enclosed, the booms retracted, the cradle opened its side caissons to the onrushing force of the water and the extra weight slowly overcame the balancing mass of the counter-weight, now deep under the pool beneath.

Cradle and barge tipped slowly outward and down, descending amongst the thunder and mist toward the turmoil of waters below.

Ziller, dressed in a waistcoat and leggings that were thoroughly saturated, stood with the Hub avatar on a forward-facing promenade deck just below the bridge of the barge *Ucalegon,* on the River Jhree, Toluf Plate. The Chelgrian shook himself, unleashing spray, as the cradle's downstream gates opened and the barge made its way, thudding and bumping against the inflatable sides of the cradle, into the maelstrom of clashing waves and surging hummocks of water beyond.

He leaned over to the avatar and pointed up through the churning clouds of vapor toward the falls' lip, two hundred meters above. "What would happen if the barge missed the cradle up there?" he yelled over the sound of the waterfall.

The avatar, looking drenched but uncaring in a thin dark suit which clung to its silvery frame, shrugged. "Then," it said loudly, "there would be a disaster."

"And if the downstream gates opened while the cradle was still at the top of the falls?"

The creature nodded. "Again, disaster."

"And if the cradle's supporting arms gave way?"

"Disaster."

"Or if the cradle started to descend too soon?"

"Ditto."

"Or either set of gates gave way before the cradle reached the pool?"

"Guess what."

"So this thing does have an anti-gravity keel or something, doesn't it?" Ziller shouted. "As back-up, redundancy? Yes?"

The avatar shook its head. "No." Droplets fell from its nose and ears.

Ziller sighed and shook his head, too. "No, I didn't really think so."

The avatar smiled and leaned toward him. "I take it as an encouraging sign that you're beginning to ask that sort of question after the experience concerned is past the dangerous stage."

"So I'm becoming as thoughtlessly blasé about risk and death as your inhabitants."

The avatar nodded enthusiastically. "Yes. Encouraging, isn't it?"

"No. Depressing."

The avatar laughed. It looked up at the sides of the gorge as the river funnelled its way onward to join Masaq' Great River via Ossuliera City. "We'd better get back," the silver-skinned creature said. "Ilom Dolince will be dying soon, and Nisil Tchasole coming back."

"Oh, of course. Wouldn't want to miss either of your grotesque little ceremonies, would we?"

They turned and walked around the corner of the deck. The barge powered its way through the chaos of waves, its bows smacking into surging piles of white and green water and throwing great curtains of spray into the air to land like torrential squalls of rain across the decks. The buffeted vessel tipped and heaved. Behind it, the cradle was slowly and steadily submerging itself again in the raging currents.

A lump of water crashed onto the deck behind them, turning the promenade into a surging river half a meter deep. Ziller had to drop to all threes and use one hand on the deck rail to steady himself as they made their way through the torrent to the nearest doors. The avatar walked sloshing through the stream surging around its knees as though indifferent. It held the doors open and helped Ziller through.

In the foyer, Ziller shook himself again, spattering the gleaming wooden walls and embroidered hangings. The avatar just stood and the water fell off it, leaving its silvery skin and its matte clothes completely dry while the water drained away from its feet across the decking.

Ziller dragged a hand through his face fur and patted his ears. He looked at the immaculate figure standing smiling opposite him while he dripped. He wrung some water out of his waistcoat as he inspected the avatar's skin and clothing for any remaining sign of moisture. It appeared to be perfectly dry. "That is a very annoying trait," he told it.

"I did offer earlier to shelter both of us from the spray," the avatar reminded him. The Chelgrian pulled one of his waistcoat pockets

inside out and watched the resulting stream of water hit the deck.
"But you said you wanted fully to appreciate the experience with all
your senses including that of touch," the avatar continued. "Which I
have to say I did think was a little casual at the time."

Ziller looked ruefully at his sodden pipe and then at the silver-
skinned creature. "And that," he said, "is another one."

A small drone carrying a very large, neatly folded white towel of
extreme fluffiness banked around a corner and sped along the passage
toward them, coming to a sudden stop at their side. The avatar took
the towel and nodded to the other machine, which dipped and raced
away again.

"Here," the avatar said, handing the Chelgrian the towel.

"Thank you."

They turned to walk down the passageway, passing saloons where
small groups of people were watching the tumbling waters and roil-
ing mists of spray outside.

"Where's our Major Quilan today?" Ziller asked, rubbing his face
in the towel.

"Visiting Neremety, with Kabe, to see some sworl islands. It's the
first day of the local school's Tempt Season."

Ziller had seen this spectacle himself on another Plate six or seven
years earlier. Tempt Season was when the adult islands released the
algal blooms they'd been storing to paint fabulous swirling patterns
across the craterine bays of their shallow sea. Allegedly the display
persuaded the sea-floor-dwelling calves of the year before to surface
and blossom into new versions of themselves.

"Neremety?" he asked. "Where's that?"

"Half a million klicks away if it's a stride. You're safe for now."

"How very reassuring. Aren't you running out of places to distract
our little message-boy with? Last I heard you were showing him
around a factory." Ziller pronounced the last word through a snort-
ing laugh.

The avatar looked hurt. "A starship factory, if you please," it said,
"but yes, a factory nevertheless. Only because he asked, I might add.
And I've no shortage of places to show him, Ziller. There are places

on Masaq' you haven't even heard of you'd love to visit if only you knew about them."

"There are?" Ziller stopped and stared at the avatar.

It halted too, grinning. "Of course." It spread its arms. "I wouldn't want you to know all my secrets at once, would I?"

Ziller walked on, drying his fur and looking askance at the silver-skinned creature stepping lightly at his side. "You are more female than male, you know that, don't you?" he said.

The avatar raised its brows. "You really think so?"

"Definitely."

The avatar looked amused. "He wants to see Hub next," it told him.

Ziller frowned. "Come to think of it, I've never been there myself. Is there much to see?"

"There's a viewing gallery. Good outlook on the whole surface, obviously, but no better than most people get when they arrive, unless they're in a terrible hurry and fly straight up to the undersurface." It shrugged. "Apart from that, not much to see."

"I take it all your fabulous machinery is just as boring to look at as I imagine it to be."

"If not more so."

"Well, that ought to distract him for a good couple of minutes." Ziller towelled under his arms and—rising to walk, stooped, on his hind legs alone—around his midlimb. "Have you mentioned to the wretch that I may well not appear at the first performance of my own symphony?"

"Not yet. I believe Kabe might be raising the subject today."

"Think he'll do the honorable thing and stay away?"

"I really have no idea. If the suspicions we share are correct, E. H. Tersono will probably try and talk him into going." The avatar flashed Ziller a wide smile. "It will employ some sort of argument based on the idea of not giving in to what it will probably characterize as your childish blackmail, I imagine."

"Yes, something as shallow as that."

"How fares *Expiring Light*?" the avatar asked. "Are the primer pieces ready yet? We're only five days away and that's close to the minimum time people are used to."

"Yes, they're ready. I just want to sleep on a couple of them one more night, but I'll release them tomorrow." The Chelgrian glanced at the avatar. "You're quite sure this is the way to do it?"

"What, using primer pieces?"

"Yes. Won't people lose out on the freshness of the first performance? Whether I conduct it or not."

"Not at all. They'll have heard the rough tunes, the outlines of the themes, that's all. So they'll find the basic ideas recognizable, although not familiar. That'll let them appreciate the full work all the more." The avatar slapped the Chelgrian across the shoulders, raising a fine spray from his waistcoat. Ziller winced; the slight-looking creature was stronger than it appeared. "Ziller, trust us; this way works. Oh, and having listened to the draft you've sent, it is quite magnificent. My congratulations."

"Thank you." Ziller continued drying his flanks with the towel, then looked at the avatar.

"Yes?" it said.

"I was wondering."

"What?"

"Something I've wondered about ever since I came here, something I've never asked you, first of all because I was worried what the answer would be, later because I suspected I already knew the answer."

"Goodness. What can it be?" the avatar asked, blinking.

"If you tried, if any Mind tried, could you impersonate my style?" the Chelgrian asked. "Could you write a piece—a symphony, say— that would appear, to the critical appraiser, to be by me, and which, when I heard it, I'd imagine being proud to have written?"

The avatar frowned as it walked. It clasped its hands behind its back. It took a few more steps. "Yes, I imagine that would be possible."

"Would it be easy?"

"No. No more easy than any complicated task."

"But you could do it much more quickly than I could?"

"I'd have to suppose so."

"Hmm." Ziller paused. The avatar turned to face him. Behind Ziller, the rocks and veil trees of the deepening gorge moved swiftly past. The barge rocked gently beneath their feet. "So what," the Chelgrian asked, "is the point of me or anybody else writing a symphony, or anything else?"

The avatar raised its brows in surprise. "Well, for one thing, if you do it, it's you who gets the feeling of achievement."

"Ignoring the subjective. What would be the point for those listening to it?"

"They'd know it was one of their own species, not a Mind, who created it."

"Ignoring that, too; suppose they weren't told it was by an AI, or didn't care."

"If they hadn't been told then the comparison isn't complete; information is being concealed. If they don't care, then they're unlike any group of humans I've ever encountered."

"But if you can—"

"Ziller, are you concerned that Minds—AIs, if you like—can create, or even just appear to create, original works of art?"

"Frankly, when they're the sort of original works of art that I create, yes."

"Ziller, it doesn't matter. You have to think like a mountain climber."

"Oh, do I?"

"Yes. Some people take days, sweat buckets, endure pain and cold and risk injury and—in some cases—permanent death to achieve the summit of a mountain only to discover there a party of their peers freshly arrived by aircraft and enjoying a light picnic."

"If I was one of those climbers I'd be pretty damned annoyed."

"Well, it is considered rather impolite to land an aircraft on a summit which people are at that moment struggling up to the hard way, but it can and does happen. Good manners indicate that the picnic ought to be shared and that those who arrived by aircraft express awe and respect for the accomplishment of the climbers.

"The point, of course, is that the people who spent days and sweated buckets could also have taken an aircraft to the summit if all they'd wanted was to absorb the view. It is the struggle that they crave. The sense of achievement is produced by the route to and from the peak, not by the peak itself. It is just the fold between the pages." The avatar hesitated. It put its head a little to one side and narrowed its eyes. "How far do I have to take this analogy, Cr. Ziller?"

"You've made your point, but this mountain climber still wonders if he ought to re-educate his soul to the joys of flight and stepping out onto someone else's summit."

"Better to create your own. Come on; I've a dying man to see on his way."

Ilom Dolince lay on his death bed, surrounded by friends and family. The awnings which had covered the aft upper deck of the barge while it had descended the falls had been withdrawn, leaving the bed open to the air. Ilom Dolince sat up, half submerged in floating pillows and lying on a puff mattress that looked, Ziller thought, appropriately like a cumulus cloud.

The Chelgrian hung back, at the rear of the crescent of sixty or so people arranged standing or sitting around the bed. The avatar went to stand near the old man and took his hand, bending to talk to him. It nodded then beckoned over to Ziller, who pretended not to see, and made a show of being distracted by a gaudy bird flying low over the milky white waters of the river.

"Ziller," the avatar's voice said from the Chelgrian's pen terminal. "Please come over. Ilom Dolince would like to meet you."

"Eh? Oh. Yes, of course," he said. He felt quite acutely awkward.

"Cr. Ziller, I am privileged to meet you." The old man shook the Chelgrian's hand. In fact he did not look that old, though his voice sounded weak. His skin was less lined and spotted than that of some humans Ziller had seen, and his head hair had not fallen out, though it had lost its pigment and so appeared white. His handshake was not strong, but Ziller had certainly felt limper ones.

"Ah. Thank you. I'm flattered you wanted to, ah, take up some of your, ah, time with meeting an alien note dabbler."

The white-haired man in the bed looked regretful, even pained. "Oh, Cr. Ziller," he said. "I'm sorry. You're a little uncomfortable with this, aren't you? I'm being very selfish. It didn't occur to me my dying might—"

"No, no, I, I . . . Well, yes." Ziller felt his nose color. He glanced around the other people nearest the bed. They looked sympathetic, understanding. He hated them. "It just seems strange. That's all."

"May I, Composer?" the man said. He stretched out one hand and Ziller allowed one of his to be grasped again. The grip was lighter this time. "Our ways must seem odd to you."

"No odder than ours to you, I'm sure."

"I am very ready to die, Cr. Ziller." Ilom Dolince smiled. "I've lived four hundred and fifteen years, sir. I've seen the Chebalyths of Eyske in their Skydark migration, watched field liners sculpt solar flares in the High Nudrun, I've held my own newborn in my hands, flown the caverns of Sart and dived the tube-arches of Lirouthale. I've seen so much, done so much, that even with my neural lace trying to tie my elsewhere memories as seamlessly as it can into what's in my head, I can tell I've lost a lot from in here." He tapped one temple. "Not from my memory, but from my personality. And so it's time to change or move on or just stop. I've put a version of me into a group mind in case anybody wants to ask me anything at any time, but really I can't be bothered living anymore. At least, not once I've seen Ossuliera City, which I've been saving for this moment." He smiled at the avatar. "Maybe I'll come back when the end of the universe happens."

"You also said you wanted to be revived into an especially nubile cheerleader if Notromg Town ever won the Orbital Cup," the avatar said solemnly. It nodded and took a breath in through its teeth. "I'd go with the universe-ending thing, if I were you."

"So you see, sir?" Ilom Dolince said, his eyes glittering. "I'm stopping." One thin hand patted Ziller's. "I'm only sorry I won't be here to listen to your new work, maestro. I was very tempted to stay, but . . . Well, there is always something to keep us, if we are not determined, isn't there?"

"I dare say."

"I hope you're not offended, sir. Little else would have made me even think of delaying. You're not offended, are you?"

"Would it make any difference if I was, Mr. Dolince?" Ziller asked.

"It would, sir. If I thought you were especially hurt, I could still delay, though I might be straining the patience of these good people," Dolince said, looking around those gathered by his bedside. There was a low chorus of friendly-sounding dissent. "You see, Cr. Ziller? I have made my peace. I don't think I have ever been so well thought of."

"Then I'd be honored to be included in that regard." He patted the human's hand.

"Is it a great work, Cr. Ziller? I hope it is."

"I can't say, Mr. Dolince," Ziller told him. "I'm pleased with it." He sighed. "Experience would indicate that provides no guide whatsoever either to its initial reception or eventual reputation."

The man in the bed smiled widely. "I hope it goes wonderfully well, Cr. Ziller."

"So do I, sir."

Ilom Dolince closed his eyes for a moment or two. When they flickered open his grip gradually loosened. "An honor, Cr. Ziller," he whispered.

Ziller let the human's hand go and stepped gratefully away as others flowed in around him.

Ossuliera City emerged from the shadows around a corner of the gorge. It was partly carved from the fawn-colored cliffs of the chasm itself, and partly from stones brought in from other areas of the world, and beyond. The River Jhree was tamed here, running straight and deep and calm in a single great channel from which smaller canals and docks diverged, arched over by delicate bridges of foametal and wood both living and dead.

The quaysides on either bank were great flat platforms of golden sandstone running into the blue-hazed distance, speckled with people and animals, shadeplant and pavilions, leaping fountains and tall twisted columns of extravagantly latticed metals and glittering minerals.

Tall and stately barges sat moored by steps where troupes of chaurgresiles sat grooming each other with solemn intensity. The mirror sails of smaller craft caught fitful, swirling breezes to slide angled shadows along the quiet waters behind and cast flitting, shimmering reflections along the bustling quays to either side.

Above, the stepped city rose in set-back terrace after set-back terrace from these vast and busy shelves of stone; awnings and umbreltrees dotted the galleries and piazzas, canals disappeared into vaulted tunnels cut into the chiselled cliffs, perfume fires scnt thin coils of violet and orange smoke rolling up toward the pale blue sky, where flocks of pure white lucent plowtails wheeled on outstretched wings inscribing silent spirals in the air, and arcing overhead a layered succession of higher and longer and more tenuously poised bridges bowed like rainbows made solid in the misty air, their intricately carved and dazzlingly inlaid surfaces brimming with flowers and strung with leafchain, storycreep and veilmoss.

Music played, echoing amongst the canyons, decks and bridges of the city. The barge's sudden appearance caused a volley of excited trumpeting from a shambling pack of cumbrosaurs arranged on a flight of steps descending to the river.

Ziller, at the deck rail, turned from the tumult of the view to look back to the bed where Ilom Dolince lay. A few people seemed to be crying. The avatar was holding a hand over the man's forehead. It smoothed its silver fingers down over his eyes.

The Chelgrian watched the beautiful city glide past for a while. When he looked back again a long gray Displacement drone was hovering over the bed. The people gathered around stood back a little, forming a rough circle. A silvery field shimmered in the air where the man's body was, then shrank to a point and vanished. The bedclothes settled back softly over the place where the body had been.

"People always look up to the sun at such moments," he remembered Kabe pointing out once. What he was witnessing was the conventional method of disposing of the dead both here and throughout most of the rest of the Culture. The body had been Displaced into the core of the local star. And, as Kabe had pointed out, if they could see it, the people present always looked up to that sun, even though it would usually be a million years or more before the photons formed from the dispatched corpse would shine down upon wherever it was they stood.

A million years. Would this artificial, carefully maintained world still be here after all that time? He doubted it. The Culture itself would probably be gone by then. Chel certainly would. Perhaps people looked up now because they knew there would be nobody around to look up then.

There was another ceremony to be carried out on the barge before it left Ossuliera City. A woman called Nisil Tchasole was to be reborn. Stored in mind-state only eight hundred years earlier, she had been a combatant in the Idiran War. She'd wanted to be reawakened in time to see the light from the second of the Twin Novae shine down upon Masaq'. A clone of her original body had been grown for her and her personality was to be quickened inside it within the hour, so she would have the next five or so days to re-acclimatize herself to life before the second nova burst upon the local skies.

The pairing of this rebirth with Ilom Dolince's death was supposed to take some of the sadness out of the man's departure, but Ziller found the very neatness of the pairing trite and contrived. He didn't wait to see this overly neat revival; he jumped ship when it docked, walked around for a while and then took the underground back to Aquime.

"Yes, I was a twin, once. The story is well known, I think, and very much on record. There are any number of tellings and interpretations of it. There are even some fictive and musical pieces based on it, some more accurate than others. I can recommend—"

"Yes, I know all that, but I'd like you to tell the story."

"Are you sure?"

"Of course I'm sure."

"Oh, all right then."

The avatar and the Chelgrian stood in a little eight-person module, underneath the outer-facing surface of the Orbital. The craft was an all-media general run-about, capable of traveling under water, flying in atmosphere or, as now, voyaging in space, albeit at purely relativistic speeds. The two of them stood facing forward; the screen started at their feet and swept above their heads. It was like standing in the nose of a glass-nosed spaceship, except that no glass ever made could have transmitted such a faithful representation of the view ahead and around.

It was two days after the death of Ilom Dolince, three before the concert in the Stullien Bowl. Ziller, his symphony completed and rehearsals under way, felt consumed by a familiar restlessness. Trying to think of sights on Masaq' he hadn't yet seen, he'd asked to be shown what the Orbital looked like from underneath as it sped by, and so he and the avatar had descended by sub-Plate access to the small space port deep under Aquime.

The plateau Aquime sat on was mostly hollow, the space inside taken up by old ship stores and mostly mothballed general-product factories. Sub-Plate access over the majority of the Orbital's area was a matter of descending a hundred meters or less; from Aquime there was a good kilometer straight down to open space.

The eight-person module was slowing now, relative to the world above them. It was facing spinwards, so the effect was of the Orbital fifty meters above their heads starting to move past overhead, slowly at first but gradually more and more quickly, while the stars beneath their feet and to either side, which had been slowly wheeling, appeared now to be slowing down to a stop.

The undersurface of the world was a grayly shining expanse of what looked like metal, lit dimly by the starlight and the sunlight reflected from some of the system's nearer planets. There was something intimidatingly flat and perfect about the vast plain hanging above their heads, Ziller thought, for all that it was dotted with masts and access points and woven by the underground car tracks.

The tracks rose slowly in places to cross other routes which sank halfway into the fabric of the under-surface before returning to the vast and level plain. In other places the tracks swung around in vast loops that were tens or even hundreds of kilometers across, creating a vastly complicated lacework of grooves and lines etched into the under-surface of the world like a fabulously intricate inscription upon a bracelet. Ziller watched some of the cars zip across the under-surface, in ones or twos or longer trains.

The tracks provided the best gauge of their relative speed; they had moved above them languidly at first, seeming to slide gradually away or come curving smoothly back. Now, as the module slowed, using its engines to brake, and the Orbital appeared to speed up, the lines started to flow and then race by above.

They went under a Bulkhead Range, still seeming to gather speed. The ceiling of grayness above them raced away, disappearing into a darkness hundreds of kilometers in height, strung with microscopic lights way above. The car tracks here rested on impossibly slender sling-bridges; they flashed past, perfectly straight thin lines of dim light, their supporting monofils invisible at the relative speed the module had built up.

Then the far slope of the Bulkhead Range came swooping down to meet them, flashing toward the module's nose. Ziller tried not to duck. He failed. The avatar said nothing, but the module moved further out, so that they were half a kilometer away from the under-surface. This had the temporary effect of seeming to slow the Orbital down.

The avatar started to tell Ziller its story.

Once, the Mind that had become Masaq' Hub—replacing the original incumbent, who had chosen to Sublime not long after the end of the Idiran War—had been the mind in the body of a ship called the *Lasting Damage*. It was a Culture General Systems Vehicle, built toward the end of the three uneasy decades when it gradually became clear that a war between the Idirans and the Culture was more likely to occur than not.

It had been constructed to fulfil the role of a civilian ship if that conflict somehow didn't happen, but it had also been designed to play a full part in the war if it did come, ready to continually construct smaller warships, transport personnel and matériel and—packed with its own weaponry—become directly involved in battle.

During the first phase of the conflict, when the Idirans were pressing the Culture on every front and the Culture was doing little more than falling further and further back and mounting only very occasional holding actions where time had to be bought to carry out an evacuation, the number of genuine warships ready to fight was still small. The slack was mostly taken up by General Contacts Vehicles, but the few war-prepped GSVs took their share of the burden as well.

There were frequent occasions and battles when military prudence would have dictated the dispatch of a fleet of smaller war craft, the non-return of some—even most—of which would be deplorable but not a disaster, but which, while the Culture was still completing its preparations for full-scale war production, could only be dealt with by the commitment of a combat-ready GSV.

A tooled-up General Systems Vehicle was a supremely powerful fighting machine, easily outgunning any single unit on the Idiran side, but it was not just inherently less flexible as an instrument of war compared to a fleet of smaller craft, it was also unique in the binary nature of its survivability. If a fleet ran into serious trouble usually some of its ships could run away to fight another day, but a similarly beset GSV either triumphed or suffered total destruction—at its own behest if not because of the actions of the enemy.

Just the contemplation of a loss on such a magnitude was sufficient to give the strategic planning Minds of the Culture's war command the equivalent of ulcers, sleepless nights and general conniptions.

In one of the more desperate of those engagements, buying time while a group of Culture Orbitals was readied for flight and slowly accelerated to a velocity sufficient to ensure the worlds' escape from the volume of space under threat, the *Lasting Damage* had thrown itself into a particularly wild and dangerous environment deep inside the blossoming sphere of Idiran hegemony.

Before it had departed on what most concerned, including itself, thought would be its last mission, it had, as a matter of course, transmitted its mind-state—effectively its soul—to another GSV which then sent the recording onward to another Culture Mind on the far side of the galaxy, where it might be held, dormant and safe. Then, along with a few subsidiary units—barely meriting the name warships, more like semi-devolved powered weapon pods—it set off on its raid, climbing up and out above the lens of the galaxy on a high, curving course, hooked above the swell of stars like a claw.

The *Lasting Damage* plunged into the web of Idiran supply, logistic support and reinforcement routes like a berserk raptor thrown into a nest of hibernating kittens, devastating and disrupting all it could find in an erratic series of pulverizingly murderous full-speed attacks spread throughout centuries of space the Idirans had thought long since swept free of Culture ships.

It had been agreed that there would be no communication from the GSV unless by some miracle it made it back into the rapidly withdrawing sphere of Culture influence; the only sign that reached its comrade craft that it had escaped immediate detection and destruction was that the pressure on the units remaining behind to resist the direct thrust of the Idiran battle fleets lessened appreciably, as enemy vessels were either intercepted before they reached the front or diverted from it to deal with the emerging threat.

Then there came rumors, through some of the refugee craft of neutrals fleeing the hostilities, of a knot of Idiran fleets swarming around a volume of space near a recent raid location on the very outskirts of the galaxy, followed by a furious battle culminating in a gigantic annihilatory explosion, whose signature, when it was finally picked up and analyzed, was exactly that produced when a beleaguered military GSV of the Culture had had time to orchestrate a maximally extraneously damaging destruct sequence.

News of the battle and the GSV's martial success and final sacrifice was headlining, main-menu stuff for less than a day. The war, like the Idiran battle fleets, swept onward, burgeoning with distraction and ruse, incident and havoc, horror and spectacle.

Gradually the Culture implemented its shift to full-scale war production; the Idirans—already slowed by the commitments they'd had to make to control the colossal volumes of their newly conquered territories—found the pace of their advance faltering in places, initially through their own inability to bring the requisite combat apparatus to bear but increasingly due to the growing ability of the Culture to push back, as whole fleets of new warships were produced and dispatched by the Culture's Orbital manufactures, far away from the war.

New evidence of the destruction of the GSV *Lasting Damage*—and the Idiran war vessels it had taken with it—came in from a neutral ship of another Involved species which had passed near the battle site. The stored personality of the *Lasting Damage* was duly resurrected from the Mind it had been stored with and emplaced into another craft of the same class. It joined—rejoined—the encompassing struggle, thrown into battle after battle, never knowing which might be its last, and holding within itself all the memories of its earlier incarnation, intact right up until the instant it had cast off its fields and set its looping, trajectorial course for Idiran space, a full year earlier.

There was just one complication.

The *Lasting Damage,* the original ship Mind, had not been destroyed. As a GSV it had struggled to the end and fought to the last, dutifully, determinedly and without thought for its own safety, but finally, as an individual Mind, it had escaped in one of its slaved weapon pods.

Having suffered its due portion of the profoundly focused attentions of not one but several Idiran war fleets, the not-quite-warship was by then little more than a wreck; a not-quite-not-quite-warship.

Thrown from the erupting energies of the self-destructing GSV, flung out of the main body of the galaxy with barely sufficient energy to maintain its own fabric, it flew above and away from the plane of the galaxy more like a gigantic piece of shrapnel than any sort of ship, largely disarmed, mostly blind, entirely dumb and not daring to use its all-too-rough and barely ready engines for fear of detection until, at length, it had no choice. Even then it turned them on for only the minimum amount of time necessary to stop itself colliding with the energy grid between the universes.

If the Idirans had had more time, they would have searched for any

surviving fragments of the GSV, and probably they would have found
the castaway. As it was, there had been more pressing matters to
attend to. By the time anybody thought to double-check that the
GSV's destruction had been as complete as it had first appeared, the
half-ruined vessel, now millennia distant from the upper limit of the
great disc of stars that was the galaxy, was just about far enough away
to escape detection.

Gradually it had started to repair itself. Hundreds of days passed.
Eventually it risked using its much worked-upon engines to start
tugging it toward the regions of space where it hoped the Culture
still held sway. Uncertain who was where, it abstained from signaling
until, at last, it arrived back in the galaxy proper in a region which it
was reasonably confident must still be outside Idiran control.

The signal announcing its arrival caused some confusion at first,
but a GSV rendezvoused with it and took it aboard. It was informed
it had a twin.

It was the first but not the last time something like this would happen during the war, despite all the care the Culture took to confirm
the deaths of its Minds. The original Mind was re-emplaced in
another newly built GSV and took the name *Lasting Damage I*. The
successor ship renamed itself *Lasting Damage II*.

They became part of the same battle fleet following their mutual
request and fought together through another four decades of war.
Near the end they were both present when the Battle of the Twin
Novae took place, in the region of space known as Arm One-Six.

One survived, the other perished.

They had swapped mind-states before the battle began. The sur-
vivor incorporated the soul of the destroyed ship into its own personality, as they had agreed. It too was almost annihilated in the fighting, and again had to take to a smaller craft to save both itself and the
salvaged soul of its twin.

"Which one died," Ziller asked, "I or II?"

The avatar gave a small, diffident smile. "We were close together at
the time when it happened, and it was all very confused. I was able
to conceal who died and who survived for a good many years, until

somebody did the relevant detective work. It was II who was killed, I who lived." The creature shrugged. "It didn't matter. It was only the fabric of the craft housing the substrate which was destroyed, and the body of the surviving ship met the same fate. The result was the same as it would have been the other way round. Both Minds became the one Mind, became me." The avatar seemed to hesitate, then gave a dainty little bow.

Ziller watched the Orbital race by overhead. Car lines whipped past, almost too fast to follow. Only the vaguest impressions of actual cars, even in long trains, were visible unless they were moving in the same direction as the module appeared to be. Then they seemed to move more slowly for a while, before drawing away, pulling ahead, falling behind or curving away to either side.

"I imagine the situation must have been confused indeed if you were able to hide who'd died," Ziller said.

"It was pretty bad," the avatar agreed lightly. It was watching the Orbital under-surface whiz by with a vague smile on its face. "The way war tends to be."

"What was it made you want to become a Hub Mind?"

"You mean beyond the urge to settle down and do something constructive after all those decades spent hurtling across the galaxy destroying things?"

"Yes."

The avatar turned to face him. "I'd have to assume you've done your research here, Cr. Ziller."

"I do know a little of what happened. Just think of me as old-fashioned enough, or primitive enough, to like hearing things straight from the person who was there."

"I had to destroy an Orbital, Ziller. In fact I had to blitz three in a single day."

"Well, war is hell."

The avatar looked at him, as though trying to decide whether the Chelgrian was trying too hard to make light of the situation. "As I said, the events are all entirely a matter of public record."

"I take it there was no real choice?"

"Indeed. That was the judgment I had to act upon."

"Your own?"

"Partially. I was part of the decision-making process, though even if I'd disagreed I might still have acted as I did. That's what strategic planning is there for."

"It must be a burden, not even being able to say you were just obeying orders."

"Well, that is always a lie, or a sign you are fighting for an unworthy cause, or still have a very long way to develop civilizationally."

"A terrible waste, three Orbitals. A responsibility."

The avatar shrugged. "An Orbital is just unconscious matter, even if it does represent a lot of effort and expended energy. Their Minds were already safe, long gone. The human deaths were what I found affecting."

"Did many people die?"

"Three thousand four hundred and ninety-two."

"Out of how many?"

"Three hundred and ten million."

"A small proportion."

"It's always one hundred percent for the individual concerned."

"Still."

"No, no Still," the avatar said, shaking its head. Light slid across its silver skin.

"How did the few hundred million survive?"

"Shipped out, mostly. About twenty percent were evacuated in underground cars; they work as lifeboats. There are lots of ways to survive: you can move whole Orbitals if you have the time, or you can ship people out, or—short-term—use underground cars or other transport systems, or just suits. On a very few occasions entire Orbitals have been evacuated by storage/transmission; the human bodies were left inert after their mind-states were zapped away. Though that doesn't always save you, if the storing substrate's slagged too before it can transmit onward."

"And the ones who didn't get away?"

"All knew the choice they were making. Some had lost loved ones, some were, I suppose, mad, but nobody was sure enough to deny them their choice, some were old and/or tired of life, and some left it too late to escape either corporeally or by zapping after watching the fun, or something went wrong with their transport or mind-state record or transmission. Some held beliefs that caused them to stay." The avatar fixed its gaze on Ziller's. "Save for the ones who experienced equipment malfunctions, I recorded every one of those deaths, Ziller. I didn't want them to be faceless, I didn't want to be able to forget."

"That was ghoulish, wasn't it?"

"Call it what you want. It was something I felt I had to do. War can alter your perceptions, change your sense of values. I didn't want to feel that what I was doing was anything other than momentous and horrific; even, in some first principles sense, barbaric. I sent drones, micro-missiles, camera platforms and bugs down to those three Orbitals. I watched each of those people die. Some went in less than the blink of an eye, obliterated by my own energy weapons or annihilated by the warheads I'd Displaced. Some took only a little longer, incinerated by the radiation or torn to pieces by the blast fronts. Some died quite slowly, thrown tumbling into space to cough blood which turned to pink ice in front of their freezing eyes, or found themselves suddenly weightless as the ground fell away beneath their feet and the atmosphere around them lifted off into the vacuum like a tent caught in a gale, so that they gasped their way to death.

"Most of them I could have rescued; the same Displacers I was using to bombard the place could have sucked them off it, and as a last resort my effectors might have plucked their mind-states from their heads even as their bodies froze or burned around them. There was ample time."

"But you left them."

"Yes."

"And watched them."

"Yes."

"Still, it was their choice to stay."

"Indeed."

"And did you ask their permission to record their death throes?"

"No. If they would hand me the responsibility for killing them, they could at least indulge me in that. I did tell all concerned what I would be doing beforehand. That information saved a few. It did attract criticism, though. Some people felt it was insensitive."

"And what did you feel?"

"Appalled. Compassion. Despair. Detached. Elated. God-like. Guilty. Horrified. Miserable. Pleased. Powerful. Responsible. Soiled. Sorrowful."

"Elated? *Pleased?*"

"Those are the closest words. There is an undeniable elation in causing mayhem, in bringing about such massive destruction. As for feeling pleased, I felt pleasure that some of those who died did so because they were stupid enough to believe in gods or afterlives that do not exist, even though I felt a terrible sorrow for them as they died in their ignorance and thanks to their folly. I felt pleasure that my weapon and sensory systems were working as they were supposed to. I felt pleasure that despite my misgivings I was able to do my duty and act as I had determined a fully morally responsible agent ought to, in the circumstances."

"And all this makes you suitable to command a world of fifty billion souls?"

"Perfectly," the avatar said smoothly. "I have tasted death, Ziller. When my twin and I merged, we were close enough to the ship being destroyed to maintain a real-time link to the substrate of the Mind within as it was torn apart by the tidal forces produced by a line gun. It was over in a micro-second, but we felt it die bit by bit, area by distorted area, memory by disappearing memory, all kept going until the absolute bitter end by the ingenuity of Mind design, falling back, stepping down, closing off and retreating and regrouping and compressing and abandoning and abstracting and finessing, always trying by whatever means possible to keep its personality, its soul intact until there was nothing remaining to sacrifice, nowhere else to go and no survival strategies left to apply.

"It leaked away to nothingness in the end, pulled to pieces until it just dissolved into a mist of sub-atomic particles and the energy of chaos. The last two coherent things it held onto were its name and the need to maintain the link that communicated all that was happening to it, from it, to us. We experienced everything it experienced; all its bewilderment and terror, each iota of anger and pride, every last nuance of grief and anguish. We died with it; it was us and we were it.

"And so you see I have already died and I can remember and replay the experience in perfect detail, any time I wish." The avatar smiled silkily as it leaned closer to him, as though imparting a confidence. "Never forget I am not this silver body, Mahrai. I am not an animal brain, I am not even some attempt to produce an AI through software running on a computer. I am a Culture Mind. We are close to gods, and on the far side.

"We are quicker; we live faster and more completely than you do, with so many more senses, such a greater store of memories and at such a fine level of detail. We die more slowly, and we die more completely, too. Never forget I have had the chance to compare and contrast the ways of dying."

It looked away for a moment. The Orbital streamed past above their heads. Nothing stayed in sight for longer than the blink of an eye. The underground car tracks were blurs. The impression of speed was colossal. Ziller looked down. The stars appeared now to be stationary.

He'd done the maths in his head before they entered the module. Their speed relative to the Orbital was now about a hundred and ten kilometers per second. Long-range express car-trains would still be overtaking them; the module would take an entire day to circle the world hovering here, while Hub's travel-time guarantee was no more than two hours from any express port to any other, and a three-hour journey from any given sub-Plate access point to another.

"I have watched people die in exhaustive and penetrative detail," the avatar continued. "I have felt for them. Did you know that true subjective time is measured in the minimum duration of demonstrably separate thoughts? Per second, a human—or a Chelgrian—might have twenty or thirty, even in the heightened state of extreme distress associated with the process of dying in pain." The avatar's eyes seemed to shine. It came forward, closer to his face by the breadth of a hand.

"Whereas I," it whispered, "have billions." It smiled, and something in its expression made Ziller clench his teeth. "I watched those poor wretches die in the slowest of slow motion and I knew even as I watched that it was I who'd killed them, who was at that moment engaged in the process of killing them. For a thing like me to kill one of them or one of you is a very, very easy thing to do, and, as I discovered, absolutely disgusting. Just as I need never wonder what it is like to die, so I need never wonder what it is like to kill, Ziller, because I have done it, and it is a wasteful, graceless, worthless and hateful thing to have to do.

"And, as you might imagine, I consider that I have an obligation to discharge. I fully intend to spend the rest of my existence here as Masaq' Hub for as long as I'm needed or until I'm no longer welcome, forever keeping an eye to windward for approaching storms and just generally protecting this quaint circle of fragile little bodies and the vulnerable little brains they house from whatever harm a big dumb mechanical universe or any consciously malevolent force might happen or wish to visit upon them, specifically because I know how appallingly easy they are to destroy. I will give my life to save theirs, if it should ever come to that. And give it gladly, happily, too, knowing that the trade was entirely worth the debt I incurred eight hundred years ago, back in Arm One-Six."

The avatar stepped back, smiled broadly and tipped its head to one side. It suddenly looked, Ziller thought, as though it might as well have been discussing a banquet menu or the positioning of a new underground access tube. "Any other questions, Cr. Ziller?"

He looked at it for a moment or two. "Yes," he said. He held up his pipe. "May I smoke in here?"

The avatar stepped forward, put one arm around his shoulders and with its other hand clicked its fingers. A blue-yellow flame sprang from its index finger. "Be my guest."

Above their heads, in a matter of seconds, the Orbital slowed to a stop, while beneath their feet the stars started to revolve once again.

14

Returning to Leave, Recalling Forgetting

How many will die?"
"Perhaps ten percent. That is the calculation."
"So that would be . . . five billion?"
"Hmm, yes. That is about what we lost. That is the approximate number of souls barred from the beyond by the catastrophe visited upon us by the Culture."
"That is a great responsibility, Estodien."
"It is mass murder, Major," Visquile said, with a humorless smile. "Is that what you are thinking?"
"It is revenge, a balancing."
"And it is still mass murder, Major. Let us not mince our words. Let us not hide behind euphemisms. It is mass murder of non-combatants, and as such illegal according to the galactic agreements we are signatory to. Nevertheless we believe it is a necessary act. We are not barbarians, we are not insane. We would not dream of doing something so awful, even to aliens, if it had not become obvious that it had become—through the actions of those same aliens—something which had to be done to rescue our own people from limbo.

293

There can be no doubt that the Culture owes us those lives. But it is still an appalling act even to be contemplating." The Estodien sat forward and grasped one of Quilan's hand in his. "Major Quilan, if you have changed your mind, if you are beginning to reconsider, tell us now. Do you still have the taste for this?"

Quilan looked into the old male's eyes. "One death is an appalling thing to contemplate, Estodien."

"Of course. And five billion lives seems an unreal number, does it not?"

"Yes. Unreal."

"And do not forget; the gone-before have read you, Quilan. They have looked inside your head and know what you are capable of better than you do yourself. They pronounced you clear. Therefore they must be certain that you will do what must be done, even if you feel doubts about that yourself."

Quilan lowered his gaze. "That is comforting, Estodien."

"It is disturbing, I would have thought."

"Perhaps that a little, too. Perhaps a person who might be called a confirmed civilian would be more disturbed than comforted. I am still a soldier, Estodien. Knowing that I will do my duty is no bad thing."

"Good," Visquile said, letting go Quilan's hand and sitting back. "Now. We begin again." He stood up. "Come with me."

It was four days after they'd arrived in the airsphere. Quilan had spent most of that time within the chamber containing the temple ship *Soulhaven* with Visquile. He sat or lay in the spherical cavity that was the innermost recessional space of the *Soulhaven* while the Estodien attempted to teach him how to use the Soulkeeper's Displacer function.

"The range of the device is only fourteen meters," Visquile told him on the first day. They sat in the darkness, surrounded by a substrate holding millions of the dead. "The shorter the leap, and of course the smaller the size of the object being Displaced, the less power is required and the less likelihood there is of the action being detected. Fourteen meters should be quite sufficient for what is required."

"What is it I'm trying to send, to Displace?"

"Initially, one of a stock of twenty dummy warheads which were loaded into your Soulkeeper before it was emplaced within you. When the time comes for you to fire in anger, you will be manipulating the transference of one end of a microscopic wormhole, though without the wormhole attached."

"That sounds—"

"Bizarre, to say the least. Nevertheless."

"So, it's not a bomb?"

"No. Though the eventual effect will be somewhat similar."

"Ah," Quilan said. "So, once the Displacement has taken place, I just walk away?"

"Initially, yes." Quilan could just make out the Estodien looking at him. "Why, Major, were you expecting that to be the moment of your death?"

"Yes, I was."

"That would be too obvious, Major."

"This was described to me as being a suicide mission, Estodien. I would hate to think I might survive it and feel cheated."

"How annoying that it is so dark in here I can't see the expression on your face as you say that, Major."

"I am quite serious, Estodien."

"Hmm. Probably just as well. Well, let me put your mind at rest, Major. You will assuredly die when the wormhole activates. Instantaneously. I hope that doesn't conflict with any desire you might have harbored for a lingering demise."

"The fact will be enough, Estodien. The manner is not something I can bring myself to be concerned with, though I would prefer it to be quick rather than slow."

"Quick it will be, Major. You have my word on that."

"So, Estodien, where do I carry out this Displacement?"

"Inside the Hub of Masaq' Orbital. The space station which sits in the middle of the world."

"Is that normally accessible?"

"Of course. Quilan, they run school trips there, so their young can see the place where the machine squats that oversees their pampered lives." Quilan heard the older male gather his robes about him. "You simply ask to be shown around. It will not seem in the least suspicious. You carry out the Displacement and return to the surface of the Orbital. At the appointed time the wormhole mouth will be connected with the wormhole itself. The Hub will be destroyed.

"The Orbital will continue to run using other automatic systems situated on the perimeter, but there will be some loss of life as particularly critical processes are left to run out of control; transport systems, largely. Those souls stored in the Hub's own substrates will be lost, too. At any given moment those stored souls can number over four billion; these will account for the majority of the lives the Chelgrian-Puen require to release our own people into heaven."

QUILAN THOUGHTS.

The words rang suddenly in his head, making him flinch. He sensed Visquile go quiet beside him.

~ Gone-before, he thought and bowed his head. ~ Just one thought, really. The obvious one; why not let our dead into the beyond without this terrible action?

HEROES HEAVEN. HONORING KILLED BY ENEMIES WITHOUT REPLY DISGRACES ALL COME BEFORE (MANY MORE). DISGRACE ASSUMED WHEN WAR BELIEVED OUR FAULT. OWN RESPONSIBILITY: ACCEPT DISGRACE/ACCEPT DISGRACED. KNOW NOW WAR CAUSED BY OTHERS. FAULT THEIRS DISGRACE THEIRS RESPONSIBILITY THEIRS: DEBT THEIRS. REJOICE! NOW DISGRACED BECOME HEROES TOO ONCE BALANCE OF LOSS ACHIEVED.

~ It is hard for me to rejoice, knowing that I will have so much blood on my hands.

YOU GO TO OBLIVION QUILAN. YOUR WISH. BLOOD NOT ON YOU BUT ON MEMORY OF YOU. THAT RESTRICTED TO FEW IF MISSION WHOLLY SUCCEEDS.

THINK ACTIONS LEADING TO MISSION NOT RESULTS. RESULTS YOUR NOT CONCERN. OTHER QUESTIONS?

~ No, no other questions, thank you.

"Think of the cup, think of the interior of the cup, think of the space of air that is the shape of the inside of the cup, then think of the cup, then think of the table, then of the space around the table, then of the route you would take from here to the table, to sit down at the table and take up the cup. Think of the act of moving from here to there, think of the time it would take to move from this place to that place. Think of walking from where you are now to where the cup was when you saw it a few moments ago . . . Are you thinking of that, Quilan?"

". . . Yes."

"Send."

There was a pause.

"Have you sent?"

"No, Estodien. I don't think so. Nothing has happened."

"We will wait. Anur is sitting by the table, watching the cup. You might have sent the object without knowing it." They sat a few moments longer.

Then Visquile sighed and said, "Think of the cup. Think of the interior of the cup, think of the space of air that is the shape of the inside of the cup . . ."

"I will never do this, Estodien. I can't send the damn thing anywhere. Maybe the Soulkeeper is broken."

"I do not think so. Think of the cup . . ."

"Don't be disheartened, Major. Come now; eat. My people come from Sysa originally. There's an old Sysan saying that the soup of life is salty enough without adding tears to it."

They were in the *Soulhaven's* small refectory, at a table apart from the handful of other monks whose watch schedule meant it was their lunchtime too. They had water, bread and meat soup. Quilan was drinking his water from the plain white ceramic cup he had been using as a Displacement target all morning. He stared into it morosely.

"I do worry, Estodien. Perhaps something has gone wrong. Perhaps I don't have the right sort of imagination or something; I don't know."

"Quilan, we are attempting to do something no Chelgrian has ever done before. You're trying to turn yourself into a Chelgrian Displacement machine. You can't expect to get it right first time, on the first morning you try it." Visquile looked up as Anur, the gangly monk who had shown them around the behemothaur's exterior the day they had arrived, passed their table with his tray. He bowed clumsily, nearly tipping the contents of his tray onto the floor, only just saving it. He gave a foolish smile. Visquile nodded. Anur had been sitting watching the cup all morning, waiting for a tiny black speck—possibly preceded by a tiny silver sphere—to appear in its white scoop.

Visquile must have read Quilan's expression. "I asked Anur not to sit with us. I don't want you to think of him sitting looking at the cup, I want you to think only of the cup."

Quilan smiled. "Do you think I might Displace the test object into Anur by mistake?"

"I doubt that would happen, though you never know. But in any event, if you start to see Anur sitting there, tell me and we'll replace him with one of the other monks."

"If I did Displace the object into a person, what would happen?"

"As I understand it, almost certainly nothing. The object is too small to cause any damage. I suppose if it materialized inside the person's eye they might see a speck, or if it appeared right alongside a pain receptor they might feel a tiny pin-prick. Anywhere else in the body it would go unnoticed. If you could Displace this cup," the Estodien said, lifting his own ceramic cup, identical to Quilan's, "into somebody's brain then I dare say their head might explode, just from the pressure produced by the sudden extra volume. But the dummy warheads you are working with are too small to be noticed."

"It might block a small blood vessel."

"A capillary, perhaps. Nothing large enough to cause any tissue damage."

Quilan drank from his own cup, then held it up, looking at it. "I shall see this damn thing in my dreams."

Visquile smiled. "That might be no bad thing."

Quilan supped his soup. "What's happened to Eweirl? I haven't seen him since we arrived."

"Oh, he is about," Visquile said. "He is making preparations."

"To do with my training?"

"No, for when we leave."

"When we leave?"

Visquile smiled. "All in due time, Major."

"And the two drones, our allies?"

"As I said, all in good time, Major."

"And send."

"Yes!"

"Yes?"

". . . No. No, I hoped . . . Well, it doesn't matter. Let's try again."

"Think of the cup . . ."

"Think of a place you know or knew well. A small place. Perhaps a room or a small apartment or house, perhaps the interior of a cabin, a car, a ship; anything. It must be a place you knew well enough to be able to find your way around at night, so that you knew where everything was in the darkness and would not trip over things or break them. Imagine being there. Imagine going to a particular place and dropping, say, a crumb or a small bead or seed into a cup or other container . . ."

That night he again found it difficult to sleep. He lay looking into the darkness, curled on the broad sleeping platform, breathing in the sweet, spicy air of the giant bulbous fruit-like thing where he, Visquile and most of the others were billeted. He tried thinking about that damn cup, but gave up. He was tired of it. Instead he tried to work out exactly what was going on here.

It was obvious, he thought, that the technology inside the specially adapted Soulkeeper he had been fitted with was not Chelgrian. Some other Involved was taking a part in this; an Involved species whose technology was on a par with the Culture's.

Two of their representatives were probably housed inside the pair of double-cone-shaped drones he'd seen earlier, the ones who had spoken to him inside his head, before the gone-before had. They had not reappeared.

He supposed the drones might be remotely operated, perhaps from somewhere outside the airsphere, though the Oskendari's notorious antipathy toward such technology meant that the drones probably did physically contain the aliens. Equally, that made it all the more puzzling that the airsphere had been chosen as the place to train him in the use of a technology as advanced as that contained within his Soulkeeper, unless the idea was that if the use of such devices escaped attention here, it would also go unnoticed in the Culture.

Quilan went through what he knew of the relatively small number of Involved species sufficiently advanced to take the Culture on in this way. There were between seven and twelve other species on that sort of level, depending which set of criteria you used. None were supposed to be particularly hostile to the Culture; several were allies.

Nothing he knew of would have provided an obvious motive for what he was being trained to do, but then what he knew was only what the Involveds allowed to be known about some of the more profound relationships between them, and that most certainly did not include everything that was really going on, especially given the time scales some of the Involveds had become used to thinking on.

He knew that the Oskendari airspheres were fabulously old, even by the standards of those who called themselves the Elder races, and had succeeded in remaining mysterious throughout the Scientific Ages of hundreds of come-and-gone or been-and-Sublimed species. The rumors had it that there was some sort of link left between whoever it was who had created the airspheres and subsequently quit the matter-based life of the universe, and the mega and giga fauna which still inhabited the environments.

This link with the gone-before of the airspheres' builders was reputedly the reason that all the hegemonizing and invasive species—not to mention the unashamedly nosy species, such as the Culture—who had encountered the airspheres had thought the better of trying to take them over (or study them too closely).

These same rumors, backed up by ambiguous records held by the Elders, hinted that, long ago, a few species had imagined that they could make the big wandering worlds part of their empire, or had taken it upon themselves to send in survey devices, against the expressed wishes of the behemothaurs and the megalithine and gigalithine globular entities. Such species tended to disappear quickly or gradually from the records concerned thereafter, and there was firm statistical evidence that they disappeared more rapidly and more completely than species which had no record of antagonizing the inhabitants—and by implication the guardians—of the airspheres.

Quilan wondered if the gone-before of the airspheres had been in contact with the gone-before of Chel. Was there some link between the Sublimed of the two (or more, of course) species?

Who knew how the Sublimed thought, how they interacted? Who knew how alien minds worked? For that matter, who was entirely satisfied that they knew how the minds of one of their own species worked?

The Sublimed, he supposed, was the answer to all those questions. But any understanding seemed to be resolutely one-way.

He was being asked to perform a sort of miracle. He was being asked to commit mass murder. He tried to look into himself—and wondered if, even at that moment, the Chelgrian-Puen were listening in to his thoughts, watching the images that flitted through his mind, measuring the fixity of his commitment and weighing the worth of his soul—and was faintly, but only faintly, appalled to realize that while he doubted his ability ever to perform the miracle, he was, at the very least, quite resigned to the commission of that genocide.

· · ·

And, that night, not quite gone over to sleep, he remembered her room at the university, where they discovered each other, where he came to know her body better than his own, better than he had known any thing or subject (certainly better than anything he was supposed to be studying), and knew it in darkness and light and indeed placed a seed in a container over and over again.

He could not use that. But he remembered the room, could see the shape of darkness that was her body as she moved about it some-times, late at night, switching something off, dousing an incense coil, closing the window when it rained. (Once, she brought out some antique script-strings, erotic tales told in knots, and let him bind her; later she bound him, and he, who had always thought himself the plainest of young males, bluffly proud of his normalcy, discovered that such sex-play was not the preserve of those he'd considered weak and degenerate.)

He saw the pattern of shadow her body made across the tell-tale lights and reflections in the room. Here, now, in this strange world, so many years of time and millennia of light away from that blessed time and place, he imagined himself getting up and crossing from the curl-pad to the far side of the room. There was—there had been—a little silver cuplet on a shelf there. Sometimes when she wanted to be absolutely naked, she would take off the ring her mother had given her. It would be his duty, his mission to take the ring from her hand and place the gold band in the silver cuplet.

"All right. Are we there?"
    "Yes, we're there."
    "So. Send."
    "Yes . . . No."
    "Hmm. Well, we begin again. Think of—"
    "Yes, the cup."

"We are quite certain the device is working, Estodien?"
    "We are."
    "Then it's me. I just can't . . . It's just not in me." He dropped some

bread into his soup. He laughed bitterly. "Or it is in me, and I can't get it out."

"Patience, Major. Patience."

"There. Are we there?"

"Yes, yes, we're there."

"And; send."

"I—Wait. I think I felt—"

"Yes! Estodien! Major Quilan! It worked!"

Anur came running through from the refectory.

"Estodien, what do you think our allies will gain from my mission?"

"I'm sure I don't know, Major. It is not really a subject it would benefit either of us to worry ourselves with."

They sat in a small runabout; a sleek little two-person craft of the *Soulhaven*, in space, outside the airsphere.

The same small airship that had carried them from the airsphere portal the day they'd arrived had taken Quilan and Visquile on the return trip. They had walked through the solid-seeming tube of air again, this time to the runabout. It had drifted away from the portal, then picked up speed. It seemed to be heading toward one of the sun-moons which provided the airsphere with light. The moon drifted closer. Sunlight poured from what looked like a gigantic near-flat crater covering half of one face. It looked like the incandescent eyeball of some infernal deity.

"All that matters, Major," Visquile said, "is that the technology appears to work."

They had conducted ten successful trials with the supply of dummy warheads loaded inside the Soulkeeper. There had been an hour or so of failed attempts to repeat his initial success, then he'd managed to perform two Displacements in succession.

After that the cup had been moved to different parts of the *Soulhaven;* Quilan had only two unsuccessful attempts before he became able to Displace the specks wherever he was asked. On the third day he attempted and conducted only two Displacements, to either end of the ship. This, the fourth day, was the first time Quilan would attempt a Displacement outside the *Soulhaven*.

"Are we going to that moon, Estodien?" he asked as the giant satellite grew to fill the view ahead.

"Nearby," Visquile said. He pointed. "You see that?" A tiny fleck of gray floated away to one side of the sun-moon, just visible in the wash of light pouring from the crater. "That is where we are going."

It was something between a ship and a station. It looked like it could have been either, and as though it might have been designed by any one of thousands of early-stage Involved civilizations. It was a collection of gray-black ovoids, spheres and cylinders linked by thick struts, revolving slowly in an orbit around the sun-moon configured so that it would never fly over the vast light beam issuing from the side facing the airsphere.

"We have no idea who built it," Visquile said. "It has been here for the last few tens of thousands of years and has been much modified by successive species who have thought to use it to study the airsphere and the moons. Parts of it are currently equipped to provide reasonable conditions for ourselves."

The little runabout slid inside a hangar pod stuck to the side of the largest of the spherical units. It settled to the floor and they waited while the pod's exterior doors revolved shut and air rushed in.

The canopy unsucked itself from the little craft's fuselage; they stepped out into cold air that smelled of something acrid.

The two big double-cone-shaped drones whirred from another airlock, coming to hover on either side of them.

There was no voice inside his head this time, just a deep humming from one of them which modulated to say, "Estodien, Major. Follow."

And they followed, down a passageway and through a couple of thick, mirror-finish doors to what appeared to be a sort of broad gallery with a single long window facing them and curving back behind where they had come in. It might have been the viewing cupola of an ocean liner, or a stellar cruise ship. They walked forward and Quilan realized that the window—or screen—was taller and deeper than he had at first assumed.

The impression of a band of glass or screen fell away as he under-stood that he was looking at the single great ribbon that was the slowly revolving surface of an immense world. Stars shone faintly above and below it; a couple of brighter bodies which were, just, more than mere points of light must be planets in the same system. The star providing the sunlight had to be almost directly behind the place he was looking from.

The world looked flat, spread out like the peel from some colossal fruit and thrown across the background stars. Edged top and bottom in the glinting gray-blue translucency of enormous containing walls, the surface was separated into long strips by numerous, regularly positioned verticals of gray-brown, white and—in the center—stark gray-black. These enormous mountain ranges stretched from wall to wall across the world, parcelling it up into what must have been a few dozen separate divisions.

Between them there lay about equal amounts of land and ocean, the land partly in the form of island continents, partly in smaller but appreciably large islands—set in seas of various hues of blue and green—and partly in great swathes of green, fawn, brown and red which extended from one retaining wall to the other, sometimes dotted with seas, sometimes not, but always traversed by a single darkly winding thread or a collection of barely visible filaments, green and blue tendrils laid across on the ochers, tans and tawns of the land.

Clouds swirled, speckled, waved, dotted, arced and hazed in a chaos of patterns, near-patterns and patches, brush strokes strewn across the canvas of terrain and water below.

"This is what you will see," one of the drones hummed.

The Estodien Visquile patted Quilan on the shoulder. "Welcome to Masaq' Orbital," he said.

~ Five billion of them, Huyler. Males, females, their young. This is a terrible thing we're being asked to do.

~It is, but we wouldn't be doing it if these people hadn't done something just as terrible to us.

~ These people, Huyler? These people right here, on Masaq'?

~ *Yes, these people, Quil. You've seen them. You've talked to them. When they discover where you're from they tone it down for fear of insulting you, but they're so obviously proud of the extent and depth of their democracy. They're so damned smug that they're so fully involved, they're so proud of their ability to have a say and of their right to opt-out and leave if they disagree profoundly enough with a course of action.*

So, yes, these people. They share collective responsibility for the actions of their Minds, including the Minds of Contact and Special Circumstances. That's the way they've set it up, that's the way they want it to be. There are no ignorants here, Quil, no exploited, no Invisibles or trodden-upon working class condemned forever to do the bidding of their masters. They are all masters, every one. They can all have a say on everything. So by their own precious rules, yes, it was these people who let what happened to Chel happen, even if few actually knew anything about the details at the time.

~ Do only I think that this is . . . harsh?

~ *Quil, have you heard even one of them suggest that they might disband Contact? Or reign-in SC? Have we heard any of them even suggesting thinking about that? Well, have we?*

~ No.

~ *No, not one. Oh, they tell us of their regret in such pretty language, Quilan, they say they're so fucking sorry in so many beautifully expressed and elegantly couched and delivered ways; it's like it's a game for them. It's like they're competing to see who can be most convincingly contrite! But are they prepared to really do anything apart from tell us how sorry they are?*

~ They have their own blindnesses. It is the machines we have our real argument with.

~ *It is a machine you are going to destroy.*

~ And with it five billion people.

~ *They brought it upon themselves, Major. They could vote to disband Contact today, and any one or any group of them could leave tomorrow for their Ulterior or for anywhere else, if they decided they no longer agreed with their damned policy of Interference.*

~ It is still a terrible thing we're asked to do, Huyler.

~ *I agree. But we must do it. Quil, I've avoided putting it in these terms because it sounds so portentous and I'm sure it's something you've thought about yourself anyway, but I do have to remind you; four and a half billion*

Chelgrian souls depend on you, Major. You really are their only hope.

~ So I'm told. And if the Culture retaliates?

~ *Why should they retaliate against us because one of their machines goes mad and destroys itself?*

~ Because they will not be fooled. Because they are not so stupid as we would like them to be, just careless sometimes.

~ *Even if they do suspect anything, they will still not be certain it was our doing. If everything goes according to plan it will look like the Hub did it itself, and even if they were certain we were responsible, our planners think that they will accept that we brought about an honest revenge.*

~ You know what they say, Huyler. Don't fuck with the Culture. We are about to.

~ *I don't buy the idea that this is some piece of wisdom the other Involveds have arrived at thoughtfully after millennia of contact with these people. I think it's something the Culture came up with itself. It's propaganda, Quil.*

~ Even so, a lot of the Involveds seem to think it's true. Be even slightly nice to the Culture and it will fall over itself to be still nicer back. Treat them badly and they—

~ *—And they act all hurt. It's contrived. You have to come on really evil to get them to drop the ultra-civilized performance.*

~ Slaughtering five billion of them, at least, will not constitute what they'd regard as an act of evil?

~ *They cost us that; we cost them that. They recognize that sort of revenge, that sort of trade, like any other civilization. A life for a life. They won't retaliate, Quil. Better minds than ours have thought this through. The way the Culture will see it, they'll confirm their own moral superiority over us by not retaliating. They'll accept what we're going to do to them as the due payment for what they did to us, without provocation. They'll draw a line under it there. It'll be treated as a tragedy; the other half of a débâcle that began when they tried to interfere with our development. A tragedy, not an outrage.*

~ They might wish to make an example of us.

~ *We are too far down the Involved pecking order to be worthy opponents, Quilan. There would be no honor for them in punishing us further. We have already been punished as innocents. All you and I are trying to do is even up that earlier damage.*

~ I worry that we may be being as blind to their real psychology

as they were to ours when they tried to interfere. With all their experience, they were wrong about us. We have so little training in sec-
ond-guessing the reactions of alien species; how can we be so certain
that we will get it right where they failed so dismally?

~ *Because this matters so much to us, that's why. We have thought long
and hard about what we're going to do. All this began exactly because they
failed to do the same thing. They have become so blasé about such matters that
they try to interfere with as few ships as possible, with as few resources as possible, in search of a sort of mathematical elegance. They have made the fates of
entire civilizations part of a game they play amongst themselves, to see who
can produce the biggest cultural change from the smallest investment of time
and energy.*

*And when it blows up in their faces, it is not they who suffer and die, but
us. Four and a half billion souls barred from bliss because some of their inhu-
man Minds thought they'd found a nice, neat,* elegant *way to alter a society
which had evolved to stability over six millennia.*

*They had no right to try to interfere with us in the first place, but if they
were determined to do it they might at least have had the decency to make sure
they did it properly, with some thought for the numbers of innocent lives they
were dealing with.*

~ We still may be committing a second mistake upon a first. And
they may be less tolerant than we imagine.

~ *If nothing else, Quilan, even if there is some retaliation by the Culture,
however unlikely that might be,* it doesn't matter! *If we succeed in our mission here then those four and a half billion Chelgrian souls will be saved;
they'll be admitted to heaven. No matter what happens after that they'll be
safe because the Chelgrian-Puen will have allowed them in.*

~ The Puen could allow the dead in now, Huyler. They could just
change the rules, accept them into heaven.

~ *I know, Quilan. But there is honor to be considered here, and the future.
When it was first revealed that each of our own deaths had to be balanced by
that of an enemy—*

~ It wasn't revealed, Huyler. It was made up. It was a tale we told
ourselves, not something the gods graced us with.

~ *Either way. When we decided that was the way we wanted to lead our* lives with honor, don't you think that people realized then that it might lead to what looked like unnecessary deaths, this instruction to take a life for a life? Of course they knew that.

But it was worth doing because in the long run we benefited as long as we maintained that principle. Our enemies knew we would not rest while we had deaths unavenged. And that still applies, Major. This is not some dry bit of dogma consigned to the history books or the string-frames in monastic libraries. This is a lesson that we have to keep reinforcing. Life will go on after this, and Chel will prevail, but its rules, its doctrines must be understood by each new generation and each new species we encounter.

When this is all over and we are all dead, when this is just another piece of history, the line will have been held, and we'll be the ones who held it. No matter what happens, as long as you and I do our duty, people in the future will know that to attack Chel is to invite a terrible revenge. For their good— and I mean this, Quil—for their good as well as Chel's, it's worth doing now whatever has to be done.

~ I'm glad you seem so certain, Huyler. A copy of you will have to live with the knowledge of what we are about to do. At least I'll be safely dead, with no back-up. Or at least not one that I know about.

~ I doubt they'd have made one without your consent.

~ I doubt everything, Huyler.

~ Quil?

~ Yes?

~ Are you still on board? Do you still intend to carry out your mission?

~ I do.

~ Good fellow. Let me tell you; I admire you, Major Quilan. It's been an honor and a pleasure to share your head. Just sorry it's coming to an end so soon.

~ I haven't carried it out yet. I haven't made the Displace.

~ You'll do it. They suspect nothing. The beast is taking you to its bosom, to the very center of its lair. You'll be fine.

~ I'll be dead, Huyler. In oblivion. That's all I care about.

~ I'm sorry, Quil. But what you're doing . . . there's no better way to go.

~ I wish I could believe that. But soon it won't matter. Nothing will.

• • •

Tersono made a throat-clearing noise. "Yes, it is a remarkable sight, isn't it, Ambassador? Quite stunning. Some people have been known to stand here or sit here and drink it in for hours. Kabe; you stood here for what seemed like half a day, didn't you?"

"I'm sure I must have," the Homomdan said. His deep voice echoed around the viewing gallery, producing echoes. "I do beg your pardon. How long half a day must seem for a machine that thinks at the pace you do, Tersono. Please forgive me."

"Oh, there is nothing to forgive. We drones are perfectly used to being patient while human thoughts and meaningful actions take place. We possess an entire suite of procedures specifically evolved over the millennia to cope with such moments. We are actually considerably less boreable, if I may create a neologism, than the average human."

"How comforting," Kabe said. "And thank you. I always find such a level of detail rewarding."

"You okay, Quilan?" the avatar said.

He turned to the silver-skinned creature. "I'm fine." He gestured toward the sight of the Orbital surface sliding slowly past, gloriously bright, one and a half million kilometers away but apparently much closer. The view from the gallery was normally magnified, not shown as it would have been if there was nothing between viewer and view but glass. The effect was to bring the interior perimeter closer, so that one could see more detail.

The rate it was sliding past at also gave a false impression; the Hub's viewing gallery section revolved very slowly in the opposite direction to the world's surface, so that instead of the entire Orbital taking a day to pass in front of the viewer, the experience commonly occupied less than an hour.

~ *Quilan.*
   ~ Huyler.
     ~ *Are you ready?*
       ~ I know the real reason they put you aboard, Huyler.

~ *Do you?*

~ I believe I do.

~ *And what would that be, Quil?*

~ You're not my back-up at all, are you? You're theirs.

~ *Theirs?*

~ Of Visquile, our allies—whoever they are—and the military high-ups and politicians who sanctioned this.

~ *You'll have to explain, Major.*

~ Is it supposed to be too devious for a bluff old soldier to have thought of?

~ *What?*

~ You're not here to give me somebody to moan to, are you, Huyler? You're not here to provide me with company, or to be some sort of expert on the Culture.

~ *Have I been wrong about anything?*

~ Oh, no. No, they must have loaded you with a complete Culture database. But it's all stuff anybody could get from the standard public reservoirs. Your insights are all secondhand, Huyler; I've checked.

~ *I'm shocked, Quilan. Do we think this counts as slander or libel?*

~ You are my co-pilot though, aren't you?"

~ *That's what you were told I was to be. That's what I am.*

~ In one of those old-fashioned, manual-only airplanes the co-pilot is there, at least partly, to take over from the pilot if he's unable to perform his duties. Is that not true?

~ *Perfectly.*

~ So, if I changed my mind now, if I was determined not to make the Displacement, if I decided that I didn't want to kill all these people . . . What? What would happen? Tell me. Please be honest. We owe each other honesty.

~ *You're sure you want to know?*

~ Quite perfectly.

~ *You're right. If you won't make the Displace, I make it for you. I know exactly the bits of your brain you used to make it happen, I know the precise procedures. Better than you, in a way.*

~ So the Displace takes place regardless?

~ *So the Displace takes place regardless.*

~ And what happens to me?

~ *That depends on what you try to do. If you try to warn them, you drop down dead, or become paralyzed, or undergo a fit, or start babbling nonsense, or become catatonic. The choice is mine; whatever might arouse the least suspicion in the circumstances.*

~ My. Can you do all that?

~ *I'm afraid so, son. All just part of the instruction set. I know what you're going to say before you say it, Quil. Literally. It's only just before, but that's enough; I think pretty quickly in here. But Quil, I wouldn't take pleasure in doing any of that. And I don't think I'm going to have to. You're not telling me you just thought of all this?*

~ No. No, I thought of it a long time ago. I just wanted to wait until now to ask you, in case it spoiled our close relationship, Huyler.

~ *You are going to do it, aren't you? I won't have to take over, will I?*

~ I haven't really had those hours of grace at the beginning and end of each day at all, have I? You've been watching all the time to make sure I didn't give any sign to them, just in case I had already changed my mind.

~ *Would you believe me if I told you that you did have that time without me watching?*

~ No.

~ *Well, it doesn't really matter anyway. But, as you might imagine, I will be listening in from now on, until the end. Quilan, again; you are going to do it, aren't you? I won't have to take over, will I?*

~ Yes, I'm going to do it. No, you won't have to take over.

~ *Well done, son. It is truly hateful, but it does have to be done. And it will all be over soon, for both of us.*

~ And many more besides. All right then. Here we go.

He had made six successful Displacements in a row within the mock-up of the Hub which had been constructed within the station orbiting the sun-moon of the airsphere. Six successes out of six attempts. He could do it. He would do it.

They stood within the mock-up of the observation gallery, faces lit by the image of an image. Visquile explained the thinking behind his mission.

"We understand that in a few months' time the Hub Mind of Masaq' Orbital will mark the passing of the light from the two exploding stars that gave the Twin Novae Battle of the Idiran War its name."

Visquile stood very close to Quilan. The broad band of light—a simulation of the image that he would see when he really stood in the viewing gallery of Masaq' Orbital Hub—seemed to pass in one of the Estodien's ears and out the other. Quilan fought the urge to laugh, and concentrated on listening intently to what the older male was saying.

"The Mind that is now that of Masaq' Hub was once embodied within a warship which played a major part in the Idiran War. It had to destroy three Culture Orbitals during the same battle to prevent them falling into enemy hands. It will commemorate the battle, and the two stellar explosions in particular, when the light of first one and then the other passes through the system Masaq' lies within.

"You must gain access to the Hub and make the Displacement before the second nova. Do you understand, Major Quilan?"

"I do, Estodien."

"The destruction of the Hub will be timed to coincide with the real-space light from the second nova arriving at Masaq'. It will therefore appear that the Hub Mind destroyed itself in a fit of contrition due to its guilty conscience over the actions it was responsible for during the Idiran War. The death of the Hub Mind and the humans will look like a tragedy, not an outrage. The souls of those Chelgrians held in limbo by the dictates of honor and piety will be released into heaven. The Culture will suffer a blow that will affect every Hub, every Mind, every human. We will have our numerical revenge and no more, but we will have that extra satisfaction that costs no more lives, only the additional discomfiture of our enemies, the people who, in effect, carried out an unprovoked surprise attack on us. Do you see, Quilan?"

"I see, Estodien."

"Watch, Major Quilan."

"I'm watching, Estodien."

They had quit the orbiting space station. He and Visquile were in the two-person runabout. The two alien drones were in a slightly larger cone-shaped black-body craft alongside.

One of the ancient space station's pressurized containment vessels had suffered a carefully contrived blowout which looked exactly like a chance catastrophe due to long-term neglect. It started to fall away on an altered orbit, its new heading taking it quickly toward the vast outpouring of energies erupting from the airsphere-facing side of the sun-moon.

They watched for a while. The station curved closer and closer to the edge of the invisible light column. The little runabout's head-up display printed a line across the canopy for each of them, showing where that edge was. Just before the station encountered the column's perimeter, Visquile said, "That last warhead was not a dummy, Major. It was the real thing. The other end of the wormhole is located possibly inside the sun-moon itself, or possibly inside something very like it, a long way away. The energies involved will be very similar to what will happen to Masaq' Hub. That is why we are here rather than anywhere else."

The station never quite hit the edge of the light column. An instant before it would have, its slowly spinning, erratically configured shape was replaced with a shockingly, blindingly bright blast of light which caused the runabout's canopy to black out over half its area. Quilan's eyes closed instinctively. The after-image burned behind his eyelids, yellow and orange. He heard Visquile grunt. Around them, the small runabout hummed and clicked and whined.

When he opened his eyes only the after-image was still there, glowing orange against the anonymous black of space and jumping ahead of his gaze every time he shifted it about, trying, in vain, to see what might be left of the stricken, tumbling space station.

~ There.
     ~ That looked good to me. I think you've done it. Well done, Quil.

"There," Tersono said, placing a ring of red light onto the screen, over a group of lakes in one continent. "That is where the Stullien Bowl is. The venue for tomorrow's concert." The drone turned to the avatar. "Is everything ready for the concert, Hub?"

The avatar shrugged. "Everything except the composer."

"Oh! I'm sure he is just teasing us," Tersono said quickly. Its aura field positively shone with ruby light. "Of course Cr. Ziller will be there. How could he not be? He'll be there. I'm quite certain."

"I wouldn't be too sure about that," Kabe rumbled.

"No, he will! I'm quite positive."

Kabe turned to the Chelgrian. "You will be taking up your invitation, won't you, Major Quilan? . . . Major?"

"What? Oh. Yes. Yes, I'm looking forward to it. Of course."

"Well," Kabe said, nodding massively, "they'll find somebody else to conduct, I dare say."

The major seemed distracted, Kabe thought. Then he seemed to pull himself together. "Well, no," he said, looking to each of them in turn. "If my presence is really going to prevent Mahrai Ziller from attending his own first night then of course I'll stay away."

"Oh no!" Tersono said, aura flushing briefly blue. "There's no need for that. No, not at all; I'm sure that Cr. Ziller has every intention of being there. He may leave it until the last moment before he sets off, but set off he will, I'm quite positive. Please, Major Quilan, you must be there for the concert. Ziller's first symphony in eleven years, the first ever première outside Chel, you, coming all this way, you two the only Chelgrians for millennia . . . You *must* be there. It will be the experience of a lifetime!"

Quilan looked steadily at the drone for a moment. "I think Mahrai Ziller's presence at the concert is of more importance than mine. To go knowing that I would be keeping him away would be a selfish, impolite and even dishonorable act, don't you think? But please, let's talk no more of it."

He left the airsphere the next day. Visquile saw him off from the little landing stage behind the giant hollowed-out husk which had provided their quarters.

Quilan thought the older male seemed distracted. "Is everything all right, Estodien?" he asked.

Visquile looked at him. "No," he said, after what looked like a little thought. "No, we had an intelligence update this morning and our wizards of counter-espionage have come up with two pieces of worrying news rather than the more common single bombshell; it appears that not only do we have a spy amongst our number, but also there may be a Culture citizen here somewhere in the airsphere." The Estodien rubbed the top of his silver stave, frowning at his distorted reflection there. "One might have hoped they could have told us these things earlier, but I suppose later is better than never." Visquile smiled. "Don't look so worried, Major, I'm sure everything is still under control. Or soon will be."

The airship touched down. Eweirl stepped out. The white-furred male smiled broadly and bowed minutely when he saw Quilan. He bowed more deeply when he faced the Estodien, who patted him on the shoulder. "You see, Quilan? Eweirl is here to take care of things. Go back, Major. Prepare for your mission. You will have your co-pilot before too long. Good luck."

"Thank you, Estodien." Quilan glanced at the grinning Eweirl, then bowed to the older male. "I hope everything goes well here."

Visquile let his hand rest on Eweirl's shoulder. "I'm sure it will. Goodbye, Major. It's been a pleasure. Again, good luck, and do your duty. I'm sure you will make us all proud."

Quilan stepped aboard the little airship. He looked out through one of the gauzy windows as the craft lifted away from the platform. Visquile and Eweirl were already deep in conversation.

The rest of the journey was a mirror-image of the route he had

taken on the way out except that when he got to Chel he was taken
from Equator Launch City in a sealed shuttle straight to Ubrent, and
then by car, at night, directly to the gates of the monastery at
Cadracet.

He stood on the ancient path. The night air smelled fragrant with
sigh tree resin, and seemed thin like water after the soup-thick atmosphere of the airsphere.

He had returned only to be called away. As far as the official
records were concerned, he had never left, never been taken away by
the strange lady in her dark cloak all those months ago, never
descended with her to the road that led back to the world and was
spotted with fresh blood.

Tomorrow he would be summoned to Chelise itself, to be asked
to undertake a mission to the Culture world called Masaq', to
attempt to persuade the renegade and dissident Mahrai Ziller, composer, to return to his home-place and be the very symbol of the
renaissance of Chel and the Chelgrian domain.

Tonight, while he slept—if all went according to plan and the
temporary microstructures, chemicals and nano-glandular processes
which had been imparted into his brain had the desired effect—he
would forget all that had happened since Colonel Ghejaline had
appeared out of the snow in the courtyard of the monastery those
hundred and more days ago.

He would remember what he needed to remember, no more, bit
by bit. His most available memories would be kept safe from intrusion and comprehension by all but the most obvious and damaging
procedures. He thought he could feel the process of forgetting starting to happen even as he recalled the fact that it would take place.

Summer rain fell gently around him. The engine sound and the
lights of the car that had brought him here had disappeared into the
clouds below. He raised his hand to the little door set within the
gates.

The postern opened quickly and silently and he was beckoned to
come in.

· · ·

~ Yes. Well done.

It had crossed his mind that now he had done what he was supposed to do, now that the mission was over, he might start—or try to start—telling the drone Tersono, or the Hub avatar itself, or the Homomdan Kabe, or all three, what he had just done, so that Huyler would have no choice but to disable him, hopefully kill him, but he did not.

Huyler might not kill him, after all, just disable him, and besides, he would be partially jeopardizing the mission. It was better for Chel, better for the mission, to make everything appear as normal, until the light from the second nova poured through the system and across the Orbital.

"Well, that completes the tour," the avatar said.

"So. My friends; shall we go?" the drone E. H. Tersono said chirpily. Its ceramic casing was surrounded by a healthy pink glow.

"Yes," Quilan heard himself say. "Let's go."

15

A Certain Loss of Control

He woke slowly, a little fuzzy-headed. It was very dark. He stretched lazily and could feel Worosei at his side. She moved sleepily toward him, curling into his body to fit. He put one arm around her and she snuggled closer.

Just as he was waking more completely and deciding that he wanted her, she turned her head to his, smiling, her lips opening.

She slid on top of him, and it was one of those times when the sex is so strong and balanced and exalted that it is almost beyond separate genders; it is as though it doesn't matter who is male and who is female, and which part belongs to which person, when the genitalia seem somehow at once shared and separate, both belonging to each and to neither; his sex was a magical entity that penetrated both of them equally as she moved over him, while hers became like some fabulous, enchanted cloak that had spread and flowed to cover both their bodies, turning every part of them into a single sexually sensual surface.

It brightened very gradually as they made love, and then, after they had each finished and their pelts were matted with saliva and sweat and they were both panting heavily, they lay side by side, staring into each other's eyes.

He was grinning. He couldn't help it. He looked around. He still wasn't entirely sure where he was. The room looked anonymous and yet extremely high-ceilinged and very bright. He had the odd feeling it ought to be making his eyes hurt, and yet it wasn't.

He looked at her again. She had her head propped up on one fist and was looking at him. When he saw that face, took in that expression, he felt a strange shock, and then an exquisite, perfectly intense terror. Worosei had never looked at him like this; not just at him but around him, through him.

There was an utter coldness and a ferocious, infinite intelligence in those dark eyes. Something without mercy or illusion was staring straight into his soul and finding it not so much wanting, as absent.

Worosei's fur turned perfectly silver and smoothed into her skin. She was a naked silver mirror and he could see himself in her long, lithe frame, perversely distorted like something being melted and pulled apart. He opened his mouth and tried to speak. His tongue was too big and his throat had gone quite dry.

It was she who spoke, not him:

"Don't think I've been fooled for a moment, Quilan."

It was not Worosei's voice.

She pushed down on her elbow and rose from the bed with a powerful, fluid grace. He watched her go, and then became aware that behind him, on the other side of the curl-pad, there was an old male, also naked and staring at him, blinking.

The old fellow didn't say a thing. He looked confused. He was at once utterly familiar and a complete stranger.

Quilan woke, panting. He stared wildly around.

He was in the broad curl-pad in the apartment in Aquime City. It looked to be about dawn and there was a swirl of snow beyond the dome of the skylight.

He gasped, "Lights," and looked around the huge room as it brightened.

Nothing appeared to be out of place. He was alone.

It was the day that would end with the concert in the Stullien

Bowl, which would climax with the first performance of Mahrai Ziller's new symphony *Expiring Light,* which itself would end when the light from the nova induced upon the star Junce eight hundred years ago finally arrived at the Lacelere system and Masaq' Orbital.

With an ignoble and tearing feeling of nausea he remembered that he had done his duty and the matter was out of his hands, out of his head, now. What would happen would happen. He could do no more about it than anybody else here. Less, in fact. Nobody else here had another mind aboard, listening to their every thought—

Of course; since last night, if not before, he no longer had his hour of grace at the end and beginning of each day.

~ Huyler?

~ *Here. Have you had dreams like that before?*

~ You experienced it too?

~ *I'm watching and listening for any sign you might give which would warn them what's going to happen this evening. I'm not invading your dreams. But I do have to monitor your body, so I know that was one hell of a hot dream that seemed to suddenly turn pretty frightening. Want to tell me about it?*

Quilan hesitated. He waved the lights off and lay back in the darkness. "No," he said.

He became aware that he had spoken rather than thought the word at the same time as he realized that he couldn't say the next word he'd thought he was going to say. It would have been "No" again, but it just never made it to his lips.

He found that he could not move at all. Another moment of terror, at his paralysis and the fact he was at the mercy of somebody else.

~ *Sorry. You were speaking there, not communicating. There; you're, ah, back in charge.*

Quilan moved on the curl-pad and cleared his throat, checking that he controlled his own body again.

~ All I was going to say was, No, no need. No need to talk about it.

~ *You sure? You haven't been that distressed until now, not in the whole time we've been together.*

~ I'm telling you I'm fine, all right?

~ *Okay, all right.*

~ Even if I wasn't it wouldn't matter anyway, would it? Not after tonight. I'm going to try and get more sleep now. We can talk later.

~ *Whatever you say. Sleep well.*

~ I doubt it.

He lay back and watched the dry-looking dark flurries of snow fling themselves whirling at the domed skylight in a soundless fury that seemed poised in meaning exactly halfway between comic and threatening. He wondered if the snow looked the same way to the other intelligence watching through his eyes.

He didn't think any more sleep would come, and it did not.

The dozen or so civilizations which would eventually go onto form the Culture had, during their separate ages of scarcity, spent vast fortunes to make virtual reality as palpably real and as dismissibly virtual as possible. Even once the Culture as an entity had been established and the use of conventional currency had come to be seen as an archaic hindrance to development rather than its moderating enabler, appreciable amounts of energy and time—both biological and machine—had been spent perfecting the various methods by which the human sensory apparatus could be convinced that it was experiencing something that was not really happening.

Thanks largely to all this pre-existing effort, the level of accuracy and believability exhibited as a matter of course by the virtual environments available on demand to any Culture citizen had been raised to such a pitch of perfection that it had long been necessary—at the most profoundly saturative level of manufactured-environment manipulation—to introduce synthetic cues into the experience just to remind the subject that what appeared to be real really wasn't.

Even at far less excessive states of illusory permeation, the immediacy and vividness of the standard virtual adventure was sufficient to make all but the most determinedly and committedly corporeal of humans quite forget that the experience they were having wasn't authentic, and the very ubiquity of this common-place conviction was a ringing tribute to the tenacity, intelligence, imagination and determination of all those individuals and organizations down the ages who had contributed to the fact that, in the Culture, anybody anytime could experience anything anywhere for nothing, and never need worry themselves with the thought that actually it was all pretend.

Naturally, then, there was, for almost everybody occasionally and for some people pretty well perpetually, an almost inestimable cachet in having seen, heard, smelled, tasted, felt or generally experienced something absolutely and definitely for real, with none of this contemptible virtuality stuff getting in the way.

The avatar gave a snort. "They're really doing it." It laughed with surprising heartiness, Kabe thought. It was not the sort of thing you expected a machine, or even the human-form representative of a machine, to do at all.

"Doing what?" he asked.

"Reinventing money," the avatar said, grinning and shaking its head.

Kabe frowned. "Would that be entirely possible?"

"No, but it's partially possible." The avatar glanced at Kabe. "It's an old saying."

"Yes, I know. 'They'd reinvent money for this,' " Kabe quoted. "Or something similar."

"Quite." The avatar nodded. "Well, for tickets to Ziller's concert, they practically are. People who can't stand other people are inviting them to dinner, booking deep-space cruises together—good grief— even agreeing to go camping with them. Camping!" The avatar giggled. "People have traded sexual favors, they've agreed to pregnancies, they've altered their appearance to accommodate a partner's desires, they've begun to change gender to please lovers; all just to get tickets." It spread its arms. "How wonderfully, bizarrely, romantically barbaric of them! don't you think?"

"Absolutely," Kabe said. "Are you sure about 'romantically'?"

"And they have indeed," the avatar continued, "come to agreements that go beyond barter to a form of liquidity regarding future considerations that sounds remarkably like money, at least as I understand it."

"How extraordinary."

"It is, isn't it?" the silver-skinned creature said. "Just one of those weird flash-fashions that jumps out of the chaos for an instant every now and again. Suddenly everybody's a live symphonic music fan." It looked puzzled. "I've made it clear there's no real room to dance." It shrugged, then swept an arm around to indicate the view. "So. What do you think?"

"Most impressive."

The Stullien Bowl was practically empty. The preparations for that evening's concert were on schedule and under way. The avatar and the Homomdan stood on the lip of the amphitheatre near a battery of lights, lasers and effects mortars each of which quite dwarfed Kabe and, he thought, looked a lot like weapons.

The crisp blue day was a couple of hours old, the sun rising at their back. Kabe could just make out the tiny shadows he and the avatar were casting across a pattern of seats four hundred meters away.

The Bowl was over a kilometer across: a steeply raked coliseum of spun carbon fibers and transparent diamond sheeting whose seats and platforms focused around a generously circular field which could adapt itself to accommodate various sports and a variety of concert and other entertainment configurations. It did have an emergency roof, but that had never been used.

The whole point of the Bowl was that it was open to the sky, and if the weather had to be of a certain type, well then Hub would do something it almost never did, and interfere meteorologically, using its prodigious energy projection and field-management capabilities to manipulate the elements until the desired effect was arrived at. Such meddling was inelegant, untidy and blunderingly coercive, but it was accepted that it had to be done to keep people happy, and that was, ultimately, Hub's whole reason for being.

Technically, the Bowl was a giant specialized barge. It floated within a network of broad canals, slowly flowing rivers, broad lakes and small seas which stretched across one of Masaq's more varied

continent-Plates and along, through and across which it could—
albeit rather slowly—navigate itself, so providing a wide choice of
external backgrounds visible through the supporting structure and
above the stadium's lip, including jagged, snow-strewn mountains,
giant cliffs, vast deserts, carpeting jungles, towering crystal cities, vast
waterfalls and gently swaying blimp tree forests.

For a particularly wild event, there was a rapids course; a giant,
quickly flowing river the Bowl could descend like a monstrous inflatable riding the world's biggest flume, monumentally spinning, tipping and bobbing until it encountered the vast cliff-encircled
whirlpool at the bottom, where it simply revolved atop a swirling
column of spiraling water being sucked plunging into a set of colossal pumps capable of emptying a sea, until one of Hub's Superlifters
came to hoist it bodily back up to its normal elevation among the
waterways above.

For tonight's performance the Bowl would be staying where it
was, at the point of a small peninsula on the shores of Bandel Lake,
Guerno Plate, a dozen continents to spinward from Xaravve. The
peninsula's point housed a collection of underground access points,
various elegantly disguised storage and support buildings, a broad
concourse lined with bars, cafés, restaurants and other entertainment
venues, and a giant bracket-shaped dock where the Bowl underwent
any necessary maintenance and repair.

The Bowl's in-built strategic tactile, sound and light systems, even
without any in-person participatory enhancement, were as good as
they could possibly be; Hub took responsibility for the remaining
external conditions.

The Bowl was one of six, all specifically constructed to provide
venues for events which needed to be held outside. They were distributed across the world so that there ought always to be one in the
right place at the right time, no matter what the required conditions.

"Though of course," Kabe felt bound to point out, "you could
have just one, and then slow down or speed up the whole Orbital, to
synchronize."

"Been done," the avatar said sniffily.

"I rather thought it might."

The avatar looked up. "Ah ha." Directly overhead, just visible through the morning haze above, a tiny roughly rectangular shape was glowing with reflected sunlight.

"What is that?"

"That is the Equator Class General Systems Vehicle *Experiencing A Significant Gravitas Shortfall*," the avatar said. Kabe saw its eyes narrow fractionally and a small smile formed about its lips and eyes. "It changed its course schedule to come and see the concert too." The avatar watched the shape grow bigger, and frowned. "It'll have to move from there though; that's where my air-burst meteorites are coming through."

"Air burst?" Kabe said. He was watching the glowing rectangle of the GSV enlarge slowly. "That sounds, ah, dramatic." Dangerous might seem a more suitable word, he thought.

The avatar shook its head. It too was watching the giant craft as it lowered itself into the atmosphere above them. "Na, it's not that dangerous," the avatar said, apparently but presumably not actually reading his mind. "The shower choreography is pretty much all set up. There might be a few bits of soft stuff that could still outgas and need retrajectoring, but they all have their own escort engines anyway." The avatar grinned at him. "I used a whole bunch of old knife missiles; reactivated war stock, which seemed appropriate. Reckoned they needed the practice."

They looked back up into the sky. The GSV was now about the same size as a hand held out at full arm's stretch. Features were starting to appear on its golden-white surfaces. "All the rocks are fully set up; fired up and forgotten long ago," the avatar continued, "sliding in simple as rings on an orrery. No danger there either." It nodded at the GSV, which was close and bright enough now to be casting its own light over the surrounding landscape, like a strangely rectangular golden moon floating over the world.

"*That* is the sort of thing Hub Minds can't help get worried about," the avatar said, hoisting one silvery eyebrow. "A trillion tons of ship capable of accelerating like an arrow out of a bow coming close enough to the surface for me to feel the curve of the fucker's gravity well if it wasn't fielded out." It shook its head. "GSVs," it said, tutting as though over a mischievous but cute child.

"Do you think they take advantage of you because you used to be one?" Kabe asked. The giant craft seemed to have come to a halt at last, filling about a quarter of the sky. Some wispy clouds had formed underneath its lower surface. Concentric shells of field showed up as barely visible lines around it, like a set of cavernous nested bubbles floating in the sky.

"Damn right," the avatar said. "Any native-to-Hub Mind would be baking its fuses at the very thought of letting something that big come inside perimeter; they like ships on the outside where if anything ever did go wrong they'd just fall away." The avatar laughed suddenly. "I'm telling it to get the hell out of my jet stream now. It is, of course, being rude."

The clouds forming underneath the giant ship started to flow in and flute upwards; the *Experiencing A Significant Gravitas Shortfall* was starting to draw away. Clouds boiled up around it like a million contrails forming at once, and lightning flickered between the blossoming towers of vapor.

"Look at that. Ruining the whole morning." The avatar shook its head again. "Typical GSV. That little display had better not stop my nacreous clouds forming this evening or there'll be big trouble." It looked at Kabe. "Come on; let's ignore this show-off and go below. I want to show you the engines on this thing."

"But, Cr. Ziller; your public!"

"Is back on Chel and would probably pay good money to see me hung, drawn and burned."

"My *dear* Ziller, that is exactly my point. I'm sure what you say is a gross if understandable exaggeration, but even if it were remotely true, quite the opposite applies here; on Masaq' there are huge numbers of people who would gladly give their own lives to save yours. It is them I was referring to, as I'm sure you well know. Many of them will be at the concert tonight; the rest will all be watching, immersed.

"They have waited patiently for years, hoping that one day you might feel inspired to complete another long work. Now that it has finally happened they cannot wait to experience it as fully as possible and pay you the homage they know you deserve. They are desperate to be there and hear your music and see you with their own eyes. They *crave* to see you conduct *Expiring Light* this evening!"

"They can crave all they like but they're going to be disappointed. I have no intention of going, not if that suppurating piece of desk-fodder is going to be present."

"But you won't meet! We'll keep you separate!"

Ziller stuck his big black nose up toward Tersono's pink-blushed ceramic casing, causing the drone to shrink back from him. "I do not believe you," he told it.

"What? Because I'm from Contact? But that's ridiculous!"

"I bet Kabe told you that."

"It doesn't matter how I found out. I have no intention of trying to force you to meet Major Quilan."

"But you'd like it if I did, wouldn't you?"

"Well . . ." The drone's aura field suddenly rainbowed with confusion.

"Would you or wouldn't you?"

"Well, of course I would!" the machine said, wobbling in the air with what looked like anger, frustration or both. Its aura field looked confused.

"Ha!" Ziller exclaimed. "You admit it!"

"Naturally I would like you to meet; it is absurd that you haven't, but I would only want it to happen if it occurred naturally, not if it was contrived against your expressed wishes!"

"Shh. Here comes one now."

"But—!"

"*Shh!*"

Pfesine Forest, on Ustranhuan Plate—which was about as far away from the Stullien Bowl as it was possible to get without leaving Masaq' altogether—was famous for its hunting.

Ziller had journeyed there from Aquime late the night before, stayed in a very jolly hunting lodge, woken late, found a local guide and gone to neck-jump Kussel's Janmandresiles. He thought he could hear one of them coming now, shouldering its way through the dense bush bordering the narrow path directly beneath the tree he was hiding in.

He looked over at his guide, a stocky little guy in antique camouflage gear who was squatting on another bough five meters away. He was nodding and pointing in the direction of the noise. Ziller held onto a branch above him and peeked down, trying to see the animal.

"Ziller, please," the drone's voice said, sounding very odd in his ear.

The Chelgrian turned sharply to the machine floating at his side and glared at it. He held one finger to his lips and shook it. The drone went muddy cream with embarrassment. "I am talking to you by directly vibrating the inner membrane of your ear. There is no possibility that the animal you—"

"And I," Ziller whispered through clenched teeth, leaning very close to Tersono, "am trying to concentrate. Now will you fucking *shut up?*"

The drone's aura blanched briefly with anger, then settled to gray frustration mixed with spots of purple contrition. It quickly rippled into yellow-green, indicating mellowness and friendliness, hatched with bands of red to show it was taking this as a bit of a joke.

"And will you stop that fucking rainbow shit?" Ziller hissed. "You're distracting me! And the animal can probably see you too!"

He ducked away as something very large and mottled blue passed underneath the branch. It had a head as long as Ziller's whole body and a back broad enough to have accommodated half a dozen Chelgrians. He stared down. "God," he breathed, "those things are big." He looked over at his guide, who was nodding down at the animal.

Ziller gulped and dropped. The fall was only about two meters; he landed on all fives and was at the beast's neck in one bound, swinging his feet over its neck on either side of its fan-like ears and grabbing a handful of its dark brown crest mane before it had time to react. Tersono floated down to accompany him. The Kussel's Janmandresile realized it had something stuck to the nape of its neck and let out a deafening shriek. It shook its head and body as vigorously as it could and charged off along the path through the jungle.

"Ha! Ha ha ha ha *ha!*" Ziller yelled, clinging on while the huge animal bucked and shook beneath him. The wind whipped past; leaves, fronds, creepers and branches went zinging by, making him duck and dodge and gasp. The fur around his eyes pushed back in the breeze; the trees to either side of the path passed in a blue-green blur. The animal shook its head again, still trying to dislodge him.

"Ziller!" the drone E. H. Tersono shouted, riding the air just behind him. "I can't help noticing you aren't wearing any safety equipment! This is very dangerous!"

"Tersono!" Ziller said, teeth rattling as the beast beneath him went thudding along the winding trail.

"What?"

"Will you bugger off?"

There was some sort of break in the canopy ahead, and the animal's pace increased as it went downhill. Pitched forward, Ziller had to lean way back toward the thing's pounding shoulders to stop himself from being pitched over the animal's head and trampled underfoot. Suddenly, through the trailing fronds of moss and pendulous leaves, there was a glint of sunlight from the forest floor. A broad river appeared; the Kussel's Janmandresile thundered down the path and through the shallows in great kicking lines of spray, then threw itself into the deep water in the center, ducking down and buckling its front knees as it went to throw Ziller off head first into the water.

He woke up spluttering in the shallows, being dragged on his back toward the river bank. He looked up and behind and saw Tersono pulling him with a maniple field colored gray with frustration.

He coughed and spat. "Was I out for a bit there?" he asked the machine.

"A few seconds, Composer," Tersono said, hauling him with what looked like enormous ease up onto a sandy bank and sitting him up.

"It was probably just as well you went under," it told him. "The Kussel's Janmandresile was looking for you before it crossed to the far side. It probably wanted to hold you under or drag you to shore and stamp on you." Tersono went behind Ziller and thumped his back while he coughed some more.

"Thank you," Ziller said, bent over and spitting up some of the river water. The drone kept thumping away. "But don't," the Chelgrian continued, "think this means I'm going to go back to conduct the symphony in some fit of gratitude."

"As if I would expect such graciousness, Composer," the drone said in a defeated voice.

Ziller looked around, surprised. He waved away the machine's field doing the thumping. He blew his nose and smoothed his face-fur down. "You really are upset, aren't you?" he said.

The drone flashed gray again. "Of course I'm upset, Cr. Ziller! You nearly killed yourself there! You've always been so dismissive, even contemptuous, of such dangerous pastimes. What is the matter with you?"

Ziller looked down at the sand. He'd torn his waistcoat, he noticed. Damn, he'd left his pipe at home. He looked around. The river flowed on past; giant insects and birds flitted over it, dipping, diving and zooming. On the far bank, something sizeable was making the deep fractaleaf sway and quiver. Some sort of long-limbed, big eared furry thing was watching curiously from a branch high in the canopy. Ziller shook his head. "What am I doing here?" he breathed. He stood up, wincing. The drone put out thick maniple fields in case he wanted to lean on them, but did not insist on helping him up.

"What now, Composer?"

"Oh, I'm going home."

"Really?"

"Yes, really." Ziller squeezed some water from his pelt. He touched his ear, where his terminal earring ought to be. He glanced out at the river, sighed and looked at Tersono. "Where's the nearest underground access?"

"Ah, I do have an aircraft standing by, in case you don't want to bother with the—"

"An aircraft? Won't that take forever?"

"Well, it's more of a little space craft, really."

Ziller took a breath and drew himself up, brows furling. The drone floated back a little. Then the Chelgrian relaxed again. "All right," he breathed.

Moments later a shape that looked like little more than an ovoid shimmer in the air swooped down between the trees overhanging the river, rushed toward the sandbank and came to an instant stop a meter away. Its camouflage field blinked off. Its sleek hull was plain black; a side door sighed open.

Ziller looked narrow-eyed at the drone. "No tricks," he growled.

"As if."

He stepped aboard.

The snow flew up against the windows in swirls and eddies that seemed sometimes to take on patterns and shapes. He was looking out at the view, at the mountains on the far side of the city, but every now and again the snow forced him to focus on it, just half a meter in front of his eyes, distracting him with its brief immediacy and taking his mind off the longer perspective.

~ *So, are you going to go?*

~ I don't know. The polite thing would be not to go, so that Ziller will.

~ *True.*

~ But what is the point of politeness when some of these people will be dead at the end of the evening, and when I certainly will be?

~ *It's how people behave when they're faced with death that shows you what they're really like, Quil. You discover whether they really are as polite, and even as brave, as—*

~ I can do without the lecture, Huyler.

~ *Sorry.*

~ I could stay here in the apartment and watch the concert, or just do something else, or I can go to hear Ziller's symphony with a quarter of a million other people. I can die alone or I can die surrounded by others.

~ *You won't be dying alone, Quil.*

~ No, but you will be coming back, Huyler.

~ *No, only the me I was before all this will be coming back.*

~Even so. I hope you won't think I'm being too sorry for myself if I regard the experience as being rather more profound for me than for you.

~ *Of course not.*

~ At least Ziller's music might take my mind off it for a couple of hours. Dying at the climax to a unique concert, knowing you produced the final and most spectacular part of the light show, seems a more desirable context for quitting this life than collapsing over a café table or being found slumped on the floor here next morning.

~ *I can't argue with that.*

~ And there's another thing. The Hub Mind is going to be directing all the in-atmosphere effects, isn't it?

~ *Yes. There's talk of aurorae and meteorite showers and the like.*

~ So if the Hub's destroyed there's a good chance something could go badly wrong at the Bowl. If Ziller's not there he'll probably live.

~ *You want him to?*

~ Yes, I want him to.

~ *He's little better than a traitor, Quil. You're giving your life for Chel and all he's done is spit on all of us. You're making the greatest sacrifice a soldier can make and all he's ever done is whine, run away, soak up adulation and please himself. You really think it's right that you go and he survives?*

~ Yes I do.

~ *That son-of-a-prey-bitch deserves . . . Well, no. I'm sorry, Quil. I still think you're wrong about that, but you're right about what happens to us tonight. It does mean more to you than me. I guess the least I can do is not try to argue the condemned male out of his last request. You go to the concert, Quil. I'll take my satisfaction from the fact it'll annoy the hell out of that scumbag.*

• • •

"Kabe?" said a distinctive voice from the Homomdan's terminal.

"Yes, Tersono."

"I have succeeded in persuading Ziller to return to his apartment. I think there's just the hint of a chance he might be wavering. On the other hand, I have just heard that Quilan is definitely going. Would you do me—all of us—the possibly incalculably enormous favor of coming here to help try and persuade Ziller to attend the concert nevertheless?"

"Are you sure I'd make any difference?"

"Of course not."

"Hmm. Just a moment."

Kabe and the avatar stood just in front of the main stage; a few technician drones were floating about and the orchestra were filing off stage after their final rehearsal. Kabe had watched but hadn't wanted to hear; a trio of earplugs had fed him the sounds of a water-fall instead.

The musicians—not all human, and some of them human but very unusual looking—went back to their rest suite, doing a lot of muttering. They were troubled that one of Hub's avatars had con-ducted the rehearsal. It had done a creditable impression of Ziller, though without the short temper, bad language and colorful curses. One might, Kabe thought, have imagined that the musicians would have preferred such an even-tempered conductor, but they seemed genuinely concerned that the composer might not be there for the real performance to conduct the work himself.

"Hub," Kabe said.

The silver-skinned creature turned to him. It was dressed very for-mally in a severe gray suit. "Yes, Kabe?"

"Could I get to Aquime and back in time to catch the start of the concert?"

"Easily," the machine said. "Is Tersono looking for reinforcements on the Ziller front?"

"You guessed. It appears to believe I may be of assistance in per-suading him to attend the concert."

"It might even be right. I'll come too. Shall we underground it or take a plane?"

"A plane would be quicker?"

"Yes, it would. Displacing would be quickest."

"I have never been Displaced. Let's do that."

"I have to draw your attention to the fact that a Displace incurs an approximately one in sixty-one million chance of utter failure resulting in death for the subject." The avatar smiled wickedly. "Still willing?"

"Certainly."

There was a pop, preceded by the briefest impression of a silver field disappearing alongside them, and another avatar stood beside the one he'd been talking to, dressed similarly but not identically.

Kabe tapped his nose-ring terminal. "Tersono?"

"Yes?" said the drone's voice.

The silver-skinned twins bowed fractionally to each other.

"We're on our way."

Kabe experienced something he would later characterize as like having somebody else perform a blink for you, and as the avatar's head rose back up after its brief bow, suddenly they were both standing in the main reception room of Ziller's apartment in Aquime City, where the drone E. H. Tersono was waiting.

16

Expiring Light

The late afternoon sun shone through a kilometer-high gap between the mountains and the cloud. Ziller came out of the bathroom puffing his fur dry with a powerful little hand-held blower. He frowned at Tersono and looked mildly surprised to see Kabe and the avatar.

"Hello all. Still not going. Anything else?"

He threw himself down onto a big couch and stretched out, rubbing the fluffed-up fur over his belly.

"I took the liberty of asking Ar Ischloear and Hub here to attempt to reason with you one last time," Tersono said. "There would still be ample time to get to the Stullien Bowl in a seemly manner and—"

"Drone, I don't know what you don't understand," Ziller said, smiling. "It's perfectly simple. If he goes, I don't. Screen, please. Stullien Bowl."

A screen, out-holo'd, burst into life across the whole of the wall on the other side of the room, protruding just beyond the furniture. The projection filled with a couple of dozen views of the Bowl, its surroundings and various groups of people and talking heads. There was no sound. With the rehearsal finished, some enthusiasts could be seen already making their way into the giant amphitheater.

The drone swivelled its body quickly, jerking once, to indicate it was looking at first the avatar and then Kabe. When neither said anything, it said, "Ziller, please."

"Tersono, you're in the way."

"Kabe; will you talk to him?"

"Certainly," Kabe said, nodding massively. "Ziller. How are you?"

"I'm well, thank you, Kabe."

"I thought you were moving a little awkwardly."

"I confess I am a little stiff; I was neck-jumping a Kussel's Janmandresile earlier this morning and it threw me."

"You are otherwise uninjured?"

"Some bruises."

"I thought you disapproved of such activities."

"All the more so now."

"You wouldn't recommend it, then?"

"Certainly not for you, Kabe; if you neck-jumped a Kussel's Janmandresile you'd probably break its back."

"You are probably correct," Kabe chuckled. He put one hand to cup his chin. "Hmm. Kussel's Janmandresiles; they're only found on—"

"Will you *stop it?*" screeched the drone. Its aura field burned white with anger.

Kabe turned, blinking, to the machine. He spread his arms wide, setting a chandelier tinkling. "You said talk to him," he rumbled.

"Not about him making an exhibit of himself indulging in some ridiculous so-called sport! I meant about going to the Bowl! About conducting his own symphony!"

"I did not make an exhibit of myself. I rode that giant beast for a good hundred meters."

"It was sixty at the most and it was a hopeless neck-jump," the drone said, doing a good vocal impression of a human spitting with fury. "It wasn't even a neck-jump! It was a back jump followed by an undignified scramble. Do that in a competition and you'd get negative style marks!"

"I still didn't—"

"You *did* make an exhibit of yourself!" the machine shouted. "That simian in the trees by the river was Marel Pomiheker; news-feeder, guerrilla journalist, media-raptor and all-around data-hound. Look!" The drone swept away from the screen and pointed a strobing gray field at one of the twenty-four rectangular projections protruding from the screen. It showed Ziller squatting on a branch, hiding up a tree in a jungle.

"Shit," Ziller said, looking aghast. The view cut to a large purple animal coming down a jungle path. "Screen off," Ziller said. The holos disappeared. Ziller looked at the three others, brows furled. "Well, I certainly can't go out in public now, can I?" he said sarcastically to Tersono.

"Ziller, of course you can!" Tersono yelped. "Nobody cares you got thrown off some stupid animal!"

Ziller looked at the avatar and the Homomdan and briefly crossed his eyes.

"Tersono would like me to try and argue you into attending the concert," Kabe told Ziller. "I doubt that anything I might say would change your mind."

Ziller nodded. "If he goes, I stay here," he said. He looked at the timepiece standing on top of the antique mosaikey on a platform near the windows. "Still over an hour." He stretched out more fully and clasped his hands behind his head. He grimaced and brought his arms down again, massaging one shoulder. "Actually I doubt I could conduct anyway. Pulled a muscle, I think." He lay back again. "So, I imagine our Major Quilan is dressing now, yes?"

"He's dressed," the avatar said. "In fact, he's gone."

"Gone?" Ziller asked.

"Left for the Bowl," the avatar said. "He's in a car right now. Already ordered his interval drinks."

Ziller looked briefly troubled, then brightened and said, "Ha."

The car was a large one, half full; crowded by local standards. At the far end, through a few embroidered hangings and a screen of plants, he could hear a group of young, all shouting and laughing. One calm adult voice sounded like its owner was trying to keep them in order.

A child burst through the screen of plants, looking back the way it had come, almost tripping. It glanced around at the adults in this end of the car. It looked to be about to throw itself back through the plants again until it saw Quilan. Its eyes widened and it walked over to sit beside him. Its pale face looked flushed and it was breathing hard. Its dark straight hair was plastered to its forehead with sweat.

"Hello," it said. "Are you Ziller?"

"No," Quilan said. "My name is Quilan."

"Geldri T'Chuese," the child said, putting out its hand. "How do you do."

"How do you do."

"Are you going to the Festival?"

"No, I'm going to a concert."

"Oh, the one at the Stullien Bowl?"

"Yes. And you? Are you going to the concert?"

The child snorted derisively. "No. There's a whole bunch of us; we're going around the Orbital by car until we get bored. Quem wants to go around at least three times in a row because Xiddy's been around twice with his cousin, but I think twice is enough."

"Why do you want to go around the Orbital?"

Geldri T'Chuese looked oddly at Quilan. "Just for a laugh," it said, as though it ought to be obvious. A gale of laughter burst through the screen of plants from the far end of the car.

"Sounds very noisy," Quilan said.

"We're wrestling," the child explained. "Before that we had a farting competition."

"Well, I'm not sorry I missed that."

Another peal of high-pitched laughter rang down the car. "I'd better get back," Geldri T'Chuese said. It patted his shoulder. "Nice to meet you. Hope you enjoy the concert."

"Thank you. Goodbye."

The child took a run at the screen of plants and jumped through between two of the clumps. There were more screams and laughs.

~ I know.

~ You know what?

~ I can guess what you're thinking.

~ Can you?

~ That they will probably still be in the underground car system when the Hub is destroyed.

~ Is that really what I was thinking?

~ It's what I'd be thinking. It is tough.

~ Well, thank you for that.

~ I'm sorry.

~ We're all sorry.

The journey took a little longer than it would normally; there were a lot of people and cars stacking up to unload at the Bowl's sub-surface access points. In the lift, Quilan nodded to a few people who recognized him from the news-service pieces he'd done. He saw one or two frowning at him, and guessed they knew that by coming he was probably going to prevent Ziller from attending. He shifted on his seat and inspected an abstract painting hanging nearby.

The lift arrived on the surface and people walked out into a broad, open concourse beneath a colonnade of tall, straight-trunked trees. Soft lights shone against the dark blue of the evening sky. Smells of food filled the air and people thronged cafés, bars and restaurants at the sides of the concourse. The Bowl filled the sky at the end of the broad way, studded with lights.

"Major Quilan!" a tall, handsome man in a bright coat shouted, rushing up to him. He offered his hand and Quilan shook it. "Chongon Lisser. Lisser News; usual affiliations, forty percent take-up and rising."

"How do you do?" Quilan kept on walking; the tall male walked to one side and a little in front, keeping his head turned toward Quilan to maintain eye contact.

"I'm very well, Major, and I hope you are too. Major, is it true that Mahrai Ziller, the composer of tonight's symphony here at the Stullien Bowl, Guerno Plate, Masaq', has told you that if you attend the concert tonight then he won't?"

"No."

"It's not true?"

"He hasn't told me anything directly."

"But would it be correct to say that you must have heard that he wouldn't attend if you did?"

"That is correct."

"And yet you have chosen to attend."

"Yes."

"Major Quilan, what is the nature of the dispute between you and Mahrai Ziller?"

"You would have to ask him that. I have no dispute with him."

"You don't resent the fact that he's put you in this invidious position?"

"I don't think it is an invidious position."

"Would you say that Mahrai Ziller is being petty or vindictive in any way?"

"No."

"So would you say he's behaving perfectly reasonably?"

"I am not an expert on Mahrai Ziller's behavior."

"Do you understand people who say you're behaving very selfishly by coming here tonight, as that means Mahrai Ziller won't be here to conduct the first performance of his new work, so reducing the experience for everybody concerned?"

"Yes, I do."

By now they were near the end of the wide concourse, where what looked like a tall, broad wall of glowing glass extending over the breadth of the pavement was slowly alternately brightening and dimming. The crowds thinned out a little beyond here; the barrier was a field wall, set up to admit only those who'd won out in the ticket lottery.

"So you don't feel that—"

Quilan had brought his ticket with him, though he'd been told it was really just a souvenir and not required for entry. Chongon Lisser obviously didn't have a ticket; he bumped softly into the glowing wall and Quilan stepped around him and passed on through with a nod and a smile. "Good evening," he said.

There were more news service people inside; he continued to answer politely but minimally and just kept on walking, following his terminal's instructions, to his seat.

Ziller watched the news feeds following Quilan with an open mouth. "That son-of-a-bitch! He's really going! He's not bluffing! He's actually going to take his seat and keep me away! From my own fucking concert! The stub-cocked son-of-a-prey-bitch!"

Ziller, Kabe and the avatar watched as several remotes followed Quilan to his seat, a specially prepared Chelgrian curl-pad. There was a Homomdan seat next to it, a space for Tersono, and a few other seats and couches. The camera platform showed Quilan sitting, looking around at the slowly filling Bowl, and calling up a function on his terminal which created a flat screen in front of him holding the concert program notes.

"I think I see my seat," Kabe said thoughtfully.

"And I mine," Tersono said. Its aura field looked agitated. It turned to face Ziller, seemed about to say something, then did not. The avatar did not move, but Kabe had the impression that there had been some communication between Hub Mind and the Contact Section drone.

The avatar folded its arms and walked across the room to look out at the city. A cold clear cobalt sky arched over the jagged surround of mountains. The machine could see the bubble that was Aquime's Dome Square. There was a giant screen there, relaying the scenes at the Stullien Bowl to a swelling crowd.

"I confess I didn't think he'd go," the avatar said.

"Well, he fucking has!" Ziller said, spitting. "The puss-eyed bollock-dragger!"

"I was under the impression he was going to spare you this too," Kabe said, squatting on the floor near Ziller. "Ziller, I'm most terribly sorry if I misled you in any way, even if it was inadvertently. I am still convinced that Quilan strongly implied he would not be going. I can only assume that something has changed his mind."

Again, Tersono seemed to be on the brink of saying something, its aura field altering and its casing rising a little in the air, and again it appeared to subside again at the last moment. Its field was gray with frustration.

The avatar turned from the window, arms still folded. "Well, if you don't need me, Ziller, I'll be getting back to the Bowl. Can't have too many ushers and general helpers at something like this. Always some cretin who's forgotten how to operate an automatic drinks dispenser. Kabe, Tersono? Can I offer you a Displace back?"

"Displace?" Tersono said. "Certainly not! I'll take a car."

"Hmm," the avatar said. "You should still make it. I wouldn't hang around, though."

"Well," Tersono said hesitantly, fields flickering. "Unless Cr. Ziller wants me to stay, of course."

They looked at Ziller, who was still watching the wall of screens. "No," he said faintly, waving one hand. "Go. Go, by all means."

"No, I think I ought to stay," the drone said, floating closer to the Chelgrian.

"And I think you ought to go," Ziller said sharply.

The drone stopped as though it had hit a wall. It flushed creamily rainbow with surprise and embarrassment, then bowed in the air and said, "Just so. Well, see you there. Ah . . . Yes. Goodbye." It thrummed through the air to the doors, whisked them open and closed them quickly but silently behind it.

The avatar looked quizzically at the Homomdan. "Kabe?"

"Instantaneous travel appears to agree with me. I will be happy to accept." He paused and looked at Ziller. "I too would be perfectly happy to stay here, Ziller. We don't have to watch the concert. We could—"

Ziller leapt to his feet. "Fuck it!" he said through his teeth. "I'm going! That piece of wriggling vomit isn't going to keep me from my own fucking symphony. I'll go. I'll go and I'll conduct and I'll even hang around and schmooze and be schmoozed at afterwards, but if that little turd Tersono or anybody else tries to introduce that selfish litter-fucker Quilan to me, I swear I'll bite the shit-head's throat out."

The avatar suppressed most of a grin. Its eyes twinkled as it looked at Kabe. "Well, that sounds eminently reasonable, don't you think, Kabe?"

"Absolutely."

"I'll get dressed," Ziller said, bounding toward the internal doors. "Won't take a moment."

"We'll have to Displace to give us enough time!" the avatar yelled.

"Fine!" Ziller called out.

"There's a one in sixty—"

"Yes, yes, I know! Let's just risk it, eh?"

Kabe looked at the broadly smiling avatar. He nodded. The avatar held out its arms and gave a little bow. Kabe mimed applause.

~ *You guessed wrong.*

   ~ What about?

   ~ *About how Ziller would jump. He's coming after all.*

   ~ Is he?

Even as he thought the question, Quilan became aware of people around him starting to mutter, and heard the word "Ziller" mentioned a few times as the news spread. The Bowl was mostly full now, a gigantic buzzing container of sound and light and people and machines. The brightly lit center, the empty stage where the various instruments glittered, looked still and silent and waiting, like the eye of a storm.

Quilan tried not to think anything very much. He spent some time fiddling with the magnifying field built into his seat, adjusting it so that the stage area seemed to swell in front of him. When he was happy that—like everybody else apart from the real no-magnification purists—he had what appeared to be a ringside seat, he sat back.

   ~ He is definitely on his way?

   ~ *He's here; they Displaced.*

   ~ Well, I tried.

   ~ *You're probably worrying needlessly. I doubt anything will go so far wrong here that anybody's going to be in any real danger.*

Quilan looked at the sky above the Bowl. It was probably dark blue or violet but it looked pitch black beyond the vague haze of the Bowl's rim lights.

~ There are several hundred thousand lumps of rock and ice heading straight this way. Converging on the sky above this place. I wouldn't be too sure this is safe.

~ *Oh, come on. You know what they're like. They'll have back-ups on the back-ups, octuple redundancy; safety to the point of paranoia.*

~ We'll see. Another thing occurred to me.

~ *What?*

~ Supposing our allies, whoever they might be, have made their own plans for what's really going to happen when they trigger their surprise.

~ *Go on.*

~ As I understand it, there's no limit to what you could squeeze through the wormhole's mouth. Supposing instead of just enough energy to destroy the Hub, they put through enough to annihilate it, suppose they shoot an equivalent mass of antimatter through the hole? How much does the Hub unit weigh?

~ *About a million tons.*

~ A two-million-ton matter/antimatter explosion would kill everybody on the Orbital, wouldn't it?

~ *I suppose it would. But why would our allies—like you say, whoever they might be—want to kill everybody?*

~ I don't know. The point is that it would be possible. You and I have no idea what our masters have agreed to, and from what we've been told, they too might have been deceived. We are at the mercy of these alien allies.

~ *You are worrying too much, Quil.*

Quilan watched the orchestra begin to take to the stage. The air filled with applause. It was not the full orchestra, and Ziller would not appear yet because the first piece was not one of his, but even so the reception was tumultuous.

~ Maybe. I suppose it doesn't matter much, anyway. Not anymore.

He saw the Homomdan Kabe Ischloear and the drone E. H.

Tersono appearing from the nearest access way as the lights began to dim. Kabe waved. Quilan waved back.

Tersono! We're going to blow up the Hub!

The words formed in his mind. He would stand up and shout them.

But he did not.

~ *I didn't intervene. You never meant to really do it.*

~ Really?

~ *Really.*

~ Fascinating. Every philosopher should experience this, don't you think, Huyler?

~ *Easy, son, easy.*

Kabe and Tersono joined the Chelgrian. Both noticed he was weeping quietly but thought it polite not to say anything.

The music rang around the auditorium, a vast invisible clapper in the inverted bell of the Bowl. The stadium's lights had sunk to darkness; the light show in the skies above flickered, flowed and flashed.

Quilan had missed the nacreous clouds. He saw the aurorae, the lasers, the induced layers and levels of clouds, the flashes of the first few meteorites, the strobing lines that hatched the sky as more and more streaked in. The distant skies all around the Bowl, way out over the plains bordering the lake, coruscated with silent horizontal lightning, darting from cloud to cloud in streaks and bars and sheets of blue-white light.

The music accumulated. Each piece, he realized, was slowly contributing to the whole. Whether it was Hub's idea or Ziller's, he didn't know, but the whole evening, the entire concert program had been designed around the final symphony. The earlier, shorter pieces were half by Ziller, half by other composers. They alternated, and it became clear that the styles were quite different too, while the musical philosophies behind the two competing strands were dissimilar to the point of antipathy.

The short pauses between each piece, during which the orchestra enlarged and decreased according to the requirements of each work, allowed just sufficient time for the strategic structure of the evening to filter through to people. You could actually hear the coin drop as people worked it out.

The evening was the war.

The two strands of music represented the protagonists, Culture and Idirans. Each pair of antagonistic pieces stood for one of the many small but increasingly bitter and wide-scale skirmishes which had taken place, usually between proxy forces for both sides, during the decades before the war itself had finally broken out. The works increased in length and in the sensation of mutual hostility.

Quilan found himself checking the history of the Idiran War, to confirm that what felt like they ought to be the final pair of preparatory pieces really were so.

The music died away. The applause was barely audible, as though everybody was simply waiting. The complete orchestra filled the central stage. Dancers, most in float harnesses, distributed themselves about the space around the stage in a semi-sphere. Ziller took his place at the very focus of the circular stage, surrounded by a shimmer of projection field. The applause zoomed suddenly then dropped as quickly away. The orchestra and Ziller shared a mutual moment of silence and stillness.

A blanking field somewhere in the heavens above blinked off, and—up near one edge of the Bowl's lip—it was as though the first nova, Portisia, had just appeared from behind a cloud.

The symphony *Expiring Light* began with a susurration that built and engorged until it burst into a single clashingly discordant blast of music; a mixture of chords and sheer noise that was echoed in the sky by a single shockingly bright air burst as a huge meteorite plunged into the atmosphere directly above the Bowl and exploded. Its stunning, frightening, bone-rattlingly loud sound arrived suddenly in a hypnotic lull in the music, making everybody—certainly everybody that Quilan was aware of, including himself—jump.

Thunder rippled around the greater amphitheater of sky around the lake and Bowl at its center. The bolts struck earth now, lancing to the distant ground. The sky hatched with squadrons and fleets of darting meteorite trails while the folds of aurorae and sky-wide effects whose origin it was hard to guess at filled the mind and beat at the eye even as the music pounded at the ear.

Visuals of the war and more abstract images filled the air directly above the stage and the whirling, tumbling, interlacing bodies of the dancers.

Somewhere near the furious center of the work, while the thunder played bass and the music rolled over it and around the auditorium like something wild and caged and desperate to escape, eight trails in the sky did not end in air bursts and did not fade away but slammed down into the lake all around the Bowl, creating eight tall and sudden geysers of lit white water that burst out of the still dark waters as though eight vast under-surface fingers had made a sudden grab at the sky itself.

Quilan thought he heard people shriek. The entire Bowl, the whole kilometer-diameter of it, shook and quivered as the waves created by the lake-strikes smashed into the giant vessel. The music seemed to take the fear and terror and violence of the moment and run screaming away with it, pulling the audience behind like an unseated rider caught in the stirrup of their panic-stricken mount.

A terrible calmness settled over Quilan as he sat there, half cowering, battered by the music, assailed by the washes and spikes of light. It was as though his eyes formed a sort of twin tunnel in his skull and his soul was gradually falling away from that shared window to the universe, falling on his back forever down a deep dark corridor while the world shrank to a little circle of light and dark somewhere in the shadows above. Like falling into a black hole, he thought to himself. Or maybe it was Huyler.

He really did seem to be falling. He really did seem to be unable to stop. The universe, the world, the Bowl really did seem to be unreachably distant. He felt vaguely upset that he was missing the rest of the concert, the conclusion of the symphony. What price clarity and proximity, though, and where lay the relevance of being there and using or not using a magnification screen or amplification when everything he'd seen so far had been distorted by the tears in his eyes and all he'd heard had been drowned out by the clamor of his guilt at what he had done, what he had made possible and what was surely going to happen?

He wondered, as he fell into that encompassing darkness, and the world was reduced to a single not especially bright point of light above—no more luminous than a nova distant by most of a thousand years—if he'd somehow been fed a drug. He supposed the Culture people would all be enhancing the experience with their glanded secretions, making the reality of the experience both more and less real.

He landed with a bump. He sat up and looked around.

He saw a distant light to one side. Again, not particularly bright. He got to his feet. The floor was warm and with just a hint of pliancy. There was no smell, no sound except his own breathing and heartbeat. He looked up. Nothing.

~ Huyler?

He waited for a moment. Then a moment longer.

~ Huyler?

~ HUYLER?

Nothing.

He stood and gloried in the silence for a while, then walked toward the distant glow.

The light came from the band of the Orbital. He walked into what looked just like the mock-up of the Hub's viewing gallery. The place seemed to be deserted. The Orbital spun around him with a vast, implicit unhurriedness. He walked on a little, past couches and seats, until he came to the one that was occupied.

The avatar, lit by the reflected light of the Orbital's surface, looked up as he approached and patted the curl-seat next to it. The creature was dressed in a dark gray suit.

"Quilan," it said. "Thank you for coming. Please; sit down." The reflections slid off its perfect silver skin like liquid light.

He sat down. The curl-seat fitted perfectly.

"What am I doing here?" he asked. His voice sounded strange. There were no echoes, he realized.

"I thought we should talk," the avatar said.

"What about?"

"What we're going to do."

"I don't understand."

The avatar held up a tiny thing like a jewel, grasping it in a pincer of silver fingers. It glittered like a diamond. At its heart was a tiny flaw of darkness. "Look what I found, Major."

He did not know what to say. After what seemed like a long time he thought,

~ Huyler?

The moment went on. Time seemed to have stopped. The avatar could sit perfectly, utterly, inhumanly still.

"There were three," he told it.

The avatar smiled thinly, reached into the top pocket of the suit and produced another two of the jewels. "Yes, I know. Thank you for that."

"I had a partner."

"The guy in your head? So we thought."

"I have failed then, haven't I?"

"Yes. But there is a consolation prize."

"What is that?"

"Tell you later."

"What happens now?"

"We listen to the end of the symphony." It held out one slim silver hand. "Take my hand."

He took its hand. He was back in the Stullien Bowl, but this time everywhere. He looked straight down, he watched from a thousand other angles, he was the stadium itself, its lights and sounds and very structure. At the same time he could see everywhere around the Bowl, into the sky, out to the horizon, all around. He experienced a long moment of terrifying vertigo; vertigo which seemed to be pulling him not down but in every direction at once. He would fly apart, he would simply dissolve.

~ Stick with it, the avatar's hollow voice said.

~ I'm trying to.

The music and the sights swamped him, overwhelmed him, ran him through with light. The symphony rolled onward, approaching a sequence of resolutions and cadenzas that were a small yet still titanic reflection of the whole work, the rest of the earlier concert, the war itself.

~ Those things I Displaced, they are—

~ I know what they are. They've been taken care of.

~ I'm sorry.

~ I know that.

The music rose like the bulging bruise of water from an undersea explosion, an instant before the smooth swell ruptures and the spout of white spray bursts forth.

The dancers rose and fell, swirled and flocked and spread and shrank. Images of war strobed above the stage. The skies filled with light, flickering staggeringly brief shadows that were obliterated almost instantly by the next detonation in the vast bombardment of fire.

Then all fell away, and Quilan sensed time itself slow down. The music faded to a single hanging line of keening ache, the dancers lay like fallen leaves scattered about the stage, the holo above the stage vanished and the light seemed to evaporate from the sky, leaving a darkness that pulled at the senses, as though the vacuum was calling to his soul.

Time slowed still further. In the sky near the tiny remaining light that was the nova Portisia, there was just the merest hint of something flickering. Then that stopped, held, frozen, too.

The moment that was *now*, that for all his life had been a point, became that line, that long note of music and that drawing sough of black. From the line extended a plane, which folded and folded until there was space for the viewing gallery again, and there he sat, still holding the hand of the silver-skinned avatar.

He looked into himself and realized that he felt no fear, no despair and no regret.

When it spoke, it was as though it used his own voice.

~ You must have loved her very much, Quilan.

~ Please, if you can, if you will, look into my soul.

The avatar looked levelly at him.

~ Are you sure?

~ I'm sure.

That long look went on. Then the creature slowly smiled. ~ Very well.

It nodded after a few more moments. ~ She was a remarkable person. I see what you saw in her. The avatar made a noise like a sigh. ~ We surely did do a terrible thing to you, didn't we?

~ We did it to ourselves, in the end, but yes, you brought it upon us.

~ This was a terrible revenge to contemplate, Quilan.

~ We believed we had no choice. Our dead . . . well, I imagine you know.

It nodded. ~ I know.

~ It is over, isn't it?

~ A lot is.

~ My dream this morning . . .

~ Ah yes. The avatar smiled again. ~ Well, that could have been me messing with your mind, or just your guilty conscience, don't you think?

He guessed he would never be told. ~ How long have you known? he asked.

~ I have known since a day before you arrived. I can't speak for Special Circumstances.

~ You let me make the Displacements. Wasn't that dangerous?

~ Only a little. I had my back-up by then. A couple of GSVs have been here or hereabouts for a while, as well as the *Experiencing A Significant Gravitas Shortfall*. Once we knew what you were up to, they could protect me even from an attack like the one you envisaged. We let it happen because we'd like to know where the other ends of those wormholes are. Might tell us something about who your mysterious allies were.

~ I'd like to know myself. He thought about this. ~ Well, I used to.

The avatar frowned. ~ I've discussed this with some of my peers. Want to know one ugly thought?

~ Are there not enough in the world already?

~ Assuredly. But sometimes ugly thoughts can be prevented from becoming ugly deeds by exposing them.

~ If you say so.

~ One should always ask who has most to gain. With respect, Chel does not, in this measure, count.

~ There are many Involveds who might like to see you suffer a reverse.

~ One may come on its own; they tend to. Things have been going very well with the Culture over the last eight hundred years or so. Blink-of-an-eye stuff for the Elders, but a long time for an Involved to stay quite as determinedly in-play as we have. But our power may have peaked; we may be becoming complacent, even decadent.

~ This seems to be a pause I am meant to fill. By the way, how long do we have, before the second nova ignites?

~Back in reality, about half a second. The avatar smiled. ~ Here, many lifetimes. It looked away, to the image of the Orbital hanging in space before them, slowly rotating.

~ It is not impossible that the allies who made all this possible are, or represent, some rogue group of Culture Minds.

He stared at the creature. ~ Culture Minds? he asked.

~ Now isn't that a terrible thing to have to think? That our own might turn against us?

~ But why?

~ Because we might be becoming too soft. Because of that complacency, that decadence. Because some of our Minds might just think that we need a bit of timely blood and fire to remind us the universe is a perfectly uncaring place and that we have no more right to enjoy our agreeable ascendancy than any other empire long fallen and forgotten. The avatar shrugged. ~ Don't be so shocked, Quilan. We could be wrong.

It looked away for a moment. Then it said,

~ No luck with the wormholes. It sounded sad. ~ We may never know now. It turned to look at him again. There was an expression of terrible sorrow on its face. ~ You've wanted to die since you realized you'd lost her, since you recovered from your wounds, haven't you, Quilan?

~ Yes.

It nodded. ~ Me too.

He knew the story of its twin, and the worlds it had destroyed. He wondered, assuming it was telling the truth, how many lifetimes of regret and loss you could fit into eight hundred years, when you could think, experience and remember with the speed and facility of a Mind.

~ What will happen to Chel?

~ A handful of individuals—certainly no more—may pay with their lives. Other than that, nothing. It shook its head slowly. ~ We cannot let you have your balancing souls, Quilan. We will try to reason with the Chelgrian-Puen. It's tricky territory for us, the Sublimed, but we have contacts.

It smiled at him. He could see his broad, furred face reflected in the image's delicate features.

~ We still owe you for our mistake. We will do all we can to make amends. This attempt does not absolve us. Nothing has been balanced. It squeezed his hand. He had forgotten they were still holding each other. ~ I am sorry.

~ Sorrow seems a common commodity, doesn't it?

~ I believe the raw material is life, but happily there are other by-products.

~ You are not really going to kill yourself, are you?

~ Both of us, Quilan.

~ Do you really—?

~ I am tired, Quilan. I have waited for these memories to lose their force over the years and decades and centuries, but they have not. There are places to go, but either I would not be me when I went there, or I would remain myself and so still have my memories. By waiting for them to drop away all this time I have grown into them,

and they into me. We have become each other. There is no way back
I consider worth taking.

It smiled regretfully and squeezed his hand again.

~ I'll be leaving everything in good working order, and in good
hands. It'll be a more-or-less seamless transition, and nobody will suffer or die.

~ Won't people miss you?

~ They'll have another Hub before too long. I'm sure they'll take
to it, too. But I hope they do miss me a little. I hope they do think
well of me.

~ And you'll be happy?

~ I won't be happy or unhappy. I won't be. Neither will you.

It turned more toward him and held out its other hand.

~ Are you ready, Quilan? Will you be my twin in this?

He took its other hand.

~ If you will be my mate.

The avatar closed its eyes.

Time seemed to expand, exploding all around him.

His last thought was that he'd forgotten to ask what had happened
to Huyler.

Light shone in the sky above the Bowl.

Kabe, lost in the silence and the darkness, watched the light of the
star called Junce as it flickered and then blazed, close enough to the
earlier, fading nova of Portisia to all but drown it out.

At his side, Quilan, who had been very quiet and still for some
time, suddenly slumped forward in his curl-pad and collapsed to the
floor before Kabe could catch him.

"What?" he heard Tersono screech.

The applause was starting.

Breath flowed out of the Chelgrian's mouth, then he went quite still.

Noises of shock and consternation built up around Kabe, and—as
he hunkered down and tried to revive the dead alien creature—
another bright, bright light shone above; exactly, precisely overhead.

He called Hub for help but there was no answer.

Space, Time

*—fear and the sudden tearing pain, the huge white-furred face suddenly fill-
ing his vision; the despair and terror and the anger at having been betrayed as
he woke and tried—too late, far too late—to bring his hands up in what
would have been a futile gesture anyway, then the ferocious thud as the creature's huge jaws slammed into his neck, and the agony of the steel-like hold
and the instant constriction, the cutting-off from air, and the shaking; neck
snapping, brain rattling, dislodging him from sense and life . . .*

*Something rasped against his neck; there went aunt Silder's necklace. The
shaking went on. Something thin and broken whipped tinily against his neck
as the blood sprayed out and the breath was worried out of him. You bastard,
he thought, slipping away again from the savage side-to-side thrashing.*

*The pain went on, fading, as he was dragged now, held by the neck,
through the alien ship. His limbs hung limp, cut off from his brain; he was a
rag, a broken puppet. The corridors still smelled of rotting fruit. Eyes gummed
with his own blood. Nothing to be done, nothing to hope for.*

*Mechanical noises. Then the feeling of being dropped. A surface
beneath him. Released, his head felt barely joined to his body, rolling
onto its side.*

*Sounds of growling and tearing and slashing, sounds he felt ought to con-
nect to pain, to some sensation at least, but which meant nothing. Then*

silence, and darkness, and the inability to do anything but witness this slow fading-away of sensation itself. And another small pain near the nape of his neck; a final, tiny jab, like an afterthought; almost comical.

Failed. Failed to get back. Failed to warn. Failed to be the hero. It was not supposed to end this way, dying a lonely, painful death, conscious only of betrayal, fear and hopelessness.

Hissing. Fading. Cold. Movement; being scraped along inside a sudden, chill breeze.

Then utter silence, utter cold, and no weight whatsoever.

Uagen Zlepe, scholar, felt cheated that his blood-gummed eyes prevented him from seeing the distant stars in their vacuum-naked state as he died.

—Great Yoleusenive, this is that which was found in the without by the servants of the Hiarankebine six thousand and three hundred beats to aft. It was brought within the world for the inspection of the Hiarankebine, which sends these remains with its esteem and compliments, believing that your self might add to the sum of knowledge with its revered evaluation.

—This form may have been known to the one to whom you address your remarks. Its appearance brings associations, memories. They are old, though. Now beginning is a deep search of our long-term memory archival storage capacity. This will take some time to complete. Let us talk further on the subject before us while said search is taking place.

—Very well. Of interest is that the analysis of the creature's cellular instruction set indicates that the form in which it appears here is not that with which it was first birthed. A representation of the form it would have according to the original cellular instruction set is shown here:

—That form was once known to us, we are sure, just as this one might have been once known to us. The representation that you have shown here corresponds to the form which is, or was, known as human. Appended to the deep search of our memory archives which was mentioned earlier will be the image that you are showing here. This search has not discovered anything of note thus far. It will take a little longer to complete because of the appendment of the visual image of the human form to it.

—Human. This is interesting to us, though the nature of the interest is historical.

—The creature concerned would appear to have accrued injuries that are not those one would associate with exposure to the conditions which prevail in the without, that is primarily the lack of medium, which absence is commonly termed vacuum, and the associated lack of any temperature save the most negligible.

—Yes. The creature's neck is not supposed to be of the appearance that one may see here, either in the form shown physically before us or in the form which has been recreated in visual form from the biological assignment array. Similarly, its torso appears to have been forcefully and injuriously opened, while these surfaces seem to have been lacerated.

—The creature has been bitten, gouged and slashed.

—Such are the actions one would most naturally associate with the alterations to the creature's physiology.

—What is known of these injuries, and in particular what is known of their timing relative to the apprehension of the object from the without?

—It is believed that this damage was incurred very shortly before the creature was expelled from whatever medium-containment artifact it inhabited prior to said expulsion. The various injuries indicate that the creature was in a state not compatible with the continuance of its life—save for immediate and most highly enabled medical assistance—before its expulsion into the without, where it would, naturally, die. The circulatory fluid has sprayed out here, here and here and then frozen subsequently as a result of the low temperatures encountered in the without.

—The frozen nature of the creature as we see it here is as it was when it was found originally, then.

—That is the case. The medium-repelling bubble in which it can be seen to reside was emplaced before its induction from the without. Only very small particles of its body have been brought to ambient conditions to allow the analyzes concerning which we have already communicated.

—These small and widespread tissue damages would indicate that the creature was at least still of a temperature approximate to its normal and healthy operating state and possibly still in an alive condition when it was expelled into the without. Would it be the case that the Hiarankebine might agree?

—It is the case.

—This level of most-small damage would indicate that the creature's remains have been exposed in the without for a long time, an interval which might be of the order of a significant proportion of a Grand Cycle, though not in the order of many such intervals.

—The Hiarankebine is of a similar belief.

—Is it the case that the direction and velocity of the creature's remains at the time of its discovery have been recorded?

—It is. The creature's remains were static in the without according to accepted definition number three to within approximately the speed of slow breath at standard temperature and pressure. Such vectoriality was of an orientation similar to the world's to within a quarter-paring.

—The deep search which it was intimated was begun remains under way but has still failed to discover anything of interest. What other results from the particles that have been brought to ambient conditions have been added to the store of knowledge?

—Some of the frozen liquid taken from the edges of the wound which the creature suffered upon its neck region has provided biological instruction set information which tends to indicate that the wound-inflicting agent may have been an individual of the species known as the Lesser Reviled.

—That is interesting. Their name was earlier the Chelgrians, or the Chel, before the outrage that befell the Sansemin occurred. To what level of completeness was the analysis of the human form which was found to be implicit in the creature that we see before us taken?

—Sufficient to provide the image which is seen here.

—It is the case that a more complete image of the creature, even

to the order of recreated biological corporeality, might further refine
and focus the knowledge of the creature's species' place in the greater
world of all life.

—This might be accomplished with equal honor and ability by
the Hiarankebine or by that to which these remarks are respectfully
addressed.

—The task is one we are happy to assume. It is noted that the creature is still clothed and has about its neck a piece, or the remains of a
piece, of jewelry. Is it the case that an analysis of any depth regarding
these extraneous objects has been carried out?

—It is not, mighty Yoleusenive.

—The deep search of our stored and non-volatile and off-system
recall functions which it was intimated was earlier begun has now
concluded. The creature that is before us was of the name Uagen
Zlepe, a scholar who came to study the embodiment of the self to
which you speak from the civilization which was once known as the
Culture.

—These names are not known to us.

—No matter. The body of this creature must have drifted in the
without for a little over the period accounted for by one complete
world-cycle, waiting here with that close-to-imperceptible fore-
directed drift which was earlier mentioned, until the world fulfilled
another revolution about the galaxy and sailed again into this region
of space. This is good to know. This piece of information ramificates
and completes. It adds considerably to the sum of knowledge, as will
be explained in a report to be prepared for the Hiarankebine. Is it
possible for that to whom these remarks are addressed to attend the
finalization of said report, the more expeditiously to convey it to the
Hiarankebine?

—It is.

—Good. It may then be worthwhile carrying out further investigations, which that to whom you have addressed your remarks would
be glad to undertake. It is to be hoped that the Hiarankebine will
share the pleasure that is both experienced and anticipated by the
Yoleusenive. A series of events which before had no conclusion now
may have. This is satisfying to ourselves.

• • •

His eyes flicked open. He stared straight ahead. Where there should have been the awful white-furred face above him, jaws hinging open, or the cold stars spinning slowly as he tumbled, there was instead a familiar figure, hanging upside down from a branch inside a large, brightly lit circular space.

He was sitting up in a sort of cross between a bed and a giant nest. He blinked, ungumming his eyes. It did not feel as though it had been blood keeping them shut.

He squinted at the creature hanging a few meters in front of him. It blinked and turned its head a little.

"Praf?" he said, coughing. His throat felt sore, but at least it was properly connected to his head again.

The small, dark creature shook its leathery wings.

"Uagen Zlepe," it said, "I am charged with welcoming you. I am 8827 Praf, female. I share the bulk of the memories associated with the fifth-order Decider of the 11th Foliage Gleaner Troupe of the dirigible behemothaur Yoleus which was known to you as 974 Praf, including, it is believed, all those regarding yourself."

Uagen coughed up some fluid. He nodded and looked around. This looked like the interior of Yoleus' Invited Guests' Quarters, with the sub-divisions removed.

"Am I back on Yoleus?" he asked.

"You are aboard the dirigible behemothaur Yoleusenive."

Uagen stared at the hanging creature in front of him. It took him a moment or two to work out the implications of what he'd just heard. He felt his mouth go dry. He swallowed. "The Yoleus has . . . evolved?" he croaked.

"That is the case."

He put his hand up to his throat, feeling the tender but whole flesh. He looked slowly up and around. "How was I," he began, then had to stop and swallow and start again. "How was I brought back? How was I rescued?"

"You were found in the without. You wore a piece of equipment which stored your personality. The Yoleusenive has repaired and reconstructed your body and quickened your mind-life within said body."

"But I wasn't wearing any . . ." Uagen began, then his voice trailed off as he looked down to where his fingers were stroking the skin around his neck where, once, there had been a necklace.

"*The piece of equipment that stored your personality was where your fingers are now,*" 8827 Praf confirmed, and clacked her beak once.

Aunt Silder's necklace. He remembered the tiny sting at the back of his neck. Uagen felt tears well in his eyes. "*How much time has passed?*" he whispered.

Praf's head tipped to one side again and her eyelids flickered.

Uagen cleared his throat and said, "*Since I left the Yoleus; how much time has passed?*"

"*Nearly one Grand Cycle.*"

Uagen found he could not speak for a little while. Eventually he said, "*One . . . one, ah, galactic, umm Grand Cycle?*"

8827 Praf's beak clacked a couple of times. She shook herself, adjusting her dark wings as though they were a cloak. "*That is what a Grand Cycle is,*" she said as though explaining something obvious to someone just hatched. "*Galactic.*"

Uagen swallowed on a dry, dry throat. It was as though it was still ripped out and open to the vacuum. "*I see,*" he said.

Closure

S he went bounding across the grass toward the cliff, nostrils flared to the wind and the tang of ozone, her face-fur flattened in the breeze. She came to the great double bowl where the land had long ago been vaporized and blown away. The grass fell curving beneath her. Beyond lay the ocean. In front, the seastacks rose like the trunks of immense fossilized trees, their bases awash with creamy foam. She leapt.

A small drone had been sent to investigate the running figure. Its weapons were armed and ready to fire. Just as it was about to intercept the female and shout a challenge, she came to the grassy edge of the crater and jumped. What happened next was unexpected. The drone's camera showed the leaping figure disintegrate and turn into a flock of birds. They flew past the drone, flowing around its casing like water about a stone. The machine twitched this way and that, then turned and followed.

The order came to attack the flock of birds. The drone instigated a prey-rich-environment targeting regime, but then another order countermanded the first and told it to attack a group of three more defense drones which had just risen from the nearest seastack. It curved away, zooming to gain height.

Lasers flickered from cupolas high on two of the seastacks, but the flock of birds had become a swarm of insects; the weapon light found few of them and those it did simply reflected it. Then the two laser towers began to fire at each other, and both exploded in balls of flame.

The first drone attacked the other three as they spread out and accelerated toward the swarm of insects. It shot down one before it was itself destroyed. Then the other two drones attacked each other, swooping in and ramming at high speed in a flash and a single sharp detonation of sound; much of the resulting wreckage was composed of pieces small enough to drift in the wind.

Several small- and medium-sized explosions shook each of the seastacks, and smoke began to drift across the blue sky.

The insect swarm collected on a broad balcony and resumed the form of a Chelgrian female. She knocked the balcony doors down and stepped into the room. Alarms warbled. She frowned and they fell silent. The only sensory or command system not fully under her control was a tiny passive camera in one corner of the room. She was to leave the complex's security monitoring system uncorrupted, so that what was done was seen to be done, and recorded. She listened carefully.

She strode into the bathroom and found him in the emergency one-person lift which had been disguised as a shower cabinet. The lift had jammed in the shaft. She flowed over the hole, formed a partial vacuum and sucked the capsule back up. She pulled open the door and reached in for the naked, cowering male.

Estodien Visquile opened his mouth to scream for mercy. She became insects—they represented something of a phobia for the Estodien—and poured into his throat, choking him and forcing open the route to his lungs and to his stomach. The insects packed each tiny air-sac in his lungs tight; others bulked out the Estodien's stomach to the point of bursting and beyond, then invaded his body cavity, while others rammed down into the rest of his digestive system, forcing an explosion of fecal matter from his anus.

The Estodien crashed and battered about the shower cabinet lift capsule, smashing the ceramic fittings and denting the plastics. More insects streamed into his ears and forced their way around his horrified, staring eyes, burning their way into his skull while his skin crawled and writhed with the insects which had invaded his body cavity and gone onto slide their way under his flesh.

The insects infested his entire body eventually, as he lay thrashing on the floor on a film of his own blood. They continued to insinuate their way into every bodily part of him until, about three minutes after the attack had begun, Visquile's movements gradually ceased.

The insects, the birds and the Chelgrian female were made of EDust. Everything Dust was composed of tiny machines of varying sizes and capabilities. With the exception of one type, none was larger than a tenth of a millimeter in any direction. Interestingly, the dust had originally been designed as the ultimate building material.

The one class of exception to the tenth-of-a-millimeter rule was that of AM nanomissiles, which were only a tenth of a millimeter in diameter, but an entire millimeter in length. One of those lodged in the center of the Estodien's brain, beside his Soulkeeper, while all the other components withdrew and reformed into the Chelgrian female.

She padded away from the deflated body lying in its bloody pool. The nanomissiles were, she thought, a give-away to the identity of her makers; an integral part of the message she was delivering. She went out of the bathroom and the apartment, down some stairs and across a terrace. Somebody shot at her with an ancient hunting rifle. It was the only projectile weapon left working for several kilometers around; she let the bullet pass through a hole in her chest and out the other side, while a set of components in one of her eyes briefly lased and blinded the male who had shot at her.

In the accommodation block behind her, the nanomissile embedded in Visquile's brain sensed his Soulkeeper about to read and save his mind. The explosion of the missile's warhead destroyed the whole building. Debris rained down, around and through her as she walked calmly away.

She found her second target trapped in a small two-person flyer, trying to smash his way out of the cockpit canopy with an oxygen cylinder.

She pulled the canopy open. The white-furred male lashed out with an antique knife; it penetrated her chest and she let it hang there while she took him by the throat and lifted him bodily out of the machine. He kicked and spat and gurgled. The knife in her chest was swallowed inside her as she walked to the edge of the terrace. He hung easily in her grip, as though he weighed nothing; his kicks seemed to have no appreciable effect on her whatsoever.

At the terrace edge she held him over the balustrade. The drop to the sea was about two hundred meters. The knife he had tried to harm her with appeared smoothly out of the palm of her hand, like magic. She used it to skin him. She was ferociously quick; it took a minute or so. His screams wheezed out through his partially crushed windpipe.

She let his bloody white pelt drop away toward the waves like a heavy, sodden rug. She threw the knife away and used her own claws to rip him open from midlimb to groin, then reached inside, pulling and twisting at the same time as she let go of his neck.

He tumbled away, finally screaming in a high, hoarse voice. She was still holding his stomach in her hand. His intestines unravelled, whipping out of his body in a long, quivering line as he fell.

Skinned and disembowelled, he was light enough—and his entrails sufficiently elastic as well as firmly anchored—for him to bounce up and down on the end of his own guts for a while, jerking and quivering and shrieking, before she let him fall into the salty waves.

She watched the splashes with Chelgrian eyes for a while, then became a cloud of dust in which the biggest single components were the nanomissiles.

By the time the warhead in Eweirl's brain exploded a few minutes later, she had become an attenuated column of grayness sucking itself up into the sky high above.

Epilogue

It is good to have a body again. I enjoy sitting here in this little café in this quaint hill village, smoking a pipe and drinking a glass of wine and looking out over distant Chelise. The air is clear and the view is sharp and autumn is just beginning. It is definitely good to be alive.

I am Sholan Hadesh Huyler, an admiral-general of the Chelgrian Combined Forces, retired. I did not suffer the same fate as that shared by the Hub Mind of Masaq' Orbital and my one-time colleague and charge, Major Tibilo Quilan. The Hub pulled me out of Quilan's Soulkeeper device, saved me, transmitted me to one of its guardian GSVs and—much later—I was united with my old self, the one which Quilan rescued twice: once—with his wife Worosei—from the Military Institute in Cravinyr City on Aorme, and once—with the Navy drone—from the wreck of the *Winter Storm*.

Now I am a free citizen on Chel again, with a reasonable pension (in fact two) and the respect of my superiors (actually two sets of them, though only one lot know of the existence of the other bunch, and they would resist being called my superiors). I hope that I may never be needed again, but if I am, I will do my duty not for my old masters but for my new equals. For I am, by the definition I would have used up to a few years ago, a traitor.

The Chelgrian High Command thought that I might have been got at in some way—even turned—before the wreck of the ship was found, however I seemed to check out and I certainly made all the right responses.

They were both right and wrong. I was turned by the Culture while I was still in the substrate in the Institute on Aorme. They hadn't thought of that, long before the Caste War.

The best way to turn an individual—person or machine—is not to invade them and implant some sort of mimetic virus or any such nonsense, but to make them change their mind themselves, and that is what they did to me, or rather what they persuaded me to do to myself.

They showed me all there was to be shown about my society and theirs and, in the end, I preferred theirs. Essentially I became a Culture citizen and at the same time an agent of Special Circumstances, which is the uncharacteristically coy name they employ for their combined intelligence, espionage and counter-espionage organization.

I went along with everything else to keep Masaq' and its people safe, not to ensure its destruction. I was SC's insurance policy, their get-out clause, their parachute (I heard many colorful analogies). If I had been told to do so, I would have prevented Quilan from making his Displacements, not taken over and done them for him had he demurred. In the end it was decided that sufficient other safeguards had been put in place for the Displacements to go ahead, with the aim of back-tracking along the attempted wormhole link to discover and even attack the Involveds behind the attack (this failed and to the best of my knowledge it is still not known who those mysterious allies were, though I'm sure SC has its suspicions).

I spend most of my time on Masaq' these days, often in the company of Kabe Ischloear; we have similar roles. I come back here to Chel on occasion, but I prefer my new home. Only recently Kabe pointed out that he had lived in the Culture for nearly a decade before he realized that when the Culture calls somebody from an alien society who lives amongst them "Ambassador," what they mean is that that person represents the Culture to their original civilization, the assumption being that the alien concerned will naturally consider the Culture better than their home and so worthy of promotion within it.

Such hubris!

Nevertheless.

I have met Mahrai Ziller. He was wary at first but eventually warmed to me. Lately we have been talking about him accompanying me back here, to Chel, for an informal visit, perhaps early next year. So I may yet accomplish the task that was only ever Quilan's covering story.

They tell me that the Hub and Quilan went together into total oblivion, with no back-ups, no copies, no mind-states, no souls left behind.

I suppose it must have been what they both wanted. In the case of the Major, I believe I can understand, and I still feel deeply sorry for him and the effects of a loss he could neither mourn away nor stand, though—like a lot of people, I think—I find it hard to understand how something as fabulously complicated and comprehensively able intellectually as a Mind might also want to destroy itself.

Life never ceases to surprise.